A RESCUE ME SERIES NOVEL

CHIMERA

NOT EVERYTHING IS AS IT SEEMS

LISA COLODNY

Copyright

Chimera is a work of fiction. All names, characters, locations, and incidents are the products of the author's imagination or are used fictitiously. Any resemblance to actual events, locales, or persons, living or dead, is entirely coincidental.

CHIMERA: A NOVEL
Copyright © 2019 by Lisa Colodny
All rights reserved.

Editing by KP Editing
Cover Design by KP Designs
Published by Kingston Publishing Company

The uploading, scanning, and distribution of this book in any form or by any means—including but not limited to electronic, mechanical, photocopying, recording, or otherwise—without the permission of the copyright holder is illegal and punishable by law. Please purchase only authorized editions of this work, and do not participate in or encourage electronic piracy of copyrighted materials. Your support of the author's rights is appreciated.

Table of Contents

Copyright..3
Table of Contents...5
Dedication..7
Chapter 1..9
Chapter 2..20
Chapter 3..34
Chapter 4..46
Chapter 5..58
Chapter 6..66
Chapter 7..76
Chapter 8..88
Chapter 9..100
Chapter 10..110
Chapter 11..121
Chapter 12..133
Chapter 13..148
Chapter 14..157
Chapter 15..170
Chapter 16..179
Chapter 17..195
Chapter 18..204
Chapter 19..213
Chapter 20..222
Chapter 21..232
Chapter 22..244

Chapter 23	261
Chapter 24	275
Chapter 25	284
Chapter 26	298
Chapter 27	308
Chapter 28	321
Chapter 29	333
Chapter 30	342
Chapter 31	356
Chapter 32	369
Chapter 33	380
Chapter 34	391
Chapter 35	401
Chapter 36	410
Chapter 37	422
Chapter 38	437
Chapter 39	449
About the Author	460
About the Publisher	461
Extras	462

Dedication

To my cousin, Leoda who has been my rock these last two years. I don't have a memory that you aren't in and I'm so grateful to have you in my life.

Chapter 1

Today's newspaper folded neatly atop the far corner of her desk was a distraction. Catherine glanced anxiously at it again, before turning her attention back to the patient profile on her hospital's computer screen. Just a peek, she thought, a quick look at the news to see what all the buzz today was about. But she didn't reach for it, instead, she relaxed back against the worn cushions of her desk chair, trying not to notice the cracking sounds as the old leather of the chair moaned and groaned.

So many years, she thought as her eyes moved over the faded framed photographs hanging slightly uneven on her office walls. No matter how many times she adjusted them straight, the frames would reacclimate themselves crooked against the wall every time someone wanted privacy and closed her office door. Over the fifteen years, she'd been a hospital risk manager, her picture frames shifted often, several times a day sometimes.

"Hey?" her visitor announced, causing Catherine to jerk in surprise as the newcomer rushed through the office door and fell into the empty wooden chair across from her desk. Like the other chair, it squeaked and cracked under the weight of the visitor, even though her visitor was a woman of small proportions.

"I didn't realize you were in the office already, Virginia. It's early for you." Catherine smiled, pulling her reading glasses off her face and dropping them on the pile of paperwork in front of her. She took a moment to study her friend, recognizing how well Virginia had weathered the years. The hospital system had a reputation of aging people far beyond their years, yet, Virginia seemed to be unphased by the passage of time or the challenges faced.

Virginia had only recently come into the position of administrative assistant to the Chief Executive Officer at the hospital , but she and Catherine had worked together before on various assignments at the other hospitals within the system. "Did you get him settled back into the office?"

Virginia pushed her wire glasses tighter against her face and glanced over her shoulder before answering. "Yes, Jay from facilities transported Andrew's stuff back from the corporate offices. Mostly I just put everything back where it was before and retrieved his phone back from the corporate office."

"You had to turn in his phone?" Catherine didn't have to relay she was confused. Her expression said it all. Why corporate would need his phone returned after his promotion was a mystery. After all, he was still part of the same system, just moving higher up on the food chain.

"I'd already submitted his phone to the communications department to be reconfigured for his new role as Chief Executive Officer of the system." Virginia paused. "Felt kind of bad having to ask for it to be changed back to the way it was since he didn't get the promotion."

"Did he say anything?" Catherine didn't know why she'd asked the question. She knew Andrew Caser well enough to know he'd never confide any of his true feelings to anyone outside of his inner circle.

"You mean about the article in the paper or about not getting the job?" Virginia tugged at her hair cropped close to neck, as if she were wearing a wig and it needed adjusting,

"Both, I guess. I mean, Andrew's spent the last ten years, waiting patiently for the incumbent, Alvin Erickson, to retire." She paused, rubbing her ice blue eyes before continuing. "Everyone has known for years that the next CEO of this hospital system would be Andrew or Wesley Bowers."

Virginia rose to her feet, smoothing the front of her skirt into place. "Just Wesley's bad luck to get picked up for drunk and disorderly at a gay bar, Huh?" She leaned in closer to whisper even though they were alone in the office. "It's not like we can have a gay man running the system, right?'

"Wesley's done okay since he transferred to the Booker system." Catherine reminded her. She folded her arms across her chest as if she were cold. "Booting Erin out of the Chief Nursing Officer role at Booker was a good move." She paused and placed her hand over her mouth as if she didn't want the rest of the words to spill out. "Maybe it was a payback. He knew she'd show up here."

"True," Virginia laughed, and checked her watch before making her way closer to the door. "Still Andrew had to be disappointed. No one thought the appointment would go to anyone other than Andrew, not even Andrew."

Catherine pulled her glasses back on and reopened the file folder on her desk. "Governor Smith has always been a wild card. We should have known he wouldn't do what was expected. And his reputation at GHF wasn't exactly one of transparency." She'd finished speaking. Yet, her thoughts continued to rattle around in her mind. It was no secret that in a corporation, any corporation, things were seldom as they seem. Healthcare was no exception; it was more the rule.

She paused, folding her hands out in front and laying them against the desktop as if she were a judge presiding over an arraignment. "I mean, it's still unfathomable to me how Smith was even elected governor in the first place. How many times did he plead the 5th during the state inquisition regarding fraudulent Medicare charges paid to the GHF system?"

"Too many to count," Virginia added, her mouth poised against a small piece of chewing gum she'd trapped under her bottom lip. "Speaking of unexpected, I saw on Facebook that Ryan has a new friend? She didn't post any pictures. Just that she was seeing someone."

Even without looking up from the file, Catherine knew Virginia was smiling, waiting for the details. "Yes, it's been a rough year for her. She lost her mother and her ex-husband announced his engagement about the same time."

"There's that and she's the director of the pharmacy." Virginia wiped at her blouse where a soup stain from the hospital cafeteria was prominent. "Seriously, I'm happy she's dating again. She's been divorced for as long as I've known her."

"Although she won't admit it, I think Ryan always thought she'd get back with her ex-husband." Her gaze settled on a framed picture on the second shelf of the bookcase near the office door. Catherine smiled, remembering her own wedding so many years ago. She'd been a different person then, young, fueled with the hope and dream of a content life. It was impossible to look at the old picture and not see how her eyes had been filled with purpose and determination. Sometimes she thought the woman in the photo was a stranger. It was like finding an old photo in a family trunk and not knowing any of the people in it.

Her stare transfixed on the picture and the way she smiled. She'd been confident in the life she'd chosen, the role she'd play in the lives of so many people around her. She'd never been happier or prouder as the day that picture was taken. She glanced quickly at a more recent holiday picture of her and her family, It was hard not to focus on Gordon's receding hairline tinged with grey around his ears or how much her youngest son, Ronnie, looked like Gordon in the wedding picture poised close by. If Ronnie had been wearing a black tuxedo instead of a holiday sweater, he'd easily have passed for his father in the picture of so many years ago.

She exhaled a breath she hadn't meant to hold and thought of another wedding, a marriage that preempted the one in her picture. A marriage her sons weren't even aware of and she and Gordon seldom spoke of. There were no pictures of that wedding but still, she saw the moment in her mind's eye, flashing forward until it was over, almost as soon as it had begun. A storm, she thought. They'd come into each other's lives like a whirlwind raging with white-hot streaks of lightning and the crash of thunder moaning just over the horizon. Her thoughts spun, intermingled, battling one over the other, the past and present merged like the start of a summer storm. The rain fell, dripping at first until it spilled into puddles already on the ground. Her mind stilled, made peaceful as the storm came to its end.

Catherine was proud, confident it the choices she made when she was younger. There had never been a moment of remorse, not once where she'd regretted any transgression of her youth. She was grateful for what she'd learned, what she'd taken away from both experiences. She was a better person because of it. Her first husband had been a good man, he had made her a better person.

She studied the folded newspaper on her desk again wondering what the bad news today might be. It was getting harder and harder to distinguish the good from the bad guys. She shook her head as if to still her thoughts and let the old memories settle to the bottom like sand.

"When Ryan's ex-husband announced his engagement earlier this year, I thought she'd have a breakdown; sort of like losing him all over again." Catherine went on, "After her Mother's death in the spring, I wasn't surprised at all when she went out on medical leave."

"I'm glad she's back." Virginia stood, pushing the chair tight against the front of the desk.

"Me too," Catherine smiled. "There's a few medication incident reviews I need her to prioritize, especially the error that happened in the operating room."

Virginia smiled before taking her exit. "I've got to get back to work, see if Andrew needs anything else before his meeting starts." She stopped at the doorway and turned back to Catherine. "Is your phone working okay now?"

"Yes," Catherine tapped on the phone lying nearby. "Thanks for sending it out for me. I appreciate it." She grabbed it from her desktop in a single motion as if studying it. "I really don't know what happened. It just stopped working."

"There were several phones with issues, not just yours." Virginia leaned in close so she could whisper. "The new Chief Information Officer doesn't play around. He had the phones turned back around in only a few days."

"I heard he's friends with one of the Commissioners on the board?"

"I heard that, too." Virginia smiled, pausing before adding. "For all the good it did Warren, though. He and Commissioner Burns have been friends for years," she whispered, "They worked together at Pine Bluff many years ago. Warren was a good guy; I don't think he knew he was on the chopping block."

"Does anyone ever know?" Catherine laid her phone near a pile of paperwork, her mind racing to the next topic on her mind.

"Have you spoken to Lorraine?"

"Beliard's new administrative assistant?" Virginia stopped at the door and announced in celebration, as if she had an award to present.

"Yes."

"Just in passing; she's been busy moving Billiards stuff into the corporate executive suite?"

"Is she excited about the promotion?" Catherine paused. "I assume there's a difference in pay between being an administrative assistant to a regional CEO, compared to the chief executive officer for the entire system."

Virginia looked at the empty middle desk. "She didn't really say. I know she's been helping him pack up his office. True, there's probably not much to pack. Beliard's spent the last eight years as the Medical Director for the Emergency Department. He really shouldn't have that much to transport. I mean, he's not going to actually see patient's anymore, right?"

"Do you know Beliard?" Catherine asked, glancing at her computer screen where notification lights of incoming emails left the monitor looking more like a well- lit Christmas tree than an electronic mailbox.

"Not very well, no. Why?"

"We worked together many years ago before coming to this system." She smiled remembering him young and energetic as a third-year resident just as she was graduating from nursing school. "

"According to the strategic plan he presented last month to the Board of Commissioners," Catherine went on, "he's going to run the entire system and still pick up a few shifts each month in the Emergency Department to keep his practice current."

Virginia disappeared through the office door. "I will believe that when I see it."

"My thoughts exactly." Catherine smiled again, thumbing through the first pages of the stack of paper. The time she'd worked with Beliard years ago seemed far away, distant as if she were reading It among the pages of documents under her nose. They'd both been young, single, care-free. She smiled remembering his laughter, his scent as he leaned in closer to her, and the feel of his lips on hers, sweet, soft, and warm.

She shook her head, wiping at her eyes as if to erase the pictures playing on the imaginary screen in her mind. "Was a long time ago," she whispered into the confines of her empty office.

****

The task had been difficult, focusing on her work when her mind kept wandering back to the time she and Beliard spent together. As challenging as it was, she managed to get through several of the stacks of documents as evidenced by the large amount of empty desk space currently visible. She'd just started reviewing the last case when her work was interrupted by a noise from outside her office.

"Virginia?" She looked to the doorway. "I thought you'd left already?" Her desk chair made a loud noise as she stood on her feet and it scraped against the tile floor. She crept to the hallway where Virginia and the other administrative assistant's empty desks were. "Who's in here?" she asked, trying to control her anxiety. It was nearly seven pm, most everyone had been gone for hours.

She took several steps so that she was well in the middle of the room before noticing one of the office doors was ajar. Odd, she thought, all of the chief administrators locked their offices before leaving for the day, especially the chief financial officer. His was always shut, sometimes even during the day when he was still on site. "Hello?" she asked again. "Cliff, is that you." She tried not to laugh; he'd been the first one out the door at five o'clock.

The door swung open quickly causing Catherine to jump out of the path as Michele, the cleaning lady, pulled her cart from the private office and into the waiting area of the administrative offices.

"Michele?" Catherine clutched at her chest. "You scared me to death. What are you doing in there?"

Michele pushed a long strand of gray hair behind her ear and yanked the earphone from her ear in the same motion. "I'm sorry, Miss Catherine." Michele smiled largely, so that her many missing teeth was evident. "I didn't know you were still here."

"I'm always here at this time, Michele." Catherine stepped back so that Michele could pull the cleaning cart the rest of the way from the office. "Which is how I know, you usually aren't. How did you get into Cliff's office? It's usually locked."

"I switched shifts with Bertha." Michele pulled at her hands until the knuckles popped. "Bertha said there was a note on the schedule to clean the CFO's office." She turned to look at the name on the door, running her fingers under the plaque where the name was printed. "Did I get the wrong office?"

"No," Catherine felt badly, knowing Michele couldn't read very well. "It's the right office. I'm just surprised you were able to get in. Do you have a key?"

Michele shook her head. "No, it was unlocked. I just turned the handle. I'm sorry."

"Don't be," Catherine smiled. "We'll have to sort this out in the morning when everyone is in the office. "Are you cleaning out here now?" She pointed to the three desks of the administrative assistants.

"Yes, I'll try not to disturb you." Michele replaced the earbuds and collected a fuzzy duster from her cart as Catherine made her way back to her office. She had a deceased new mother's chart to review. She doubted anything Michele might do would be enough of a distraction. Over the years there was hardly anything she hadn't encountered at least once. There were parts of her job, she just didn't like. Dead babies and mothers were at the top of that list.

****

The walk from the parking lot to the hospital seemed longer this morning, mostly because of the building's new construction. No one was happier about the hospital's expansion than Catherine but, maneuvering around the temporary parking areas was becoming more and more challenging. She glanced from side to side checking for traffic before running across the street and through the physician's parking lot. Although it was only a two-lane street, sometimes the cars flew by so quickly, it felt more like an obstacle course than a pedestrian walkway. It had been a miracle no one had been hurt trying to cross the street from the makeshift parking area to the hospital.

Once she was safely on the other side of the street, she cataloged the parked cars. Jaguar, Mercedes, Porsche, the luxury car list was endless. Yet the doctors carried out food from the cafeteria and lounge as if they hadn't a penny to their name. Ironically, Dr. Lee emerged from the physician's exit, a green cloth grocery bag over his shoulder filled with food and drinks from the hospital cafeteria.

"Morning," she said, as he passed by, his face searching the pavement as if he'd lost something.

He smiled at her but didn't respond. Instead, he gripped the straps of the bag tighter atop his shoulder and made his way quickly around to the far side of the parking lot where his black BMW was parked.

Her gaze drifted to an unfamiliar vehicle, a white van whose front doors were faded several shades lighter than the rest of the vehicle's body parked a few spaces away from Dr. Lee's. Curious, she made her way closer, waving to the doctor as he slid behind the steering wheel without responding to her greeting.

She blew of sigh of frustration. Surely the driver of the van had seen the huge sign that read no parking. How could he have missed it; he'd nearly ran over it. As if the driver had read her thoughts, a male figure wearing gray work coveralls and a baseball cap emerged from the shadows of the building's easement. At first, she thought he'd come from the older part of the hospital but, as she closed the gap between them, another worker emerged from the alley between the old building and the new building still under construction. It was obvious they were both exiting the new building. Wherever they'd come from, they'd been together.

"Good morning!" she called, still a fair distance away.

The first man waved her off as he slid into the driver's seat and started the vehicle waiting patiently. as the second man made his way toward the van.

"You can't park there," she called out, walking faster hoping to catch up to them before they left the physician's parking lot. She thought she might actually engage them before they could pull away as the second man's pace was slow as if he were injured.

"Sorry," the other man called out, as he swung the passenger door open and eased himself onto the passenger seat.

"Do you need medical attention?"

"No," the driver yelled back as he rolled the window up.

"I'd like to see your identification?" Her words were lost amidst the roaring of the van's engine as it backed from the space and pulled away toward the exit gate.

She rumbled quickly through her purse, searching for something to write with and on, all she needed was the license number to pass along to the hospital's captain of security.

"Hey!" a familiar voice called from the back of the physician's lot.

Catherine turned to see her friend, Ryan, stepping from a silver Mazda. "Welcome back."

Ryan moved the briefcase from one hand to the other and pulled anxiously at the strap of her purse slung over her shoulder. "Saw Dr. Lee as I was driving in. Is today grocery day?"

"Yeah, not much has changed while you've been away." She looked past Ryan to where the van's taillights were barely visible. "Did you happen to notice any markings on that van?"

"No, just that its doors were an odd color." Ryan spun around, searching for the van.

"I noticed that too, the driver parked in the fire lane. I think they're working in the new building. Probably didn't want to park down the street with all the other construction workers."

"Did you tell them they can't park in the physician's lot?"

"Didn't get the chance. They took off before I could get close enough to tell them."

"Guess they thought they were in trouble and bolted."

Catherine nodded. "Probably," she paused. "Glad to have you back. We've missed you."

"I know that's your own way of telling me you have lots of things pending for me."

"Yes, I do. But I did miss you." She paused, taking a moment to assess the younger woman with perfect blonde hair, wearing an expensive suit and conservative heels. She looked exactly like the picture hanging outside the pharmacy offices except she was older.

It was her eyes, however, that held Catherine captive. The pain was evident, intermixed with the green and blue hues of color. Catherine knew her friend's personal losses had changed her; she knew her friend was different and would be for the rest of her life.

"I missed you, too." Ryan stopped before entering the building, her attention focused on a window several floors above them. "I've already told Andrew; I can't round in CCU right away."

Catherine held the door to the employee entrance open and motioned for Ryan to go first. "No one expects you to do any more than you're comfortable with."

"I'm just being silly?" Ryan's heels clicked loudly against the hallway tile before coming to a stop at the intersection of the hallway. "It's just a hospital room, right. CCU bed four?"

"It's the room where your Mom died, Ryan." Catherine's eyes were watery. "Everyone understands. You aren't superwoman. It's not silly at all."

"I'll see you at lunch?" Ryan asked abruptly, wiping at her eyes and disappearing around the corner and into the back entrance to the pharmacy. No doubt, Catherine thought where she'd slip quietly past the pharmacy assistant and into her office.

"Sure," Catherine answered anyway, knowing Ryan couldn't hear her and was probably already inside the pharmacy.

Chapter 2

Virginia handed Catherine a Styrofoam cup filled with coffee and paused at the doorway watching as Catherine pulled items from her briefcase. "She seemed okay?" Virginia asked.

"She will be, I think. It will help her to be back at work. Just not in CCU." Catherine watched as her mind's eye replayed her own Mother's death years earlier. It had been a hard time for Catherine and her family, coordinating work and school around her mother's deteriorating health. At first, the assisted living facility had seemed a good, albeit expensive idea. However, her mother hadn't been there very long at all before the calls for assistance started, calls from nurses and administrators that her mother really wasn't able to live alone independently. She needed more one on one care, something more extensive than the assisted living facility was able to provide.

Ironic how her mother fell just before the plans to move her from one facility to another could be finalized. Once she'd been admitted to the hospital, Catherine's intuition was more like a sixth sense than true nursing skill. She'd known as soon as she'd walked into the emergency room and took the chair next to her mother's frail form. She knew her mother was dying; It was simply a matter of time.

"I wouldn't imagine she'd want to go up there for a while." Catherine thought briefly about triage room fourteen in the trauma area, the room her mother had been treated in. It was the same room she'd died in; a room Catherine hadn't been inside since.

"I'm just glad she's back at work." Catherine tapped several file folders. "I've got a feeling she'll be over at some point today, once she catches up on her emails. You know she hates for things to be unresolved."

"If she doesn't make it over here, I'll take a walk to the pharmacy." Virginia smiled.

"Did you need something?" Catherine asked, hoping her question wouldn't be unwelcomed, wouldn't be perceived by Virginia as prying.

"No, I just have to have her retake possession of the department phone and sign for it."

"You'd think corporate would be too busy to police the phones the way they do." She paused. "I mean, what would have been the harm if her phone were locked safely in her office while she was on leave?"

"New corporate policy implemented by the system's new chief information officer," Virginia called out, as if she were rehearsing in a church choir. "God forbid anyone might make a personal call on a corporate phone."

Catherine motioned for Virginia to follow her toward the CFO's office. "Did you know Cliff left his door unlocked yesterday? After you left last night, I found Michele, coming out of it. She said, she was told to clean it."

"Who unlocked it?" Virginia asked, her words were loud and rushed as she stopped what she was doing, her attention focused on Catherine.

"She said It was unlocked." Catherine monitored Virginia's reaction, hoping her words didn't sound accusatory. Virginia was efficient and responsible; there was never ever any doubt, she'd locked it before leaving.

"All the offices were locked when I left" Virginia advised. "I checked; I always do."

"It was reopened at some point."

"I'll check with the Supervisor. Greg knows no one can be in these offices after hours."

"Check what with Greg?" A tall, thin man asked, as he entered the office and sped past where Virginia and Catherine were standing.

"Morning Cliff," Virginia said. "Did you come back last night for something and leave your office unlocked?"

"No," he rubbed at the red hairs of his goatee. "I left at five and didn't return." He slid out of his suit jacket and draped it across the back of his chair. "Why?"

"Michele was here last night cleaning."

"How'd she get in?"

"We aren't sure. Catherine asked her and was told the door was unlocked."

He opened and closed several drawers, his eyes reconciling its contents. "No one should have access to my office except me. The janitorial service needs to clean it before five o'clock. Greg knows that."

"I'll put in a variance report," Virginia advised.

"Don't bother," Catherine responded. "I'll submit it. All the variance reports come to me to review anyway. Will save me a step."

Cliff held up the morning newspaper. "Has Andrew seen this morning's article?"

Virginia looked to the closed door of the chief executive's office. "Yep."

"How'd he take it?" Cliff made his way to the breakroom and made a beeline for the coffee pot, pouring a large cup to sip on as Virginia answered.

"The article implies that Andrew didn't get the system CEO job because of our hospital's current quality and patient satisfaction scores. This reporter, Tim Hartmann, implied that Andrew is incompetent and shouldn't be the CEO here, much less the system." Virginia paused. "How do you think he's taking it? He's mad as hell."

"Best thing to do is to just focus on work. No one except Beliard and the Governor think this change in leadership is a good thing for the system. I don't think Beliard will be in charge long. Then Andrew will get his shot. He's been groomed for it for years. Right?" Cliff fell into his chair, not bothered by the creaking of the wood and crackling of the worn leather.

"Right," Virginia nodded, making her way to her desk with Catherine following close behind her.

"Virginia?" Catherine asked, once Virginia was comfortably seated behind her desk. "Do you happen to know if Aiden is back from vacation?" She hesitated, her attention on the physician's parking area clearly visible from the window of the chief operations officer's empty office. From her perspective, it was easy to see the fire lane was empty. There was no sign of the white van with the mismatched doors.

"He's back in the morning," Virginia answered, as she scrolled through her computer's address book looking for a specific phone extension.

"Who's covering for security until he's back?"

"Jessica is listed as the officer in charge until Aiden is back." Virginia read from the computer screen. "You want her number?"

"No, I completed an incident report regarding a white van parked in the fire lane of the physician's lot this morning. Two men emerged from the building without any identification, and I wasn't able to confront them before they jumped in their vehicle and drove away."

"Did you try and question them?"

"Yes, but they took off." Catherine smiled. "More than likely, it's nothing. Probably thought they were in trouble because they didn't park in the approved construction area." She walked back toward her office. "If Jess comes while I'm out of the office, can you just give her the envelope with the incident report in it?"

"Of course," Virginia said, as she typed rapidly on the keyboard, not looking away from the monitor.

****

"Why didn't you call me?" Ryan's question hung pregnant in the air between them, as if watching a tennis match and the ball was in a holding pattern waiting to be returned.

"You were on medical leave," Catherine's response was calm, precise. She was hoping to avoid an argument but knew there was only a slight chance of that. Ryan wasn't the kind of woman who liked to be excluded from discussions where she was responsible and accountable. Catherine compared it to peering through a dirty window and only able to ascertain a portion of what was on the other side. She knew it could go either way.

"A pharmacist helped a thief empty all fifteen operating rooms of controlled substances. You don't think that warrants a call to the person legally responsible for all those narcotics?"

"First of all, it wasn't like that. Theo didn't know the person pretending to be a doctor at the pharmacy window as a thief. She told him she was a new anesthesiologist and needed immediate access to the automated dispensing cabinets."

"So, he gave her access without getting an approval from anyone in the OR?" Even though she asked the question, she didn't wait for a response. "Then proceeds to walk upstairs with her to make sure her access was working." Ryan paused. "I bet she was pretty, right?"

"He said he was trying to be helpful." Catherine didn't respond to the second question and for good reason. There was only one way the discussion was going to go down, avoiding an argument was going to be impossible. It was like the calm before the storm.

"Sounds like he was helpful, very helpful. Over the next hours, the pharmacy was inundated with calls from the operating room, reporting that their dispensing cabinets were empty and needed to be refilled. All fifteen!" She paused, "She emptied them all."

There was a moment Catherine thought the tantrum might be over. Instead, it was like Ryan needed the time to recover. She took a deep breath before continuing. "Were we at least able to identify her on the camera for the police report?"

"Not exactly."

"Don't tell me the cameras weren't working."

"Oh, they were working." Catherine opened the file folder and handed Ryan several black and white photographs taken from the cameras that were outside the pharmacy, and along the hallway to the operating rooms. In all the photos, the woman had her face down, baseball cap pulled low against the bridge of her nose. In every frame, only the pharmacist was identifiable.

Ryan flipped through the photos one by one. "You've got to be kidding me?"

"No, it's almost like she knew where the cameras were and when to look away." Catherine tapped on the photo. "She might have some kind of tattoo on her shoulder." She pushed the photo closer to Ryan and indicated to the image. "I can't make it out for sure, but I think it might be a bird of some kind."

"Unbelievable!" Ryan shook her head, holding the picture tight against her face for a better look. "It could have been anyone. I'm not even sure it's a woman."

"Hi ladies," the young man said, as he tapped against the door frame. "Sorry, to bother you. Virginia isn't at her desk. And I have the rest of Andrew's things for his office." He leaned in closer to the photo and laughed, "You guys don't take pictures of us in the mechanical room, do you?"

"No, of course not." Catherine closed the folder.

"I didn't mean to interrupt—"

"It's okay, Jay," Ryan said, standing. "We were done here anyway." She pointed to the big office across the room. "Andrew just went inside."

"Just tap before you go in," Catherine advised.

"Will do," he hummed, before pulling a large, plastic-wrapped pallet of furniture from the hallway and into the executive office. "Am I putting everything back where it was?"

"Yes," Catherine called out, following Ryan to the door. "I'll see you for lunch?"

"Sure, am I notifying the police or do you want to?" Ryan paused at the door.

"Police?" Catherine was frantic, thinking she missed something. She thought back to several years ago when she'd found the remote control in the refrigerator at home. If had been missing for several days. It felt just like that. "For what?"

"Controlled substances," Ryan words were in cadence. "OR rooms?"

"Let me get with Andrew first. I'm not sure how he wants to handle it."

"Handle it?" Ryan paused at the door and retreated back inside Catherine's office. "Do we have a choice?" She chewed on her bottom lip. "Shouldn't we have actually reported the incident in real time instead of waiting?"

"We don't usually involve the police when we suspect a healthcare provider is diverting?" Catherine felt the tiny hairs on the back of her neck stand at attention. There was no way around the discussion, and she knew Ryan was not going support where the dialogue was going.

"This isn't as simple as a nurse diverting controlled substances. Someone posed as a physician and stole a significant amount of controlled substances from us," Ryan argued, her words bold and almost angry.

"I'm not disagreeing with you, but we have a chain of command that we have to follow. I just want to make sure everyone is on board." Catherine knew she was towing the company line and she also knew Ryan would as well in the end. It would just take her a little longer to get there.

Ryan shook her head, before disappearing into the hallway and pulling the door closed.

Catherine turned toward Andrew's office and looked back at her own, where piles of work were waiting for her. She walked past Cliff's office and the empty office of the chief nursing officer to Andrew's office. Jay was moving a table to one side to accommodate a black sofa into the corner.

"Andrew left?" she asked, once she paused at the doorway.

"Yeah," Jay didn't look up from his work. "He said to lock the door on my way out."

She nodded. "Are you happy with the transfer out of the Information services department?" She really wasn't sure why she was making small talk. She had plenty of her own work waiting across the hallway. Yet, she waited for him to respond.

"Yeah," he smiled. It was hard for Catherine not to notice how perfect his smile was. He was either born with perfect teeth or for sure, there was an orthodontist in the family. "I like working with my hands more than my head." He smacked at his stomach. "Besides, I was getting fat!"

"I'm glad you were able to find something you like to do," she laughed. "It certainly makes life more rewarding if you enjoy what you do, don't you agree?" As she waited for his answer, she recognized she was only partially speaking in reference to him. Job satisfaction had always been important to her, even as a youngster growing up in a rural community.

Was she as happy with her career path today, as she was when she first started out? She thought again of the wedding pictures she didn't have anymore. Old, she whispered to no one. She felt old.

"Yes Ma'am," he smiled, his lips clenched around his teeth and not looking up from his task.

He aligned the table in front, as if it were a coffee table before pulling a large knife from a pocket sheath and slicing the plastic wrap away from the boxes.

Her attention was on the knife, weapons of any kind were not allowed on hospital property, except by police officers. "That's quite a knife, Jay."

He smiled, his dark eyes lighting up. "Thanks, I've had it for a long time." He paused. "It was my grandfather's, I think, before it was my dad's."

"I see. Do you have family nearby? she asked, but she wasn't sure why she kept bringing up new topics to discuss. She could hear her stack of work calling her from inside her office, screaming louder and louder with each passing minute.

"Not really," he slashed the plastic ties holding the plastic around the ends of the sofa, so that it fell away in a thick pile at his feet. "My father was a marine. He died when I was very young. I don't remember my mom at all. She died when I was a baby." He bent at the waist and wrapped the thick string of plastic around his arms, before thrusting it into a black recycling bag. "My grandparents raised me." He paused. "Got a few cousins up North, but I don't know them, not really."

"I'm sorry," she said, as she watched as he cut a large cardboard box away from a large color printer. His strokes with the knife were almost artistic and she found it hard to look away. She folded her arms across her chest like she used to do when her boys were in trouble. "When you were hired, did Steven talk to you about weapons not being on hospital grounds?"

"No," he continued cutting the plastic away. "My orientation was with Barry, not Steven. Neither mentioned anything. Why?"

"You can't have that knife on hospital property. It's in the guidelines of conduct and is grounds for termination." From the look on his face, she knew he was expecting her to pull the code of conduct manual from her pocket and show him.

He stopped cutting the plastic away from the pallet, folded the knife closed, and returned it to the sheath on his belt. "All of us in facilities use them, Catherine." Jay paused, wiping his chin and forehead. "I didn't mean to do anything wrong. I'm sorry." He pulled the knife from his sheath again and held it out to her. "Here you can have it."

"No," she stepped away, toward the hallway, surprised he'd part so easily with a family heirloom. "Just take it home and don't bring it back here."

She mentally negotiated if the event required an incident report or not. God knows she was still a dozen or so reviews behind. But, she reasoned, if in the future should there be an event or question unresolved from this event, she didn't want the liability of knowing and having reported nothing.

"Do you need help?" she asked, hoping he didn't. She had plenty of her own to do.

"No," he dropped an armload of books on the top shelf. "I won't be very long. Only one more load to bring back. It's mostly stuff that sets on his desk, I think."

"I'm going to send Steven an email about the knives." She turned to take her exit. "I'll be in my office in you need something." She paused at the door. "Make sure you take that knife home".

"I will," he promised, balling the plastic into a tight knot, before pushing it into the trash.

****

There had been many times over the years, Catherine had wished she had a window in her office. It didn't have to be very big; the size of a car window would have been just fine. Today wasn't one of those days. If she'd had a window, she'd had watched the sunset, hours ago.

Twice she'd called Gordon to let him know she wasn't ready to leave yet. Both times, she'd implied it wouldn't be much longer. Although, she only half believed what she said was true.

Absentmindedly, she flipped on the small television that she kept on the second shelf of her bookcase. Usually, she only utilized it during hurricane season when the managers were locked in during the storm. Jay had finished with Andrew's office a while ago; she'd heard him leave earlier. She'd been alone for hours. There was no one in the office who might be bothered with the sound of the television. Therefore, she adjusted the volume as low as it would go, but that she could still hear it. It would be for background noise anyway.

She was nearly done with the first of several stacks of file folders, when a news bulletin interrupted the repeat of whatever sitcom she was pseudo-listening to. Catherine watched as the report was broadcast live from an area downtown, in a park near the beach. The television screen was bursting with police cars, up and down the walkway, parked at irregular angles and blocking any and all traffic from the immediate area.

"A police officer's been killed in the line of duty," she repeated to no one, as the reporter spoke and the screen was filled with pictures of a policeman. The officer was older and he looked very familiar to her. She rose from her desk to get a better look, her hand covering her mouth as if the words once spoken couldn't be taken back.

Abruptly, she grabbed her office phone and dialed as quickly as she could, hoping Gordon wouldn't have given up and called it a night already. She tapped her manicured nails against the desktop, wondering who else might be up that she could talk to. At this hour, only Ryan was most likely not in the bed yet. Still, she dialed her own number and waited as the phone rang several times.

She pulled the phone away from her ear to end the call, just as she heard his sleepy voice.

"You on your way home?" Gordon's words were slurred, and she felt guilty for waking him up. His workday at the school started before seven am every morning, and he liked to get in early. As the principal, he had a thing about being the first one to arrive. After all the years they'd been married, she wasn't sure if it was because he was just that motivated, or he enjoyed keeping the silence of a sunrise to himself.

"No," she was distracted, listening for more information on the deputy who'd been killed. "I shouldn't have called; it could have waited till in the morning."

"I'm up now," he yawned the last word. "What is it? What's wrong?"

"Remember last fall. The prisoner we had who was also a patient on the med surg floor and being guarded by that older Deputy Sheriff?"

"Vaguely," he answered. "Is this the prisoner who escaped from the Deputy, but was thwarted by the nursing staff as he tried to run down the hallway?"

"Yes," she couldn't get the words out quickly enough. "A nurse in another room pushed a gurney into the prisoner's path, so that the Deputy could catch him."

"Yeah," Gordon answered, in a way that made her realize he was only partially listening.

"Did you watch the news tonight?"

"Oh man!" The words were such she knew she'd startled him wide awake, "The Deputy who was killed this afternoon?"

"Yes," she whispered, even though she didn't know why. She knew there was no else in the office, no one was listening.

"Based on the report, he was transporting two prisoners back to lock up from an arraignment at the courthouse." Gordon paused. "Not sure what happened, but his van and body were found near the beach."

She paused as the news reporter went on, repeating what he was reporting. "Preliminarily, the authorities believe he removed the handcuffs from one of the prisoners for some reason and was overpowered, Once the deputy was subdued, the prisoner released the other prisoner," she exhaled. "It's not clear which one killed him."

"It's almost the same scenario as what happened when he had that prisoner in custody here." She paused. "I don't know what to do."

"About what?"

"Should I call BSO and tell them what happened last fall?"

"What would be the point now, Catherine? He's dead, the prisoners have escaped."

"I think both are in custody already. I'm watching the press conference now." She paused. "Maybe if I'd reported what happened last fall, he wouldn't have been killed tonight."

"You don't know that. If it's his time, he steps off the sidewalk and boom, bus cuts the curb too close. He's a goner." He blew a long breath. "Shut down your computer and lock up the office, come home."

"I will," she whispered, trying to hear the last words from the reporter at the scene. "He was a nice old man. I didn't want to get him into any trouble."

"I know," his words were slurred. "It's one of the things I love about you."

"Love you," she blew the words across the receiver. "Be home in about a half hour."

She waited to hear him hang up, holding the receiver to her ear longer than she needed to. She wiped her eyes as if she could erase the sleepiness and rub herself into a new day. It only took a few minutes to shut down her computer and lock the office door. By the time she walked through the empty physician's parking lot to the pedestrian walkway, she was literally moving on the fumes of her residual energy stores, she'd stored up for the winter.

At that time of the night, there wasn't that much traffic on the road between the hospital and the parking lot. But she could see at least two sets of headlights at the intersection a short distance away. There was no doubt in her mind, she could have made it safely to the other side. But she was too tired to run the last few steps to be sure. So, she waited for the cars to pass by before stepping into the crosswalk.

Maybe it was the way the moon lit the backside of the new building or maybe her sixth sense was on overdrive, sparked, no doubt, by the news of the deputy's death. The headlights of an approaching car reflected off the taillights of the van as it sat parked almost completely hidden behind the new hospital building.

Catherine stopped, debating between stepping into the crosswalk and getting into her car, or going back toward the hospital to investigate what the occupants of the van were doing in the building at that time of night. She scanned the rest of the area for other workers or construction vehicles. It was no surprise to her that there weren't any.

She pulled the phone from her pocket and dialed the front desk. Several rings passed before an operator answered. Catherine introduced herself and asked to have a security officer meet her at the hospital entrance near the physician's lot.

The young officer arrived within minutes; Catherine was grateful security had been attentive. She was in no mood to be kept waiting for a long period of time. Quickly she explained what happened the other day and how she was almost certain it was the same van that was presently parked in the shadows of the new building.

"Are you armed?" she asked, once they were out of the physician's lot and nearly to the ease way of the new building.

"No," the security officer advised. "But I do have mace and handcuffs." He tapped the radio pinned on his shoulder. "And this radio is in direct contact with BSO."

"Good," her smile was anxious, hadn't he been watching the news. "Didn't he realize BSO was no doubt busily mourning the loss of one of their own."

"Where is it?" he asked, coming to an abrupt stop once he stepped off the sidewalk that ran alongside the back wall of the front entrance.

"It was right here." She pointed to the empty spot in the space between the buildings.

"Maybe some one's putting in some overtime?" he offered.

"I didn't see any lights inside the building, nothing to suggest anyone was inside working."

"I'll put in my report that you believe it was the same van you saw illegally parked." He paused, resting his hands on his hips and scanning the area as if he were looking for the van. "Where are you parked?"

"Across the street, toward the back of the lot."

"Come on." He smiled. "I'll walk you over."

She put her hand up to refuse but hesitated. "Thank you, that's very kind of you." She followed him toward the front of the visitor's lot and across the street to the area that had been designated for staff parking. He waited until she was safely inside her car and started the engine, before walking away back toward the hospital.

Catherine waved to him as she pulled onto the street feeling a little silly about allowing an escort. The fact was, she wasn't even sure it was the same van. It could have been any color including white. True, she had no proof but, she felt it in her gut. She knew it. Even without a trace of evidence to support her theory. She knew it was the same van, she felt it.

Chapter 3

Andrew Caser wasn't a very big man, no taller than five feet six inches, maybe seven depending on the thickness of the heel of his shoes. Catherine studied him through her office door as he paced around in between the desks of the assistants.

His office across the hallway was huge. Why was he always milling about in the area of others? He'd had a haircut, since she'd seen him last week. No doubt, preparing to look the part for the new role he thought he'd be assuming. And from the way he kept looking at his fingernails, he'd had a manicure as well.

"You sure Jay didn't leave a box with some files out here?" He asked Virginia.

"No," Virginia didn't get up from her desk. "I've looked everywhere. It's not here. It has to be somewhere in your office."

"Nope," he walked past Virginia's desk toward Catherine's office. "It's not in there. Can you check with facilities and see if there's a pallet still to be delivered?"

"Yes," she dialed the phone having most of the phone numbers memorized. "But Jay 's note reads that the boxes delivered last night were the last of the items he needed to bring over."

"Can you just confirm? It's important." He asked once he'd passed her desk and was nearly to Catherine's office door. "Is Ryan getting acclimated back into the grind?" He asked through the door not coming fully into the office.

"I think so, she's got a lot of things to catch up on though and I need her to prioritize several unexpected outcomes."

"Probably best, don't you think?" He leaned against the doorframe his arms crossed at the waist as if he were posing for a photograph. She'd been right about his manicure. There was a clear coat visible on his thumbs where the nails were bigger.

"Yes, I know her mom is on her mind a lot. She misses her."

"I know they were very close," he offered. "Her mother had been living with Ryan for a few years now?"

"Yes, since her Father's death."

"Ryan's tough," he smiled. "Always has been, even as a student."

"You knew her when she was a student?" Catherine was surprised. Why hadn't she known that?

"Yeah, she did several rotations with the system before she got her doctorate." He paused. "Thought we'd recruited her during her residency but, she took a job with another system. Was about a year before she came back around asking for the opportunity."

"I didn't know that. It was good of you to give her a second chance."

"She's always been good with the details, even when she was still in training. I knew she'd grow into a competent department head."

"Speaking of," Catherine paused, choosing her words carefully. "Ryan wants to make sure a police report is completed and that the DEA is notified."

"Regarding?" Andrew answered, but she knew he already knew what she meant.

"The event in the OR." she exhaled, hating the games he sometimes played.

"That's not a matter for the police." His response was prompt, his expression angry.

"She feels she has an obligation to file the report."

"It's not her decision to make. The surgery was completed successfully without further complications and no negative outcome for the patient."

"That's not the event, Andrew. I'm talking about the controlled substances that were taken from the automated dispensing cabinets in the operating room."

"Still not her call." His demeanor was all different. Gone was the friendly, conversation making person. Instead, he was defensive and anxious.

"I think it's something we have to discuss. She and I both share accountability to notify practice specific boards." She paused. "I don't think the parenteral directive of 'just because' is going to work this time." There was another pause as she considered her next words. "I'm not sure it should."

"Set up a meeting to discuss it, but I'm not changing my mind." He looked behind to the office area as if realizing the conversation might have been overheard. "I don't need any more negative publicity."

His head turned toward the exterior door as the door burst open and a large, dark-haired distinguished-looking man dressed in an expensive suit strode into the administrative office with an assortment of women and men following behind him, as if he were the emperor, but not in need of any new clothes.

"Dr. Beliard?" It wasn't clear who or where the salutation was from. It seemed to come from all the occupants of the offices at the same time as they piled out one by one, lining up like bees attending to their Queen as Beliard stepped further into the office.

"Anwar," Andrew was the first person in the procession; he held his hand out to him, pumping furiously once Beliard's hand was inside his. Andrew seemed small, almost tiny standing next to Beliard. Catherine couldn't help but consider the battle of David and Goliath, smiling to know the outcome of the confrontation between these two would have had a very different outcome.

Beliard's stance was self- important as he paused to survey the area, nodding and smiling to everyone who stood waiting patiently as if he was going to deliver a speech. He pulled away from Andrew's personal space and made his way to Catherine, stopping to drop a kiss on her cheek.

"Been a while, Catherine." His smile was wide, revealing long rows of straight, white teeth. "How's Gordon and the boys?"

"Boys have moved out, busy with lives of their own. Gordon's doing well looking forward to retiring from the school system." She followed him to the office door, stopped to fold her arms, one over the other, before leaning into the door jam and waiting. She waited, knowing he had more to say.

Instead, Beliard spun around to face the other administrators and assistants before looking directly at Virginia. "If I could just get a cup of coffee?" He took Andrew's elbow and led him toward the large conference room behind Andrew's office. "Just need a few minutes with the boss."

Virginia disappeared into the small kitchen next to Catherine's office and reappeared moments later with two Styrofoam cups of steaming hot coffee. She walked quickly toward Andrew's office, not making eye contact with anyone she passed before disappearing into Andrew's office.

****

"They've been in there for a long time?" It sounded more like a question than Catherine meant for it to. She looked anxiously at the closed door before stepping into the tiny area and pulling a small plastic bottle of water from the refrigerator. She took little sips before recapping it and dropping the bottle into the pocket of her laboratory coat. Truth was she wasn't even thirsty, not really, she was just looking for an excuse to venture out and snoop around near Andrew's office.

She glanced at her watch to validate how much time they'd spent behind closed doors. Beliard had been meeting with Andrew for a long time and she doubted whatever they were discussing was positive. If Andrew had been receiving kudos from Beliard, the meeting would have been over hours ago.

Almost as if Beliard read her mind, the door swung open and he emerged, red-faced and pushing his giant glasses higher on his nose until they were flush against his forehead so that the creases bled stark white against the pink skin around his eyes. He nodded to each of the assistants as he strode past their desks and stopped to wave to at Cliff who was pounding his computer's keyboard as if he was performing a concert. He was nearly through the door when he stopped and called out to her.

"I'll see you soon, Catherine." He stepped to the side to allow another visitor into the administrative office. Once the newcomer was through the door, Beliard waved once more and strode purposefully out of the office.

"Was that the new boss?" the visitor asked, pointing at the door Beliard had just left through.

"Yes," Virginia called from her desk. "You here for Catherine?"

He nodded before taking baby steps toward her office and tapping on the door frame.

"Aiden," Catherine waved him inside. "Welcome back. How was your vacation?"

"Too short," The captain of the security team pushed his bulky form into the chair across from her desk.

She pointed to a small bandage over his right brow. "Vacation bragging rights?"

He waved her off. "Nah, a buddy of mine got a little too energetic at a pickup game at the park." He rubbed the top of the bandage gently. "Seven stitches." He repositioned himself in the chair. "I saw your incident report about the van that was illegally parked." He reviewed what was written in a small black note he'd removed from his belt. Unlike the security officer last night, Aiden was armed, his sidearm was clearly visible against his hip.

"You weren't able to confirm that it was the same van?" He read before looking up to her. "My officer said by the time he got there; the vehicle had vacated the property."

"Yes," she confirmed. "I saw the reflection of its taillights from the headlights of oncoming traffic." She paused and shook her head. "I guess I should have walked over and made sure it was the same van before I called security but.."

He interrupted her. "No, you did the right thing, Catherine. There should never be a situation where you are investigating something late at night by yourself on the property."

He forced his way out of the confines of the chair. "We'll keep an eye out for that van."

"Thanks, Aiden." She glanced at her caller ID and motioned to the ringing phone, picking the receiver up before adding. "I've got to take this."

"Of course," he took his leave, pulling her door closed behind him.

****

"So that's the plan?" Ryan asked, falling back against the creaky back cushions of Catherine's office chair. "Andrew's putting all nursing leadership on notice that if the satisfaction scores aren't better over the next six months, he's going to replace them all with new managers who can get the job done?"

"Beliard was here yesterday, with Andrew for almost three hours." She paused as if she could be heard through her closed office door into the administrative waiting area. "Rumor has it, Andrew was put on a performance improvement plan."

"Really?" Ryan paused, eyes racing as if she needed more time to comprehend what Catherine was saying. "What about the rest of us?"

"Andrew's planning an organizational staff meeting later today. I'm sure he'll go over everything then." Catherine hesitated, maybe she should wait for the meeting for Ryan to get all her answers. Instead, she leaned in closer, whispering into the space between them. "The rest of us are going to be directed to focus on the quality scores."

"That's fine by me," Ryan stood, pushing the chair against the desk so she could step closer to the door. "I'm always looking at the quality end of things," She smiled, stopping when her hand touched the handle. "It's who I am, remember?"

"Speaking of," Catherine smiled. Her friend was correct. No one focused more on the quality processes for how medications were used within the facility than Ryan. She'd been practicing pharmacy there most of her career. She knew more about the pharmacy policies and procedures than anyone else in the system. Chances were she'd written most of them. "We had two medication errors while you were out. One in the operating room during a coronary bypass procedure and one more recently related to an outpatient prescription that was filled incorrectly."

"Were you able to sequester the products involved?" Ryan turned back toward the desk; her hands extended toward Catherine as if receiving a gift.

"Yes," Catherine stood and walked quickly to a locked metal cabinet. The padlock fell open quickly, the bulkiest piece tapping loudly against the surface of the drawer. "Once you take possession of these, they're all yours. Chain of custody, etc." She smiled as she handed a medium sized plastic bag of partially infused solution and a large amber prescription vial to Ryan.

"I'll start on these as soon as I can." She held her hands just as Catherine started to respond. "Don't worry, I'll make sure they are secured. No one has keys to my office."

"Well," Catherine lamented. "That's what Cliff thought too, but I'm learning things aren't always as they seem."

"Don't worry," Ryan interrupted. "I have a safe inside a secure filing cabinet in my locked office." She was partially out of the door when she added. "It's like Fort Knox and I'm the only one in the building with a master pharmacy key."

"I'll look forward to the results of your investigation."

"Since we're on the subject. Any update on notification of the appropriate authorities regarding the theft of those controlled substances?"

"Andrew doesn't believe it's an event for that needs to be reported."

"Do you agree with that summation, Catherine?"

"I could go either way on this one." She hesitated, "But I am supposed to set up a meeting with the three of us to discuss it."

"Don't bother," Ryan barked. "Discussing it would be a waste of time. His mind is made up. He won't change it."

"I'm sorry, I know it's not the answer you were hoping for. I've got so much on my plate right now; I'm really having to prioritize my battles." Her mind drifted back to the BSO officer who'd been killed.

"What else is going on?" Ryan fell back into the chair she'd just vacated.

"I can't decide if I should follow up with BSO regarding an incident that happened with one of their officers last fall." The words spilled out of her mouth. Even if she'd wanted to stop them, she couldn't. She was drowning in self-doubt and overwhelming guilt. If she'd taken her concern up the proper chain of command, would the Deputy's death had been prevented? It was time for another opinion. Ryan was one of the best sounding boards she knew. Catherine was sometimes in awe of how Ryan was able to compartmentalize her emotions and focus solely on the facts.

"You had no legal obligation to report it" Ryan words were soft once Catherine shared the events of last fall. Additionally, Ryan pulled the chair around so that she and Catherine were on the same side of the desk.

"What about a moral obligation?" Catherine hoped as the words crawled from her mouth they didn't sound as indignant to Ryan's ears as did to hers.

"I think your heart was in the right place," Ryan advised. "You didn't want to get him in trouble."

"Yes, and now he's dead." Catherine willed the tears behind her eyes to maintain a holding pattern. More than anything, she did not want to cry.

"And that's not your fault." Ryan paused before leaning back more fully into the chair's cushion. "He was in the wrong place at the wrong time."

"I know," Catherine cleared her throat. "What would you do?"

"I'd leave it alone," Ryan answered. "He's gone and nothing you do is going to change that." She stood up. "As it stands now he was killed in the line of duty. His widow will be taken care of financially."

The office wasn't very big, but it seemed to Catherine as if it took forever for Ryan to walk the short distance to the door. "Who knows, if you share what happened, it might make him look as if he was clumsy, careless even and support that he had a pattern of reckless endangerment. You know how insurance companies can be. They're always looking for an excuse not to process a payout."

"I hadn't thought of that." Catherine rubbed at her chin. "That's a really good point, actually."

"Good." Ryan opened the door, stepping back in surprise as the Captain of the security jumped back as if he'd been startled.

"Aiden?" Catherine questioned through the door and wondered how much he'd overheard. "Everything ok?"

He held up a note card size piece of paper that he'd written on. "I was just leaving you a note."

"We're done, Ryan's late for patient satisfaction rounds, right?"

"Uh," Ryan's face contorted as if she smelled something foul. "Speaking of things not being as they seem." She leaned in closer. "We round every day on the same patients and ask the same questions that we log onto the sheets and turn into administration." She paused. "Seven years of patient rounding, our scores haven't improved even a single percentage point."

Ryan grunted and disappeared through the door, addressing the administrative assistants as she moved from one office to another before nearly colliding with Priscilla as she pulled the heavy cart from the empty COO's office. "Sorry," Ryan said, bending to collect her rounding sheets from the floor. "I didn't know you were in there, it being empty and all.

"Still got to dust and all, Miss Ryan," Priscilla explained. "Even if there's no one in there."

"It's okay," Catherine smiled as she listened to Ryan's farewell to Virginia in the front office area before turning back to Aiden. "She hates rounding."

"Doesn't everyone," he agreed. "How much did we pay that service company to reeducate us?"

"Quarter of a million," Catherine could hardly get the words out. It was hard even for her, to imagine how much money had been wasted on improving the service scores. Why could the leaders at the corporate level understand, if they want better service scores, ensure the staff had the resources needed to provide better service to the patients.

"What a waste," he shook his head.

"Grab a seat," Catherine pointed to one of the chairs in her office.

"I can't stay, I'm late for a meeting with the Captains from the other sites." But he dropped down into the chair anyway.

"Anything I can help with?" She smiled noticing he'd removed the bandage over his eye, The pink skin was healing black and blue barely visible amidst the dark hairs of his brow. Rumor was the handsome captain of the security team hadn't been injured during a basketball game as he'd said. The story was he'd had a little plastic surgery completed while he was out on vacation. She hadn't paid much attention to the small triangular shaped birthmark above his eye. It was interesting the things people chose to keep private.

"No," he shook his head. "There's a rumor going around that the system is considering contracting with an outside vendor to provide security at the hospitals."

"Oh no," her words were sincere. "I hope that's not the case. I really like working with you." She smiled. "What's up?"

"I wanted to follow up with you on the white van." He flipped pages in his notebook. "Buddy of mine downtown at the sheriff's office, ran ownership records for all white vans registered in the area." He paused. "There are thousands."

"Dead end." She chimed in, hoping he hadn't how she'd averted her eyes when he'd mentioned the sheriff's office.

"So, I watched the video from the day you saw the driver coming from the new building."

Catherine's face lit up. "That's a good idea. Anything?"

"The cameras in the new building are not functioning yet so I only had the one camera in the back of the old building to review. There is a picture of two male subjects of the unknown race on the tape for that morning." He paused. "They are not carrying tools or any kind of equipment. The camera only caught them leaving the building. So, they must have come in through one of the other access points." He paused.

"I spoke with the foreman of the project. The van wasn't familiar to him. He doesn't think they are part of his crew, but he said he would remind everyone the importance of wearing identification and parking in the designated areas."

"The doors of the van are pretty specific, If they'd been part of the construction crew, he'd have been able to identify the vehicle. Now I'm even more concerned. No way to identify them?" She paused, her mind racing how to ask the question without making him defensive. "It's odd that none of the cameras in the existing building caught them coming in or crossing over at the second-floor walkover."

Her eyes met his. "You watched all the tapes?"

"Yes. I did." His words were flat. She knew he was thinking it had been a waste of his time.

"There's nothing more we can do to identify them?" She paused thinking back to her encounter in the parking lot. "One of them might have been injured, limping maybe?"

"No, I'm sorry." He paused. "But we will start patrolling the area and we'll be on the lookout for the vehicle."

"Did any of your police contacts provide any update on the death of the deputy sheriff?" she asked, hoping her anxiety wasn't evident.

"No," he shook his head and rubbed nervously at the material of his trousers around his knees. "One of my guys mentioned an incident here involving the same deputy."

"It was nothing," Catherine added. "Just an accident that didn't amount to much." She spun the wedding ring around on her finger and looked away again. "I'd forgotten about it."

"I can pull the incident report, if you'd like." He paused before adding, "it was before my time."

"I keep forgetting how new you are to the system." She was being truthful. He knew so much about the facility and the people; it was almost as if he'd studied the site and its people.

"Don't bother," she went on. "I don't need to review the report." That would be just perfect she thought. As discreet as she'd tried to be, all she needed was to attract attention to the event. The deputy's widow would surely lose his pension if everyone continued to dig around in the past.

Aiden checked his watch, jumping up quickly. "I've got to go."

"One more thing, Aiden. If you don't mind?"

He loitered near the doorway. "Of course not."

"Can you put together a recommendation to administration to provide a catwalk over the busy street out front. Once the parking garage is completed, we'll need something one way or another." She watched as he scribbled in his notebook. "From a safety perspective, I think we need it sooner rather than later."

"That's a good idea." He smiled." I can't tell you how many times I've nearly been run over trying to get across the street."

"Me too," she joined in, hoping it could be built sooner rather than later.

Chapter 4

"Can you meet me somewhere privately?" Catherine heard Beliard whispering, pleading from the phone's receiver. "Catherine, it's important, I need to talk to someone I can trust."

"Anwar," her words were slow, mentally assessing what he could possibly need to speak to her about. True, they'd been close once, but that had been many years ago. She could count the number of times she'd talked to him independently on a single hand. Funny, over the last three weeks, she'd already seen him at least that many times. "What's this about?"

"I'm not sure what to do, who I can trust to help make me this right." His words were tight, breathless. "Please," he begged. "Meet me at that coffee shop we used to go to."

"Now?" She glanced at her watch. It was more of a nervous gesture than any actual interest in the time. Plus, what reason would she give for leaving early? Everyone knew Catherine's hours weren't nine to five, not even close.

"No!" His words were harsh. Gone was his simple, pathetic, pleas. "It will have to be after work. Just go on as if it's a normal day."

"You're scaring me," she responded, her heart pounding so hard she could feel the vibration all the way down to the tips of her fingers. "Just tell me what's wrong?"

"I can't now, but I will as soon as know it's safe to talk."

"Ok," she nodded at the phone as if he could see her and licked her dry lips. She imagined him, folding his big form small enough to hide behind a door or inside a closet. "I'll be there as soon as I can get away."

"It was so long ago." He rambled on, pensively. Whatever was bothering him was big and personal. "I never thought, after all these years have passed. It would come to this."

"Does this have something to do with Mae?" she asked, thinking how he seldom spoke of his second wife, the wife after her. Her own marriage to him had lasted less than a year and his second marriage only slightly longer. The difference was he and Mae hadn't walked away from their relationship, hadn't decided to call it quits after a long weekend at an isolated, lonely cabin in the woods.

Mae's leaving hadn't been a voluntary or even a conscious one. She died only minutes after giving birth to their baby, a son who lived barely long enough to suck in three breaths of air before following his mother to the other side.

Catherine recalled Anwar's words, desolate and angry describing how much he missed Mae and longed to hold the baby in his arms just once. Why the midwife had insisted the baby's body be taken to the coroner so abruptly had always troubled Catherine. She'd always though Anwar might have dealt better with the loss of the child had he held it in his arms, kissed its soft, tender cheek, and had the opportunity to say goodbye.

After Mae and the baby's death, he was different, sadder, more serious than Catherine had ever known him to be. There was no laughter, only work. No one was more surprised than she was when he announced he was getting married again, to someone he'd met at a medical conference. Like him, she was a physician, a widow whose husband had died during a military exercise.

Even after his marriage and the birth of his two children, he wasn't the same. It might have appeared to some as if he'd recovered, managed to put his life in order. But Catherine knew the truth, his truths. He wasn't the same man she'd married all those years ago. Sometimes, she felt as if she didn't know him at all, as if the person she'd known never existed. She missed the man he was, the man she'd married once when the world, like them, was new, fresh, and innocent. They'd been like Superman and Wonder Woman with the world waiting at their feet for salvation. It was hard to entertain the thought that Superman and the man on the phone were one and the same.

"Come alone," he said before the line went dead.

****

Okay," Catherine reiterated, settling into a small table near the back of the coffee shop. "I'm here, all alone per your request." There weren't many people in the shop, the few in attendance were stationed on the other side of the shop. She took his hand across the table, grateful for the privacy. "Tell me what this is about."

Beliard twisted and turned around in the wooden chair. "It wasn't supposed to be like this." He rubbed his palm across his chin. "All I wanted was a chance to make things right,"

"You haven't been in the role very long, Anwar, but already things are starting to move in a more positive direction. You are making a difference; you just have to give yourself some time." She paused deliberating if she should continue. "My God, you're still recovering from open heart surgery."

"I'm fine." He pulled his hand away from hers and tapped his fist to his chest, right where his heart was. "I've never felt better."

"I've been working with the FBI," he blurted out so fast she feared he was trying to get the words out before he changed his mind.

"FBI?" Had she heard his correctly? What could he possibly have to work with the FBI on?

"Yes," he was whispering again. "I don't know where the money's going, so much money." He was silent as if he wasn't sure what else to say. "There's things, things I'm not proud of, from a long time ago. I made some compromises when I was young."

"What kind of compromises?" He had her interest now. As a risk manager she more than anyone how important a company's compliance and ethics programs could be.

He cleared his throat and straightened up in his chair. It was as if he'd changed gears, changed his mind on what he wanted to say. "It's the tax funds." He leaned in closer to her after checking no one had taken any seats patrons behind them.

"The funds we collect from the county taxes to care for the uninsured?"

"Yes, it's over a hundred million dollars annually that is entrusted to us to disperse in a manner so that the care of the uninsured can be maximized."

"And?" It seemed simple enough to her, what was struggling with?

"I'm not sure who's responsible for the current state of events. But the amount of money we paid out to select groups of key physicians is bordering on criminal." His timing, tone, every word out of his mouth was different. And she couldn't help but consider he wasn't telling her the truth. She knew this man like no one else and was aware he was lying to her.

"I don't understand?" A part of her wanted to take him by the shoulders and shake him until he told her what was really on his mind, what was eating away at him.

"By law, the tax funds can only be used for contracts that fall within a specific practice of common market pricing." He went on as if he were a weatherman, delivering an update on an upcoming storm, his words were calm, controlled, objective, and without emotion. His conversation couldn't have been more different from the one he'd started when he'd initially sat down.

She didn't try to conceal her confusion. He moved his chair closer around the table so that they were nearly sitting side by side. "For example, if the normal and customary price for a consultation by, say, a cardiologist is five hundred dollars per patient. There's an expectation that what we are paying them is within a reasonable range of that."

"And we aren't?" She opened her hand out to him, as an invitation to continue.

"No, Take the contract we currently have in place with Dr. Grayson. We paid him over three million dollars last year. Yet he saw only three patients."

"That can't be right." She wanted to laugh but couldn't. Deep in her gut, she felt a rumble, knowing it wasn't going to end well. She didn't doubt his facts at all.

"It's only one example. There are hundreds of other contracts where we've paid physicians for minimal to no service with the tax money. "He gulped from the cup, wiping at his lip where the liquid caused it to turn, thick and red. "And there's wire transfers in and out of the system, to hundreds of accounts that I can't reconcile to any type of patient encounter or invoice for services."

He shook his head in a way that reminded her of the night he'd lost his first patient. It was a child, a friend of another physician whose young son drowned in the pool during a family event. She recalled the sad look in his eyes as he had tried to comfort the child's family. "It's so messed up, I don't know where to begin to fix it, make things right again."

"What does the FBI want you to do?"

"I've been recording discussions, copying documents. I thought they'd step in by now. I don't know what they are waiting for."

"Are any of the Commissioner's involved?"

"I can't be sure but Commissioner Fleming continues to inquire about what's holding up some of the new physician contracts. She wants them signed and executed like yesterday. I've been dragging my feet, citing how I'm signing around the time I'm on vacation and out of the office."

"Fleming?" Catherine repeated. "She's the new commissioner just appointed by the Governor?"

"Yes," he nodded. "She's the only one with any experience in healthcare. I think she worked with the Governor before his appointment, when he worked with GHF."

"She also applied for the chief operations officer positions at two different hospitals within our system." She knew this man like the back of her hand. His mind was racing with questions about the application.

"I didn't know that," surprise evident on his face and in his words.

"You wouldn't. You were still the medical director for the emergency room when she interviewed. I was on the panel for Ridge Point Medical Center."

"Why wasn't she considered?"

"The panel felt like she didn't have the experience needed in operations."

"Even for Pleasant Ridge? It's significantly smaller?"

"Guess they didn't think so."

"Yet she's running the entire system, now? And in a position to govern those people who rejected her?" He didn't wait for Catherine to answer. "Perfect, I'm not even surprised. I told you. I don't know how far up this goes."

"You have to contact the FBI, Anwar and tell them you're in too deep and you need help."

"I will but first…" The shrill ring of his cell phone was a distraction and he fumbled to retrieve his cellphone from his jacket pocket.

"Beliard," he barked into the phone.

Whoever was on the other end of the call, barely spoke a minute. Beliard disconnected his call and dropped it back into his jacket pocket. "I have to go." He stood up, gathering his overcoat and umbrella.

"Who was that?"

"Victoria Wales. Corporate compliance is following a complaint regarding the Director of Procurement."

"What kind of complaint?" She knew she was pushing him but she needed to know. She'd known the Director of procurement for years. He was an ass, everyone knew that.

"Several female vendors have come forward, claiming that Aaron forced them to have sex with him if they wanted their products, devices, whatever to be used within the system."

"Is the FBI aware of these charges?" She stood to join him, watching as he slid into his overcoat.

"Yes, they're aware." He clipped his corporate identification to the lapel of his overcoat.

"You're not going back to work at this hour? You're recovering from heart surgery? You shouldn't be under all this stress" She followed him toward this door.

"I have to." His smile wasn't genuine. "I'll try and get back to you in a day or two once I know more."

"I'd like that." She walked quickly through the door while he held it open for her. "What could possibly be going on that can't wait till the morning?"

"I'm suspending Aaron in the morning, pending the outcome of the FBI's investigation." He made his way quickly down the walkway.

"Does he have any idea?"

"I think he may know something is going on. I saw him going through his office like it was spring cleaning or something. I'm pretty sure he knows something is up." He kissed her on the cheek. "Thank you for meeting me." He hesitated, his eyes searching hers as if he'd lost something.

"You remember the first time I kissed you?" he asked his words were thick, stuck tight against his lips.

"Yes, why are you bringing all this up?" She knew she should pull away, put some distance between them but she didn't. She couldn't. Her eyes were fixated on his lips as he spoke. "We're different people now. It was a long time ago."

"I'd never been more afraid of anything as I was that night." He smiled. "You were always so tough and intimidating. I was afraid you'd slap me."

"You weren't afraid of me," She laughed. "We were in a mausoleum. You were afraid of ghosts, not me."

"It wasn't ghosts. It was always you. I've always feared hurting you, disappointing you."

"You have a funny way of showing it." She paused then added when she realized he didn't understand. "You walked away from me. I didn't leave you."

"I know." He dropped his forehead to hers. "My mother never forgave me for walking away from our marriage." He smiled, remembering his mother's nickname. "Babi always said you were the one, my soul mate."

Catherine considered responding but she didn't. It was as if she knew he had more to say, other things he wanted her to know. "She never acknowledged my marriage to Mae or the baby." He swallowed.

"I thought that after I lost them, she might reconsider but she didn't." He paused; his eyes sad. "My divorcing you was the beginning of the estrangement between my mother and me."

"She was at their funeral; I spoke to her." Catherine saw their caskets in her mind, one long, shiny silver casket covered with sprays of brightly colored yellow, red, and blue flowers and the other small white casket barely distinguishable under the blue floral arrangement that covered the top of the casket.

"My mother made the arrangements for the services." He paused. "She was there that night at the house when Mae and the baby passed." He cleared his throat. "She made the calls, contacted the coroner's office. I was in no shape."

He paused, his hand drawing closer to her as if to stroke her cheek. "I know I hurt you."

She backed away just enough to avoid his touch. "You wanted another life; a life you didn't think I could give you." She reached for his hand and placed hers over his. "We've both moved on."

"And there isn't a day that goes by that I don't regret it." His lips touched hers, but just briefly before she backed just barely out of his reach. It wasn't that she didn't want him to kiss her, she did. And that was the problem.

She blinked in the direction of her left hand as if the small, gold band on her finger was her

lifeforce. It was and she felt herself push away from him in response.

"I'm sorry," he whispered, and pulled her closer. "You are the only person who has ever really known me." His were soft, pleading. "Everyone got the me for show, but not you." He stepped backward. "I have to go; I'll call you soon and give you an update."

"Anwar," her words were hushed, pained. "Be careful."

"I will," he said before disappearing down the street and climbing into an expensive black BMW parked at the curb.

A ticket, she thought to herself. If he wasn't careful, he was going to get a ticket. But no, she reconsidered, he was one of the most powerful men in the county. He knew everyone associated with law enforcement or public service. His years of managing the emergency department had left him with many important allies and more than likely just as many omnipotent enemies. She couldn't help but say a prayer for him, knowing there was really no way to predict with of those encounters might put him in compromise.

****

"I don't know any more than you do, Virginia really." Catherine insisted. "As was discussed at the emergency organizational staff meeting this morning, The Office of the Inspector General has filed corruption charges against the hospital system." She looked away, hoping Virginia wouldn't see through her lies. They have been friends for a long time and she hated lying but she didn't have a choice. Anwar's warning had been specific, say nothing to no one.

"How much more stress can the staff can take?" Virginia shook her head, biting at the nail on her pinky finger. "Everyone is getting inundated with questions from the staff and outside vendors. Not to mention the shock of seeing all this on the evening news. It would have been nice if we'd had a heads up and not find out about it on the television."

"You'd think."

"Dr. Beliard didn't mention anything to you. I know you're friends."

"We were friends a long time ago. He's nothing more to me than he is to you."

"Huh huh," she smiled. "He shook my hand when he was here last week. Couldn't help but notice you were greeted with a kiss."

"Knock, knock" came a voice just on the other side of the door. Catherine couldn't help but be thankful she'd been saved by the visitor. She really didn't have an answer she could share, why he'd greeted her differently than the others.

"Ryan, come in." Catherine hoped her greeting didn't reveal anyhow grateful she was for the interruption. She pointed toward the empty chair next to Virginia.

"I can come back later," Ryan said, from the doorway. Sorry, Virginia. I didn't know you were in here."

"No worries." Virginia stood and pushed the chair closer toward the desk. "I've got some calls to make anyway." She paused at the door. "The catwalk company will be in later this afternoon. I'm assuming you want to sit in on the meeting?"

"Yes, I do," she waved at Virginia and motioned for Ryan to come in.

"What's up?" Catherine asked motioning to the chair Virginia had vacated.

"I've spent all morning reviewing that infusion bag you saved from the event in the operating room."

Catherine looked away, unable to meet her gaze. Presently, it was quiet all the home front but the storm was brewing again. It felt like watching the black clouds rolling in on a clear sky on a summer morning. You knew what the rest of the day was going to be like.

"Why didn't you tell me the bag was from Dr. Beliard's cardiac surgery?" Ryan asked, her words circumstantial.

"Would it have made a difference?" Catherine tried to sound more confident than she felt.

"Should it?" Ryan fired back, adjusting her cell phone more comfortably in her jacket pocket.

"No, of course not." Catherine swallowed, wishing for a sip of water, knowing she was backed against the ropes and wishing she could tap out.

"Then why the secrecy?"

Catherine rubbed the bridge of her nose. "I didn't think it warranted any different treatment. Our process has always been that you reviewed them as soon as you could. I didn't want to set a different precedent because it was an error relating to Dr. Beliard's cardiac surgery."

"I think it might be too late for that."

"Why's that?"

"See this?" Ryan slid a large black and white photograph under Catherine's nose and pointed to a small speck on the neck of the infusion bag."

"What am I looking at?" Catherine slid her reading glasses on and took a closer look.

"It's an injection mark on the neck of the bag."

"So, isn't that how your technicians usually make the bags?"

"We would never inject into the neck of the bag like that only into the port. And not this one." Ryan tossed another photo on top of the other. "This was a premixed product."

"Meaning what?" Catherine wasn't deliberately trying to pick a fight. It seemed odd that if an order changed, the pharmacy staff wouldn't just inject the additive and change the label.

"We didn't have to do anything with this bag except smack a patient label on it. There's no reason to inject anything into the bag. It comes premixed and ready to hang."

"Any chance the order changed and an additive was added to the bag?"

"It's against our policy to inject anything into a premixed bag. We'd have made a new bag in the IV room reflecting the change in concentration."

"What are you saying?" Catherine asked she was a racing horse and the gate was within sight.

"I'm saying something was injected into this bag by someone other than pharmacy after it was sent to the operating room, either by accident or on purpose. I have no way of determining which premise is accurate." She collected her photos and stood to leave. "What do I do now?"

"Write it up and sign it, like always." Catherine paused, her eyes darting back and forth as if she were reading pages from her risk management policy manual.

"And the bag?"

"Keep it secured in your office just as we'd normally do." She hesitated, adding as Ryan opened the door. "And Ryan?"

"Yes?" She turned to look back at her friend.

"Say nothing about this to no one. Not even your supervisors." Funny, she thought how that theme seemed to be repeating itself.

Chapter 5

"No comment, Mr. Hartmann, as I've said before." Catherine heard Virginia explaining to the visitor, her words sharp and tinged with sarcasm.

"Just a few questions?" Tim Hartmann, senior reporter for the Chronicle asked hopefully.

"No!" Virginia answered. Catherine knew Virginia hadn't made eye contact with him. She could

hear the sound of the keys striking the keyboard furiously in pace with the reporter's barrage of questions.

"One question."

"Do you have an appointment, Mr. Hartmann? If you don't I'm going to have to ask you to leave."

"As a tax-supported entity, an expectation of transparency exists." He paused to look at the

closed offices in succession as if he were counting the doors. "As a taxpayer, I have a right to ask. Where is everyone?"

"Most of the administrators are in a closed-door meeting." Virginia's response was curt,

bordering on rude. She stopped typing and looked up to meet him, her lips contorted in frustration.

"Is there something I could help you with?" Catherine asked, finally making an appearance from

her office to stand near Virginia's desk for reinforcement.

"You are?" He pulled a small notepad from his jacket pocket and awaited her response with pen

in hand.

"Catherine Masters, I'm the Risk Manager." She didn't bother to extend her hand.

"Wow," he laughed even though Catherine had said nothing funny. "I bet you've been busy."

Catherine took a minute to study him. She supposed he could be described as handsome, if he wasn't so annoying with his constant negative editorial barrage of the hospital system. Even before the current problems with the office of the inspector general, he'd been a thorn in the hospital's side.

He flipped the notebook back several pages and wrapped the pages around the book's back spine. "As you know, the monthly Board of Commissioners meeting is open to the public."

"Huh huh." She folded her arms over her chest and leaned against Virginia's desk knowing he wasn't going away anytime soon. She thought about pretending to yawn as he talked but didn't want to appear openly antagonistic.

"Do you have anything to say regarding the corruption charges made by the Office of the Inspector General?" His words methodical, as if he were marking questions off an imaginary list.

"No," Catherine answered looking to Virginia for validation.

"It's been several days since the office of the inspector general initiated the corruption investigation." He watched her closely for chinks in her armor.

"And?" She stood down his stare.

"Why do you think it wasn't discussed as an agenda item at yesterday's board meeting?"

"I couldn't say except discussion seldom ensues around open investigations." She paused, smiling. "I'd think an experienced reporter like yourself, would know that Mr. Hartmann."

"Okay then," He ignored her criticism and scribbled on the page as if she'd said something.

"What about the sexual misconduct charges filed against your Director of Procurement?" He paused before firing another question. "What about the termination of Victoria Wales? I was under the assumption; the board was reviewing all terminations of tenured employees?"

"No comment," she said again.

"There's rumor Andrew Caser is about to be replaced with a leader who can deliver better

quality and satisfaction scores?" He fired again.

"I wouldn't know anything about that." She returned fire.

"I see, what about the concerns expressed regarding physician gratuities, billing inconsistencies,

and violations related to the DEA?"

"Can't speak to any of those concerns." She turned away from him, her brow furrowed in

frustration. *Who else had Ryan talked about the incident with the automated cabinets?* "Mr. Hartmann, you can take a seat in the waiting area and hope you can get an appointment with someone."

"Maybe you'll know the answer to this one," he said sarcastically. "My research has revealed a connection between the Governor and the newly appointed Commissioner Fleming."

"Was that a question?" She pointed toward the chairs in the waiting area for him to take a

seat.

"No," he said with great arrogance. "I already know the answer." He paused and eyed her in a way that made her feel uncomfortable. "I was wondering if you were aware."

"Aware of what?" She didn't know why she was still engaging him. She should have walked

away already.

"Fleming's husband and Dr. Beliard went to college together."

"That's not so unusual. A lot of people in healthcare are or were connected. It's a small world."

"Maybe," he walked toward the office door. "But don't you think it's odd how the new commissioner couldn't even get a job as the chief operations officer at the smallest of the hospitals. Yet, she is now one of a handful of people managing and overseeing the executives in charge of all the hospitals including the small one she wasn't qualified to supervise?"

"No comment," she blurted out, making her way back into her own space as he exited the office and the door snapped shut. She couldn't help but think, however, what a very good question that was.

****

"Did Chloe know she was on the chopping block?" Ryan asked, as she and Catherine made their way back from the hospital cafeteria. "That's the fourth manager fired over the last two weeks?"

Catherine pulled her by the arm into the hospital chapel where they could have a more private conversation. "I'm not sure. Chloe's been so preoccupied with planning the obstetrics expansion in the new building, she's had a hard time trying to oversee the existing care and plan for the needs of the building's expansion at the same time."

"That event with the anesthesiologist surely didn't help."

"Which event?" Catherine hated to admit at any moment, there was usually more than one event. Most were insignificant with little or no negative outcomes.

"The delivery where the anesthesiologist pulled meds from his locker instead of the automated cabinet, not checking to make sure they were not expired before administering to the patient." Ryan reminded her.

"That was more a reflection of the Director of Anesthesiology's performance than Chloe's. She doesn't oversee the anesthesiologists or nurse anesthetist, Dr. Paine does." Catherine advised. "And Dr. Paine responded that he'd look into the event and see if the anesthesiologist should have done something different."

"Paine's looking into it?" Ryan asked, exhaling and shaking her head once the words were out of her mouth. "That will be a waste." She paused. "But they are all interrelated, don't you agree? You'd think one of the nurses would have questioned where the med came from." Ryan stifled a laugh. "How many doctors actually pull their own medications from the dispensing cabinets. Wouldn't you think one of them would have questioned where the vial came from?"

"I don't think any of these terminations have anything to do with performance or improving patient care. It's more to related to retaliation." There, Catherine thought, she'd said the words aloud. For weeks, they'd been circulating in her mind as if searching for an escape. Now that they were out of her mouth, there was no going back. She felt naked and exposed.

"Retaliation for what?"

"Chloe didn't support the termination of the nursing supervisor. Chloe was very verbal about giving her another chance?" Catherine wished she was near to a window to assess the weather, there might be an impending storm coming.

"Angela was diverting steroids from my cabinets and trading it to her personal trainer for sessions." Ryan paused. "If anyone deserved to be terminated, it was her," Ryan argued, sounding more like an attorney than a pharmacist.

"You're never going to be an unbiased reviewer when it comes to medication diversion. You always take it personally." Yes, she thought, they'd entered turbulent weather. If she'd been on a plane, she'd expected the airbags to drop.

"It is personal, my machines, my meds, and my accountability."

"See," Catherine stifled a laugh. "Is that why you're leading the charge to have Dr. Paine fired for setting up his own pharmacy in the physician sleep room."

"Once again, my meds, my responsibility. Besides, he allowed the anesthesiologists to hoard in the sleep room medications they didn't use on patients during procedures." She stumbled over her tongue not able to get the words out quick enough. "My God, they'd fashioned a makeshift IV pole from a metal hanger draped over the ceiling tile. They were giving themselves infusions of antibiotics and vitamin supplements. Legally I'm responsible for the regulation of these medications. Medications removed from the dispensing cabinets and not administered to a patient are to be returned to the cabinet and the patient's account credited. Unused medications aren't supposed to be hoarded in the anesthesiologist's sleep room for their own personal use."

"I know and I do understand. That's why I supported his suspension." Catherine said calmly, thankful the storm was passing.

"He should have been fired not suspended." Ryan caught her breath. "Is that why aren't you more supportive of reporting that event to the DEA?"

"Because I need my job, Ryan. And so, do you. You're a single Mom functioning on an independent income. You should consider that before making any more confessions to regulatory agencies."

"I haven't said a word about any of our events, as you requested." Ryan folded her arms as if she were six years old, sitting at the dinner table, and refusing to eat her broccoli.

"Tim Hartmann stopped by the office a few days ago," Catherine stated, but once she finished talking, she realized it came out as more of a question.

"He should write novels instead of newspaper articles, he has an amazing imagination." It was said with great scorn and Catherine knew Ryan meant it sarcastically.

"Maybe but truth be told, he never prints anything he can't substantiate. When he was here, he mentioned the DEA in a way that led me to believe he knew about the physician event with your OR machines."

"He didn't get it from me," Ryan said defensively.

"You sure?" Forget the storm, Catherine braced for a hurricane, instead.

"Have I ever lied to you? If I did it, you know me. I'll bend over and grab my ankles and take it." She paused. "But if I didn't, you'll never get to cop to it. I didn't say anything to anyone." She made her way closer to the chapel's exit. "But I'm not going to be anyone's scapegoat either. I'm not going to follow in Chloe's footsteps."

"I think we're all just holding our breath waiting for the other shoe to drop. All you can do is your best and hope it's enough." Catherine fiddled with the cell phone clipped at her waistband.

"Nevertheless, it seems like they'd have given her some administrative support while the new building is going up."

"Do they ever?" Catherine concealed a laugh. "Did you get any help with designing the medication rooms in the new building?"

"No, but that's different."

"How so?"

"My involvement is less direct. I'm not at the bedside with my hands in someone's wound or worse?" Ryan paused and checked to make sure her words were still private. "I heard Victoria Wales was let go a few days ago?"

Catherine looked away, hoping Ryan would move to another topic. "I heard that too."

"She's been here a long time too. Was any reason given?"

"I only heard that the board thought she should have acted timelier in investigating the charges made against Aaron Lewis."

"Like what? She can't really do anything until the charges are substantiated."

"With charges so extreme, he should have been suspended with pay pending the outcome of the HR review." She hesitated before adding, "Course it takes so long for HR to do anything, I guess Victoria knew that wouldn't work. Think of the outcry when the public finds out a sexual predator was given three weeks paid vacation while HR reviewed the charge."

"Doesn't sound like Victoria really had a choice?" Ryan offered. Catherine knew the firing of the corporate compliance director violated Ryan's strong sense of right versus wrong. It was one of the things she liked most about her friend.

"Probably not and I don't think it helped Victoria 's cause that Fleming doesn't like her," Catherine whispered.

"Why doesn't she like her?" Ryan whispered back.

"Fleming's best friend is the compliance director for the Booker system. She wants to bring him here but needs a high-level position to move him into. With Victoria gone, the door for Peter is open." She paused. "I think that's what happened with Kushion, too? Fleming wanted to move Mason Riley into that role and Kushion wasn't ready to retire yet."

"Warren Kushion has been the Chief Information Officer her for over ten years. He was well liked. I still can't believe they fired him." Ryan added.

"Severed," Catherine corrected her. "Not fired. Kushion's seat was still warm when Mason moved his ass into it."

"That's just wrong," Ryan's words were in sync, precise as if she was marching. "What's wrong with these people? How do they sleep at night?" She hesitated. "Sheep in wolves clothing. Sometimes I really hate being a part of all this."

"Be careful what you wish for." Catherine meant it as a joke but she knew her words came out as more of a warning.

Ryan paused, reaching for her cell phone as it vibrated from her suit pocket. "Do you know something that I don't? Should I be worried?"

"I think we should all be worried," Catherine responded, as the chapel door opened and Michele appeared before pushing her cleaning cart into view and through the door.

"Sorry," she smiled. "I didn't mean to interrupt. Is it okay to clean?" She stuttered and pulled the cart back toward the door. "I can come back later.

"No," Catherine insisted. "We were just taking a break." She opened the door and directed Ryan from the chapel.

Chapter 6

"I can't believe Beliard fired Andrew." Cliff's words were soft, empathic. "He's been here for so long; he grew up in this system."

"I can't say I'm surprised." Catherine joined him next to the copier, waiting for the coffee to finish brewing. "But still it's a shock."

"Did Beliard come here to do the deed?" Cliff asked, as Virginia moved closer to the group so that they were nearly elbow-to-elbow.

"No," she was shaking her head before he finished the question. "They never do it within your comfort zone." She paused. "He got a call early this morning to meet Beliard in his office at noon."

"Is he coming back for his things?" Ron asked, looking to Andrew's office where the door was closed, no doubt Virginia had turned the lights off.

"Was odd," Virginia swallowed the last drink of her water. "He called about an hour after being fired and asked if his missing box had surfaced yet."

"I told him it hadn't and that we'd pack up the rest of his office and call him when he could pick it up." Virginia words were barely above a whisper.

"You think he knew?" Catherine wasn't sure why she asked. It was common knowledge his days were numbered. Still, she felt compelled to ask.

"I think he suspected," Virginia poured each of them a cup of coffee. "It was obvious when Beliard was here things weren't good between them." She looked at Catherine. "Didn't you think?"

"I wasn't really paying attention."

"Anyone home?" a voice was heard as the door rushed open.

"Hey Virginia, I got a message you needed me to stop back by?" Jay asked, silencing his radio once he was fully into the room and only a foot or two away from the group.

"Sorry," Virginia pointed toward Andrew's office. "But I need you to pack up Andrew's stuff so I can call him to come by and pick it up."

Jay looked around curiously, "But I just finished bringing it all back here?"

"I know and I'm sorry," Virginia explained, tugging at her hair.

Jay exhaled and took several large steps toward the office. "Where am I moving it to this time?"

"You haven't heard?" Someone asked, it wasn't clear who.

"Heard what?" Jay opened the office door and flipped the light on.

"Andrew was fired this morning, he'll be picking up his things over the next day or two," Virginia answered, and walked closer to the office. "Focus on the big things, I'll come in and help you with the smaller stuff."

"Ok," he called from inside the office as Virginia rejoined the group, taking the space next to Cliff.

"No doubt Beliard will be by some time this afternoon to try and smooth things over." Cliff's words were straight forward but the expression he made with his face showed pure skepticism. He looked at Catherine. "I have this fear; he's going to tap me to be the interim CEO?"

"Does he have any other choice?" Virginia laughed. "Andrew fired the chief operating officer two months ago, citing him as incompetent."

"Did you spend any time with Michael?" Catherine tried to curtail her sarcasm but the man had been an imbecile. How he'd gotten the position in the first place had been a mystery to her and others since day one.

"What about Erin?" Cliff offered up the chief nursing officer frantically as if the decision was being made by the three of them.

"She just got here," Virginia added. "She has her hands full managing the nursing staff."

"If you don't want to do it, just say no when he asks you?" Catherine, the voice of reason, stated confidently and almost poetically.

She jumped as the exterior door opened abruptly and Beliard stepped inside, looking anxiously around the room.

"Afternoon," his words were precise. He shook his head as if he'd heard part of their conversation. However, his eyes locked on Catherine's. "Everyone doing ok?"

Virginia and Catherine nodded as Cliff motioned toward the coffee pot. "Can we offer you some coffee?"

"No." Beliard waved them off. "I need to appoint an interim CEO until we can refill the position." He looked to Cliff. "I was hoping I could count on you?"

"Of course, Dr. Beliard." He turned and followed Beliard back toward his own office. "Whatever you need me to do."

Catherine couldn't help but think of her oldest son after having been grounded. Cliff slumped his shoulders and bowed his head, looking up just as he closed the office door behind Beliard.

****

"Do you have a minute?" Beliard poked his head around the wall and into Catherine's office. She knew he'd finished talking with Cliff about a half hour ago. She'd felt Cliff's door opening and listened as Beliard made the circle around the office ad-libbing small talk from person to person until he'd found his way to her doorway.

She looked up from the stack of incident reports and smiled to him before tossing her glasses on top of the pile. "Something tells me I shouldn't say no to the CEO of the system?"

"Don't be silly." He fell into the empty chair. "It's just us. Anwar and Catherine."

"We haven't been those people in a long, long time, Anwar." She couldn't help but giggle at how out of place his big body looked as he squeezed himself into the small wooden desk chair. Like Cliff, earlier, he looked like a child in a time out.

She smiled and scooted as close against the desk as she could. It was almost as if she couldn't get close enough. He'd been in the sun, his skin was golden, almost bronze but not in a George Hamilton kind of way. His tan made the scar tissue on his forehead noticeably white, pale even. The scar hadn't been as obvious when they were younger, partially hidden by the dark locks of hair. Over the years as his hairline receded, the scar had become a more prominent characteristic.

Distinguished, she thought. It gave him a more distinguished persona, even if he'd gotten the scar wasn't very flattering. Slopping pigs, she remembered the story he'd shared with her in bed one night after she had asked about it. He'd gotten too close to the pig inside the pen and it had charged at him, tossing him and his slop pail four feet into the air before coming to rest atop the feed bin. Twelve stitches he had said, pulling his hair away so she could get a better look at the scar. And not twelve pretty ones he admitted before wrapping her into a bear hug and initiated making love to her again.

She was lost in the recollection not comprehending what he was saying until he called her name.

"Catherine, I wanted to apologize." He blurted out as if he'd been practicing. "When he met offsite a few days ago. I said some things that might have been considered controversial."

He seemed nervous as if he was filtering the words he wanted to use. She thought back to their life together before and couldn't remember a time when he'd ever exhibited anxiety about anything.

"What is it?"

"Nothing really." He smiled but not in the way she knew to be genuine. "Last time we met," the words tumbled around on his tongue as if in battle. "I'd just started taking those antidepressants."

"Antidepressants?" She tried to conceal her surprise. He wasn't the type of man who'd she thought would ever admit to needing or taking antidepressants.

"After my open-heart surgery, I had several episodes where I was…" He paused as if he didn't have anything else to add. "I wasn't myself."

"It's not uncommon." She comforted wishing she'd moved around to the empty chair next to him. It would have been okay to have taken the seat when he first entered her office but now it didn't feel right. It was too personal. In hindsight, she was grateful now for the desk between them.

"I'm thinking some of what I talked about to you was more than likely medication induced." He fiddled with the seat cushion of the chair.

"But you said.."

"I shouldn't have said anything to you. The office of the inspector general's investigation is confidential and probably won't amount to very much at all."

"Anwar, what are you hiding? Why aren't you being truthful with me?"

"I don't want you to get hurt." He leaned closer to her, whispering so softly she could barely hear him. "I want you to forget everything we talked about." He stood up abruptly. "You understand?"

"I don't understand, are you being threatened?"

"No, nothing like that." She knew his words weren't true, she knew how his voice changed when he was lying. It was like reliving the past over again. "But something from my past has popped up. It's something I hadn't thought about in years but it's come up nevertheless."

"Something to do with Mae and the baby?"

"No, no" he shook his head for effect. "It has nothing to do with them. It was before that when I was very young, when I was in medical school."

"Does this have something to do with Commissioner Fleming's husband?"

"What do you know about Jacob?" His eyes were soft as he said his friend's name.

"Nothing really, just that you were friends in school. You knew each other before he married Rachel."

"Jacob and I grew up on the same block in the Bronx." He smiled. "He was the brother I always wanted. We did everything together." He paused. "Even went to medical school together."

"I thought Jacob Fleming died in the military, I didn't know he was a doctor."

"He wasn't." Beliard cleared his throat, "He only went one semester then dropped out. We were both going through medical school on army scholarships. When he dropped out of school, he was enlisted to active duty."

"I'm sorry, I didn't know you'd lost someone else, someone other than Mae."

"I hadn't spoken to him in many years when he died. Over the years we drifted apart like people do." His stare was intense, searching her eyes as he went on. "You know how that happens, right?"

"Yes," her smile was warm. It was easy to remember why she'd fallen in love with him all those years ago. "Please," she paused staring him down as if he were under interrogation. "Tell me what's going on."

"I've told you everything I can." He squeezed himself out of the chair. "It's for your own good. I don't want anything to happen to you."

"Anwar, I'll do as you've requested, but I know you aren't being truthful with me."

"Just do what I ask, please." His words were pleading, desperate.

He closed the distance between so quickly, she jumped away in surprise before he took her by the shoulders and pulled her closer to him. Seconds past before he kissed her, on the cheek again, like he had the last time he'd been onsite. "I'll see you soon."

"Of course." Her smile was narrow, reserved.

He checked his watch. "I'm going to be late for a meeting."

She watched as he switched the chair he'd been sitting in for the other one, tucking the one he'd used as close against the wall as he could.

Before she could inquire, he added. "I think I might have broken your chair. It has a wobbly leg."

"I'll get facilities to look at it tomorrow."

"No rush." He stopped abruptly at Catherine's door just as Jay closed Andrew's office door and stepped across the room.

"Anwar Beliard," he offered his hand. "You are?" He bent at such an angle to read Jay's name badge.

"Jay Flowers," Jay hesitated before offering his hand.

Beliard studied him for a second. "Where have we met before?"

"I don't think we have, Sir." Jay pushed his hands in his pockets and rocked on the tips of his work boots. "Met, that is. I'm relatively new to the system."

Catherine stepped closer, "Jay transferred to facilities from IT a few months ago. Maybe you ran into him there?"

"Maybe," He said, hesitating to take a second look at Jay. "But I seldom forget a face." With that said he disappeared through the door, taking his exit almost as quickly as he'd entered.

It seemed like it took forever for the door behind him to swing closed. It made a resonating thump as it collided with the door frame and the pictures on her wall moved just enough to be uneven. She was grateful for the distraction.

What was going on? The question hung pregnant in the emptiness of her office.

****

"Knock, knock" A familiar unwelcomed voice announced before stepping into Catherine's office and motioning someone else in from the foyer to join her.

"Hi Erin," Catherine tossed her glasses atop the stack of file folders in the middle of her desk and pushed herself to her feet, hoping Erin couldn't read between the lines and identify the disdain in Catherine's smile.

Erin Lighter was tall, and thin with dark hair cropped close against her neck and curls that made a broad line across her forehead just above her eyebrows. Unlike most of the other chief nursing officers, Catherine had known and worked with over the years, Erin seldom wore a tailored suit. Instead, she was dressed more like a staff nurse in light-colored scrubs, an obviously too big, long white laboratory coat that hung almost to her knees and white Nike running shoes on her feet. The only time Catherine had even seen Erin dressed more formally was when the hospital was undergoing a regulatory survey.

During those times, Erin Seemed almost uncomfortable in a navy skirt and off-white blouse. Sometimes, Catherine wondered if that was the only suit Erin owned. She'd never seen her in anything else, scrubs or the navy ensemble. There was nothing in between.

"I wanted to introduce you to the new nurse manager for Labor and delivery." Erin pointed to the other visitors to the office. "Madison Byles,"

"Hi," Madison pumped Catherine's hand and smiled. "I've heard so many great things about you."

"Thank you," Catherine smiled. "And welcome." She looked to Erin and motioned to the empty chairs in front of the desk. "Have a seat."

Madison stepped past the empty chair closest to Catherine's desk, aiming to utilize the second chair that was flush against the wall. She tugged it away from the wall positioning it near the empty one in front of Catherine's desk.

"Be careful," Catherine warned. "My last visitor indicated the chair was broken and moved it away so that I'd remember to put in a work order and have it fixed. She jumped to her feet. "Let me grab another chair."

"Don't bother," Erin explained. "I can't stay. I'm late for a meeting," She pointed to the functional chair for Madison to take the seat before asking Catherine. "Would you mind, spending a few minutes with and then escorting her to lunch? I've got to meet the representative from the American Stroke Council to review our application for the gold award."

"No problem at all," Catherine smiled, thinking she had little choice anyway. Even though it had been presented as a request. Catherine knew it really hadn't been. "If there's anything you have questions about, I'd be happy to try and answer them for you."

"No, "Madison shook her head. "It's the first day, my head is spinning just trying to keep the names of the department heads straight."

"I bet," Catherine smiled. "There's so many new managers, you're in good company."

"That's what I heard." Madison cleared her throat, coughing into her hand. "I heard you've been here a while?"

"Yes, I've been at this site for ten years." She couldn't be sure but she felt as if her statement should have concluded with an apology. "So, you worked with Erin when she was with the Booker system?"

"Yes," Madison nodded. "We've worked together for over ten years." She paused. "I'm excited about this opportunity and to work with her again."

"You're going to have your work cut off for you, we're building a new building and the entire top floor is devoted to labor and delivery patients."

"I worked with Chloe many years ago when she first got out of nursing school" She paused swallowing as if it hurt. "I liked her. I'm sorry about what happened."

"Chloe was a good manager." Catherine nodded. "She was very well liked by her staff and the patients." There was a little voice inside her head that wanted to add. "But being a good manager here has nothing to with your continued employment." But Catherine didn't. Instead, she bit her lip and smiled, hoping Madison wouldn't detect how tainted with sarcasm her words were.

"Why was she fired?"

"I can't answer that," Catherine moved folders from one side of the desk to the other. "You'd need to speak to Erin about that."

"I did,"

"What did she say?"

"That the department was moving in a different direction." She looked behind to the foyer to see if anyone was nearby. "It's interesting, she'd been the manager here for a while, yes?"

Catherine nodded.

"And with the exception of one year, the hospital was recognized with the March of Dimes Caesarean section rate reduction award every year."

"I don't understand?" Catherine was genuinely confused but impressed by the fact that Madison had done her homework. She knew a lot about her predecessor as well as her accomplishments.

"What other direction would there be, except down?" She smiled. "I feel as if there's another agenda that maybe I'm not privy to?"

"If there is, I'm not aware either." Catherine couldn't have been more uncomfortable if she'd been standing there naked in front of her. "I think sometimes, it's more about the people than the work." She jumped to her feet and hoped to change the subject. "Are you about ready for lunch?"

"Yes," stood to join her. "And thank you for taking the time to meet me today. I'm looking forward to working with you."

"You, too." Catherine grabbed the telephone. "Let me call my friend."

"Friend?"

"Yes, the director of pharmacy, she has a bad habit of eating lunch in her office." Catherine punched in the extension number she knew by heart. "I've been getting her away from the desk and to the cafeteria at least three times a week since the new year started."

"You ready?" she spoke into the receiver once Ryan answered the phone.

"Yes," Ryan words were distracted on the other end. "I'm just finishing up meeting with Emiley?"

"The pharmacy technician?"

"Uh huh, I'll meet you in the cafeteria."

"Good, I'm with the new nurse manager for labor and delivery. She's joining us."

"Okay, I'll be there in a minute."

Chapter 7

"You mean her car's been in the parking garage all this time?" Catherine's words were loud, easily discernible over the chatter of the other occupants in the hospital cafeteria.

"Apparently," Ryan swallowed the last bite of a grilled cheese sandwich.

"I don't understand," Madison's face contorted with such confusion, Catherine felt sorry for her.

"When security called and told me that one of the vehicles left in the garage this morning belonged to someone in my department needed to be moved, so the garage floor could be repaved. I asked who it belonged to." She looked around to make sure their conversation was still private. "I called Emiley into the office and told her she needed to move her car."

"What car?" Emiley had asked.

"A blue Honda Civic," Ryan advised.

"I don't have that car anymore," Emiley continued to explain. "It was stolen from the parking garage like seven years ago." She had paused. "I filed a police report and everything. The insurance company paid me for it already,"

"You're kidding!" Madison exclaimed, laughing until she wiped tears away from her eyes. "The car's been sitting there in the garage all this time. She just forgot where she parked it?"

"Yes," Ryan laughed and nudged Catherine's arm noticing she wasn't laughing. "You don't' think that's funny?"

"Yes, of course, but as the risk manager I'm more concerned that it sat there all this time and no one from the security department noticed or investigated it." Catherine sliced her grilled chicken into small pieces and forked it unto the fork with several bites of salad. "Sort of leaves us with a false sense of security, don't you think?'

"Chimera," Ryan explained as she tossed the empty paper plate unto the tray for disposal.

"What?" Catherine questioned, adding her leftovers to the tray.

"A chimera is an illusion of something that can never exist."

"Is this from that show you're always watching, the X-files?"

"No," Ryan laughed. "In Greek mythology, it's a creature with the head of a lion, the body of a goat, and a serpent's tail. It can never exist genetically. It's an illusion of something that can never be."

"You're saying the security here is a chimera because the safety they provide is an illusion?" Madison moved anxiously in her chair.

"No, of course not," Ryan said

Catherine stood, grabbing the tray for disposal. "Good but it sure makes you wonder what security was thinking every time they patrolled past that old blue Honda civic?"

****

"Good to see you again. Sarah." Catherine heard Virginia address the visitors before she was able to get out of the office and join them in the main waiting area. She stopped short to find Beliard with Sarah Richardson and another fashionably dressed woman she wasn't familiar with.

"You look well, Catherine." Sarah smiled, falling into a semi-embrace before righting her posture and returning to line up with Beliard and the newcomer.

Catherine knew Sarah Richardson well. She'd spent almost six years at Sarah's site before coming to her present position. Sarah had been a fair but tough, chief executive officer who'd gained a bit of notoriety, partly because she was a woman and partly because she was the first African American woman appointed as the chief executive officer of any of the hospitals. Sarah's hospital was smaller than the one Catherine was currently assigned to but was renowned for its Neurological programs. Like Sarah, Catherine was proud of the work, they'd done together there.

"Thanks, you too," Catherine answered, waiting for either Beliard or Sarah to introduce the other woman.

Beliard offered his hand, taking Catherine's and pointing to the other woman with his remaining hand. "Wanted to introduce you to Lindsey Danson. She'll be acting as interim CEO here until the position is filled permanently."

"Welcome," Catherine tried to hide her surprise, knowing Virginia was doing the same. Neither was aware the interviews for CEO had even started, let alone finished with a candidate already selected.

Lindsey Danson was a pretty woman, older than she looked with red hair trimmed fashionably into place and pale freckles on her face that made her complexion seem almost white. Her suit wasn't terribly expensive, but it wasn't cheap either. The off-white jacket no doubt had a designer label on its collar and Catherine was sure it cost more than twice what hers probably had.

"I've heard so many nice things about you." Lindsey's voice was deep and scratchy as she shook Catherine's hand before moving around to engage everyone standing nearby as well as those who'd ventured out of the office.

"Ah," Beliard smiled as Erin emerged from her office, with several file folders against her hip. "Lindsey, let me introduce you to Erin Lighter. She's the new chief nursing officer here."

Erin did no better at hiding her surprise than either Virginia or Catherine. Catherine had to look away to avoid breaking out into laughter. She couldn't help but consider how surprising it was that Erin hadn't hand-picked the CEO. After all, she had alliances with all the other people recently hired both at the regional and corporate level. Odd, she'd have no influence in Lindsey's appointment.

"Welcome," Erin offered her hand, "So nice to meet you."

Catherine looked away, knowing Erin's words weren't genuine and feeling as if Lindsey knew it, too.

****

"Did you get Lindsey moved into the office?" Catherine asked, as she and Virginia took large strides toward the cafeteria.

"Mostly," Virginia answered, chewing quietly on a small piece of gum in her mouth. "Andrew didn't keep that much stuff in the office. And Lindsey didn't bring that much with her. It hadn't taken long for Jay to move his out and hers in." She paused and looked at the CEO's closed office door. "Jay stayed late last night to sit up her office. He even connected the computer and printer. His IT training is really coming in handy." She waved to numerous staff as she passed the cashier, straining to look around those already in line to see what food selections were available. "I had Michele come in early this morning and clean everything up really well."

"That was thoughtful of you," Catherine grabbed a tray and placed a paper plate of eggs on the top. "Did you see Erin's face when Dr. Beliard introduced Lindsey as the interim CEO?"

Virginia snorted, holding back a laugh. "Yeah, I about wet my pants." She moved deeper into the cafeteria; her eyes lit on the makeshift omelet bar. She took a place at the end of the line at the breakfast bar, tapping her fingers against the shell of the hard-boiled egg she'd already selected from the bar. "Did you know Beliard had selected an interim?"

"No, I was just as surprised as you. It didn't appear as if the other chiefs knew either. It was obvious Erin didn't know."

"Didn't know or didn't approve?" Virginia whispered.

"Won't really matter. I've a feeling if she's not an associate of Erin, I doubt she'll last very long." Catherine scooped several portions of scrambled eggs on her plate, looking longingly at a tray of biscuits. Carbs, she thought to herself. They were a no-no.

"I get the feeling that Beliard isn't a fan of Erin's?"

"Is that a statement or a question?"

"You and Beliard are tight, I just thought he might have said something-"

"He hasn't said anything about her one way or another." Catherine interrupted.

"Really?"

Catherine knew by the way Virginia asked the question that she didn't believe her. Still, she didn't reply.

"Lindsey seems okay." Virginia went on without missing a beat. "I haven't really spent that much time with her. She left for Maryland to present our stroke data and collect the award."

"Still can't believe we're being recognized with a quality award." Catherine exhaled as her words concluded, hoping her embarrassment wasn't evident by the way she'd said the words.

"Why's that?" Virginia's question seemed defensive to Catherine and she felt guilty.

"Have you seen the variance reports on my desk? I get one problem resolved and three more take its place. It's as if I added water and multiple gremlins appeared." She laughed, shaking her head. "Ryan called it a chimera."

"Chimera?" Virginia stopped near the cashier, waiting for Catherine to catch up.

"Yes, seems like the errors and the awards are contradictions, one stacked against the other. She called it an illusion of something that can't really exist." Catherine blew a sigh, hoping she'd remembered the description correctly.

"That's an interesting analogy but it won't really matter, Erin will never let Lindsey have any credit for any recognition."

"I'm not sure Lindsey should get any accolades. She wasn't involved in the award. Then again, neither should Erin. The award is a result of data from last year. Erin wasn't working here either. Actually, everyone that did the work has been fired or quit." Catherine saw the faces of Chloe, Janet, and Ana in her mind's eye. These were the people who should be recognized for the work.

"I think Ryan's right. It is an illusion." Catherine said as she motioned Virginia toward a table in the back of the cafeteria and hoped they could enjoy a peaceful albeit brief breakfast.

****

"What has Lorraine said about moving to the corporate office?" Catherine sliced her grilled chicken into pieces and forked a large bite. She had sucked breakfast down in record time and barely tasted a bite. She hoped she'd be able to at least taste some of her lunch as she cut the remnants of the chicken breast into smaller more manageable bites. "As Beliard's executive assistant, she must have lots of inside news?"

"If she does, she's not sharing much. Although she did say, Fleming was there about an hour after Beliard left here and returned to his office." Virginia looked around behind their table. "She didn't say much except their discussion was very loud and Lindsey's name was mentioned several times."

"Lindsey?" Catherine whispered. "She's hasn't been here long enough to have gotten into trouble already?"

"I think Fleming's upset Lindsey's here at all. It doesn't appear as if Lindsey's appointment was approved by the board. Beliard hired her all on his own."

Sounds like Anwar, Catherine thought but didn't say it aloud. "There's Ryan." She waved to the pharmacy manager as she entered the cafeteria.

"So, about this guy, Ryan's dating. Has she said anything?" Virginia asked, watching as Ryan was lost in the food line.

"No, just that he's not in healthcare."

"What does he do?"

"A police officer, maybe but I'm not sure."

"Seriously with a gun and badge?"

"Yes, I think so."

"She hasn't said anything about him?"

"Only that he's nothing like her ex-husband."

****

"Why'd Virginia take off as soon as I sat down?" Ryan asked, twisting the top off her plastic bottle of soda and watching Virginia's back as she walked away from the table..

"I think she had a meeting to set up for," Catherine explained. "Mostly just keeping me company till you arrived."

"Have you spent much time with the new CEO?" Ryan asked, watching as the chief administrators emerged from the physician's dining room, clustered together and talking like they were the popular kids in high school.

"Not really, I've been inundated with variances?" Catherine answered trying not to let her disdain be evident as she watched the administrators exit the physician's dining room and pass through the cafeteria. These people were the highest paid employees on site. Yet, they entertained squatter's rights in the domain of the physician dining room even though none of them were physicians.

She thought of Dr. Lee and the green grocery bags of food he pilfered from the physician's lounge every morning. If anyone's meals should be free, she thought. It should be someone making minimum wage, not the physicians and administrators.

Fairness, integrity, doing the right thing, it was all an illusion. It wasn't fair and they no longer even bothered to pretend that it was. Ryan's chimera description had been a perfect analogy.

"Not medication variances?" Ryan asked, rolling her eyes and shaking her head. "I haven't finished with the others yet." She looked around and moved her chair closer toward Catherine. "I sent that IV bag from Beliard's surgery to a chemist friend of mine for analysis."

"Why would you do that?" Catherine stopped eating. "I told you this was a confidential matter."

"I removed the name and made up a fake medical record number."

"What made you think it needed further assessment?" Catherine was calmer, her words precise.

"I ran a sample through the spectrometer we have in the pharmacy."

"And?" Catherine was intrigued. She hadn't thought of that. They seldom needed to test anything in the house.

"There was something in the sample. I couldn't identify." She paused, wiping a string of melted cheese from her mouth. "I want to know what it is."

"When will we know?"

"About a week, maybe less depending on how busy he is."

"And you're sure you can trust this man?"

"Yes, we went to pharmacy school together and college before that. We've been friends for a long time."

Ryan paused and leaned closer into Catherine's space. "Did Beliard really code during the surgery?"

"Twice," Catherine nodded.

"Who ran the code?"

"Ana," Catherine tossed her trash on the tray in the middle of the table. "Good thing, she had so

much experience in the emergency room."

"Lot of good that did her. Wasn't she one of the first that was fired?" Ryan's phone went off just as they stood to leave.

"It's Virginia," she said, looking up from the phone and redialing.

"Hey, Virginia," Ryan announced into the receiver.

"Is Catherine still with you?' Virginia asked.

"Yes, we're just finishing lunch."

"I need you both in administration as soon as is possible."

"What's going on?"

"A representative from the OIG is here to see you both."

"The office of the inspector general? We're on our way."

****

Catherine looked anxiously around the conference room, hoping they'd find out soon what the meeting was about. She looked across the table to Ryan, wishing she knew what had prompted the invite. Usually, whenever regulatory audits were conducted, there'd be ample time to prepare the staff to answer the questions completely and specifically, focusing on just answering the question and nothing else.

She smiled across the table. Ryan was a pro; she'd done more than her share of interviews. She was experienced enough to know exactly how to answer. Too bad, Catherine thought, the same couldn't be said for the other two-thirds of the management team. They were all newer than shiny dimes and their discomfort was more than evident as they took their seats at the conference table.

The inspector waited until everyone was seated before introducing herself and asking everyone at the table for name and function at the hospital. She was younger than the agents that usually ran the investigations. And by the way, she sat perched at attention like an eagle watching and waiting to swoop down and collect its prey, she was aiming to more than make up for any weakness her age might imply. Name, rank, and serial number, Catherine considered thinking there were times when it did feel as if she was a prisoner of war.

She waited until everyone around the conference table had spoken before she tucked her chair so tight against the table's edge, it pushed into her stomach and spilled her breasts on top of the table. She cleared her throat as she folded her hands together as if in prayer. "I'd like to thank everyone for coming."

Her eyes made contact with each person as she went on. "Now, if you don't mind. Everyone except for the risk manager and pharmacy manager, please vacate the room."

"Pardon?" Erin asked first, looking across the table to where Lindsey sat, as if they were in alliance.

"My request to interview was directed to specific people. This is an active Inspector General investigation. It's a need to know, only." She glanced around the room again. "And frankly, most of you don't need to know." She straightened a stack of papers. "You're all excused, except for Ms. Masters and Ms. Allen."

Quietly, everyone except for Catherine and Ryan, stood and pushed their chairs up against the table before quickly taking their exit. Once everyone except the designated people had left the room, she turned in her seat to face Ryan.

"How do you know Aaron Lewis?" There were no pleasantries exchanged, her words were thick and confident.

Catherine couldn't help but feel as if the investigator already knew the answer she was looking for.

"Aaron Lewis?" Ryan repeated.

"Yes," the investigator slid more comfortably into her chair. "He's the corporate director of procurement."

"I know who he is." Ryan's said before the investigator had finished making the clarification. "But I really don't know him very well."

"How often would you say you encounter him?"

"In person encounters or any encounter?" Ryan cleared her throat and adjusted herself more comfortably in the chair.

Catherine smiled thinking Ryan sounded more like a lawyer than a pharmacist.

"Any." The investigator tapped her manicured nails against the table's top.

"Aaron is the director of procurement for materials, not pharmaceuticals."

"Meaning?"

"Meaning, he shouldn't have any involvement with any pharmacy formulary considerations or decisions."

"Formulary? Please explain." The agent picked up her pen to take notes.

"Formulary is a list of medications reviewed by the pharmacy that we agree to have available to the physicians for patients they treat here within the system."

"Having a product available on formulary is a big deal?"

"Yes, for the company that manufactures the product. It can be a very big financial deal."

"Just meds?"

"No, most devices and non-pharmaceutical products also go through a review process but it's usually a panel of practitioners who are familiar with the products."

"Mr. Lewis had oversight of these types of products but not medicines?"

"Correct." Ryan snatched a water bottle from the center of the table and sipped delicately.

"Who controls the pharmaceuticals?"

"Pharmacy" Her words were confident and bold. Catherine knew it was an argument Ryan had made before.

"Specifically, who in Pharmacy, you?"

"No, not really. There are five managers who work closely with the pharmacy clinical coordinators to manage the formulary."

"Explain, how you manage the individual projects, Ryan," Catherine put in, seeing the confusion on the inspector's face.

"It depends on which manager is championing what medication. For example, two of the four sites do not treat pediatric patients. So, for any treatment regimen for pediatrics, just us and Pleasant Ridge would decide. The other two sites wouldn't care."

"Ever been a time when the five of you didn't agree?"

"Sure, but we usually come to some kind of agreement. We work very well together."

"You work well with Mr. Lewis?"

"I don't understand the question." Ryan's gaze met Catherine's across the table. Catherine couldn't help but experience a sense of pride. Ryan had learned well.

"We've spent the last few weeks interviewing a variety of staff and managers, even some vendors."

"And?"

"We're just curious about *your* relationship with Mr. Lewis?"

Catherine knew Ryan wasn't being evasive. She genuinely was confused. "I don't understand." Ryan recanted.

"You are the only female pharmacy manager." The investigator added, tossing the pencil down atop the table.

"I don't like what you're implying." Ryan's response was curt.

"If you have a question for her, please ask it." Catherine chimed in. "Otherwise, move on."

"You're aware of the charges made against Mr. Lewis?"

"Yes, of course." Ryan took another sip of water.

"Was there ever a time, he conducted himself in a manner to you that made you feel threatened or uncomfortable?"

"Look," Ryan pushed away from the table. "Let's get something straight. I didn't like Aaron, that's no secret. He was constantly interfering with the contractual processes for the pharmacy formulary."

"And you didn't like that?"

"No, I didn't. And I dropped the hammer on him every chance I got." She stood up. "I don't know what happened between Aaron and those women. But I promise you, if he'd pulled any of that crap with me, I'd snapped him like a bug."

"Ms. Allen?' the investigator stood and moved to stand between Ryan and Catherine.

"Dr. Allen," Ryan corrected him.

"Dr. Allen, please take a seat. We aren't done."

"Actually, I think we are." Ryan looked at Catherine. "I believe I'm entitled to have my own legal representation present, yes?"

"Yes," Catherine nodded and gathered her paperwork. "She is."

"It's okay," the investigator nodded. "That won't be necessary. I'm finished with you, Dr. Allen." She turned to Catherine. "But I do have a few questions for you?"

Catherine watched as the conference room door closed behind Ryan. "What's this about?"

She checked her watch. "Just as soon as my colleague from the FBI arrives with your system's legal advisor."

As if cued, a knock at the conference room door startled them both. Catherine moved to an empty chair across the table and watched as Virginia led the newcomers into the room and exited almost as quickly. They took a seat on either side of the investigator without exchanging pleasantries.

Chapter 8

"Do you recognize these invoices?" One agent asked as Catherine watched him display several documents across the table. They were patient accounts Catherine had approved to either be written off or reduced depending on the outcome of the patient's care.

He waited while she reviewed the documents, his suit wrinkled and worn as if he'd slept in it. Agent Frank Bronson was middle-aged and probably not that far away from retirement, Catherine considered. He was good-looking in a rugged Paul Newman kind of way with thinning blonde hair and intense blue eyes. He could have used a shave; she doubted all the overgrowth was from today.

"Of course." She pointed to her signature on the documents.

"Can you elaborate on the circumstances that led to these accounts be credited or reduced?" The way he'd asked the question Catherine knew he'd already formed an opinion regarding the document's legitimacy.

"This one," she pointed to the one furthest away from where she sat at the conference table. "Came after we failed to properly complete a fall assessment for an elderly female patient. To further complicate things, the bed alarm wasn't properly set by the PCA assigned to the patient."

"So, what happened?" He smiled, a dazzling smile, she thought of Newman's picture on the commercial bottles of salad dressing.

"The patient fell on her way to the bathroom and broke her hip." Focus, she told herself, hoping he didn't see the chip in her armor.

"You authorized a reduction of the patient's bill?"

"I had the charges associated with her hip fracture wiped from the bill, yes."

"Was that a decision you made independently?"

"No, I collaborated with our previous CEO, Andrew Caser."

"What about this one?" The agent pushed another file closer to her so that she could see it better.

"We discovered there was a problem with the sterilization process for several non-disposable surgical items."

"I'm not in healthcare, Mrs. Masters. Give me the lay version."

Catherine blinked as if she'd been slapped. "Many of the instruments are disposable, others are not. Instead, they are sterilized here on site." She paused, waiting to see if anyone had questions. As there were none, she went on. "It's a two-step process, where the instruments are secured into a tray and placed in the sterilizer for a specific period of time. When it's finished, the tray is flipped over and sterilized again. When both cycles are finished, the flashing process is completed and a light indicates it is ready to be used on the next surgical case."

"So where did this sterilization break down?"

"We realized there were several cases where the tray was removed before the second cycle was complete."

"The instruments weren't clean?"

"They were clean but not sterilized." Catherine clarified.

"Tomato, tomatoe," the inspector sang before adding, "How many people were affected?"

"Twenty-two." She answered without making eye contact.

"How was it handled once the hospital was made aware?" The inspector wrote quickly on her notepad, not bothered by the noise her bracelet made as it that jingled and jangled against the hard surface of the table.

"We notified the patients regarding a potential exposure and paid for hepatitis and HIV panel testing." Catherine closed her eyes, hoping the bracelet wouldn't be such a distraction if she couldn't see it. "We followed these patients for the next year to ensure they'd not been compromised." Her study had failed, the sound of the bracelet tapping the desk was annoying whether she could see it or not.

"Are you aware of any negative sequela for any patient from the exposure?" Agent Bronson asked.

"No."

"And manipulations of these accounts were a result of collaboration between you and the CEO?" Inspector Winters clarified.

"My office was involved in this recommendation as well." Ms. Heights, the system legal advisor, added. "We agreed it was best to divert any negative publicity and put the patient's best interest above any financial considerations." Gayle Heights was an odd-looking woman, especially considering she was the chief counsel for the entire system. Her hair seemed to always be in desperate need of a good combing, maybe even a cut and some highlights. No matter what time of the day, her suit looked as if it belonged to someone else, someone, significantly bigger and she'd simply slid into the suit and when on her way to the next meeting.

"Was it a successful venture?" The inspector's question was curt as if she already knew the answer to the question. Catherine disliked her more and more every time she opened her mouth.

"We believe it was, yes." Ms. Heights answered before Catherine could.

"If you've nothing else for me, gentlemen. I have some other things I need to attend to." Catherine waited as they looked from one to the other before shaking their heads at one another.

"Appreciate your time." The agent offered his hand and handed her a business card. "If you think of anything else, you'll give me a call?"

"Of course." She moved to the door, glancing at Ms. Heights before making her way out of the conference room.

It was no surprise to see Virginia rise from her desk and follow her into the office. "Janitorial services called while you were in with the FBI. They found something in the visitor bathroom you should see. Can I call and tell Greg you're out of your meeting?"

"Yes, give me a few minutes to use the restroom." She dropped her keys on the desktop and disappeared out of the office and into the hallway.

****

"Where'd you get these again?" Ryan snapped the latex glove against her wrist and picked up one of the three empty intravenous syringes from Catherine's desk. She studied the one and then another, not bothering with the third syringe.

"One of the janitors found them in the guest bathroom just off the lobby," Catherine explained, pulling a fresh pair of gloves from the box she kept on the shelf.

"Which bathroom?"

"Men's."

"Just these three?"

Catherine nodded and held another one up in the space between them. "Is there any way you can determine if these are ours?"

"Possibly," Ryan examined the syringe more closely. "There should be a barcode here. I just need to compare it what we have currently in the house and see if the lot numbers match."

"What about the contents?" Catherine knew she was probably pushing it, but she also knew Ryan loved a good mystery. Sometimes she thought Ryan would have made a good detective. No one was better at putting the pieces than she was.

"There's a bit of liquid still in the barrel of the syringes." Ryan held them up against the fluorescent lights on the ceiling. "If it's a narcotic, I might be able to identify what it is with the spectrometer. Otherwise, I'll have to send it to my chemist friend."

"Try to determine what it is first by yourself. Then send it to your friend but I'd rather keep as few people in the loop as I can."

"Of course." Ryan collected the syringes and dropped them into a plastic bag motioning for Catherine to give her the chain of custody log to sign.

"Standard rules apply," Catherine reminded her. "You can't talk to anyone about it."

"Of course," Ryan paused at the door. "Leaving soon?"

Catherine pointed to a stack of documents. "I've some clerical stuff to do before I leave."

"Clerical stuff?"

"I need to make file folders for all those incident reports."

"Want some help?"

"No, I need to get a box of folders the closet in the main office." She tapped her phone to check the time. "It won't take long, then I'm leaving."

"I can wait?"

"No, don't be silly. I'll see you tomorrow."

Ryan nodded before disappearing through the door and out of site.

****

"So, you just stood quietly inside the supply closet and listened to their argument?" Gordon asked buttering another piece of toast and motioning for Catherine to pass him the grape jelly.

"It didn't start out that way." She handed the jar to him and jumped toward the coffee pot as it finished brewing. "I was out of file folders; it was late. All the clerical support had left for the day. I guess the door was only partially open after I went inside and they thought they were alone."

"Neither Lindsey nor Erin realized you were still there?" He asked.

She shook her head that they weren't aware anyone was nearby.

"What were they arguing about?" He prompted. She thought he sounded like she was telling a scary story. All that was missing was the campfire and smores.

"Lindsey doesn't agree with the current methodology of streamlining managers with longevity out of the system."

"Would any sane person without an ulterior motive support disposing of the most experienced people in the system, any system?"

"It's hard to say really. I've worked with CEO's before who replaced their immediate staff with managers they knew they could trust." She waved her hand between them. "But never to this level. Seems like everyone, upper and middle managers are being replaced."

"In all the years and transitions, firing to this caliber has never happened." She finished the last sip of coffee. "And I think Lindsey is concerned that everyone is being replaced with someone who worked with Erin previously."

"People who're loyalty is tied to Erin instead of Lindsey?"

"Possibly, in this business, there's always another ladder to climb. Healthcare is just as vicious as the financial industry." She smiled. "The money people are just more honest about what they'll do to get to the top." Chimera, she thought again.

"Are you worried about your job?"

"I'd be a fool not to be, but there is a rumor that Beliard has placed a hold on all patient care related terminations."

"Do you see him much?"

"Who?" She asked even though she knew he was referring to Beliard.

"Anwar?" He paused. "You know who I mean."

"Yes, he's been in the office a time or two since his appointment." She felt guilty for not mentioning his heartfelt plea to meet with her, even worse that she's actually met with him.

"Must be odd, running into each other, even peripherally."

"Was a long time ago, Gordon."

"Catherine, you were married to the man. I know you well enough to know that that in itself counts for something."

"You were married before, too." She dropped the coffee cups into the sink and ran water over their breakfast dishes.

"Yeah but I don't run into my ex-wife at company picnics." He met her at the sink and wrapped his arms around her waist. "I love you."

Catherine pointed to the clock. "You're going to be late for school."

He stuffed the last quarter of the toast into his mouth as he passed by the table and pulled his suit jacket from the back of the chair in a single motion. "Kind of late for you." He slid his arms into the jacket. "You're usually already on the road by seven am."

"There's so much tension in the administrative office right now. I'd rather work later after everyone has left for the day."

"Cliff and the others on the team aren't getting along any better either?"

"Not really, In the very short time that Cliff was interim, he was able to make budget but he did it by cutting back on resources and supplies." She handed him his briefcase, realizing that if he weren't getting ready to retire, it would probably be time for a new one. "Erin's requested all those nursing positions plus new ones back and Lindsey's been approving it."

"You're no longer making a budget?"

"No, we aren't and he's mad at the world."

****

"I forgot we had to set through this two-hour training session this afternoon." Catherine moaned into her hands and covered her face as Madison Byles took the empty seat behind her.

"Me, too." Madison whispered before getting fully into the seat." I'm supposed to train the two new nurse managers starting tomorrow. I could really use these two hours to catch up."

"You're training already?" Catherine hoped she didn't sound as surprised as she felt. Madison hadn't even been on staff a month. Yet, she was training new staff. What was the term Ryan had used to describe the illusion that things were one way when they were really another?

"How much longer?" Ryan whined, as she leaned closer toward Catherine and whispered. "This is torture."

"I can't believe the person sent by corporate to deliver the ethics training to us is Gayle Heights." Catherine words were so low, she knew no one else other than Ryan would be able to decipher what she'd said.

"You aren't a fan of the general counsel?" Ryan asked seriously but Catherine knew she was being sarcastic.

"No, I'm not. I don't care what recommendation I make regarding a case. She rarely supports it." She thought back to the interrogation by the FBI agents and how surprised she'd been that Gayle wasn't firing the questions off as well.

The picture Gayle painted during the OIG discussion regarding support for risk management's recommendations hadn't been exactly accurate. At first, Gayle had denied the request to pay proactively for HIV and hepatitis titers for the patients exposed by the incomplete equipment sterilization. Catherine had been called to corporate to plead her case. Fortunately for her, Beliard's predecessor had agreed and overturned Gayle's denial. The general counsel had conveniently left that fact out.

"You'd think they'd sent someone else even if only because of the indictment she's facing," Ryan whispered.

"I know, that woman has some balls. If I was charged with corruption charges, this is the last sermon I'd be giving." Catherine tried not to smile but she couldn't help it.

"Speaking of balls? What about the board of commissioner's meeting last night?" Madison asked in words so hushed, Catherine had to lean in to hear what she'd asked.

"I heard," Catherine looked around. "The board didn't approve Beliard's proposal to appoint Lindsey as CEO."

"You mean, Fleming didn't support the recommendation, don't you? The rest of the board couldn't care less." Madison interjected, looking behind them again to ensure no one had sat down behind them and was privy to their conversation.

"No doubt Erin's bidding." Catherine sounded bitter and she felt a tad guilty. Perhaps, she should have held her tongue altogether. It was no secret Madison had worked with Erin before. By all accounts, she was just as much a "mole" as anyone else Erin had brought into the system. But there was something about Madison that Catherine liked, something that made Catherine think Madison wouldn't say anything to Erin, wouldn't tell her anything shared in confidence.

"No doubt," Madison added, motioning to the front of the room where the speaker was scanning the room as if she'd asked a question from the audience.

"How long did you work with Erin before coming here?" Catherine threw out the line, anxious to see what she might catch.

"Honestly," Madison looked around the room. "We were part of the same system for nearly ten years but we worked at different sites. When she came to Booker, I only worked with her for a few weeks. I'd already given my notice before she started." She smiled. "And it was a long two weeks if you know what I mean."

"Not a cohesive relationship?" Catherine smiled, pulling her imaginary line in.

"I think she and I have different management styles." Madison paused. "Erin wasn't here when I initially interviewed for this position. Truthfully, I probably wouldn't have applied if I'd known she was going to be the CNO."

Madison scribbled her name on an attendance sheet that was going from desk to desk. "I'm trying to think positively but I've my doubts this will be a long- term commitment for me."

Wow, Catherine thought, she hadn't seen that coming and she hoped her expression hadn't revealed her surprise.

"Catherine?" She heard her name from the hallway and for a second she thought, she'd been busted, thought someone might have heard what she'd said about Erin. She turned to see Virginia, hanging halfway into the room from the hallway and motioning her closer.

"ACHA is here," Virginia whispered.

"Thank God, a reprieve." She said to Virginia. In over twenty years of healthcare, she never thought she would be so happy to partake in an unannounced regulatory audit.

Virginia held the door for Catherine to get through. "I've got you set up in the conference room." They walked quickly toward the conference room, heels clicking against the polished floor almost like a clock or a ticking bomb. Catherine couldn't be sure.

The ACHA inspector across the table was young, younger than any Catherine had had in a while. The inspector flipped through the patient charts she'd requested, pausing momentarily to inspect the long, polished nails of her right hand.

She wasn't in any hurry, that was for sure. Twice she'd been offered the opportunity to take a break. Both times she'd refused.

"Can I offer you some water or coffee?" Virginia asked from the doorway, her feet only steps into the conference room.

"No," the inspector barked. "And I'd appreciate it if you'd didn't interrupt again."

Virginia backed out of the office, face, red and flushed, mumbling, "My apologies."

"When you discovered the surgical devices weren't flashed sterilized correctly, what immediate steps did you take?" Her words were fluid like she were reciting a poem as she waited for Catherine to respond.

"We contacted a surgical device company and began utilization of disposable kits until the problem could be remediated."

"These patients were notified?" She tapped the file folders on the table.

"We've already answered the FBI's questions related to this event." Catherine's words were impatient, bordering on angry.

"I'm not with the FBI." She coughed into her hand. "Contrary to popular belief we don't share notes." There was a moment's pause before she added. "Now please answer the question."

"Yes," Catherine licked her lips. "Once we identified who was affected, the patients were informed as is outlined in our sentinel event policy."

"This policy?" She held up a stapled packet of papers.

"Yes."

"Associated staff retrained?"

"Both the department manager and assistant manager were relieved of their responsibilities pending the outcome of the investigation. Once all the facts were in both were terminated." Catherine paused. "The entire department underwent retraining."

"Is surgical sterilization being monitored on your current performance measurement report?"

"Yes."

"For how long?"

"Six months."

"I'll be back in three months to reassess." The inspector stacked the charts into a neat pile.

"You aren't able to close this out today? This event was self-reported. We'd already completed the retraining and made the changes in our process before your office even notified us you'd be reviewing the event."

"No, due to the extent of the problem, as well as the number of patients affected. I feel as if it's paramount to patient safety to make sure these quality issues are resolved." Her words were like acid and Catherine felt the burn all the way to her core.

"I assure you it's been corrected."

"Then you'll have time over the next three months to focus on other more pressing things." She smiled but it wasn't a friendly one. Her words dripped with content as she added. "I read the papers; I know you have plenty of other things to worry about."

Catherine and the inspector stood up at almost the same time and pushed away from the table.

"It's odd that your chief nursing officer wasn't available to participate today."

"She had another commitment and as I am the risk manager, she knew I'd be more than happy to assist and provide you with whatever you needed." It felt odd defending Erin, especially since she didn't especially care for her. But that's how it was in families sometimes, you supported one another without question when the stakes were down.

"Still, you'd think she'd made herself available."

"She and the quality manager are in Orlando to accept the Surgical Care Improvement project award." *God, when was this lady going to leave?* She had to bite her tongue to avoid asking her the question.

"Your hospital won a SCIP award?" She couldn't have tried any less to hide her contempt. It dripped from every word and Catherine was more than aware of the restraint it had taken not to call her out.

"Two actually, one for antibiotic prophylaxis and other for DVT prophylaxis. Neither had anything to do with instrument sterilization." Catherine explained.

"Still," she rubbed her tongue across the roof of her mouth. "Seems a contradiction but I guess here in this system, things are seldom as they appear." She smiled. "Don't you agree?"

It had taken every ounce of strength for Catherine to answer. "No, not really," especially since she actually did feel that way. A chimera she thought, Ryan had said it was a chimera. And truth be told, she did agree.

Chapter 9

"Sorry, I'm late." Catherine entered Ryan's office in a rush, stopping only long enough to drop into one of the two chairs in her office.

"No, problem." Ryan pointed to the good-looking gentleman occupying the other chair. "You remember my friend, Nathan?"

"Yes," she offered her hand to the dark-haired man. "You sure you don't want to use the pharmacy conference room? There's a lot more room and--" She pointed to the walls of Ryan's office. "Not so many X-files things staring at us."

"Nathan's more than familiar with my obsession," Ryan explained. "We've been friends for years, even while the show was still on television." She laughed. "Besides, I don't want anyone to overhear us."

"So," Catherine rubbed her hands together. "What's this about?"

"Nathan's my Anderson & Black sales representative, we've known each other for many years. His girlfriend, Lauren, is also an approved vendor for the healthcare system."

"And?"

"Nathan came to me yesterday to share Lauren's story about something that happened between her and Aaron Lewis."

"Is this something you should report to the FBI or the police?" Catherine interrupted.

"Probably, she wouldn't sleep with him and he removed her devices from the approved product list. Since it's not a medication, it really has nothing to do with me. But I wanted you to know just the same."

"Give me a blank piece of paper?" Catherine reached across the desk to Ryan. "I have to make sure the details are documented exactly as he tells it to us." She turned to face Nathan. "She's aware she'll get a call from the Inspector General?"

"Yes," he nodded. "He made the proposition to her during a scheduled appointment about two months ago." He clenched his fists together. "She was able to get away from him without actually having sex with him but the very next day he sent a memo to the procurement committee that the products had been reviewed and hers had been removed from the approved product list."

He exhaled. "When she called to inquire what was going on, he told her if she wanted her products to be available. She needed to reschedule her appointment and be prepared to see it through next time."

"You mean, have sex?" Catherine asked, scribbling as quick as she could to keep up.

"Yes"

"Did she reschedule?"

"No. And her products are still not available at any system facility."

"I'm sorry, Nathan. And please extend my apologies to your girlfriend. As you know this is an active OIG investigation. There's not a lot I can tell you except I will make sure the appropriate people are aware of what happened to her."

He stood and offered his hand to her before waving to Ryan. "Thanks, and I'll talk to you soon."

"Sure," Ryan said, smiling as he left the office and pulled the door closed before asking Catherine. "Who are you going to report it to?"

"Compliance, it's their job to make the details available to the OIG?" Catherine stood to leave the office.

"Do you have another minute to talk about something else?" Ryan motioned Catherine back to the chair.

"Sure, I came in late thinking I could get a lot done once everyone left but so far all I've done is set in meetings." She took her seat again. "What is it?"

"I've been noticing discrepancies in liquid preparations for codeine-containing products."

"You mean, like they are missing?"

"Not exactly missing. Take this product." Ryan pulled a pint, a sized glass bottle filled with a thick, mucous, yellow liquid from her locked cabinet. "If we use one of these a year, that's a lot."

"So?"

"We've used three bottles this month."

"Did you review charts?"

"Of course, and there hasn't been a patient at all this month, not one."

"So, you think someone's diverting?"

"Yes, someone in the pharmacy." Her words came out as if she was in pain.

Catherine knew it wasn't something she'd bring up unless she was positive. "Any thoughts as to
 who?"

"Yes, I have a pharmacist that's part of the impaired practitioner program. He's a new hire and he's been a great asset to our team. But lately, I'm noticing changes in his temperament, the way he's interacting with the rest of the department and the nurses."

"What do you want to do?"

"I completed the variance report; it should be in your inbox." She paused. "I want him to report
 to HR for a random drug test." She took a deep breath. "I need you to sign off on it."

"There's no other reason to have gone through all the product. You didn't loan it to another
 site?"

"I checked the loan and borrow log, There's no record that we loaned any out."

"Hand me the phone and dial Brittany's number."

"Do we have to involve her so early? She'll tar and feather him before we even have a chance to
 investigate. She always overreacts."

"She's the director of human resources. We have to include her if you want the drug test to be
 legitimate."

"Fine," Ryan fell back against the back of the chair. "I have a bad feeling about this."

****

"Virginia?" Catherine called from her desk, "Do you have a minute?"

Catherine waited as Virginia made her way into the office. It only took her a few seconds to appear at Catherine's door. "What's up?"

Catherine motioned for her to shut the door. "I can't stand the suspense anymore. What the heck was going between Lindsey and Erin this morning when I walked in?"

"Lindsey is not taking any more of Erin's crap. Lindsey pretty much told her that once her appointment changes from interim to permanent, she's going to have her replaced." She paused.

"Bet that went over well." Catherine laughed wishing she'd been in the office to hear it. "I hope Dr. Beliard is more successful at having her appointed at the next board meeting."

"I'm supposing it will be on the agenda again." Virginia chuckled. "And not a minute too soon. It's obvious they don't like each other. It seems as if everyone on Erin's hit list has become Lindsey's favorite." She leaned in closer. "I shouldn't tell you this but I overheard Lindsey talking about Ryan."

"Ryan?" Catherine was worried. Ryan was one of her closest friends, not to mention the best pharmacy manager she'd ever known."

"Lindsey has scheduled a meeting with Ryan for next week. She's going to ask her to take the COO position on an interim basis."

"Ryan as the chief operations officer?' Catherine tried not to laugh. Although she knew her friend was more than a competent choice. She also recognized that Ryan was the worst politician she knew. No one hated the lies and trickery of politics more than Ryan. "There's no way she'll agree to it."

"You don't think she could do it?"

"Oh yes, I know she could do it but she won't want to. She hates the politics that plague this system. There's no way. Plus losing her Mom and her ex's wedding, I'm not sure she can handle the stress."

"She may not have a choice." Virginia nodded in a way that led Catherine to believe Virginia had heard enough to the reappointment wasn't optional.

"I hope so, otherwise. There may be another manager opening very soon." Catherine said anyway, realizing it may be a moot point.

"Has she told you anything about her mystery man?" Virginia asked abruptly.

"No, I thought she was fessing up today but she introduced me to an old friend who needed to report something regarding Aaron ."

"Why would Ryan have anything on Aaron ?"

"Ryan knows all the pharmaceutical representatives. One of them shared something personal that happened and Ryan wanted to make sure it was reported."

"So, the new man in her life wasn't this old friend?"

"No, all she's said is that he's in law enforcement. I've no idea how old he is or anything."

"Catherine?" Ryan's voice was strong through the door. "Do you have a minute?"

As Virginia jumped to her feet and yanked the door open, her expression was such, it was obvious Ryan knew they'd been talking about her.

"What's going on?" She asked looking from Virginia to Catherine as if they were serving a tennis ball between them.

"We were just talking about this mystery man you're seeing." Catherine offered.

"I'm taking the 5th." Ryan squeezed into the small office and took a seat.

"You've been doing that a lot lately." Catherine laughed.

Ryan looked awkwardly away from Virginia. "I hate to break up your little gossip-a-thon but I need to talk about something work-related."

Virginia was on her feet before Ryan finished the sentence. "I've got bunches to do anyway." She waved them off. "I'll talk to you both, soon."

"What's up?" Catherine flipped her computer screen off, a sure sign whatever she was working on was confidential.

"I just suspended Jayson."

"The pharmacist you were talking about the other day. The one you thought was diverting controlled substances?"

"Yes," She rubbed her forehead, an anxious habit Catherine had observed many times before.

"The drug test came back positive?"

"No, it's still pending."

"Then why'd you suspend him?"

"Because he disappeared for about two hours this morning and a nurse on one of his floors called down to central pharmacy asking about a missing dose of an oral chemotherapy agent he'd profiled for a patient."

"You're not usually one to discipline punitively as a result of an error."

"That's not what happened. In the process of resending the medication, it was made evident that the patient had received the medication. In fact, Jayson profiled the medication to be given, grabbed a dose off the shelf, went upstairs to the patient room, and administered it to her."

"I see," Catherine nodded, biting her lip.

"He practiced outside his scope of practice. Brittany insisted he be suspended until the facts are in but it's just an exercise. The facts are in, he did it, he admitted giving the dose. He has to be terminated."

"I'm sorry," Catherine slid her glasses atop her head. "I know you like him. It was good of you to give him a chance but it's not your fault."

"I know, but he needs help not to be fired."

"You tried to help him, Ryan. You can't save them all, you know that."

"I do."

"I was going to call you today to get an update on the IV bag you sent to your friend. Anything to share?"

"He called this morning and said he'd have it later today. I asked for a written report to be sent to me."

"Make sure he sends you a certified copy."

"My signature isn't good enough?"

"Not this time, no." Catherine looked anxiously at her watch, not really concerned about the time but needed the distraction anyway.

"Why? I get that it's Dr. Beliard but we treat our own all the time. Why are we treating this one so differently?"

"I haven't said anything to you about it because there wasn't really a need for you to know." This to fess up, Catherine thought, there was no way to put it off any longer. Soon everyone would know of the relationship she'd once had with Beliard. Last thing she wanted was for Ryan to find out from someone else.

"Know what?"

"Beliard and I didn't just work together all those years ago."

Ryan waited for Catherine to continue, waiting patiently as Catherine struggled to gather her thoughts. "Anwar and I were married a very long time ago, when our careers were just getting started."

It was a good thing; Ryan was sitting down. Catherine knew if she hadn't been, most likely she'd have fallen into the chair. "It was a long time ago; We both were young."

"What happened?"

"We just grew apart." She smiled, remembering pillow fights on Sunday mornings and eating chocolate brownies in bed. "It just happened."

"I had no idea." Ryan rose to her feet. "I'm sorry. All this time when I talked about my marriage falling apart, I assumed there's no possible way you could understand." She blew a sigh of relief. "I wish you'd told me."

"I'm sorry but there was really no need for you to know."

"So, what's different now?"

"If someone deliberately injected something into his IV bag it could only be to hurt him. So, depending on what those results are, it may take us down a whole different road. Once it comes out that he's my ex-husband, I'm sure I'll be a suspect. And I'd never do anything to compromise his safety."

****

Many times, over the years, Catherine had wished her immediate office was in a different location, a larger area far away from the administrative offices. Sometimes when she was meeting with more than one person, she dreamed of a larger area with a round conference table surrounded by several comfortable chairs. During visits from AHCA, she seemed to always need more filing cabinets and bookcases. She looked at the big stack of three-inch white binders that had fallen over across the floor between her desk and the wall. She needed to step carefully when she left or the binders would surely be crushed.

Today, however, what she wished her office had was different walls. Right now, she needed thicker walls to absorb some of the conversation currently going on in the CFO's office next door. The voices weren't muffled or distorted in any way. At one point, she thought about knocking on the door and informing Lindsey and Cliff that she could hear them. Maybe she could just knock on the wall and get her point across.

But she did none of those things. Instead, She hunkered down against her desk and listened to every word.

"Cliff," Lindsey was saying. "None of this makes any sense. You have to have a better answer than I don't know."

"Maybe, "his words were precise. "If you weren't loading the staffing roster, we wouldn't be in the budget pickle we're in."

"As CEO---"

"Interim." He clarified.

"Is that what this is about? You're still upset that I was appointed interim and Beliard asked you to step down."

"Of course not!"

"I was saying that even though I'm an interim CEO, I will always be a nurse first."

"Our staffing can't support these volumes." Catherine heard a loud knocking. One of them was pounding the desk. She thought it was most probably Cliff.

"Our patients expect the healthcare that we provide to them while they are here fit into specific quality expectations. Your staffing recommendation is not reflective of the quality of care I want us to be known for." Lindsey's words were eloquent, almost poetic.

"We have to minimize the money we are expanding on salaries. If we evaluate the roster and determine which high-cost position could be filled with less expensive labor--" Cliff's words weren't poetic or eloquent. He was angry, downright mad.

"Beliard put a hold on any further termination of long-term staff, an action I support."

"Your nose is so far up Beliard's ass –"

"Think carefully, Cliff!" Lindsey's words weren't loud but Catherine felt the wall shake between the offices.

"I can't work like this." His words were calmer.

"Are you resigning?"

"No, are you firing me?"

"I couldn't even if I wanted to, I just told you Beliard was issued a moratorium on the termination of anyone with more than ten years of service."

"That's the only reason you aren't firing me?"

"Yes!" her word dripped through the plaster board.

"Before I leave," Lindsey went on. "I have an emergency meeting with the corporate CFO this afternoon. Do you have an idea what it could be about?" She paused. "Or why you aren't a part of the meeting."

"I didn't know there was a meeting. Should I accompany you?"

"The invitation was marked confidential."

"Well, then." His words were louder, he'd opened the office door. "I'll have to wait till tomorrow."

Catherine saw the blur of his image as he dashed from his office. Although it wasn't unusual for Cliff to be the first one out the door at the end of the day, it was odd that he didn't say goodbye as he left.

Chapter 10

The OIG representative waiting outside the administration offices wasn't familiar to her. Catherine was pretty sure he hadn't been in any of the other meetings earlier in the year. *Maybe,* she thought, *Ryan would remember.*

Before she took the 5th and requested her own legal representative, she'd been given a business card. No doubt it contained the agent's name. Over the weeks of multiple meetings, dozens of business cards had been exchanged. No doubt, Ryan had kept them all.

"Thank you for seeing me, Ms. Masters, Ms. Danson." The representative looked from Catherine to Lindsey before continuing. "I know it's early but I wanted to meet with you before the preliminary results of the OIG are made public."

Catherine stole a glance at Lindsey. Although she hadn't said so, it was obvious Lindsey was aware of the purpose of the meeting.

"Do you know what these are, Ms. Masters?" Like before several documents were fanned on the desk in front of her. Not the invoices again, she thought. Hadn't she already answered those questions?

Before she could answer, the heading on the first document caught her eye. "These are statements. Bank statements."

"Yes, they are. Have you ever seen anything similar to these documents?"

"They look like a normal bank statement." She tapped the bottom of the document where the financial summary was. "Except I'd never have that much money in any account of mine."

She pushed the documents away. "What does this have to do with me?"

"Nothing really. The only capacity in which you are here is from a risk management perspective." He paused. "Several transactions have been identified as coming from computer encounters here at this site."

"I've no idea what you are talking about. Do I need a lawyer?"

"No, we have documented evidence where someone has funneled millions of dollars away from the healthcare system and into one of several private accounts."

"Private account?" Now he had her attention. She hoped the surprise wasn't as evident on her face as she felt.

"Yes, these account numbers are from several bank accounts in the Dominican Republic."

"Who's responsible for this?" She hoped they weren't trying to pin this on her. She and Gordon had barely managed to put any money aside for retirement. And no way could they afford to live out of the country when they did retire. With the little amount of money, they'd put away, they'd have no choice but to relocate up North where the cost of living was more reasonable.

She shifted her weight in her chair, biting her bottom lip as she studied the agent sitting across her desk. Catherine's mind spun as she searched the files of her memories. Who would do this? No one she knew that was for sure. She hadn't meant to stall but she was and it was obvious to her that the agent was aware of the diversion as well. "Do I need legal representation?"

"Just hoping you can answer a few questions for me. I'm not accusing you of anything." His response was confident, curt. Catherine could see him in a short-sleeved dress shirt and cheap necktie, peddling used cars on a corner lot.

"Then I have nothing more to say." She shuffled the folders laying in the space in front of her so that the edge of the folders were even. "I haven't stolen any money and am not aware of anyone who has." She dropped the files neatly on top of the desk. "If I was aware of such activity, I'd have reported it to corporate compliance."

"Corporate compliance?" the agent chided, almost laughed. "That's a joke, right?" He cleared his throat. "Everyone thinks so, right. They are the most crooked of all, aren't they?" He flipped several pages in his notebook, stopping on a page about eight pages from the beginning. "Want to know what we call your corporate compliance department at the attorney general's office?" He laughed without waiting for her to answer. "Corporate crookiance."

He flipped the memo pad around so she could read what was written on the page. "See?" There was a pause before he added. "Wasn't your compliance director just terminated?"

"One of many just fired actually." She exhaled so he'd know she was bored. "Somehow I think you already knew that. Anything else?"

He jumped to his feet and flipped the memo book closed. "For now, yes." His steps toward her door were soft, almost dance-like. "But I'll be back." The door closed quickly behind him, making the office oddly quiet again.

****

She couldn't decide what was more unnerving, the resonating of angry voices through the office walls or the deafening silence once the OIG representative had left. Lindsey and Cliff were at it again. And this time Erin had been invited in as well.

Catherine listened as Lindsey gave them both ultimatums. She could imagine Lindsey drawing an imaginary line in the air with her manicured hand. "You're either with me or against me." Lindsey had said. "There is no middle ground."

Seconds later, Cliff's office door was opened as Lauren exited first, followed by Erin. The door closed so forcefully behind Erin; Catherine's wall pictures turned at odd angles. She smiled thinking to herself, *I know how you feel.*

She leaned back into the cushions of her office chair, her mind's eye wandering past the framed photographs of her husband and sons, as well as certificates of completion of various events, and another dozen awards for quality improvements. It was there presented for inspection as if to remind her of the role she played, contributions she'd made in improving someone's life. She couldn't help but wonder when the time came to pack them away out of sight. Would the difference she'd made still exist? Or would it be like a tree in the forest that crashes to the ground with no one near enough to hear it connect with the ground? Would there be a sound when she said her goodbye or would the waves vibrate endlessly through the air until they simply just ran out of gas?

She wasn't sure how long the phone on her desk had been ringing but she knew enough time had passed so that the caller was sent to voicemail. Funny, she thought. She hadn't even heard it ring until seconds earlier. Her computer was still open to her emails, there was enough time to read a few while the caller left a message.

It was the last email that caught her attention. Although she didn't recognize the email address there was something familiar about the email identification. Anxiously she clicked on it until the call light on her phone indicated the caller was finished leaving the message. She was only partially surprised to discover the email was from Anwar. It simply read. Just left you a message. Please meet me at the coffee shop after nine tonight. I'll explain everything when I see you.

She was still reading his email as she dialed into her voice mail to hear the message. It seemed to take forever for the machine to play his message. Once again he reiterated that she should meet him at the coffee shop, tonight after 9 pm. He'd paused and laughed as if he'd thought of something funny. "I've got to make a stop by my place first and pick up an envelope. There's something I want to show you." The message quieted and for a minute, she thought he'd ended the call until she heard his voice again, hoarse, whispering. "I'll always love you, different from how I love my wife. And that first kiss with you will always be my most treasured memory." She heard him swallow on the recording. "I'll see you soon."

****

Catherine waved the server off before she was able to refill the coffee cup again. The server turned a one-eighty and made her way to another table where the only other occupants of the coffee shop were seated. After two cups of coffee, Catherine doubted she'd sleep a wink.

She checked her watch again. *Where was Anwar?* It was after ten o clock and he hadn't responded to either of the voices mails she'd left. *How long,* she thought. How long would she be able to wait for him to show before calling it a night?

Maybe if she'd eaten something, even just a little bite to absorb a fraction of the thick, black coffee, her stomach wouldn't be rolling, twisting and turning against her lungs until she found it was hard to catch her breath. Although, deep down in her gut, she knew her anxiety had nothing to do with hunger or coffee. It was hard to explain, even harder to understand but she knew something was brewing on the horizon, something blacker and stronger than Sal's coffee.

****

It wasn't unusual for Catherine to be the first one into the office every morning. In fact, over the years, it had become quite customary for most of the administrative team to arrive with coffee in one hand and the office key in the other. Only to discover, the key wasn't needed, the door was already unlocked. Catherine was already in the office.

This morning was the exception. Catherine was startled to find the knob turn easily and the door open before she could insert the key. Most of the area was dark except for a line of light coming from the CEO's office. She didn't know why but the first thought to cross her mind was the white van and its occupants. Somehow, they'd made it past security and into the belly of the beast, they'd penetrated the heart and soul of the facility.

Quietly, she rested her bag on the floor near the empty desk closest to the external door. Lorraine had removed her personal items weeks ago, Fortunately, the phone was still functional, ready and waiting for her replacement. Tenderly, she selected the button on the phone for the operator, whispering into the receiver that security needed to be dispatched to administration immediately.

"I'm sorry," the operator replied. "I can't hear you. Can you speak up?"

"No—" she jumped away from the desk with the receiver still at her ear as Aiden strode through the unlocked door.

"Never mind," she whispered into the phone before replacing the receiver into the cradle.

Catherine put her finger to her lips willing him to be quiet as pointed to the CEO's office and hoped he'd notice the light coming from under the door.

"It's okay," Aiden answered in his normal voice. "I have an appointment with---"

His words cut off as the door to the CEO's office was thrust open and Lindsey emerged from within holding a large file folder in her arms. Catherine was able to make out another figure in the room, sitting in the big comfortable chair near to the wall.

Brittany, the human resource director, looked as if she'd been in the building for a while. Instead of her customary dress or suit, she was wearing a pair of loose fitting sweatpants and jacket, She'd applied minimal make-up and her hair was tied into a loose, messy bun.

"I'm sorry," Lindsey explained, knowing she'd startled Catherine when she'd opened the door. "Didn't mean to scare you, Catherine. I should have told you I'd be in early this morning."

"Everything ok?" Catherine knelt down to retrieve her case knowing before Lindsey answered that it wasn't. Human resources and security meeting with the CEO before the sun had even risen? There was only one event that would bring these specific people together at that time of the morning. Someone at a high level was leaving. What was the terminology that was usually used when someone was fired? Left to pursue an opportunity outside of the system, wasn't that the way it was worded?

"Yes," Lindsey smiled and motioned for Aiden to join them. "Just some HR business that needs attention."

Catherine smiled but it wasn't one brought about by seeing or hearing something funny. It was a nervous smile. One that she usually reserved for those times when the sky was genuinely falling. She glanced nervously at the ceiling as if she could see through the dirty tiles. Where was chicken little when you needed him?

"I'll be in my office." She took small steps toward her office, hoping her external demeanor was calmer than her internal one. If she wasn't able to get into the office and shut the door immediately, she was sure she was going to implode. Once inside she dropped her briefcase, it made a resonating thump against the floor and leaned across the desk to dial the phone. She couldn't even expend the time to walk around the desk and make the call. She was practically ling belly first across the desk's surface.

"Gordon?" she whispered as soon as he answered the phone. "Something is going down this morning. I think they're getting rid of someone today." She paused hoping it wasn't her.

"I hope they aren't thinking you're the leak?" Gordon advised, his words anxious and shaky.

"No, I don't think it's me." At least she hoped not. She thought again of the deputy who'd been killed. Maybe she thought, they'd found out the deputy had lost his prisoner at least once before. Only a handful of people were even aware anything had occurred. Elena Stalinski, the emergency department nurse who had pushed the medicine cart in his path as made his way down the hall and Aiden. Several other officers and nurses had been summoned for questioning but no one else really knew what had transpired.

"Ryan?" Gordon asked. "I know you're worried about her."

"No, Ryan's termination wouldn't take this much juice." She remembered last month when the laboratory manager had been fired. If it were Ryan, would just be the chief operations officer and a human resources representative."

"I have a feeling Cliff or Erin is looking for a new opportunity whether they realize it or not." If she had her druthers, she was leaning toward Erin. It was no secret she and Lindsey were like oil and water. It was as if the town wasn't big enough for two sheriffs and one had to go. Catherine supposed she should be happy, there wouldn't be a dual of any kind, at least not one out in the open like was customary in the old west.

You must feel as if you spent the night there?" Gordon words were delicate and for a minute she thought maybe he knew she hadn't been working late last night. Somehow he knew she waited till almost midnight for Anwar to make an appearance at the coffee shop.

"Yeah," she mumbled. "I was working on another variance in the OR." She paused, her mind racing for something plausible. "Now that I know the OIG is reviewing every case where I've adjusted the charges, I'm making sure everything is perfect."

"It's got to be hard working under these conditions, Catherine." He paused. "Maybe it's time you start thinking about doing something else." He hesitated, the words humming on his tongue like a song. "I thought once you moved from bedside care to risk management, your quality of life would be better. But that hasn't been the way it's worked out. If anything, I think your hours are longer and more erratic than when you were a nurse on the floor."

"It's a lot of responsibility Gordon." She whispered, trying to hear what was happening in the outside office when Brittany, Aiden, and Lindsey were huddling in front of Virginia's empty desk as if preparing for a fight.

Catherine stretched her neck as close to the door as she could comfortably. "I gotta go, Gordon." She pulled the receiver away from her ear while still talking into the receiver. "See you tonight."

"Knock, knock." Aiden tapped against her open door. "Can I hang out in here with you for a bit?"

He slid into the chair without waiting for her to consent and pulled the door behind him nearly closed. Aiden adjusted himself in the chair so that he had a clear view of the administrative offices. "Go ahead with what you need to do." He advised. "Just pretend I'm not here."

"Why are you here?" She whispered.

He spun back around to face her. "There's an HR event happening this morning and per policy, a security officer must be in the general location to ensure the safety of all the staff."

"Erin or Cliff?" she mouthed, afraid to say the words.

"Cliff's being suspended pending the outcome of some investigation." He paused. "I don't know the details, don't need to. My role is to make sure everyone is safe and that there are no emotional episodes that turn violent."

"I see," but she really didn't. Anyone who knew Cliff knew he was no threat. There was nothing violent about him, Having Aiden station himself close by was simply an exercise of policy.

"How was your vacation?" She knew was making small talk but she didn't care. The silence was deafening it, it was making her more than nervous.

"Went back home for a short visit. My grandfather's not been feeling well. I wanted to see if there was anything he might need that I could provide."

"You have a big family?"

"Not really, I was raised by my grandparents, my grandfather mostly." He paused. "My mom passed away when I was very young, my grandmother while I was still in school."

"I'm sorry, was your mother ill?"

"Not that I knew but I think alcohol may have been involved."

"And your grandmother?"

"She worked as a housekeeper for several families when I was young. She was always able to find work in very well to do homes. I had a lot of opportunities I wouldn't have had."

"Like?"

"Their homes were in the best areas, good schools. No worries about gangs."

"I see. How did she die?"

"Some kind of industrial strength lung cancer. Probably from inhaling all those cleaning products over the years. She wasn't a smoker so I don't know what else it could have been,"

Catherine's attention was drawn to the outside office where Cliff was just entering the office followed closely by Virginia and the other administrative assistant, Olivia.

"That was a great game." He was saying, "My wife was at her sister's so I was able to have a few friends over to watch it on the big TV."

"Cliff?" Lindsey's voice was strained as she called to him from her office. "Can I see you for a minute?"

The view from the slit in Catherine's door didn't allow for much to be seen. Fortunately, she didn't need to see much to know what was going down. It was clear as day, Cliff was being offered up as the latest casualty of tenured employees.

"I hate this part of my job." Aiden moved around in his seat as if she had ants in his pants.

"When do you find these kinds of things out?" Catherine asked, only partially out of curiosity, mostly she asked as a distraction.

"I got a call yesterday afternoon of what was coming." He paused. "I have to ensure someone, preferably me, is available in case there's an outburst."

"Has there ever been?"

"An outburst?"

"Not at this level," he smiled. "But there have been issues with middle and lower level managers." He squinted through the door. "Mostly just yelling, sometimes crying." He ran his hand through his hair so that it stood up on it ends. "Just a precaution, mostly."

"You've got to be kidding me." They heard Cliff yell from behind Lindsey's closed office. "What about preserving the tenured employees?" There was a moment of two of silence. "Where is Beliard in this?"

Whatever Lindsey's response was, it was obvious Cliff didn't believe her. "Lies!" He yelled. "It's all lies penned by crooks!"

Aiden spun around, making his way to the door just in time for Cliff to pass by on his way into his office. "I'm getting my things."

Seconds later, he strode past, his arms wrapped around a small cardboard box of pictures and sports memorabilia from his desk. "Nice working with you, Catherine." Like a storm, he was gone. The office as quiet and tranquil as a stroll in the woods at sunset.

Lindsey appeared from her office with Brittany at her heel. She was only stepped a few steps out of the office door before asking. "Virginia?' her words were barely above a whisper. "Please gather everyone together for a brief meeting."

"Of course," Virginia answered her head bowed low as in prayer.

Chapter 11

"Does anyone have any questions that I can answer?" Lindsey asked the administrative team composed of only the highest level of managers. Catherine shifted her weight from side to side anxiously. Suspended, she heard Lindsey's words again. Cliff had been suspended pending the results of an HR investigation.

Lindsey had answered their questions as politically as she could, which meant she had told them nothing except he was suspended till further notice and he should be extended the same courtesies as any other visitor.

"His direct reports will be temporarily divided between myself and Erin at this time," Lindsey announced.

"Aren't you guys already spread thin with the chief operations officer position being vacant." Catherine hadn't asked the question but she had been wondering the same thing.

"I have someone in mind to fill the COO position on an interim basis and that should help with some of the administrative bottlenecking."

"Someone already on the team or someone new to the hospital?" Lana, the quality manager asked.

"Someone already on the team," Lindsey answered.

Catherine looked away from Virginia's stare. All the way across the room, she could hear Virginia's words in her mind. "Told you so."

"We—" her words were cut off as Aiden burst through the external door, his face red and flushed as if he'd been running.

"Turn on the television, quick! There's been an accident." He instructed not concerned that he'd interrupted the meeting.

Catherine thought of the train wreck several years ago that had rolled over several cars stalled on the tracks, There had been many casualties that day, major and minor injuries that haunted her to this day. But nothing could have prepared her for what flashed across the television screen once Olivia turned it on.

"Anwar Beliard," the reporter was saying, "is dead. The victim of an apparent self-inflicted gunshot wound."

"What?" Catherine's head was spinning, the room was so hot she thought she might vomit. This had to be a mistake, her words were lost in a maze of emotion. Her feet found their way to Lorraine's empty chair and slid down into it as if she'd just run a marathon.

"His body," the reporter went on, "was discovered about an hour ago in the home he shared with his wife, Dr. Melinda Beliard who had just returned from a medical conference in Atlanta." The reporter paused to listen to the data coming from his earpiece. "The coroner is putting the time of death at approximately eight o'clock last night."

"Eight o'clock," Catherine repeated aloud. "Eight o'clock last night." Oh God, she thought. He was already dead when she was waiting for him at the coffee shop. When she finally gave up and left at midnight, he'd been dead for several hours already.

"Catherine," she heard her name, but it seemed far away, almost like it was coming from somewhere outside in the hallway. "Catherine?" she heard it again but closer this time. "You don't look well." Virginia pushed a cup of water into her hand. "drink this. I'm calling Gordon."

"No," she whispered, drinking the water and pulling herself to her feet. "I'll be in my office in you need me."

She made her way quietly back to the office, his last words echoing in her mind like an old Barry Manilow song.

****

"Can I get you anything?" Gordon asked again, sitting down beside her on the couch as if she were fragile and he feared she might break if he moved her around on the sofa too much.

"You asked me that already?" she smiled, rubbing his arm. "In fact, you've asked me at least four times since I walked in the door almost an hour ago."

"I know you cared for him." His words were concerned, not accusing "I'm sorry."

"I can't believe he's gone." She choked on the words, her hands to her mouth, as if holding the words in would make them less real.

"Do they know what happened?" He asked, rubbing up and down her arm from elbow to wrist.

"Just that he'd been depressed since his heart surgery." She said the words even though she didn't believe them. He wasn't the kind of man to commit suicide, this she knew.

She paused as Gordon handed her a small glass of vodka and cranberry juice. "I haven't seen anything official but it's being reported that he shot himself, point blank in the chest." She pointed to an area between her breasts. "Just about where his cardiac surgery scar was."

"I'm sorry," He kissed her forehead. "Why don't you go and lay down?"

She shook her head even though she found her feet dragging her body toward the bedroom she shared with him. "If anyone calls for me, please come and get me."

He nodded as she walked away. She knew he wouldn't wake her unless the house was on fire or one of the boys was hurt.

****

Once inside the bedroom, she kicked her shoes off and crawled into the bed as if she were a child. The blanket collected around her chin, she smiled thinking it smelled of Gordon's old spice cologne. It was a scent she liked very much, almost as much as the Stetson; Anwar used to wear.

Was he still wearing that brand or had he moved into more expensive fragrances offered by various designers? Did he still eat two scrambled eggs, a piece of wheat toast, and half a grapefruit for breakfast every day? Would it be wrong to ask Melinda the next time she saw her? Most likely that would be his funeral, She doubted she'd see her or the kids before the funeral.

His funeral, the words were foreign as they fell off her tongue, almost choking her. Anwar's funeral? It just didn't seem real, someone had to have made a mistake. He couldn't be dead. If he were, she would know it, she would feel it deep in her heart.

She wondered if the apartment they'd shared after they'd first married was still there, by the beach tucked snuggly between Tom's deli and the all-night laundromat. She hadn't thought about that old place in years. It was hard to think of the apartment and not remember their first Christmas tree and how she'd cried once they got it together and discovered it was so tiny. It was barely a tree; she'd cried into his shoulder.

Money had been tight then, between living expenses, school loans, and groceries, there had been no money for any extras, including a new Christmas tree. She knew she should have been angry when he drug the new, bigger tree up the stairs to the apartment and into the living room.

An extra shift, he rationalized. Paying for the tree wouldn't be a big deal, he'd pick up an extra shift and that money would be more than enough to cover the cost of the new tree. They'd decorated it until the wee hours of the night with a box of her grandmother's old ornaments and the partridge family Christmas album playing in the background. Later as the Christmas lights twinkled and flashed in synchrony, they'd made love on the tiny sofa. It was one of her favorite memories of the life she'd had with him.

Her tears came freely, slowly at first until her pain was so great, they spilled down her cheeks like rain. I will miss you she cried into her pillow, hoping Gordon would give her the time she needed to mourn Anwar and knowing at the same time, that he would. It was one of the things she loved most about him.

****

"How are you doing?" Ryan asked, her eyes locked onto Catherine's. "I thought you might take a few days off. At least until after the funeral."

"I can't just sit there at the house and think about him. I've remembered things I haven't thought about in years. I can't stop seeing his face, earning his voice." She wiped her eyes. "I need to work."

"Have you learned anything new about his death?" Ryan had chosen her words carefully; she'd avoided the work suicide and Catherine was more than aware of the omission.

"The coroner's report isn't final but he is still saying Anwar's wound was self-inflicted."

"Was he upset or depressed when you last saw him?"

"I can't talk here," Catherine admitted. "Can you meet me at the Walk for a drink this afternoon?"

"Of course, I'll need to get a sitter,"

"Can you do me a favor?"

"If I can, sure."

"Will you bring your friend, the cop to join us?"

"Catherine, I like keeping my work and personal life separate. He won't be able to tell you anything that's not been reported to the public."

"I know and that's not why I want to meet with him. There are some things I want to tell him. Things someone else should know about. Someone in an official capacity."

"You're scaring me. What is going on? What's this about?" Ryan whispered.

"Not here." She placed her hand atop Ryan's.

"OK, I'll see if he can meet with us. I just--"

Catherine wasn't sure what else Ryan had to say and she didn't get a chance to ask for clarification. A loud crash followed by Virginia's call for help brought both of them out of Catherine's office to determine what the commotion was about.

Catherine was first out of her office, hand on her cell phone in case she needed to call for assistance and scanning the immediate area for the origin of the noise. It was Cliff's ajar office door that grabbed her attention and she motioned Ryan behind her as they moved closer to his office.

They weren't fully inside but could already make out Virginia's prone form on the floor. Her arms lying at an odd angle away from her legs. Her glasses lay near to her face, broken into several pieces intermingling with blood from a gaze just across her forehead. The shelves above Cliff's credenza were in pieces near her feet as if they'd fallen after she did.

"Oh my God!" Catherine dropped to her knees next to Virginia. "Call 911."

Ryan picked up the phone from Lorraine's desk to make the call. "And call a code blue to administration."

"She's not breathing?"

"Yes, she is breathing, but it will get everyone here quicker. We'll do what we can before the ambulance arrives."

Ryan disconnected the call and dialed the operator first to initiate the code blue. Once she'd completed that, she redialed 911.

She'd barely started to explain to the operator when the administrative office door imploded with staff coming to assist with the code announced on the overhead pager.

"What happened?" Elena from the emergency department asked as she bent down to assess her. "Airways fine." She snapped a pair of surgical gloves on. "We need a backboard STAT and something to compress the wound with. She's losing a lot of blood."

"Coming through," the paramedics pushed their way through the administrative crowd and maneuvered the staff away from Virginia.

"What happened?" Virginia mumbled, moving anxiously against the good intentions of the paramedics.

"We're going to put you on the board, Ma'am?" The older paramedic advised. "Please don't move your neck."

"I understand," she answered holding her hand out in the air, as if she was reaching for something, "Catherine?"

"I'm here." Catherine moved closer, dropping to her knees and taking Virginia's hand.

"I didn't see him," she mumbled

"Who?"

"I don't-- know how he ---got in." Her words were jumbled as if she was unsure of what words she needed to use.

"You have a head injury, Virginia." Catherine squeezed her hand tighter. "You're confused. Don't try and talk."

"No," Virginia fought the paramedic attempting to place a brace around her neck. "There was no one in the office when I came in. He must have come in behind me."

"Who?"

"I don't know, he had a hat pulled over his face. I only know it was a man, because of his hands." She paused. "I think I hurt him though. He was limping when he ran out of the door."

"Limping?" Catherine remembered the passenger in the white van thinking how it couldn't be a coincidence.

"What happened? What were you doing in Cliff's office anyway?"

"Cliff called and asked me to get something from the top drawer of his credenza. Pictures of his kids and a disc. Just little personal things he forgot was in his office." She paused before pulling her hand from Catherine's. "I had my back to the door; I didn't see him come in or anything. Just felt something hit the back of my head and I fell against the shelves."

"Just try and relax, Virginia," Catherine advised, standing as the gurney with Virginia safely secured was adjusted to roll out of the office and into the hallway.

"Just take her around to the emergency department," Catherine advised, looking down at her blood-stained shirt and hoping she had something in her office to change into. Quickly she scanned the crowd for the faces of the people who would be needed for the assessment.

"Aiden!" she saw him almost at the end of the hallway, clearing the path for the convoy headed toward the emergency department.

He stopped and motioned that he was going with the paramedics and Virginia. "I need to wait for the police to take her statement."

"Make sure the tape is secured it's the only way we can identify him."

"Virginia said he was masked." Aiden walked away from her, a few paces behind Virginia.

"He wouldn't have been wearing a mask when he came into the hospital. I want the camera outside administration so we can see what he's wearing. Then we'll check all the exterior cameras for someone dressed similarly."

"Got it!" He practically ran to catch up.

Catherine turned to Ryan. "The police will want to speak to us since we were the first on the scene."

"But I didn't hear or see anything," Ryan reminded her. "Except the crash when Virginia fell into the shelves."

"I know but they will still want to hear that from us."

"I'm sorry." Ryan moved closer to her. "I know this is the last thing you need right now."

"I can't believe all that's happened these last few days."

"I know," Ryan pulled her into an embrace. "And I'm sorry for your loss."

****

"Virginia will only be out a few days," Catherine mentioned from Virginia's desk, where she was rummaging through a pile of papers looking for the internal mail. "Thank God she just needed a few stitches."

Lindsey appeared from her office and dropped several large envelopes in Virginia's outbox. "I still think they should have kept her a few days, just to be sure." She stopped to observe Catherine still sifting through papers and folders. "What are you looking for?"

"A risk summary corporate swears they sent a few days ago." She gathered several other envelopes addressed to her and stacked them together in a clearer space on Virginia's desk.

Lindsey glanced at the closed door into Cliff's office were remnants of tape were still visible on the door frame. "I'm glad the cops finished with his office." She smiled. "It doesn't instill a lot of good will for patient experiences to have crime scene barricade tape across the CFO's door."

"Yes, I don't suppose it promotes a lot of confidence for patients and families who are already a bit anxious." Catherine paused. "With the OIG penalties, Beliard's death, and now an attack here on the grounds, our competitors must be knee deep in celebration."

Jay stepped into the office pushing a make-shift facility cart loaded with tools and a small ladder draped over the cart. He pointed to Cliff's office, specifically the tape. "I got a work order to put the shelves back up and fix the wall?"

"It's fine," Lindsey answered, "You can take the tape down. The scene's been cleared."

He nodded and disappeared into the office and partially closed the door behind him.

"How are you doing?" Lindsey smiled and moved closer to Virginia's desk.

"Like everyone else, I'm in shock," Catherine answered, tripping on her tongue.

"I'd heard that you and Dr. Beliard worked together before, that you were friends?"

"We worked together very early in our careers." She blushed and cursed her fair skin. "Was a long time ago."

"I see," Lindsey turned away. It was evident to Catherine that Lindsey wasn't buying it. "In any event, I'm sorry for his family and friends. I didn't know him very well but he seemed like a very nice man."

"He could be," Catherine laughed. "And he could be an arrogant, stubborn, son of a bitch, too." She paused. "But he was my friend and yes, I will miss him."

****

"With everything going on I forgot to tell you," Ryan flipped through the folder in her hand. "It slipped my mind."

"Understandable," Catherine removed the contents from the first envelope in her inbox. She really wasn't sure why she'd been in such a hurry to go through Virginia's desk in search of her mail. After all that scavenging, she was just getting around to opening them.

She scanned the documents she'd just removed. It was a patient complaint regarding their hospital bill, she recognized the terminology without reading the entire paper. "This can wait." She said aloud even though she knew Ryan wasn't really interested.

Ryan's head jerked toward the wall between Catherine and Cliff's office. "Is there someone in Cliff's office?"

"Jay's repairing the wall and shelves." She turned to look where Ryan's attention was drawn. "He should be done soon, I think."

"Why's he got the door shut?" She paused and leaned closer to the wall. Catherine half expected her to ask for a glass to hold against the wall to eavesdrop better. "I hear the desk drawers opening and closing." She smiled, "he's snooping. I thought only women did that."

"He's probably moving the credenza back and has the drawers open to have better leverage to move it where it belongs."

"I suppose," Ryan turned back to face Catherine.

"So," Catherine asked once Ryan had organized the documents in the folder in the sequence she wanted. "What were the results?"

"Potassium chloride," Ryan's words were so low, Catherine wasn't sure she'd heard her

correctly. She stopped, the next envelope dropping unopened against the desktop. "Pardon?"

"Yeah," Ryan pushed the documents so that Catherine could read them better. "My friend was so surprised. He ran the sample again to confirm." She paused. "Same result."

"Is there any chance potassium chloride would be used as a diluent?"

Ryan shook her head before answering. "No, none at all. The bag that was hanging was a

presser." She pushed a manufacturer insert into Catherine's view. "Potassium Chloride isn't a normal and customary component of this product. Nor would I expect it to be. Potassium chloride can cause arrhythmias, so much so it can be deadly even in very small concentrations."

"So, it wouldn't be a stretch to conclude that it was injected into the bag after it was sent from pharmacy?" Catherine retrieved the envelope she'd been opening and ripped the sealant tape off the top.

"Yes, that is what I believe." Ryan pushed the folder and its contents across the desk to Catherine. "These copies are for you." She leaned back against the chair's back. "What do we do now?"

"When we meet with your police officer friend—"

"Cole," Ryan interjected. "His name is Cole. He's a detective with the Providence PD."

"I think we need to share everything you've uncovered about the event." She dropped the envelope atop her desk and turned to her computer, typing furiously on the keyboard. "I'm going to update the variance report to include the results of your outside reviewer." She looked up to face her. "And I'll need the contact information for the lab as well as the chemist you used."

"It's right there," Ryan advised, "On the top of each page."

"Good," Catherine pulled the folder closer and transcribed the data into the variance report for Dr. Beliard's code event during surgery. "Did you decide if you are going to the funeral?"

"I'm planning to." Ryan paused. "Obviously you are."

"Yes, Melinda, Anwar's widow, asked me to sit with her and the family." She paused. "I was hoping to avoid the specifics of our past relationship getting out but I don't think that's possible now." She finished updating the electronic variance report and grabbed another envelope.

"Whoever that's from really didn't want anyone else to open it." Ryan mused. "There must be a half a roll of tape on there."

"Yes," Catherine answered; her eyes locked on the familiar handwriting as she read her name printed in bold letters across the top. "I—"

She poured the contents outs, surprised to find only a picture with a small, yellow sticky note that read. Keep this in a safe place. AB. Her hand flew to her mouth as if her entire essence might escape out if she didn't. AB, she read it again. Anwar Beliard.

"What is it?" Ryan stretched as far over the desk as her dress suit would allow.

"A picture."

"Of?"

"Black and white picture of people I don't know."

"Who's it from?" Ryan pulled the envelope closer to inspect the writing.

"Anwar, the night he died. He said he had to pick something up from his office."

"What?" Ryan was on her feet before Catherine finished talking.

"Yeah, so apparently he makes an appointment with every intention of standing me up, stops by his place to send me this picture, and then goes back to his place and shoots himself?"

Ryan fell back in the chair. "None of this makes sense, Catherine and I think we are in over our head." She paused. "We need help."

"I don't know who to trust." She held the picture closer hoping she might identify someone in the photo. "I'm hoping we can trust your friend."

Chapter 12

She'd been to many funerals over the years. Patients, friends, and both her parents years earlier. But nothing could have prepared her for the overwhelming despair that tore through her heart as she took her seat next to Melinda Beliard and her sons. If Gordon hadn't been close by, holding onto her hand with such energy, she wasn't sure she'd been able to make it through. He was her strength right now, she felt sorry for Melinda that she had no one to hold on to.

Melinda was a pretty woman, tall and dark like Anwar. Her dark hair was longer than a woman her age probably should wear it. But if you knew Melinda, you'd know she didn't care. She was a woman who did as she pleased, yet still managed to be well-liked. Catherine thought they'd always made an attractive couple, a power couple long before Brad and Angelina. Even dressed in black, Melinda stood out from the others seated quietly in the pews. She was still, quiet, positioned against the back of her seat like a silent storm just off the horizon and making its way steadily to the shore.

Even in death, he looked good, Catherine thought. If she hadn't known better, didn't know about the huge, gaping, hole in what had been his chest and back, she might have considered that he was simply sleeping. Still, dressed in an expensive, dark, Italian suit and red designer tie with his glasses perched on his nose as if he might sit up and read a memo, it seemed that he could and might at any moment just sit up and step out of the shiny, silver casket.

"He never stopped loving you," Catherine heard the words first in her head and then again as Melinda repeated them.

"Was a long time ago," Catherine looked to Gordon trying to reconcile in her mind if her recent actions with Anwar might be construed as cheating. He had kissed her twice and not always on the cheek. She remembered the way his lips felt against hers. She glanced again at Gordon, hoping he wouldn't notice the flush that had come over her.

It was hard sometimes to rationalize relationships, especially in relation to old lovers. Isn't it written somewhere that once you love someone, you always love them? Maybe not in your brain but always in your heart? Was it really possible to stop loving someone just because they hurt you?

Catherine's eyes traveled the short distance to the front of the room where he lay in his coffin, her eyes watering more with each advancing step. She clutched Gordon's hand as tight as she could, so tight she felt him pull away in discomfort. No, she thought to herself knowing the answer that was buried deep within her heart. Love does last forever, even after we've drawn our last breath, it endures. She smiled knowing he'd have liked this realization.

****

She waited until the last of his family had walked the processional before getting in line to offer condolences and say her last farewell to him. He would have been flattered by the sheer number of people who had come to pay tribute, offer sympathies to his wife and sons. Some she recognized from all their years of service. The faces flew by in her mind as if they been dealt from a deck of cards, early morning meetings laden with strong coffee and pseudo bagels as well as dinners, conferences, and charity events. Every arm of Anwar's legacy had been in attendance, most strewn through the first few pews during his service. She watched as they made their way to the vehicles, most were foreign, expensive cars that looked new or near new.

They were nearly to Gordon's Ford Explorer when she heard him ask. "You want to go to the graveside?" He ran his hand through his hair, a sure sign to her that he was tiring. Neither of them was twenty years old anymore. It didn't take much these days to tire them out. Gordon more so than her. His diabetes kept her on her toes. He was the most noncompliant patient she'd ever known.

"No," she smiled. "I'm tired and you need to eat a little something."

"I can go for a bit," his smile was genuine. "I know this is important to you. I know he was important in your life. I'll do whatever we need to do to make you feel good about your role, past, and present."

God, she thought. What had she done to deserve this man? He was the kindest, most caring person she knew. How any woman could have let him go was beyond her. He didn't talk much about his first wife but one thing was for sure. They couldn't have been more different from her and Anwar if they'd tried. The thought comforted and terrified her at the same time and she wasn't sure why.

"I just want to go home. "She pulled herself into his arms. "I've got work tomorrow."

"You sure you can't take a day or two?" He rested his chin atop her head. "I could take a day. We could drive to the lake for the weekend?"

"We can't afford that," she offered, wishing their situation was different and they could have taken off for a day or two. Dirt under her feet, wind in her hair, it was a break they both needed.

Instead, she pulled away. "I'm meeting Ryan and her friend tomorrow after work."

"The cop?"

She nodded.

"Anything I should know about?"

"All work stuff," she smiled, sliding into the passenger's seat and hoping she was able to stay awake for the ride home. She could count the number of hours of sleep she'd had over the last three days on one hand. Given her meeting tomorrow with the Detective and Ryan, she doubted she'd get any more tonight.

****

It wasn't often Catherine had the opportunity to actually soak in a bathtub. Most mornings, she showered in seven minutes or less and air dried her hair while walking the dog prior to heading to work. She pinched herself again and slid deeper into the tub, tossing another handful of bath salts in the water and reaching for the partially full glass of wine.

Twenty minutes, she moaned to herself. That's about all she had left to soak before Gordon would probably be back with their dinner. Reluctantly, she pushed to her feet wrapping up in the fuzzy blue bath sheet usually hanging near the door and stepped out of the tub. True, the bath sheet had been meant more for decoration than actual use but she didn't care. Not tonight. Life was short and nothing was more prominent on her mind and heart than the fact she'd just come from burying her first love.

Dam the towel, she thought. It was time to turn over a new leaf, eat the carbs, drink the wine and enjoy the one and only life you're given. It played in her mind like a song, a mantra she thought to celebrate his life and whatever was left of hers.

He loved to dance, she smiled thinking of an old bar they frequented when they were married. It was a small hole in the wall place with greasy food and cheap beer with a band that only played music popular in the seventies. She remembered how the vibration felt in her bones, its music pumping loud, hard in the long bones of her legs. Anwar had loved that old place, especially the music, even if he wasn't very good at dancing. She'd given him points for trying. His chair was seldom warm, he gave it his all.

Through the imaginary music playing in her head, she could hear the rhythm, fell the cadence of the song as the continued to play. Knocking? She thought, what was that noise? Was someone at the door?

Catherine quickly slid into her bathrobe and make her way to the front door tying the belt around her waist as she flung the door open. Melinda Beliard stood solemnly; hands folded delicately at her waist. Catherine couldn't be sure but she thought Melinda was still dressed as she'd been at the funeral.

"Melinda?" Catherine stepped back, motioning for her to enter.

"I'm sorry to come unannounced." Melinda looked away as she stepped through the threshold.

"Please, come in." Catherine swaddled herself into the robe as tightly as she could and motioned Melinda into the living room. "Can I get you some coffee?"

"No," Melinda shook her head and walked almost elegantly where Catherine had indicated until stopping next to a good but used couch. It was the first time she'd made eye contact since Catherine had opened the door. Melinda didn't ask but her eyes seemed to be waiting for permission to sit.

Catherine waved to the couch with her hand but took a sofa chair nearby and pulled the ends of the robe as snuggly as she could around her knees. "Please have a seat."

Melinda did so, sitting regally on the edge of the cushion as if she was planning a quick exit and placing her handbag nearby on the coffee table's edge. "I didn't mean to impose." She waved to where Catherine was sitting and indicated to the robe. "My timing couldn't be worse."

"Nonsense," Catherine smiled as much as she could but she was aware Melinda knew the smile was a farce. They were in the same boat, she and Melinda. They both had lost someone they loved, loved in different ways, but loved just the same. "What can I do for you?"

"I wanted to thank you for coming today." She swallowed. "I know it would have meant a lot to him to see us both there, sitting together."

"Yes, I think so too but that's not why you're here?"

"No, no." Melinda was shaking her head, wiping away tears she willed wanted not to fall. "I know you've been involved with investigating Anwar's death."

"Not really," Catherine interjected noticing Melinda hadn't used the word "suicide."

"I mean, you've been following it not that you're actually part of the investigation."

"Then yes, but I'm afraid I don't have any more information that you do."

"But you have access to the police, you work closely with them all the time. You must have more information than me. You're an insider." She paused. "They told me nothing except that he put a gun to his chest and shot himself, twice." She wiped her nose with the back of her hand. "How is that even possible?" Gone was her regales. She slumped forward as if the only thing holding her up was her ribcage.

Catherine moved from the chair to the sofa and sat as close to Melinda as she thought was appropriate. They weren't friends, they'd never been close but she couldn't help but feel Anwar calling to her as if he were sitting there with them. "There's nothing I've seen that suggests anyone else was involved with his death." She paused wondering where the hell was Gordon and what was taking so long? He should have been home already. "I know the coroner report for GSW was positive."

"He shot a gun. That's all that means." Melinda's body language changed. She was rigid again as if she'd gotten her second wind. "I don't think Anwar killed himself. He just wasn't that kind of a man." Her chin rose to meet Catherine eye to eye. "And I don't think you do either."

Catherine chewed her lip thoughtfully. "No," she shook her head. "I don't think he did."

****

Business was good for the shops located up and down University Avenue that composed a commercial area known as the Walk. Even in the middle of the afternoon, most of the tables at a less popular restaurant, the Pointe, were taken and a small line of senior citizens was building outside of its doors.

"Let's go to the organic place on the corner." Catherine pointed a short distance ahead of them. "Tell Cole to meet us there in like an hour?"

"An hour?" Ryan adjusted her purse to a more comfortable position on her shoulder and pulled her cell phone from her suit pocket. "Why not now?"

"I want to talk to you first about some work-related stuff." She paused, noticing Ryan's reaction. "I mean, work related to our actual jobs."

"Everything ok?" Ryan walked close at Catherine's arm. "The suspense is killing me."

"Nothing to worry about." Catherine pointed to an outside table under a wooden pergola. "Grab that one. I'll order us a drink." She returned several minutes later with two glasses of wine, one white and one red. "I couldn't recall if you liked red or white."

"Either is fine." Ryan laughed, moving her purse to another empty seat so that Catherine could sit down. "Was good to have Virginia back today?"

"Yes, although I still don't understand what's going on. What could the intruder be looking for or why he'd wait till someone was in the office to try and get it."

"Did the tapes show anything?" Ryan sipped on a glass of white wine.

"Aiden had to turn the tapes over to the police."

"And?"

"From what I understand, the tape shows a non- descriptively dressed man walking with a slight limp pull a toboggan over his face just as he entered the office from the hallway outside. He doesn't appear anywhere else on the tapes for that day."

"That doesn't make any sense," Ryan set the glass down. "How'd he get in? He must have passed through security?"

"We both know that if someone wants to bypass the front desk, it's not that hard. They can piggyback in with a physician or with a staff member, even though we tell them to watch for tailgaters."

"Still, you'd think he'd have shown up somewhere else, leaving even?"

"I know, but according to the police, The tape is inconclusive."

"That's just odd," Ryan said dismissively and in a way, Catherine knew she was thinking hard on something else. "It's sort of like—" She paused, searching for the right inoffensive words.

"Like what?" Catherine finished the wine and indicated to the server she wanted another glass.

"It's almost like he was already inside."

"I thought that, too."

"You think he could be one of us?"

"I don't think Cliff's suspension for embezzlement is coincidental. And I don't think Cliff stole any money or funds wired offshore. I think whoever used his access is trying to clean house and Virginia was in the way."

"Is that why you wanted to meet Cole here, instead of the office?"

"I can't explain it but it seems like every conversation we've had has been leaked to someone. It almost as if my office has ears."

"You mean bugs?" Ryan looked around. "My God Catherine, what the hell is going on?"

"I'm not sure but Anwar was somehow in the middle. He was either part of it or he uncovered it. I don't think he killed himself."

"Me neither," Ryan added as she waved the server closer to order another drink.

"What brings you to that conclusion?" Catherine smiled, she loved Ryan's stories.

"I wasn't married to him or anything but I did work with him when I first started here. He had one of the worst God complexes I'd ever seen. To this day, no physician was more arrogant than he was." She smiled. "No offense."

"None taken." She sipped from the glass enjoying the way the cool liquid felt as it slid down her throat.

"I remember encountering him my first week with an issue about Ceftriaxone. It wasn't available as a generic yet and it was really expensive. I put together a usage review and discovered that one of his physicians was using it for everything from dog bites to cellulitis." She scooted closer to Catherine. "I'll never forget the smug look the son of a bitch gave me when he told me he was the physician, not me."

"Bet that went over well?"

Ryan laughed. "What happened with you guys? Why'd you split up"

"More of the same. His God complex didn't stop at the office." She paused. "He wasn't always that way. When we were younger, he was less ambitious, almost nervous at the time about some things."

"I can't see him as nervous or anxious about anything."

"You didn't know him the way I did. I think I could have learned to live with his ego."

"Why'd you leave then?"

"I didn't." She paused. "He wanted out of the relationship. I didn't know he didn't want children and although I wasn't in a hurry, I wanted to be confident that one day, we'd have kids."

"But he had kids with Dr. Melinda?"

"That was later, She's actually his third wife. His second wife died giving birth."

"I didn't know that."

"He seldom spoke of Mae or the baby."

"What happened to the baby?"

"Mae delivered early; the baby didn't make it. He died a few minutes after Mae did. Anwar was never the same. I think that's when the God complex started to really be a problem." Catherine moved her wine glass from one place on the table to another for no apparent reason than simply mediating a nervous tic.

"Speaking of problem. The results of those three syringes you found in the visitor's bathroom are back." Ryan coughed into her hand and looked around the area to ensure no one was nearby.

"What's the verdict doctor?" Catherine joked.

"The syringes contained residual amounts of ketamine, midazolam, and hydromorphone," Ryan whispered.

"Anesthesia cocktail—" Catherine mumbled under her breath.

"Yes, but there was something unusual about the ketamine syringe," Ryan added

"Unusual how?"

"It was laced with a subtherapeutic concentration of glycopyrrolate."

"Paine—" Catherine could barely form the name.

"Yes," Ryan pushed a folded piece of paper toward Catherine. "It does appear to be the surgical cocktail used primarily by one anesthesiologist, Dr. Paine."

"We have nothing to support that claim?" Catherine shook her head. "I'm not sure our suspicion is enough to even warrant a drug test."

"I don't think HR will drug test him purely on my testament that he is the only one who uses that combination." She paused. "And in actual fact, anyone could have drawn those syringes up and added glycopyrrolate to the ketamine syringe."

"You think someone is framing him?" Catherine hoped she'd been able to downplay her sarcasm. She didn't like the man and everyone knew it. She could only think of one more physician with a bigger ego and they'd just buried him.

"No, I don't but we can't prove that they aren't." Ryan nodded

Catherine thought again what a good detective Ryan would have made. Maybe sleeping with one was the next best thing, she mused, grateful Ryan couldn't read her mind.

"What's your recommendation?' Catherine asked.

"I can complete a usage review but most of the anesthesiologists administer that combination of fentanyl, midazolam, and ketamine during surgery. It's not going to help us draw any conclusions."

"When we get back on Monday, remember to complete a variance report so that the syringes and the contents are documented." She paused, tapping her fingers against the wine glass. "What do we do in the meantime?"

"I had no idea---" Ryan words were cut off as a familiar figure approach their table, his torso directly in her line of sight from the sun.

"Ladies?" He announced as if they'd won something fabulous. "Fancy running into you here."

"Hartmann?" Catherine's words were etched in frustration. "How did you know we were here?"

"I didn't" He pointed behind him to where an older couple had made themselves comfortable on a bench close to the fountain. "My parents and I meet here once a week for the early bird dinner at the Pointe. We were just finishing when I saw you." He pulled a chair from a nearby table and set between them. "Hope you don't mind."

"Actually, I do," Catherine answered. "Neither of us are on the clock. There is nothing to imply we need to answer any of your questions."

"Just hear me out," he held up his hands in surrender. "I'm not going to ask you any questions. I want to tell you a story. And when I'm done if you want to talk to me, you give me a call." He slid his business card across the table, one to each of them.

"This story is about two little boys who grew up in a middle-class section of the Bronx in the late sixties. Unlike most childhood relationships, this one continued into middle and high school. They were closer than brothers. Even looked so much alike, the neighbors thought they were."

"Does this end with them going to work for a man named Charlie that they only speak to over the phone?" Ryan asked as Catherine stifled a laugh.

"After high school, they attended college and finished their bachelor's degree in biology with the expectation they'd apply to medical school and both become doctors."

"Is there a point to this story that isn't an open book, Hartmann? This is old news." Catherine tried to sound less interested than she truly was.

"Now one of the boys came from a long line of money. Jacob Fleming's grandfather was a very successful land developer. He could have afforded any medical school he wanted. But that wasn't the case for Anwar Beliard. No way could his parents help him out financially with medical school. So, Anwar decided to join the military and attend medical school on an army grant. "

"Again, old news." Catherine looked around as if she was in need of something.

"What does Jacob do?" Hartmann went on. "He also joins the army to ensure his pal Anwar is safe. Daddy Fleming has some juice and with his money is able to ensure the boys train locally and aren't sent into active military duty. Everything is good for a while until Jacob realizes he really doesn't want to be a doctor. In fact, military life is a good fit for him, especially the intelligence branch of the army. Here his natural abilities excel and he moves through the ranks very quickly always making sure his pal, Anwar, is looked after."

He leaned in closer to Catherine and Ryan. "This is where my data gets a bit cloudy. There's some kind of falling out between Jacob and Anwar. In fact, they don't speak for years. And when they finally do meet again, Jacob is on his deathbed dying in Anwar's emergency department with Anwar hovering nearby. Jacob dies in trauma room nine alone waiting for his estranged wife to make an appearance while Anwar tends to a complete stranger in trauma room twelve."

"What was the feud about?" Ryan asked, looking at Catherine first for approval.

"Whatever it was, it changed their lives and their relationship forever." He leaned back in his chair as he was a lawyer who'd just delivered his closing argument. "You have anything to add?"

"No comment," Catherine shook her head.

"You were the first Ms. Beliard. You must have known at least parts of this?"

"I never met Jacob and Anwar rarely spoke of him but I was aware of his existence."

"What about the wife, Commissioner Fleming?" Hartmann wasn't writing down any notes but it was obvious to her that he was memorizing every word she said.

"I met her at Jacob's funeral. It was the one and only time until she showed up here for the interview as COO."

"Did she remember you?"

"Yes, but she pretended that she didn't" Catherine hoped his questions were ending soon. She was running out of discussion items to keep him at an arm's length. "Only recently has she indicated she knew who I was."

"And?" he pushed his chair closer.

"Nothing really, she just mentioned that she was finally able to place where she knew me from." She paused. "Asked how I was doing. You know it was benign."

"I was wondering—"

"Do you mind, Mr. Hartmann? I think we've been more than cooperative."

Hartmann's response was interrupted as a middle-aged man wearing a faded set of blue scrubs approached the table. "Well," the man said, scratching at his balls through the thin material of the scrub bottoms. "Fancy meeting you all here." He turned to the reporter and offered his hand. "Dr. Tyler Paine. You are?"

"Tim Hartmann, I'm—"

"You're that reporter for the Chronicle." Paine waited to shake Hartmann's hand.

"Guilty as charged." Hartmann smiled, pulling his hand away.

"You giving interviews offsite now?" Paine asked, adjusting himself again.

"No just saw Ms. Masters and Dr. Allen sitting here. Thought I'd say hello." His next words were addressed to Catherine. "How did you say I could get access to the variance report regarding the BSO deputy who died recently."

"What do you mean?" She hoped her surprise was evident. How did he even find out about that? Nevertheless, she smiled. "As I've said before Mr. Hartmann any work-related documents you require must be requested through official channels."

Paine stepped away, waving. "Nice meeting you, Mr. Hartmann. Have a great week, Ladies."

"I'll make the request on Monday." Hartmann stepped to his feet and motioned to the older couple on the bench that he was ready to leave. "I think you have me all wrong Ms. Masters."

"How's that?" Her response was curt, dismissive.

"Like you, I just want to know the truth about what happened to your friend. And I don't think what's happening here with the tenured terminations is right." He stuffed his notebook in his pocket. "I know you think no one cares but I do and so will my readers."

"Everything ok?" a tall good-looking man asked as he approached them and made his way to Ryan's side. After a quick kiss, he turned back to Catherine and Hartmann offering his hand. "Cole Spencer."

"Cole," Ryan said wrapping her arms around his. "This is my friend Catherine."

He smiled exposing perfect white teeth. "Heard a lot about you."

Ryan indicated to the reporter. "Tim Hartmann. My friend Detective Cole Spencer."

Cole stuffed his free hand into his pocket. "Do you work at the hospital too?"

"No, I'm a reporter." Hartmann pushed his chair back against the table's edge.

"A reporter?" He exchanged a quick glance with Ryan.

"You being interviewed, honey?" he asked squeezing her hand.

"No," Hartmann answered for her. "Just following some leads regarding Dr. Beliard's death." He fished in his jacket pocket. "Speaking of Detective, can I get a card from you."

Cole handed him a business card and pulled a chair for himself and watched as Hartmann took his exit.

Once the reporter was away from the table, he loosened his tie and asked. "What can I do for you guys?"

Ryan took his hand in hers. Catherine couldn't help but smile. It was an unfamiliar feeling to consider Ryan as part of a couple. In all the years they'd been friends she'd been a single woman raising a young child. As she sat there looking upon her with Detective Spencer she couldn't help but feel as if her time had finally come. And she was happy for her.

Chapter 13

"I asked Ryan to have you meet us here because there's something going on and I think we need some help. Since you're a police officer officer--."

"With the Providence PD," he reminded her. "I really have nothing to do with Butler County.".

"I know but you still have some judicial authority even if only as a courtesy."

"We just want someone else to know what we know, Cole," Ryan added. "In case something happens."

"Nothing's going to happen, honey." He kissed her hand atop his. "I promise."

****

"So that's all he said?" Cole motioned for the server to refill his water glass and pushed the mostly empty plate toward the center of the table. "That he was working with the FBI and several physicians had been paid millions of dollars to do pretty much nothing?"

"Pretty much," she pulled an envelope from her purse and pushed it towards him. "He sent this picture to me the night before he died."

"The night he asked you to meet him and didn't show?" Cole repeated.

"Yes." She slid the photograph almost tenderly across the table. It was Anwar's last request, his last words to her. She hoped she wouldn't be sorry for bringing Ryan's friend in the loop. But she trusted Ryan and if Ryan trusted him, then Catherine really had no choice. She had to trust her instincts.

Cole took a few minutes to examine the photograph. "It's old. I'd say, early eighties or late seventies by the way they are dressed. Can you identify anyone or anything in the photo?"

"No, I've studied it since I received it." She sighed. "I've no idea what it means.

"Mind if I show it to a friend of mine?" He tapped it against the table as if it were a card.

"I don't know—" Catherine hesitated.

"He's someone I trust, retired from the CIA. Knows a lot about things he probably shouldn't, if you know what I mean." Cole smiled.

"Okay," She relented. "But you should make a copy. It's the only one I have."

"What do you know about that reporter?" Cole leaned back in his chair and looked across the parking lot as if he was waiting for someone.

"Just a reporter," Ryan answered for her. "Always mulling about."

"Do you trust him?" Cole waved for the server to bring the check.

"I don't not trust him," Catherine answered. "I don't know him really." She paused, her mind recalling the numerous articles he wrote that she read. "His interest seems genuine."

He stood to his feet. "Usually when you're trying to uncover something someone wants to cover up, it's good to have a hook with the newspaper." He tossed several bills on the table. "Let me see what my friend is able to uncover."

"Hartmann did try and cover for us when Paine walked up. I mean does he really want some silly variance report?" Ryan explained without expecting a response from Catherine.

Ryan stood as he pulled his jacket from the back of the chair. "Thanks for coming." She leaned in to kiss him. "McKenzie's with her Dad this weekend."

He smiled and kissed her again. "I'll bring my jammies."

"See you tonight," she smiled and waved to him as he walked away.

"Jammies?" Catherine smiled, attempting to hide her smile.

"It's a new development." Ryan blushed.

"About time," Catherine taunted. "I hope we don't regret involving him."

"He's a good guy, Catherine." Ryan confided.

"I just don't want anyone else to get hurt." Catherine bit her bottom lip. "And I want whomever is responsible for Anwar's death to be held accountable."

"We all want the same thing, then." Ryan picked up her purse. "I'll see you on Monday?"

"Yeah" Catherine smiled. "Have fun."

"Planning on it," Ryan waved, walking away, without looking back.

****

"Good weekend, Virginia?" Catherine asked through the open door of her office. It was the third time in a half hour she'd seen Virginia's figure pass by.

"Yes, but I was so tired. All I really did was sleep. Richard wanted to go out for dinner at least one of the nights, but I was so beat, I opted for take-out and we ate in."

"How's the head?" Catherine tapped her hand against her own forehead.

"Stitches came out on Friday." She smiled, stepping farther into Catherine's office and checking the small mirror stuck to the metal filing cabinet. "I'm going to ask Dr. Fare to take a look and see if he can do anything with the scar."

"Dr. Fare the ED physician?" Catherine stopped reading the file under her nose, her eyes locked with Virginias. "You aren't thinking of using him instead of seeing a plastic surgeon are you?"

"Why not? I heard he's very good." Virginia leaned closer toward the mirror rubbing the red, angry scar gently with her index finger. "A lot of physician's are fortunate to have another specialty on the side."

"I know, they pick up shifts in an urgent care center or a stand-alone emergency department. I don't know of any specialist who moonlights in a completely different specialty, especially plastic surgery."

"I don't think it's that uncommon." Virginia stretched her bangs over the scar as much as she could. She looked back out into the waiting area. "What do you think about Sarah Richardson?"

Oh no, Catherine thought, not another tragedy. "What's happened?"

"Board of Commissioners met this morning to appoint an interim CEO for the system until a permanent one can be found." She paused. "Sarah was appointed six to one."

"Who was the one?" Catherine asked even though she felt as if she already knew the answer.

"Commissioner Fleming was the only nay." Virginia smiled.

"Not surprised. Sarah is homegrown here. She's never worked for GHF or Booker. Of course, Fleming's going to vote no." Catherine shuffled the files in front of her. "She already thinks Lindsey is a wild card, there's no way she wants to give her up monopoly." She paused to see if Virginia had anything to add. "When's the announcement?"

"Today right before lunch."

"Have you talked to Cliff?" Catherine asked even though she knew Virginia had spoken to him.

"Yes, he picked up the rest of his stuff." Virginia paused. "Now that his suspension has been modified to a termination, he didn't want anything left behind that was his."

"The feds have already taken what they wanted right?" Catherine asked, hoping they might be able to wash their hands of the entire thing.

Virginia nodded.

"Was he able to get a good lawyer?" Catherine hoped so, she liked Cliff.

"Yes, Lindsey's husband is a lawyer and offered to help him."

"Lindsey?" Catherine questioned. "Isn't she the one who fired him?"

"I know it's supposed to look that way but I don't think she had any say in the matter." Virginia pulled at her hair again. "The decision was made at a much higher level. She simply delivered the bad news."

Catherine recalled that Ryan had said something similar after terminating the impaired pharmacist. She'd mentioned that the entire review and assessment was out of her hands, she'd been nothing more than a mouthpiece. Once again in her mind's eye, Catherine saw the creature with the head of a lion, the body of a goat, and a serpent's tail.

"Steven, Lindsey's husband, doesn't think the case is very strong at all. He seems sure he'll be able to get the charges dropped. They have nothing that incriminates Cliff as the one who embezzled the money."

"But it was traced back to his computer?"

"Yes, but the hours the transactions were made are times Cliff would never have been In the office. He's going to subpoena the surveillance tapes from the dates the transactions were made to show that Cliff had left the building hours earlier or wasn't clocked in at all."

"Remote access?" Catherine tossed out feeling more and more like a prosecutor with every question she posed.

"Even easier to trace." Virginia took a seat. "Leaves a hell of an electronic footprint." She stopped chewing on the gum in her mouth. "You don't really think Cliff had money wired from the hospital into a personal account offshore?"

"I don't but it certainly seems that way."

"Aren't you the one who said things aren't always what they seem?" She hesitated. "What was it you called it?"

"Chimera," Catherine answered. Looking toward the front office where the sound of the front office opening was audible. "Who's there?"

"Sorry," he said, as the inspector from the office of the Inspector general fudged his way closer to the door. "Inspector Winters, we met before?" He pointed to another man behind him. "And you remember Agent Bronson from the FBI?"

"Yes," Catherine stood up and motioned them inside as Virginia returned to her desk.

"Have a seat," Virginia instructed and checked to see if either of them had an appointment.

"Miss Virginia?" Michele called from Lindsey's doorway. "I'm all done in here." She nodded at the visitors before addressing Virginia again. "I'm going out the other door."

"That's fine, Michele, thank you." Virginia waited until Michele disappeared back into the office and the other exterior office door snapped closed.

"I forgot she was in there," Virginia whispered to Catherine as they made their way to where the Inspector and Agent Bronson were waiting.

"Happens to me all the time," Catherine whispered under her breath and held her hand out to the visitors. "Can we offer you anything, water, coffee?"

Obediently, both slid into the chairs in front of her desk. "Sorry to come unannounced but it seems as if the encounters work out better than when we schedule an appointment." The inspector smiled and flipped his notebook open. "We won't take up much of your time. Just trying to follow up on a complaint you took regarding Mr. Lewis and a female sales representative from Anderson and Black."

"I simply handed you the complaint that was shared with me." She hadn't planned to sound as bitchy but once the words were out of her mouth, it felt odd to try and recant or back pace.

"How well do you know Ms. Horseman?" The FBI agent interjected.

"Not at all. In fact, I've never met her."

"I don't understand?" The agent asked looking at his notes for clarification.

"Her complaint was shared with me by an associate of hers."

"Yes," he flipped the pages, stopping when he found what he was looking for. "Mr. Curtaine?"

"I believe that's his name, yes."

"And how well do you know Mr. Curtaine?"

"I've met him a few times but we don't know each other well at all. Mostly just passing in the hallway or the few times he joined Dr. Allen for lunch?"

"Dr. Allen? The pharmacy manager?" He wasn't able to contain his excitement. It was evident in his voice. He was like a child at a birthday party, watching as the cake was presented.

"Yes,"

"How is she involved with this complaint?"

"I believe he confided in her and she encouraged him to report it. I asked him to write everything down that he knew." She waited a minute as he jotted down a few notes then went on once he looked up from his notepad. "That's really my extent of involvement."

"Dr. Allen didn't like Mr. Lewis very much, did she?" the inspector chimed in.

"You'd need to ask her."

"I'm asking you." He didn't say or else but Catherine knew the way he said the words, it was implied.

"I was present, as were you, during your last interview with us both. During that discussion, she did say she didn't like him and she felt as if he meddled in pharmacy issues that he shouldn't have been involved in."

"Did you ever witness his interference personally or was everything, you know, heresy?"

A rock and a hard place, she thought. No matter how she answered this question she was screwed. "I'm not aware of any situation where Mr. Lewis was involved with or managed pharmacy in any way."

"So, hearsay?" he repeated.

"Yes," she swallowed. It had taken most of her energy to get the word out.

The front office door swung open and Michele drug herself through the door pushing her cleaning cart in first.

"Michele," Catherine heard Virginia say. "I thought you were done?"

"No, I still need to clean Miss Erin's office. I tried to come back in the way I went out but the door doesn't open from the outside."

"That's right." Virginia nodded. "It only opens to the outside." She looked past where Michele was standing hoping to see that Catherine's visitors were done and standing to leave." Instead, she asked. "Are you able to come back in a half hour or so?"

Michele checked her watch, thinking thoughtfully as if she were studying the door to Ryan's office. "I may not be able to come back till tomorrow, Ms. Virginia." She smiled, "Greg said no overtime."

"Go ahead and start in Erin's office, just close the door once your inside. Catherine's in the middle of an important meeting."

"I will," Michele pushed the heavy cart toward Erin's office, stopping to steal a glance into Catherine's office before she disappeared inside.

"Thanks, Virginia," Catherine called through the door.

"Has there ever been a time when something Dr. Allen said or did turned out to be untrue or inaccurate?" The inspector went on, oblivious to the interruption. Catherine shifted uncomfortably in the chair feeling as if the FBI agent was wondering the same thing.

"No," she said. "I've never known Dr. Allen to say anything that she knew wasn't true." She shook her head not liking where she felt this discussion was headed. It seemed to her as if Ryan might be on the chopping block. "This can all be resolved quickly. Just speak with Ms. Horseman, confirm the details with her."

"We did interview Ms. Horseman." The FBI agent jumped in. "She said it was a terrible misunderstanding. Her version of the event does not implicate Mr. Lewis in any way."

"Someone's not being truthful Inspector Winters. And I don't think it's Dr. Allen." She waited for him to look up from his notepad. "I was with Dr. Allen in her office when Mr. Curtaine made the accusation. What does he say?"

"Mr. Curtaine is no longer employed by Anderson & Black. We haven't been able to reach him by any number he had on record with them."

"I don't know how to respond to that. I was there, I heard what he said. You have his signed testament."

"Unless we can validate that was his statement, the document means nothing. It could have been written by anyone."

"You mean, by Dr. Allen or myself?"

"I mean, by someone who voiced discontent with him and his processes."

"Do you have any other questions Inspector Winters, Agent Bronson? If not, I'm going to ask you to leave. I have work to do."

She called out into the office area. "Virginia, could you please show these gentlemen out?"

Virginia appeared as if by magic and motioned them toward the front office door. "Gentleman, if you don't mind?"

Inspector Winters rose first, then Agent Bronson who shuffled his feet as if he were asking her to dance. "Thank you for your time, Ms. Masters." Winters smiled. "We'll be in touch soon."

"Is it okay to come out know?" Michele stuck her head through Erin's doorway. "I'm ready for the next office."

"Yes," Virginia motioned Michele out and into Cliff's previous office. "It's okay, they're gone."

Michele nodded and pulled the cleaning cart into Cliff's office, leaving the door slightly ajar as she moved farther into the room.

Catherine was calling her phone before the officers were fully out of the front office. She hoped Ryan was close by and not in a corporate meeting downtown. It was impossible to hide her disappointment as Ryan's voicemail answered instructed the caller to leave a message. "Call me," she said, "as soon as you get this. It's urgent."

Chapter 14

"What's that?" Catherine asked as she moved the stack of mail from one side of Lorraine's vacant desk to the other and began to sort through it, pulling hers and Ryan's from the stack as Virginia emerged from Lindsey's office with a small box tucked almost underarm.

"Uh?" Virginia stuttered and startled to find Catherine at the front desk, grabbing the box anxiously as if she'd forgotten it was there. "I wonder if this was the box Andrew was so anxious about?" Virginia held up a small box about a quarter the size of a shoe box with its top so worn around the edges, it had been taped onto the box. It was just wide enough to hold several regular sized envelopes. It could have easily been a pencil box if not for the worn edges of the box where taped and been placed and tor away multiple times before.

"Any word from Ryan?" If Catherine had been standing, she'd be pacing.

"No, I saw Linda from the pharmacy when I went to the cafeteria to get some soup. She said Ryan left around mid-morning and that she seemed upset."

"Did Linda say what Ryan was upset about?"

"No, but she thought it might have had something to do with her ex-husband." Virginia pushed the box further into Catherine line of sight and repeated. "Do you think this is Andrew's box?"

"Maybe," she motioned for Virginia to open it on the desktop. "Where did you find it?"

"There was a leak in one of the OR rooms upstairs and one of the ceiling tiles in Lindsey's office was stained." She paused. "I had facilities stop by and replace the stained tile."

"Jay?" Catherine moved closer to Virginia and the box.

"No, he's off today. Barry came instead." Virginia held the box up to get a better look at it. "When he removed the ceiling tile this box was sitting just inside the ledge." She cut the tape away and pulled the top away, looking carefully inside at a handful of old pictures, handwritten documents, and letters.

"Do you think this is the box Andrew was looking for?" Virginia stacked the contents into one of the three piles, pulling the photographs out first and pushing them toward Catherine.

Catherine was only partially paying attention, her mind wandering to what could be prohibiting Ryan from returning the call. The interaction with the officers earlier that morning was burning a hole in her mind. She needed to talk to Ryan, make sure she was aware of where the investigation was headed.

It wasn't the first picture of the stack or even the second or third that made Catherine stop and take a closer look. "Oh my God," she exclaimed. "It's the same picture."

"Which one?' Virginia stopped sorting the contents.

"This one," Catherine picked up the picture and inspected it more closely "I've seen it before."

"Where?" Virginia started piling the contents back in the box.

"I'd rather not say," she smiled thinking of the picture she'd given to Detective Spencer. "I'm sorry but I made a promise to someone that I wouldn't say or share anything they'd told me." Catherine replaced the top and scotch taped the ends to the body of the box. "Just leave it, Virginia. I'll go through it and document the contents in the variance system as an incident."

"I can do that for you," Virginia offered. "There's a lot of stuff in here that you'll have to scan and enter if you're treating it as a variance."

"That's okay." Catherine laughed nervously, anxious to get a better look at the contents of the box. Other than the picture nothing else looked notable but her hands itched at the thought of getting to its bottom. She had more questions than answers and it was beginning to bother her. "I want to go through it all."

She'd just laid the final document from the box into one of three piles when the front office door opened and she heard Virginia address the visitor.

"We were getting worried about you," Virginia called from her desk.

"I'm fine." Ryan's voice was anything but. "Just needed to step off site for some personal business."

"Everything okay?" Virginia asked. She didn't wait for an answer before she added. "Can I get you a drink?"

"No, I'm responding to Catherine's voice mails," Ryan answered as she appeared at Catherine's office door,

"I was worried when you didn't answer my calls. Everything okay?"

"Yeah, my ex-husband called to let me know that he decided to get married last weekend in the Bahamas." She paused. "Was kind of a shock. Our divorce hasn't been finalized that long."

"But you've been separated for several years." Catherine meant it as a question but it didn't come out as one. Instead, it sounded more like an accusation.

"Yeah, I know." She pointed to the chair. "Got a minute?"

"Yes, and shut the door."

Catherine waited until Ryan had secured the door. "I saw you met with Lindsey this morning?"

"Yes, she's appointing me to the COO position as an interim even though I don't want the position." Ryan ran her hand over her forehead, pulling the hair across the top of her head and letting it fall messily back into place. "I don't think the additional stress will be good for me."

"Neither do I." Catherine nodded, wondering if she should even bring up the discussion she'd had with Inspector Winters and Agent Bronson. The last thing Ryan needed was something else to stress over, worry about. "When does the appointment take effect?"

"Tomorrow morning." She yawned. "But I'll be sharing my office in the pharmacy with Bailey for a while. I'll be in and out to help her manage her existing role and the new one she's taking on."

"You're doing both roles?"

"They promoted Bailey from supervisor to interim pharmacy director in the meantime." She paused. "Then when someone gets hired, everybody goes back to where they belong." Her words broke as she finished the sentence. Catherine knew Ryan was fighting to control her emotions and maintain her composure.

"I hate to add fuel to the fire, but we may have other more pressing problems to deal with."

"Like what?"

"Bronson and Winters were here again this morning."

"What did Frick and Frack want this time?"

"They were here to follow up on the pharmaceutical representative's claim that Aaron sexually assaulted her."

"And?"

"The rep has recanted her story and is saying it's all a misunderstanding."

"What did Nathan say?"

"They haven't been able to contact him." She dropped her folded arms atop the desk. "He hasn't returned any of their calls."

Ryan pulled her phone from her pocket, dialing Nathan's number as she pointed to the pictures and documents from the box. "What's all this?" She asked before adding as his voice email picked up her call. "Hey Nathan, it's me. Give me a call so I know what's going on. The FBI is under the impression that Lauren has recanted her accusation." She paused. "I need to know what's going on. Thanks."

"These were in a box in the ceiling of Andrew's office." Catherine held up one of the pictures. "This is the same picture I gave to your friend. Has he uncovered anything about it?"

"No, I don't think his friend has gotten back to him yet." Ryan waved toward the other items from the box. "What about the other stuff?"

"Letters to and from several different people I don't know." She held up another picture. "Old pictures of men in suits, posing for the camera in front of some old barn."

"You think it has something to do with Dr. Beliard?"

"I think so, yes. But I have no idea how or why."

"How do you think the box got up there? If Andrew knew where it was why all the searching for it?"

"Andrew's stuff has been moved back and forth several times by various people. Once we identify who these people are, it might help lead us to whoever wants or is hiding this information." She paused before adding. "I don't think Andrew knew it was up there or he wouldn't have been so hot to find it." Her finger's tapped anxiously against the desktop. "Maybe someone was waiting for an opportunity to get it out and that seemed like a safe place to hide it in the meantime?"

"Could be and maybe this is what the guy who broke in was looking for?"

"Maybe," Catherine gently replaced the items back into the box and taped the top into place. "Can you give this to Detective Spencer?"

"Of course." Ryan wiped at her eyes. "I'm not sure when I'm going to see him again but I'll call and ask him to pick up the box."

"What do you mean, you don't know when you'll see him again?" She stifled a smile. "I mean, he brings his jammies and all, right?"

"He misread something I said about my ex's wedding this morning before we left for work. He was angry when he left. I'm not sure he'll be back tonight." Ryan's tears fell freely down her face. In all the years they'd known each other, Catherine could only think of two times she'd seen Ryan reduced to tears. Once upstairs in CCU when her mother passed away and today.

"You have to give him a chance. The workday isn't over yet. I bet he's at your house waiting when you get there."

"I doubt it." She wiped her eyes again.

Catherine stood and pulled the broken chair; the one Anwar had placed against the wall the last time he'd been in her office closer to Ryan. "He cares about you. He'll call."

She adjusted herself more comfortably in the seat noticing something bulky just under the leather cover of the chair. Catherine moved to one hip, tugging at the object hoping she could bring it closer to the torn edge.

"What are you doing?" Ryan laughed through the tears. "You got an itch?"

"No," Catherine responded. "There something here under the leather of the seat."

"What is it?"

Catherine tugged at the leather not bothered by how much bigger she was making the hole until finally the object emerged tucked flush against her fingertips. "A key." She held it up so Ryan could see it better. "An old key? Looks like, what is it called?"

"Skeleton key," Ryan answered. "It's an old skeleton key. What's it doing in your chair?"

"I'm fairly certain Anwar put it here."

"Why would he do that? And what does it go to?"

"I can't answer either of those questions," Catherine blinked as if she could will his image from her mind.

"That's too bad." Ryan stood up, wrapping her hand around the box. "Cause there's something he really wanted you to know."

****

"Thanks for letting me stop by," Catherine dropped her purse and bag near the door and waited for Ryan to usher her into the house.

"You still think someone is listening in to our conversations in your office?" Ryan pointed towards the living room and waited until Catherine was seated before falling into a chair close by.

"I'm just taking every precaution." Catherine looked around the room, assessing if the décor had changed any now that Cole Spencer was in Ryan's domestic picture.

"Want something to drink?" Ryan asked, before sipping from a wine glass filled with what Catherine assumed was red wine.

"Maybe later after we talk with Detective Spencer," Catherine breathed a sigh. "So, everything is good again between you?"

"Yes," Ryan took another sip but Catherine knew it was more of a nervous response to the question than a desire for more wine. "He's got to be the most stubborn—"

Catherine cut her off. "You two have a lot in common."

"He accused me of trying to push him away because I was scared." Ryan finished the statement with another swallow of wine. "Can you believe that?"

Catherine smiled and nodded as Ryan went on. "My ex has remarried. I'm okay with that."

"Are you?, Really, I mean?"

"Yes," she took a big gulp. "I've recently realized what different people we are. I love him, always will but not like I did once." She paused. "But I can still mourn that loss, the death of the people we were once, right?"

Catherine nodded and thought of Anwar, "Yes, you can." She jumped to her feet. 'I think I will take that drink after all?" she asked, before disappearing into the kitchen. "What time can we expect Detective Spencer?"

"He usually stops by and eats dinner." She paused. "If McKenzie's home, he eats and leaves. If she's with her Dad, sometimes he spends the night."

"Why couldn't he tell us what he'd found out about the picture and the contents of the box over the phone?" She asked from the kitchen.

"I think you've made him paranoid with all the office bugging talk." Ryan laughed before clearing her throat. "I fired Jayson this morning."

"You fired him while you were still the pharmacy director or in your new role as COO?" Catherine reappeared holding a glass of red wine and retook her seat.

"My last official act as the Director of Pharmacy." Ryan shook her head. "Still think this is a bad idea. I already hate the little bit of politics I had." She rubbed her head. "Plus, when this is over and I'm no longer COO, my direct reports will be my colleagues again. That's going to be awkward."

"You told Lindsey you didn't want the promotion even on an interim basis?"

"Yes," Ryan stuffed her feet up under her butt. "She said it wasn't a request. She needed me to step up to the plate and take one for the team." She took another drink of wine. "I felt bad for Jayson; He needs help not to be unemployed."

"Brittany didn't give you another option?"

"No, in fact, our lovely director of human resources said the decision had already been made at a much higher level. All they needed from me was to meet with Jayson and do the deed."

"How did he take it?" Catherine asked, feeling as if she already knew. Ryan had been his last chance at getting his professional life back. He had to know his chances of working again as a pharmacist were pretty much over.

"As well as he could I guess." Ryan paused. "He kept insisting it was a misunderstanding."

"What's there to misunderstand?"

"He said the nurse was there in the room and asked him to give the patient the med."

"That doesn't make any sense," Catherine took another drink, wishing Ryan had made it a tad stronger. "Did you speak to the nurse?"

"I did," Ryan nodded. "He denied being in the room or instructing Jayson to give the medication to the patient."

"What did the patient say?"

"The patient said the medication was given to her by a man." Ryan paused, "Both care providers are male in this situation."

Catherine opened her mouth to respond but Ryan went on instead. "Both Caucasian, wire glasses, sandy blonde hair," Ryan added. "The patient is a bit confused and couldn't identify for certain which man gave her the medication." She paused again. "I showed her pictures of both the nurse and the pharmacist."

"And?

"She picked them both at different times."

"So inconclusive?"

"Yes, very." Ryan refilled their glasses, after returning from the kitchen and sitting the wine

bottle on the coffee table. "Something else odd, too."

"What?"

"When I was walking him out, he mentioned something about his termination being payback for

asking about the blue dot."

"Blue dot?"

"Yes?"

"What does that mean?"

"I don't know and he stopped talking when Aiden met us in the hallway. He wouldn't answer

any of my questions. He just kept mumbling under his breath how the retaliation started after he questioned the blue dot."

"Is that a medication or a brand of a medication?"

"I've never heard it used in any capacity. It almost seemed as if he was trying to divert my attention away from firing him by having me focus on whatever the blue dot is." She exhaled a deep breath. "In any event, I did as I was instructed. I don't have to like it."

"What happened to him is sad," Catherine agreed, wishing there was another option for the impaired pharmacist. "But as I'm constantly reminding you. You need your job."

"Yes, I do," Ryan said. "Anything new on the white van you've seen lurking about?"

"Not since the other day."

"What about the intruder who attacked Virginia?"

"No update on that either." She feigned a laugh. "It doesn't seem as if our security team is ever where you need them, Hence my concern that your pharmacy technician's car sat unabated for so long."

"One big, fat walking chimera." Ryan taunted.

****

"You didn't have to bring dinner, honey." Ryan greeted Detective Spencer with a kiss and motioned him inside.

"I figured we could eat while we talk. I'm starving." He made his way to the kitchen and dropped a large brown paper bag on top of the counter. "Hope everyone likes Chinese." He smiled at Ryan. "I know McKenzie does." He held up a container. "Pad Thai only noodles and mushrooms."

"She's at dance till eight but I know she'll love that she got her own."

"Vegetable lo Mein sans the mushrooms for you." He handed Ryan a similar size carton before turning to Catherine. "I didn't know what you liked. So, I got a sweet and sour chicken and beef with broccoli." He moved to the sink to wash his hands. "Hopefully, you'll like one of those dishes."

"Either, actually." Catherine smiled. "You didn't have to provide dinner Detective." She opened her hands for the chicken takeout box before following them into the dining room. "But I'm glad you did. Smells wonderful."

****

"I checked with a colleague on my softball team." Cole offered; his words soft almost rhythmic as he swallowed the last bite of his Chinese food. The lighted candles burning in the room gave it an almost mystical feel as he went on. "She's a detective with BSO. There is no movement on the breaking and entering an event into your CFO's office. It couldn't be colder." Cole finished the last few bites of Ryan's vegetable lo Mein and scanned the table as if looking for remnants of other leftovers to scavenge.

"What about the men driving the white van?" Catherine asked, wiping a trail of sweet and sour sauce off the table in front of her.

"I stand corrected." Cole smiled. "That might be the only complaint that is colder."

"Is it unusual to have so few leads on an open case?"

"Sometimes," he scooped up the beef and broccoli carton like a vulture closing in on its prey. "Don't take this the wrong way but in the overall scope of the complaints that come in on a daily basis, both of those events are going to be a pretty low priority."

She'd known that to be true even before she asked the question. During her years of managing the risks associated with patient care, she'd become an expert at prioritizing the lowest of risks and addressing a hierarchy of higher risks.

"Ryan mentioned she told you about the potassium chloride that was injected into Beliard's vasopressin during open heart surgery."

"Yes," he nodded. "But I can tell you that it won't amount to much since the chain of custody can't be validated." He pulled his notebook from his jacket. "I'll make sure the detectives working his suicide are aware of the event. If they have questions, I'll have them call you?"

"Yes," she nodded. "We can provide the data from the independent lab that we used."

"We would have used the coroner's lab and staff." He smiled. "Sorry to keep busting your balls but it's just the way we do things."

"Were you able to find out anything about the picture or any of the other documents that were in the box?" Catherine asked pouring another glass of wine.

"Yes and no." He sat the cartons of Chinese food down and pulled the picture from his jacket pocket. "This group of men." He tapped at the picture Beliard had given Catherine. "Are the seven physicians who were acquitted during the Doctors' Trial of the Nuremberg Trials in 1947."

"Why would Anwar have that picture?"

"That's one of the questions I haven't been able to answer. "But this man," he pointed to the man second from the right. "This is Dr. Paul Prostock, He was a consultant for the US Army in 1939 and a high-ranking surgeon in the Nazi party.

"What's the connection to Anwar?"

"Paul Rostock was Jacob Fleming's grandfather." He paused watching their reaction. "But I doubt he knew his grandfather very well. Rostock died in 1956. Jacob would have been little more than a toddler."

"What about the other things in the box?" Ryan asked, moving closer to get a better look at the picture.

Cole collected the picture. "My friend wasn't able to piece much else together." He held the picture up so they could see it better. "The man next to Rostock is Kurt Blome. He was also acquitted even though it was well known he tested vaccines against the plague on Jewish prisoners in the camps."

"Was Rostock a part of that testing?"

"That wasn't clear but whoever put the documents together seems to be tracing Blome's family tree."

"Anything else of significance?"

"Not that I can tell but one of the trails point to Albert Kligman, a dermatologist who used prisoners from the Holmesburg Prison System in Philadelphia, as a probable descendant." He rifled through the documents. "This single piece of paper is from a poll survey validated by Robert Maridian. He was one of the Watergate Seven." He returned it to the box and selected another document. "This is a copy of an invoice payable to Kornal Morawiecki, the founder of the Fighting Solidarity anti-union movement in Poland." He unfolded a wrinkled paper from the bottom of the box. "This appears to be the locations of several restaurants scattered throughout Warsaw county in Dalles, Oregon during 1984."

Cole looked around the room and for the first time, Catherine thought he seemed nervous. He went on. "My friend found mention that someone named Ma Anand Sheela was convicted of food poisoning the salad bars at those same restaurants. There's a canceled check in the box written by Richard Fleming to Sheela for half a million dollars."

"Did your friend say why Sheela wanted to poison all those people?" Ryan asked.

"To sway the vote so Sheela's candidate would win." He replaced the contents of the box and pushed the top back on. "There are notes from the aid to Casper Weinberger when he was questioned for the Iran Contra scandal. And another canceled check for half a million dollars."

"There's other, too." He went on. "Special assistants to Senators and Congressmen, District attorneys, and deputy sheriffs. They are all listed in the black book with dates and money they were paid." He feigned a laugh. "There's even a plastic surgeon listed. His payment was among the largest. He was paid more than six million dollars over a five-year period of time. If you consider the entries as cases, he performed plastic surgery on over a hundred people. Some most certainly refugees and criminals."

"Do you know his name?" Catherine asked, her mind spinning with uncertainty. Why would Anwar have had the picture? She questioned. How was he involved with these people in the ledger?

"Just his initials" Cole answered. "M.L"

Catherine exhaled a breath she didn't realize she was holding; thankful Detective Spencer hadn't recited the initials as AB. "Thank goodness," she whispered under her breath.

"Of course." Cole added, "We've no way of knowing if any of these men used their real names. It's all smoke and mirrors. Nothing is as it seems, one big illusion."

She felt her heart drop below her belt. Her mind had known this before he'd said the words but hearing him say it out loud, it was almost too much to bear. She dropped into the place of the couch next to Ryan and grabbed the bottle of red wine on the coffee table in front of them.

Chapter 15

Catherine hated to admit it but she was kind of liking having Ryan in the office next door. And truth be told they were getting a lot more work done than she expected with them being in such close proximity. There had been many visitors into Ryan's office since she'd become COO, mostly her visitors had been direct reports from the operational team, the leaders of facilities, laboratory, radiology, and of course pharmacy. Still, she managed to get a lot of projects completed. Perhaps Ryan should reconsider and assess the potentiality of taking the position full time?

Catherine knew the supervisor who'd taken over Ryan's role as pharmacy director was more than competent. Although Bailey, the interim director, had been in and out of the COO's office frequently after Ryan had initially moved from the pharmacy office, she hadn't been in administration at all yesterday. Catherine checked her watch, it was well after lunch and still, Bailey hadn't made any requests for help.

She wouldn't have called it a premonition, not really. It was simply coincidental when the front office door opened and the visitor greeted everyone before making a beeline for Ryan's office.

Bailey, Catherine thought hearing parts of the conversation and watching as Bailey's petite form passed by Catherine's open office door.

"Hey," she heard Ryan greet the visitor. "I got your voicemail this morning. Everyone ok?"

"Yeah," Bailey's voice was hushed. "I didn't leave here last night till late. Stopped at the grocery for a few things." She paused. "I was just down the street when the accident happened."

"You're ok?" Ryan asked.

"I am but my car's going to need some backend work."

"Cars can be replaced." Catherine heard Ryan say. "I'm glad you're ok? Whatever you need just let me know."

"I need your key to the office," Bailey said. "I know I had my key when I left last night but I can't find it."

"You have to find it or you'll need to call security and have the pharmacy locks changed. Our keys are master keys. They'll open any area tagged as belonging to the pharmacy."

"Can't I just wait for it to show up?"

"No," Catherine heard Ryan's chair scooted across the floor. Ryan was on her feet. "When's the last time you remember actually having it?"

"I know I put my key in my jacket pocket like always. Then draped my jacket over the passenger's front seat so it doesn't wrinkle."

"It's not in your pocket? Maybe it fell out of your pocket during the wreck. Did you check your car?"

"Yes," her words were precise. "Can I just borrow yours until we get the locks changed? I have some things I need to finish today."

"Sure, it will take a day or two to get the locks changed anyway," Ryan advised.

"Catherine?" Ryan and Bailey appeared at her office doorway. "Does Bailey need to complete a variance report if she can't find her key?"

"Yes," Catherine looked up from her paperwork. "You want me to do it?"

"No," Bailey shook her head. "I'll do it, once I get into the office."

Catherine watched as Ryan handed the pharmacy key over to Bailey. It was impossible not to think of Anwar's key. She thought of it, tucked safely away in its hiding place, a place she'd told no one about, not even Ryan.

She waited till Bailey had left them alone before motioning for Ryan to take a seat. "Where are the items you were holding for investigational review?"

"In my office safe of course."

"Don't you think you should move the items over here in the office you're currently residing in?"

"I guess I could." She rubbed her head. "I can have facilities reconfigure one of the credenza doors to a single lock, one only I'll have a key for."

"I'll put in a work order," Catherine offered, signing into her computer.

"Did you decide if you're going to update the variance report with what we know about Beliard's IV bag being tampered with?" She paused. "And what about the things Cole told us a few nights ago?"

"I'm going to omit the specifics of what Detective Spencer told us about the items. Just that we have outside agencies working on the boxes' contents. And yes, I'll scan the report from your outside chemist of the potassium chloride that was injected into the vasopressor." She pointed out the door. "Can you grab the report from the chemist for me while I pull up the incident to update?"

"Sure" Ryan disappeared from the office, returning moments later with the paper in her hand.

Catherine searched the database diligently, several times by patient name and then by date. Each time the computer screen flashed the same irritating message, no record found.

"What's wrong?" Ryan asked, dropping her arms to her side with the report still in her hand.

"I can't find the incident." Catherine typed Beliard's name again only to receive the same message."

"Maybe you forgot to save it?" Ryan paused, laughing nervously. "I can't tell you how many times I've done that."

"No," Catherine shook her head. "I've added addendums at least twice."

"That's not possible." Ryan moved to stand next to her, watching as Catherine retyped his name.

"There's only one explanation." Catherine stopped typing.

"What?"

"Someone deleted the report."

****

What a night Catherine, yawned into her hand. Even after she'd convinced Ryan to go home, she'd stayed in the office, awaiting the call from the information technology department. It had taken someone with some corporate balls to have that report deleted. She wanted to know who it was, she thought of Mason Riley, the recently appointed system CIO and supporter of Fleming. He'd certainly qualify as having the juice. It was nearly ten o'clock when she'd finally packed up her briefcase and started her trip home.

Coming home had been pointless, she hadn't been able to focus on anything except that variance report and who could have deleted it and why. It was this mantra that kept her awake most of the night, tossing and turning to the extent that Gordon had finally gotten up and retreated to the guest bedroom, hoping for an hour or two of sleep.

****

"Yes?" she answered the phone on the first ring hoping not to disturb the others already in the office. She recognized the number, knew the caller was from information technology. She could just call commissioner Fleming and ask her to call her IT friend and find out what the hell was happening. Why someone had been allowed to delete the record in the first place?

"What do you mean, there's no record?" Catherine repeated the information technology technician's summation. "That's impossible, I submitted the record myself." She paused. "I even made updates to it."

"I don't know what to tell you," the technician reiterated.

"Can I speak to a supervisor?"

"All the IT managers are at a management retreat. I can have him call you when they're back in the office tomorrow."

"Please do." Catherine disconnected the call without waiting for a response.

"Catherine?" Virginia called from her desk. "Agent Bronson is here to see you."

"He can come in."

"Knock, knock" Agent Bronson tapped against the door frame. "I got your message you needed to talk to me?"

"Yes," she motioned for him to close the door. "I need to talk to someone about some things that are going on." She paused, rubbing her forehead. "I don't know who else to turn to."

"What is it?" He took a seat in front of her desk.

"I think someone may have killed Dr. Beliard. I think he was involved in or uncovered something and he was killed for what he knew or whatever he'd found."

"I know you and he were close." Agent Bronson went on. "You were his first wife."

"It's not that." She swallowed. "He came to see me a few weeks before he died. He was very upset and talking about mismanaged money and fraudulent payments to physicians. He said he was working with the FBI and was concerned that you guys weren't stepping in."

"He was probably referring to the OIG investigation."

"Maybe," she paused. "But it felt as if there was more."

"There is nothing to suggest Anwar Beliard was working with the FBI at any level." He cleared his throat as he finished the sentence.

"But he said he was, he mentioned he was concerned that the FBI wasn't engaging quickly enough. He felt like he was in over his head and he didn't know who to turn to."

"Did he ever mention who in the FBI he was working with?"

"No, he didn't mention any names but I don't think he would lie about it, not to me." She hesitated, rubbing her forehead as if she had a headache. "He seemed genuinely frightened the night he had me meet him. He was scared. And Anwar Beliard was not an easy man to frighten."

"I've read the coroner's report, saw his body, Catherine. He killed himself. I swear."

"I knew him Agent Bronson, better than anyone else, even better than his wife Melinda. His ego would have never allowed him to commit suicide. He would have been assured he could fix himself. He was just that arrogant."

****

"Are you sure it's Sarah?" Catherine asked, her heels clicking in double time as she ran alongside Lindsey toward the emergency department.

"Yes, they just brought her in by ambulance," Lindsey said between breaths. "My understanding is she's unresponsive."

"A stroke?"

"Maybe," she pulled Lindsey by the arm toward the employee entrance into the emergency department. "Could be an MI, too." They made their way around the pediatric nursing station and stopped when they came upon the cardiac nursing station where people were lined up three and four deep.

"Get these people out of here." Catherine barked to Aiden as he ran around the corner. "Immediate family only in the trauma room, everyone else is to wait in the waiting room."

"I'll set up a perimeter!" he advised, calling into his radio for additional officers to respond to the emergency department.

She took Lindsey by the arm. "We should wait outside in the hallway, too."

"Of course." Lindsey followed her into the hallway and took one of the plastic chairs just outside the trauma room.

"The entire code team is in there," Catherine remarked, turning her head to watch as another crash cart was wheeled into the trauma room. "That's not good." She stood up "We should call Ryan and make sure she knows. I don't know how many crash carts they have in the area. We may need to have another one close by, just in case."

"Good thinking." Lindsey nodded, watching as Catherine pulled her phone from her pocket.

"It went to voicemail." She disconnected the call without leaving a message. "I'll call the pharmacy and have one brought over." She paced a few steps, her mind wandering to another night she'd paced in the hallway, the night she'd lost her mother. Her eyes traveled the short distance to trauma room twelve. She hadn't been in the room since that night.

It was oddly quiet as she neared the doorway. Just a peak she thought from the doorway, a glance to see what if any of her mother might still be there. Was it possible a hair had fallen to the floor, stuck like glue in the corner between the floor and the plastic floorboards that ran throughout the building? It was an old structure with nooks and crannies at every turn. Surely, a thin, frail gray hair might lay unnoticed for an undetermined period of time. Or maybe it was her scent that might still be lingering in the air of the room. The air was recirculated inside the rooms, if she actually went inside, might she detect the faint odor of her mom's cologne?

"She didn't make it." Elena appeared near the room. "I'm sorry. I know she was your friend."

"We worked together many years ago and we were friendly to one another but I'm not sure we could be classified as friends." Catherine looked down the hallway. "Is her family here?'

"Yes, a few were in the room when she was pronounced. Others were directed to the east waiting room." Elena waved as Lindsey approached them. "Is there anything specific you need for me or my team to do?"

"We will need a more private area for the family to gather. Can we close off this hallway?" Catherine asked straining to see into the waiting room for any familiar faces.

"Yes, I only have two patients nearby but I can move them. We can barricade the hallway."

"I'll have Aiden put an officer at the door where she is. I'm sure other members of her family will want to see her, say their goodbyes." Catherine pulled her phone from her pocket. "We will need an officer at the chapel as well."

Lindsey turned away from them, placing her phone to her ear. "I'll call the chaplain."

****

"You stayed until the funeral home arrived to take possession?" Ryan asked yawning and blowing into the plastic lid of her coffee.

"Yeah," Catherine nodded logging into her computer. "I was waiting for a call from corporate. Mason Riley was supposed to return my call regarding the deletion of my variance reports."

"Wow, who'd you have to piss off to get that high up on the food chain?" Ryan asked.

"He's the Chief Information Officer. It's his responsibility to ensure the reports are safe and confidential." Catherine paused. "He failed on both counts."

"Mason is a moron, you know that. He's only been in the position for a few months and ---"

Catherine interrupted. "He came with Fleming's appointment. My mother used to say bad news travels in pairs." She smiled. "Mom wasn't far off, huh?"

"No, she was on the mark. It's one big cluster—"Ryan's browed furrowed.

"Chimera," Catherine interjected avoiding the obvious term.

"What did Mason say?" Ryan laughed.

"His response was brief and to the point." She paused. "There's nothing to investigate as he insists nothing was deleted."

"We know that's not true." Ryan paused. "But I feel as if we're beating our heads against a brick wall." She stood, ironing the front of her skirt with her hand. "We have to accept that no one cares what's going on here."

"I met with Agent Bronson a few days ago and I told him everything that's happened to date. He assured me the completed report would be sent to the attorney general."

"What about that reporter? He seems sincere about finding out the truth." Ryan stopped at the door before turning back to Catherine.

"We have no way of knowing what story he'll tell until it's printed." Catherine paused. "He's a wild card. Besides, we're still under a gag order from the OIG but I like the way you think."

"I've got some notes to review before my meeting with the corporate COO." Her back was to Catherine once again.

"Glad to see you're playing nice."

"I'm trying." She disappeared into her office only to reappear at the door moments later. "I'm heading to the corporate office. I'll see you tomorrow?"

"Sure," Catherine waved as Ryan passed by, watching as the door drew slowly to a close.

"Ought oh," she heard Virginia moan from her desk where her face was buried in her computer screen.

"What's wrong?" Catherine didn't get up from her desk.

"Check your email," Virginia responded to her words dry and curt.

It took several attempts before Catherine was able to input her password accurately. "From who?" She called out once she was finally able to get into the program. It was there second from the top, an announcement from the corporate office.

Catherine couldn't believe her eyes, she had to read it again and again. Rachel Fleming had resigned her position on the board of commissioners. It was true, Catherine thought, she should be happy to be rid of that woman and her meddling friends. God knew over the years; the system had its share of homegrown crooks. It was hard to fathom how common place it had become for the system to hire someone else's criminals. It should have been a time of celebration but Catherine knew it wouldn't be. She was too worried waiting for the other shoe to drop. Catherine couldn't help feeling the worst was yet to come.

Chapter 16

"When you're finished with that newspaper, I'd like to have a look-see," Gordon asked, stuffing the last bite of toast into his mouth.

"I just can't believe what I'm reading." Catherine pushed the untouched breakfast plate away from her, letting it idle in the center of the kitchen table. She folded the paper into quarters and handed it across the table to him.

"You must have known Fleming would have an ulterior motive for resigning from the board?" His words were like a knife, cutting through her frontal lobe. Catherine rubbed her forehead as if to alleviate the stabbing discomfort.

"How can she appoint herself as interim CEO of the system?" She paused as if expecting an answer but went on before Gordon had a chance to answer her question. "Is that even legal?"

"Apparently she volunteered to step down as commissioner and take Sarah's position until an appropriate candidate can be hired permanently." He answered. "I don't know if it's legal but sounds kind of Hitlerish to me."

"You've no idea how grossly accurate that statement truly is," Catherine mumbled, as she finished her coffee. "I've got to get into the office, I'm sure it's a madhouse."

****

"Has anyone spoken to Lindsey this morning? Does she know?" Ryan was firing off questions faster than an executioner at a prison squad. She hadn't made it physically into her office. Her briefcase and purse were dropped ceremoniously at the threshold of her office.

"I haven't but I'm sure she read the email," Catherine answered, wishing she'd just called out for the day. Her head was spinning, the news of the leadership change had made her physically ill.

Ryan turned to Virginia who was typing furiously at her desk. "Have you spoken to her?"

"No," Virginia answered. "She and Lana were supposed to collect the oncology award first thing this morning and fly back tonight."

"Oncology award," Ryan whispered under her breath, looking to Catherine as if something else was still to be said.

"I know what you're thinking, Ryan," Catherine warned. "Don't say it."

"We fired two nurses and a pharmacist less than a year ago as a result of a major medication error related to chemotherapy." Ryan leaned in. "Why would anyone send in an application for an oncology chemotherapy award so soon after that event?"

"I guess it depends on how you look at it." Catherine motioned for Ryan to come inside. "Maybe it was to bring attention to all the wonderful process improvements the team put together afterward?" She paused. "You were a part of that team, you're aware of all that was done."

"The root cause of that error was staffing," Ryan advised, sounding more like a lawyer than Catherine liked. "We didn't hire any nurses or pharmacists. And the ratio of chemotherapy trained nurses to patients is unchanged." She paused. "Actually, it's one less because we fired the nurse caring for that patient who was affected. The last thing I'd want to do is bring any attention to that particular product line."

"Not our call," Catherine said.

"I've heard that before." Ryan bit her tongue. "Recently, actually."

"Excuse me?" a large round, young man entered through the office door and stopped close to where Ryan was standing instead of addressing Virginia at her desk. "I'm looking for the CEO, Lindsey Danson?"

"She's away at a conference," Catherine informed him, stepping from behind her desk and making her way closer to him with her hand extended. "Can I help you with something?"

"My name is Oliver Barrel." He smiled and tugged at his shirt as if to cover his protruding belly. He looked from one to the other awaiting a response before adding. "I'm the new CFO. I'm supposed to start today."

"CFO?" Virginia repeated, jumping from her desk and almost running to where the trio was standing. "Are you sure you're in the right place?" She looked to Catherine as if she needed reinforcement. "I don't think the panel interviews have even started yet." She moved back toward her desk. "Let me call. I bet you're supposed to be at Pine Bluff. They have an opening, too."

"No," his smile was polite. "I worked with Erin and Commissioner Fleming at Booker. Rachel interviewed me independently. I spoke to someone in your HR department." He put his finger to his chin, Catherine couldn't help but think if he were wearing a red suit, he'd have made a good Santa Clause. "I believe her name was Brittany."

Yep, Catherine thought to herself. The other shoe had fallen. In fact, the imaginary ground in her mind was littered with shoes falling from the sky.

"Let me call Brittany and get your information," Virginia answered, her head bowed as if she were praying. She pointed to the closed door of the office between Ryan's and Catherine's. "The door's unlocked. Just go ahead and get your desk set up." Virginia fell into her chair, spinning it around toward the computer screen before the chair had come to a stop. "If I'd have known you were coming, all your access would have been completed."

"No problem," He smiled, pulling his suit jacket off as he entered the office and draped it over the back of his chair. "I'm in no hurry. I'm sure Erin will be able to expedite my access."

"I'm sure," Ryan whispered under her breath.

He reappeared at the doorway into his office and offered his hand to Ryan. "You are?"

"Dr. Ryan Allen, I've been the Director of Pharmacy for many years but I am currently the interim COO." Ryan shook his hand and pointed to Catherine. "Catherine Masters, risk manager."

"Welcome," Catherine smiled and if Oliver had known her better, he'd have known her smile was ingenuine. "If you need anything, just ask." She turned to go back into the office just as the door opened and

Bailey entered red-faced and flushed making a beeline into Ryan's office.

"What's wrong?" Ryan asked, before Bailey had a chance to say anything and nodded to Catherine who remained perched just outside her own office door.

"I spent most of the morning trying to find my draft of the schedule." Bailey paused. "I spent most of the week working on it."

"And?" Ryan asked.

"I thought you had everything you needed out of the office?" Bailey had chosen her words carefully and Catherine watched as she drew closer to Ryan.

"I did." Ryan's eyes darted to Catherine. "I took what I needed from the safe last week. I haven't even been in the pharmacy for days." She took Bailey's arms and pulled her closer to Catherine's doorway out of the general traffic of the front office. "What's this about?"

"Yesterday when I came into the office, it seemed as if my things had been moved." She paused. "I didn't think much about it, figured you were overlooking for something specific, went on about my day." She turned to Catherine. "This morning when I came in, it was the same thing. Things weren't where I left them yesterday when I left."

"I haven't been there in a few days." Ryan restated, folding her arms across her chest.

"What were you working on that you think was messed with?" Catherine asked.

"Nothing really." Bailey rubbed her chin as is trying to remember every detail. "It felt as if someone was looking for something."

"What?"

"I don't know but I wanted you to know." She paused. "Everyone knows what happened to Virginia in the CFO's office." Bailey jumped to her feet. "I've got two small children. I can't even imagine not being here for them."

"I'll ask Aiden to review the camera." Catherine reached for the phone.

"Don't bother," Ryan shook her head. "There are no cameras anywhere except in the narcotic vault."

"Wouldn't they have to get into the pharmacy first and it's a secured area?" Catherine asked.

"Theoretically, yes but I assure you. No one was allowed into the pharmacy and no one has a key to Ryan's office, not even security." Bailey reminded her.

"Call Aiden and let's walk over?" Catherine suggested.

****

It was a tight fit with all four of them stuffed into Ryan's pharmacy office. Even with the door open, it was borderline claustrophobic. "The ceiling tile is displaced." Aiden pointed to an area above Ryan's desk.

"I'd say, whoever it was coming through the ceiling and dropped down atop the desk." Ryan moved around to the back of the office. "That's why the stuff on the desk was displaced. Probably knocked stuff off and wasn't sure where it went."

"Call facilities and ask for someone to bring a ladder. I want to take a look." Aiden asked.

"Make sure you take pictures of anything that looks out of place." Catherine reminded him. "And I think we should alert the police."

"To do what?" Aiden questioned.

"We have a potential breaking and entering," Catherine stated. She indicated to Ryan. "You're the COO, what are your thoughts?"

"I agree," Ryan smiled. "The pharmacy is the most secure area in the building. Badge readers allow access in and only authorized pharmacy staff has access. Even security's badges do not work in the readers." She looked behind to the where the pharmacy staff was busily attending to patient care orders. "If this environment isn't safe for the staff, we need a new plan in place ASAP."

She turned to Bailey. "Aiden will need an escort while he's here in the pharmacy. Please give me an update before the end of the day. We may need an additional officer manning the pharmacy if we can't ensure the area is secure."

Ryan waited as Catherine took a final look around the office before following her out the door and into the hallway. "Do you think the camera in the hallway picked up anything?"

"I doubt it," Catherine answered. "I have a feeling the entry point is elsewhere and they crawled through the ceiling until they got to your office."

"What do you think they are looking for? If they didn't find it last night, I guess there's a chance they might return?" Ryan asked.

"Drugs maybe?" Catherine followed Ryan back to the administrative offices.

"Wouldn't they just drop into the pharmacy?"

"Maybe not if they weren't looking to actually confront anyone. Maybe they were waiting for an opportunity to come out of your office and take some when no one's around." She paused. "You only have one pharmacist and one technician on the night shift, right?"

"Yes."

"So, if the technician is out of the pharmacy and the pharmacist is in the IV room preparing a sterile product, the pharmacy would in effect be unattended, yes?"

"I guess." Ryan nodded before stepping into her former office. "I've got to make a call."

"Don't forget," Catherine checked her watch. "We're scheduled with Inspector Winters and Agent Bronson in less than an hour. We should grab some lunch first."

"Frick and frack, again? I think we should start invoicing them for our time."

Catherine heard the pharmacy office door clicked shut. No doubt Ryan was calling Detective Spencer and that was probably a very good idea.

****

"So," Inspector Winters smiled and looked to Agent Bronson before addressing Ryan. "You've been promoted?"

The conference room was normally cool, even in the hot, humid months of August when the temperature was the greatest. But today it was downright cold and it has nothing to do with the climate.

Catherine fiddled with a loose piece of leather on her note ledger. How many more times, she thought, would the OIG agents show up with questions? Not only had she sat through her own interrogation by the agents but now she was sitting in on everyone else's as well. There was no one they were harder on than Ryan. It was as if they were determined to get her to admit something whether she was guilty or not.

"My role is on an interim basis." She said flatly.

"Are we waiting for your lawyer?" The Inspector's question was tinged with sarcasm, not overtly noticeable to anyone else but Catherine knew it was there like a bitter after taste.

"Not today," Ryan answered, looking down at her perfectly manicured nails. "Ask me your questions. I have work to do."

"Have you had any contact with Aaron Lewis since the last time we met?" Agent Bronson asked, his eyes locked on hers.

"No," she answered. "As I explained last time, we are barely acquaintances."

"Are you aware of any contacts Mr. Lewis might have in the Dominican Republic?"

"No," she exhaled. "As I said, I barely know him."

"We've been advised that Mr. Lewis and his family are no longer living in the Charlotte area, In fact, they aren't currently in the states." The inspector hadn't asked it as a question but he paused as if he expected an answer.

When she didn't respond. He went on. "You were presented with a subpoena, were you able to comply?"

"You'll need to be more specific, Agents." She answered. "I've only been in this role a few weeks, and I've been subpoenaed three times. Which subpoena are you referring to?"

"For all documents related to procurement including but not limited to correspondence with Mr. Lewis or anyone else representing your organization?"

"Yes, I did comply. Everything I had was copied and forwarded to your office for review."

"What about the complaint from one of your pharmaceutical representatives?"

"I reported the event once I was made aware." She answered. "It's my understanding that the woman has recanted the accusation?"

"Yes, mine too." The Inspector paused. "The representative in question is known to you?"

"Not exactly." She answered. "I don't know her, but her fiancée is a very good friend of mine. I've known him for years."

"Mr. Curtaine?" he flipped through his notebook.

"Yes," She leaned forward and snatched a bottle of water from the center of the table.

"We haven't been able to reach Mr. Curtaine. Any thoughts on his current whereabouts?"

"He hasn't answered my calls either. I've no idea how else to contact him."

"I see," Agent Branson flipped his notebook shut. "Are you concerned about him?"

"I'll admit, it's unlike him not to return my calls." She looked from one to the other. "As I said before we've been friends for a long time."

Inspector Winters pushed his thick body away from the table's edge as if were Thanksgiving and he'd just devoured a big meal. "So, you've been COO for a few weeks, you said?"

"Interim" she reiterated again.

"About the same time period as Ms. Horseman recanted her sexual assault charge against Mr. Lewis?

"What are you implying, Inspector?" Ryan's words were sharp, pointed like a spear.

"Nothing really, just maybe your interim appointment was a reward for a job well done. A task maybe that included getting an old friend to convince his girlfriend to drop the charges?"

"Of course, you have some evidence to support that claim?" Catherine piped in.

"No," Winters stood up first, then Bronson. "But we will."

"Good Luck with that," Ryan stepped in front of them, exiting the conference room ahead of everyone else. "I won't be meeting with you again without my lawyer." She paused. "So, no more pop-ins." She closed her office door behind her.

Catherine stuck her head out of the conference room to address Virginia. "Can you see the agents out, please Virginia?"

Virginia moved from behind her desk, sprinting to address the agents. "If you'll follow me, please."

Catherine looked to Lindsey's open office door. "Is Lindsey back?" Lindsey needed to be updated on the break-in and the meeting with the Agents. They were on a ghost hunt and Catherine feared Ryan was their mark. For whatever reason, they had their sites on her.

"Yes, she's back from her trip." Virginia pointed to where another award had been mounted to the wall behind the credenza against the main office wall. "She had a meeting downtown. I'm not sure when she'll be back."

"Gentlemen?' Virginia pointed to the door. Catherine smiled. Virginia wasn't a large woman by any means. But standing there facing down the two agents, if felt as if she was twenty feet tall.

"When we return it's going to be with a warrant." Winters threatened.

"Warrant?" Catherine repeated. They had moved from landing on the boardwalk to going straight to jail, literally. "For what?"

"We're going through every invoice Ms. Allen has approved and sent to accounts payable. Every single one." He disappeared through the door with Bronson on his heel.

Catherine waited for the officers to leave before she walked the short distance to Ryan's office and gently tapped on the door.

Catherine didn't wait for consent; she turned the knob easily and went inside. To say she was surprised again was an understatement. During all the time they'd been friends, Ryan prided herself on controlling her emotions. She had an amazing poker face and that was no secret to anyone who knew her in any capacity. It made Catherine uncomfortable that Ryan had reached her breaking point at least twice in a very short span of time. Catherine did not even try to hide her concern as Ryan wiped anxiously at her eyes and turned her face away.

"It's going to be okay," Catherine took a seat. It felt odd to be on the other side of the desk. She quickly assessed the office, delighted at how quickly Ryan had made it her own. Pictures of her daughter, parents, and brother were prominently displayed on the shelf to the far side of the room. Framed awards and recognitions lined the other wall in a manner similar to her own office nearby. She wondered if Ryan was still considering the appointment to be just an interim assignment.

Catherine gently picked up a framed photo of Ryan and her Mom. "This is a really good picture of you both." She touched the glass covering Ryan's mother's image. "I'd forgotten how beautiful she was. The last few years were hard on her, took its toll."

"Yes, the last year hadn't been a good one." Ryan smiled. "God how I miss her. So many times, throughout the day I pick up the phone to call her." She paused and wiped at her eyes again. "I've actually dialed the number before I realize she's not going to answer."

Ryan held out her hand for the photo. "Sometimes I feel so lost without her."

"I know," Catherine slid gently into the seat across from Ryan's desk. "We all feel like that at some point in our lives. It's the natural progression of things, don't you think."

"Maybe," Ryan paused. "Once when I was about eight. We were at a big mall in the city." She smiled remembering the event as if it were playing on the television screen in her office. "I must have wandered away from her or something because all of a sudden I looked up and she wasn't there." She laughed and cried simultaneously. "I remember walking up and down the aisle crying, looking for her in the crowd."

"Everyone has a memory like that, Ryan."

"Maybe, but I can't tell you how relieved I was when I felt her at my side. Bending down to me, making sure I was okay. I'll never forget the feeling, the relief I felt that she'd found me."

"I give just about anything to experience that kind of relief again, just for a while." Ryan's words were damaged, as if she were reciting them from inside a cavern or tunnel, desperate for someone to reach down and pull her up to the ground.

"I know." Catherine reached across the table and took Ryan's hand.

"From that day on, I never worried about being lost ever again."

"Why's that?"

"Because she told me that afternoon, if I ever got lost again to return to the last place we were together. She said that's where she'd go to find me and I'd never had to worry about being lost again." Ryan exhaled a breath. "And that's what we did. From then on, every time we were out and got separated or couldn't find one another, I'd go back to the last place we were together and there she'd be waiting for me."

"That's a nice story. You should make sure McKenzie knows that plan."

"She's aware." Ryan took a minute before continuing and collected her thoughts. "What is going on? Why are they determined to charge me with something?" She pulled a tissue from a box and wiped at her eyes. "I'm beginning to think that Aaron had the right idea?"

"Aaron?" Catherine tried to conceal her surprise. "Idea about what?"

"Running." She swallowed. "What if all of this is just one big set up? Maybe they did to him what they're doing to me."

"Him?" Catherine asked, even though she knew Ryan meant Aaron and not Anwar as a casualty in the conspiracy theory.

"It almost seems as if someone is trying to implode the system. It's like a serpent eating itself from within, starting at its tail until its devoured itself." Ryan buried her face in her hands and sighed. "Maybe we should ask to meet with the Inspector privately somewhere outside of the hospital?"

"I don't think that's a good idea." Catherine hesitated, weighing exactly how much she should say. Ryan was stressed out enough. There was no point in aggravating her and making her even more anxious. "In fact, I don't think you should meet with them again without your personal lawyer."

"You can't be serious." She shook her head, looking up to the ceiling as if she'd lost something. "Where I come from only guilty people need legal representation."

"Well," Catherine chose her words carefully. "You aren't in Kansas anymore, Dorothy."

"I—" Ryan response was interrupted by a tap from the other side of the door. It swung open gently as Aiden stepped into the office.

"I just finished assessing the crawl space over the pharmacy office." He stated, adjusting the volume on his radio so that he could update Catherine and Ryan in his usual and customary voice. "The crawl space has been compromised from the office along a path originating from one of the restrooms near the loading dock." He paused. "Anyone who used that bathroom could be the perp."

"Did you review the tapes?" Catherine asked, not hopeful it would amount to much. There were no cameras in the bathrooms, only those stationed in the hallway outside of the restrooms.

"I will," he rubbed at his chin, scratching at the thin growth of beard that was just breaking his skin. "Hundreds of people use that restroom daily. I doubt it will lead to much but I'll watch it."

"What do we do in the meantime?" Ryan asked. "The staff can't be placed in harm's way and we can't relocate the pharmacy."

"I've instructed facilities to weld the crawlspace around the exterior pharmacy walls shut. Once they finish, there will be no way anyone could enter through the ceiling."

"How long is that going to take?" Catherine asked, looking at her watch.

"Several hours, Jay's getting the supplies he needs to weld it closed," Aiden answered. "In the meantime, I'm going to station myself inside the pharmacy with the staff until the entry points are secured."

"That will work" Ryan smiled. "I appreciate your quick action and fast thinking on this matter."

Catherine smiled thinking to herself how Ryan was sounding more like a COO and less like a pharmacy director with every hour that passed.

"I'm just glad we discovered it before anyone was hurt." Aiden opened the office door. "I'll be in the pharmacy if anyone needs anything."

"I've got a meeting offsite. I'll be gone for about an hour but I'll be back." Ryan checked her watch. "Not planning on having a late night tonight. I'm meeting Cole for dinner." She paused. "McKenzie is at her Dad's tonight. I know Cole is going to want to stay over but to tell you the truth, I am not in the mood for company tonight." She slid into her suit jacket and bent to collect her briefcase.

"You like this guy?" Catherine smiled.

"I do," Ryan answered, her face turning a crimson shade of red before she pushed her hair away from her forehead.

"Then maybe, you let him stay over just for the company and not for sex."

"I'm not sure he'll go for that." She clipped her phone to the waistband of her skirt. "We both work so much and the jobs are so all-consuming. It's like we need the release to depressurize, you know?"

"I do," Catherine followed her to the doorway. "But if he's going to be a keeper, it should be about more than just sex, don't you think? If you don't give him the opportunity to comfort you, you'll never really know where his heart is, right?"

"I guess." Ryan disappeared through the doorway.

"Just think about it." Catherine watched as Ryan disappeared through the door. Just as the door snapped closed her attention was drawn to Virginia as she sat at her desk, head bowed and typing furiously.

She pointed toward Lindsey's office door where it was ajar partially open. "She in?" Catherine knew Lindsey was, she could hear someone moving around in the office. She pushed through the door without waiting for Virginia to respond.

"Hey, welcome back." Catherine stopped abruptly and wished she could grab the words and stuff them back into her mouth. Rachel Fleming looked up from Lindsey's computer where she'd made herself comfortable at Lindsey's desk.

"Sorry," Catherine stumbled over the word. "I was looking for Lindsey."

"I was just sending out an email," Fleming explained, as she waved at the screen as if Catherine could see what she was typing.

"I can come back tomorrow and talk to Lindsey." Catherine turned to leave the office.

"Actually," Fleming paused. "You can't. I'm afraid Lindsey Danson is no longer employed here."

"What?" Catherine asked, even though she'd heard every word clearly. That explained why Virginia wouldn't make eye contact when she'd passed by the desk.

"Lindsey has vacated her position as CEO. I'm going to expedite getting a panel together and hire someone quickly." Fleming returned to typing, slapping the enter button ceremoniously.

"I have someone in mind that I believe will be an awesome leader for you guys." Fleming went on, her voice was celebratory and the words cheerful. Too cheerful, Catherine thought.

"And in the meantime?" Catherine asked. She waved toward the offices. "Everyone left is either interim or brand new to the site."

"Erin will assume the CEO responsibilities until an appropriate candidate can be acquired."

"In addition to her responsibilities as CNO?" Catherine asked, even though she already knew the answer. Waiting for an answer was simply an exercise.

"She'll have no problem managing the dual roles," Fleming explained. "We worked together previously. I've no doubt she can handle it." She checked her watch before dropping her hands back to the computer keyboard. "What's the interim pharmacy manager's name again?"

"Bailey," Catherine knew her lips had responded but she wasn't sure any actual sound had escaped from her mouth. To be sure, she repeated, "Bailey's only been in the role since Ryan assumed the COO position. It might be more beneficial to just ask Ryan." She paused before adding, "if you have a pharmacy question."

"I'd like a tour of the pharmacy this afternoon." The keys clipped loudly against Fleming's manicured nails. "This was an error recently with a prescription that was filled here and I'm trying to understand how it happened."

"Medication error?" Catherine repeated even though she'd head Fleming's words perfectly. "You mean, the one while Ryan was on medical leave with the patient allergy?"

"Yes, the patient had an anaphylactic reaction to a prescription filled here in our pharmacy even though the patient's profile listed the allergy." She stopped typing and looked up to make eye contact with Catherine. "I'd like to know why that happened and how to make sure it doesn't happen again."

Fleming leaned back against the desk chair and folded her arms across her chest. "I don't see any type of process improvement plan attached to the event."

"Ryan reviewed it when she returned but I think most of her time has been looking at the two events in the OR."

"What other events?" Fleming sat at attention as if she were on a hunt and had the scent of her prey.

"Someone pretending to be a physician came to the pharmacy window and was given access to the automated medication cabinets. Over the next few hours, she emptied all the machines of all controlled substances."

"I'd like a copy of the incident report please." She began typing again. "And the other?"

"We've determined an infusion bag prepared by pharmacy was tampered with and an unknown additive added." Catherine paused.

"We've determined with the aid of an outside laboratory the additive to be potassium chloride."

"Isn't it more probable that the pharmacy prepared it incorrectly?"

"We don't think so."

"How's that?"

"The injection mark wasn't in the port but in the neck of the bag. And it was a premixed bag so the policy is that nothing is added."

"Who performed this assessment?"

"Ryan, of course."

Fleming's laugh was more of a cough. "The chicken and the coop?"

"She's always taken responsibility when one of her staff is at fault."

"I'd like a copy of that incident report as well."

"That might be a problem."

"Why is that?"

"Because someone deleted the report."

"Have IT find it."

"I tried and was told it doesn't and never did exist."

Fleming adjusted her body so that her back her nearly to Catherine. In a single motion, she grabbed her phone and dialed, waiting for someone to answer. "Mason, there's something I need your help with." She turned had to Catherine. "Do you mind?"

Catherine nodded and slipped quietly out of the room pulling the door closed behind her. She practically ran past Virginia who was still working quietly at her desk. There wasn't anything to say that would make the recent change in leadership make any sense. She envisioned the serpent eating at its tail. Ryan had hit in on the mark.

Chapter 17

"The good news is," Erin explained as Oliver, Ryan, and Catherine sat collectively around the conference table in the CEO's private office, "is my appointment as interim CEO probably will only be for a week, two at the most." She smiled so that her bottom teeth radiated brightly against the sunlight flooding into the room. Catherine thought of the cartoon her boys used to watch when they were younger. The shark in the story, smiled, its teeth shining so brightly, the other characters had to cover their eyes. It continued to smile, right up to the point in time, where it opened its mouth and devoured them whole.

The conference room was small with a dozen or so chairs pushed up against the long wooden table that shined as if it had just been polished even though Catherine knew it hadn't been. But the room seemed small especially since everyone was pushed to one side of the table nearly elbow to elbow.

"There's not going to be a panel interview?" Ryan asked.

"Was there a panel interview when you interviewed?" Erin's question was delivered as it was intended. Catherine imagined she saw Ryan's hands drop below the table and place them on her knees as if to ensure her legs her still intact.

Instead, Ryan didn't move, not a muscle. She didn't even blink, her eyes locked on Erin's as if they were connected. "I didn't interview Erin; I know you're aware of that. I was "recruited." She finally moved, making imaginary quotation marks in the air.

"I'm aware." Erin's words were specific. "And if you want to be unrecruited, you just let me know." She tossed her clipboard toward the middle of the table.

"Erin," Oliver said her name as if in a warning. "Rachel said there were to be no changes at the administrative level until Noah comes. He'll assess the team and make whatever changes he wants."

"Noah?" Catherine repeated, thinking Lindsey hadn't even removed her personal items from the CEO suite and her replacement had already been selected. Handpicked by Erin and Fleming, no doubt.

"Noah Reid," Oliver responded watching as Erin and Ryan continued to stare down one another as if they were in a shootout. "You worked with him before, didn't you Erin?"

"Yes," Erin answered; her teeth still clenched.

If Catherine hadn't heard Erin's response, she wouldn't have known Erin had spoken. Her lips hadn't moved. Catherine looked back to Ryan hoping she wasn't still glaring at Erin. No such luck, they were both still locked, eye to eye.

"When's he scheduled to arrive?" Catherine asked, mostly just to alleviate the silence and partly to distract one or the other, Erin or Ryan. It didn't matter but one of them needed to look away.

"Monday," Oliver answered. "Till then—"

"I'll make sure I make the best of whatever time I have then." Ryan stood up and left the office, making sure the door was securely closed behind her.

"Erin," Oliver's words were soft, almost pleading. "She's actually doing a really good job."

"She's not a team player." Erin retrieved her clipboard from the middle of the table.

"Maybe just not your team, Erin." Oliver challenged. "You haven't exactly been very welcoming."

"I have someone in mind for the COO position." She said. "Once Noah gets settled and brings the new guy in, Ryan can return to the pharmacy if she wants." Erin paused. "I tried to get that bitch to at least interview him but she wouldn't even entertain the thought.

No doubt, Catherine thought, Erin was referring to Lindsey as the bitch. Catherine pushed her chair away from the table. "If we are done, I've got some reports to finish."

Oliver smiled and looked to Erin waiting for a response. Instead, she said nothing. She simply watched as Catherine made her way form the conference room nearly bumping into Virginia at the door.

"Virginia," Erin asked, looking past Catherine. "Did you need something?"

"No," she pushed her chewing gum just under her bottom lip, massaging it with her tongue. "Jay is here to box up Lindsey's things and I need her phone."

"I don't see a phone in here," Erin answered, not looking up to meet Virginia's eyes. "She probably had it with her when she was fired."

"Just give her a call and ask that she bring it in when she comes to pick up her stuff." Oliver offered, motioning to Jay. "Come on in. We're done here."

Jay waved to Catherine as he passed through the CEO's threshold. "I don't think it will take very long." He mused. "She wasn't here long enough to have accumulated very much."

"Just put whatever she left in a box," Virginia said, as Catherine disappeared into her own private office and pushed the door closed.

****

Catherine pulled into Ryan's driveway, relieved to see only Ryan's silver Mazda parked in the driveway. She knew she should have called ahead before stopping by but she hadn't planned on coming over until her car was literally pulling through the security gate.

She sent a quick text message to Gordon that she wouldn't be home in time for dinner and he should eat without her, like he ended doing almost every work night she thought. Many years of managing and accessing problems before they occurred had left her almost an expert at minimizing risk. It was way past time for talking, she considered. They were in too deep; it was time to call in reinforcements.

She didn't hear the lock being turned until she'd rang the bell several times and had her cell phone in her hand to call Ryan and verify she was home. Once the door was fully open, the reason for the delay was obvious. Detective Spencer stood wearing only a pair of faded jeans, unbuttoned but zipped with a leather belt hanging loosely from the belt loop.

Catherine held her hands out as if she were surrendering. "I'm so sorry."

"Don't be," he stepped back so she could enter. "Come on in."

"I didn't see your car," Catherine said apologetically.

"It's at the restaurant." He smiled. "She'll drop me on our way into work tomorrow."

"I should have called." She mumbled stepping up through the front entryway and into the foyer.

"You're here now." He shut the door and motioned for her to follow him. "She'll be down in a minute." He stopped near the kitchen. "Want a drink?"

"No," she bit her lip hoping her the embarrassment on her face had resolved.

"Let me grab a shirt." He stopped at the bottom of the stairs. "Have a seat."

Catherine made her way into the family room and took a seat near the fireplace. A fireplace, she wondered if Ryan had ever actually used it. It was usually warm for most routine activities. She'd try and make a point to ask once things settled down and their lives were normal again.

"Hey?" Ryan's bare feet on the stair steps were a distraction. "What's up?" She buttoned the top button on her shirt as her feet hit the floor.

"I'm so sorry." Catherine flushed again.

"Don't be, we're all adults, right?"

"I thought you wanted to be alone tonight?" Catherine asked, remembering the discussion they'd had before the showdown between Ryan and Erin.

"I did but then I didn't." Ryan took the seat closest to her. "You didn't stop by to ask about that?"

"No," she shook her head. "But I'm glad Cole is here. We need help to sort this out. And I don't think we can rely on the OIG inspector. He's only worried about how the medications for Medicare and Medicaid were billed and reimbursed."

"What kind of help?" Ryan asked, smoothing down the front of her shirt to make sure she hadn't missed any buttons.

"That's what I want to ask him."

"Ask me what?" Cole appeared at Ryan's side, fully dressed in jeans and a burgundy knit shirt that emphasized his biceps so much so that Catherine hoped her acknowledgment hadn't been noticed.

"Beliard's suicide, Sarah's death, these breaking and entering events, they're all related. I can feel it; I just don't know how."

"I agree," Ryan added. "There's something else going on. Maybe individually, the clues don't amount to much but collectively, there are just too many coincidences."

"Okay," Cole nodded, taking Ryan's hand. "My friend from the CIA, the one who's retired and tracked down the names of the men in the photo. I'm going to talk to him and share what you've found. But first- " he paused. "We have to develop a timeline for all the events you believe are related. We'll need that before I meet with Erik."

"It started with Anwar's being hired as CEO instead of Andrew Caser." Catherine began. "It was completely unexpected I think even Anwar was surprised." She paused. "He wasn't feeling well when the announcement was made. He had open heart surgery very soon after he accepted the position."

"He coded twice during the surgery and Ryan identified that someone injection potassium chloride into the infusion of vasopressors used during the surgery."

"Where is this bag now, I know you said you kept it," Cole asked.

"It's in a safe place," Ryan admitted. "I have no evidence to support it but I think that's what whoever broke into the pharmacy office is looking for. I think they're looking for the evidence."

"I think so, too." Catherine nodded. "Anwar was convinced the corruption went up to the highest system ranks. He told me that he didn't know who to trust." She paused. "And he hid a key in the seat of my chair the last time he was in my office."

"A key?" Cole repeated. "Do you have it? Can I take a look at it?"

Catherine fumbled in her purse and finally pulled it out and presented it to him as if it were a trophy. "I know I should hide it somewhere but I am not sure where is safe anymore."

"May I?" Cole asked, holding his hand out for the key. "It looks really old. More like a skeleton key than an actual key that might open something up."

"Don't forget the box of pictures with all those old criminals?" Ryan added. "We still have no idea who collected all those pictures or why."

"Of how they got in Andrew's ceiling?" Catherine chimed in.

"We'll need to give everything to Erik when I meet with him, the photocopies of the lab reports, the code sheets, everything ."

He pushed to his feet to pour a drink, offering Ryan and Catherine one as well.

Ryan watched as he disappeared into the kitchen before turning to Catherine. "Why didn't you tell me Fleming was touring the pharmacy today?"

"I had to get out of there. I was afraid I might reach across the desk and smack her." She paused. "How did it go?"

"There's a thousand things for Queen Erin to fix. She's the only one who actually knows anything about everything." Ryan reached up to take the drink from Cole. "Did you know the patient related to this incident is Fleming's son?"

"No," Catherine swallowed her drink wondering if it was Cole habit of making the drinks so strong or if he'd done it because he thought she and Ryan needed the distraction.

"The last name wasn't Fleming." Ryan patted the empty place next to her for Cole to sit. "Maybe he's her stepson?"

"Maybe, you can never tell with these people. Maiden names and married names, hyphenated names. It's just too much to keep up with. It's hard to tell who belongs to by just a last name anymore."

"What's surprising," Ryan went on, "is how condescending she was, especially with the pharmacist who initiated the breakdown."

"So much for a non-punitive culture of safety." Catherine tried not to laugh. Talk about a chimera. That's the mother of all chimeras."

"Funny thing is the pharmacist swears the allergy was not listed as part of the patient's profile when she filled the script. She continues to insist it was added afterward." Ryan took another drink. "When the patient dropped off the prescription, he told the technician at the pharmacy window who his mother was."

"Why would he do that?"

"Because he didn't want to wait very long for the prescription to be filled. When he dropped it off, he was told he could pick it up within the hour. He didn't want to wait and made a scene at the window that included asking the staff if they knew who his mother was."

"The pharmacist said the script was perfect."

"What does the electronic ledger read? What's the time stamp on the allergy?"

"The allergy appears on the profile with a recorded date about the time the patient was seen in the emergency department."

"Seems undebatable then?"

"That's what I thought too until I started reviewing all the steps in the process." She paused again. "If the allergy was on the profile before the pharmacist entered the medication, an alert would have popped up that would have had to have been overridden by the pharmacist for the process to be completed."

"And? She blew through the alert. Happens all the time especially with the physicians."

"You'd think," Ryan smiled. "But there's no override notice on this allergy medication encounter. I don't see that an alert even fired."

"Maybe the alert wasn't active for that allergy?" Catherine asked, her head spinning with the possibilities.

"No, I searched for other patients in the system with the same allergy who almost received the same medication." She strode across the room and pulled two documents from her satchel. "There were only two but the alert fired both times."

"You think the allergy was added to the profile later?" Catherine thought of the missing incident report again, nothing surprised her anymore.

"I do," Ryan nodded, folding the documents and returning them to her satchel. "Is that even possible?"

"If you'd asked me that a month ago, I'd have said absolutely not. But I know for a fact someone at a very high level in corporate IT deleted Beliard's incident report." Catherine shrugged her shoulders and fell back against the couch.

"Mason Riley?" Ryan asked, but Catherine knew she really didn't mean it as a question. She was looking for validation.

"Maybe him, maybe someone else. I don't know and until we know who we can trust there's really no one who can tell us for sure."

"Speaking of trust. I know you don't trust him but I think we need to see if that reporter can help." Ryan moved to the end of the sofa using the arm to lean into.

"Tim Hartmann?" Catherine shook her head. "He's just sniffing out a story."

"He's looking to report the truth and I don't think he'll care who is affected or how up the corruption that Beliard spoke of goes? He won't care as long as it's the truth."

Cole jumped into the discussion. "And reporters are great with research."

"I still have the card he gave me when he met us at the Walk." Ryan jumped to her feet. "I'll get it."

"Let's give him a call and see if he can meet us?" Cole suggested.

"Are you sure we can trust him?" Catherine questioned.

"I don't think we have a choice." Ryan summarized, studying Hartmann's card where he'd scribbled his cell phone number on the back. "He may be the only one other than us who's looking for the truth."

She handed Cole the card. "You set up the meeting and we'll be there." She exhaled and looked at Catherine. "Will have to be after hours though, you and I have panel interviews for the site CEO almost every day this week."

"I can't believe we are interviewing so many people for Lindsey's position." Catherine yawned into her hand.

"Fleming is really trying to sell this as an authentic panel review," Cole advised.

"Which we'd be really grateful for except she's already selected Lindsey's replacement without any guidance or input from anyone on the management team." Catherine knew she sounded bitter and uncooperative but she didn't care. It was a fact. There was nothing democratic about the processes currently being followed. She couldn't help but consider if maybe that hadn't been a factor in Anwar's death. He would have never supported the current degree of turnover at the corporate level. She doubted he would have signed off an application for an oncology award so soon after a catastrophic oncology medication error. He would not have wanted to be a part of the deception and lies. He would have fought them till the very end. And any one of those reasons could have been considered the justification for his death. What other factors might have contributed to his demise that she had yet to uncover. Did she really want to know the truth, his truths?

Chapter 18

"Why are we even interviewing anyone else for the position?" Ryan asked as she, Catherine, and Virginia walked toward the cafeteria, single file across the hallway. "Fleming's already decided Noah Reid's going to get the job."

"I think she's trying to at least trick a few people into thinking the appointment is legitimate," Catherine answered.

"The candidate we're interviewing today is Wesley Bowers." Virginia smiled. "I think he's interviewing just to annoy Erin." There was a pause as she looked around to make sure no one was walking close enough to hear their conversation. "He likes where he is now and he dislikes Erin. He has no intention of coming back to this system."

"Still," Ryan collected a plastic tray and waited in the line near the grilling station. "You'd think he wouldn't waste his time."

"He's salaried." Catherine reminded them. "It's a powerplay more than anything else." She nudged Ryan as a tall, familiar figure approached them with his arms opened wide.

"Ladies?" Wesley Bowers leaned into the group, taking the time to embrace each one.

"My gosh Wesley," Catherine said. "It's been so long. How are you?"

"Good," his smile faded. "I was sorry to hear about Anwar. I always enjoyed working with him. He was a good guy."

"Thank you," Catherine swallowed the know in her throat. "Yes, he was a good man."

"Have you heard anything from Andrew?" Virginia asked curiously, as to what had befallen her former boss.

"Caser?" Wesley clarified; his expression of surprise was evident to everyone.

"Yes, I've left several messages for him," Virginia advised. "He hasn't answered any of them." She waited for him to respond. When he didn't, she went on. "I heard he applied down your way?"

"If he did, his resume never made it to me." Wesley blew a sign. "I doubt Andrew would turn to me for help anyway. Besides at his level, he probably received a year severance package so he wouldn't need to be in any hurry to go back to work."

"Just seems odd that no one has heard from him or his family. It's like they dropped off the face of the earth." Catherine noted; she'd known him for years. It was odd he hadn't reached out to her if nothing else than to say goodbye.

He looped his arm through Catherine's. "Are you part of the panel?"

"Ryan is," Catherine smiled before adding, "begrudgingly."

"I heard," his smile was genuine as he turned to Ryan. "that you were the new COO."

"Interim" she clarified. "Soon as the new CEO replaces me, I'm going back to the pharmacy."

"Not interested in the position?"

"There's no way I could work very closely with Erin."

"Not a fan?" he stopped near a secluded table near the back of the cafeteria.

"No," she answered setting her tray on the table and motioning for Catherine to select a chair.

"Me neither," he smiled taking a seat between them.

****

Catherine checked her watch before strolling into the administrative offices. The incident in the lobby had taken longer than Catherine expected, the middle-aged woman who had fallen had gone on forever with fabricated aches and pains that had finally resulted in the paramedics being dispatched. No doubt, the ambulance had delivered her to the emergency room by now, it would be several hours before any results would be made available, there was no need to go there and wait.

She checked the time again, she had just enough time to get back to her office and change into her sneakers to join Ryan in a brisk walk around the lake. God knows, they both needed not only the distraction but the physical exercise as well.

Catherine entered quietly and slipped into the office, slipping into her well-worn converse running shoes and stepping next door to Ryan's office. She could tell without saying a word that something had happened, something was different.

"What's wrong? Was there a problem with Wesley's interview?" Catherine asked, entering Ryan's office to find her twirling a hospital identification badge in her hand. At first glance, Catherine feared Ryan was resigning, thinking it was all just too much for her. But that couldn't be the case, Ryan's badge was clearly visible hanging from the lapel of her suit jacket.

"No, it's not that at all." Ryan flipped the badge around so that Catherine could read the employee's name.

"Bailey resigned?" Catherine closed the door and slid into one of the two empty seats.

"No, Erin fired her this afternoon while I was downtown at the corporate COO meeting."

"Can she even do that as interim CEO?"

"I think she can do whatever she wants to whomever she wants." Ryan tossed the badge on the desk. "I feel bad for Bailey; she really doesn't deserve this. Erin's trying to get her point across to me. Bailey's just a casualty of the war."

"Why wouldn't she wait and have you do it? Bailey does technically still report to you."

"To show me that she's in charge, not me."

"What grounds did Erin give for termination?"

"As a result of the findings from the misfiled prescription."

"Fleming's son's script?"

Ryan nodded. "Once this is all over and done, I'm going to help her file a lawsuit for wrongful termination."

"Careful," Catherine mouthed the words. "Not here."

"It doesn't matter anymore Catherine. They seem to always be a step ahead. They know every move we make."

"Maybe," Catherine whispered. "But you don't have to make it easy for them. We'll keep Bailey in our thoughts." She paused before asking. "So, Wesley interviewed well?" Catherine asked, walking around Ryan's desk to the big window that overlooked the pond on the west side of the property.

She hoped it wasn't so obvious how much she wanted to wander outside in the sunlight and take a seat under the big tree that ran alongside the lake on the backside of the hospital property. She wasn't the first person who'd considered it as was evident by the numerous concrete benches scattered around under the shaded areas. For now, walking quickly under the umbrella of the shaded areas would have to suffice.

"Yes," Ryan answered and turned to see what Catherine was focused on, "but you know it's just an exercise. Fleming already has her sights on Noah Reid."

"I know. I guess it's just wishful thinking." Catherine advised. "Crap!" she ran her hand along the waistband of her skirt. "I left my phone on my desk. You have yours with you?"

"Yes," Ryan tapped the phone clipped to her belt. "They can do without you long enough to take a twelve-minute walk around the perimeter."

"Perimeter?" Catherine laughed. "You and the Detective are spending a lot of time together."

"He's been at my house every night working on that box of stuff with Erik, his retired CIA friend." Ryan smiled, turning her face away from Catherine.

"I'm happy for you, Ryan." Catherine squeezed Ryan's arm. "You deserve someone in your life." She paused, "It's just kind of odd to see you as part of a couple, you know?"

"I know," Ryan's motioned for Catherine to walk toward the new building. "Speaking of, something weird happened as we were leaving the panel interview."

"What happened?" Catherine asked, her ears listening to every word while her eyes scanned the area for any sign of the white van with the mismatched doors.

"Dr. Paine was one of the physicians who participated on the panel."

"What moronic thing did he ask of Wesley?"

"Nothing directed at Wesley but as we were reviewing the interview notes and Wesley was already excused from the room. Paine asked Fleming where they'd met before."

"Did Paine work at Booker?"

"No," she went on. "He asked her what her maiden name was and where she was working in the mid-eighties."

"Where was Paine working in the '80s?" Catherine asked.

"Philadelphia, I think by the questions he was asking. She blew him off but you could tell she was aggravated." Ryan answered, fighting back the laughter.

"Did she ever tell him her maiden name?" Catherine's mind was swimming. Here was another piece to add to the puzzle Cole and his friend were working on. "What was her son's last name on the incident report?"

"No, she kept insisting they'd never met before." Ryan shook her head. "Although I've no idea how she could be so sure. If there's one thing I know, it's that healthcare is a very small world. The last name on that incident report was Turnhill." She paused. "Sound familiar?"

"No, I wonder where Fleming was working in the '80s?" Catherine asked, her words coming out quickly as if she was expecting an answer even though she really wasn't. There was no way Ryan would know the answer.

"Any word from your friend Nathan, the drug rep?" Catherine asked. It was a question she'd meant to inquire of earlier but it kept slipping her mind when she and Ryan were together.

"I saw his boss, Joaquin, and Lauren at a seminar last week," Ryan answered. "I got the impression Lauren was trying to avoid me so I didn't engage her." She paused. "But I've known Joaquin for many years, I couldn't get away when he approached me."

"Did you ask about Nathan?"

"Yes, she said he'd been in San Antonio at a training launch for a new drug."

"You didn't believe her?"

"No, I didn't."

"Maybe she's embarrassed and just wants the whole thing to go away."

"You mean, because nothing happened and she lied or because something did happen and she was coerced into changing her story?"

"Either," Catherine shrugged. "I'd be embarrassed either way. It's not –"

Her words were cut short as she pointed to a door propped open inside to the new building. "Why isn't that door closed?"

"I don't know." Ryan pulled out her phone and dialed. "I'm calling security." She took Catherine's arm. "Let's wait here."

"I'm just going to stick my head inside and see if I see anyone," Catherine advised.

"Wait here!" Ryan pleaded with her.

"Just stay here." Catherine pulled away. "If I'm not back in 5 minutes, call 911." She disappeared through the door, careful not to dislodge it from the door stop holding it open.

The first floor was cooler than Catherine was expecting. With so much of the building still unfinished, she expected it to be warmer, more humid. Why were they wasting all that money on the air conditioning a building that wasn't going to be in use for a while yet or completely built?

"Hello?' she called out down the corridor, not bothered by the hollow empty sound as her words traveled back around.. She thought of the lyrics to the song Please Come to Boston and how the hallway looked and smelled nothing like the canyons of Los Angeles.

Nothing, for as far as she could see, there was nothing but drywall and five- gallon paint cans scattered down the hallway as if it were part of an obstacle course.

"Is anyone there?" she called again, wishing she had her phone. Even though the walls were completed and intact, there were several areas encased in shadows, the flashlight function on her smartphone would have been a godsend to peer into the areas that would eventually be the stairwells.

She turned to return the way she'd come, knowing her five minutes would be expiring soon and she didn't want to read about the false 911 alarm in the morning paper. God knows the hospital system had been on the front page far too many times recently. She didn't want to be the source of yet another bruise on the system's reputation.

If the clatter from the corridor across the hallway hadn't been so loud, she might have thought it to be the large condenser for the air conditioning turning on. But the noise wasn't consistent with that and she made her way closer toward the sound to investigate.

She wasn't sure if the noise had come from the room that when completed would be a linen room or a medication room, it was hard to tell when all the rooms were empty and unfinished. She put her hand on the door only half hoping it was unlocked.

It wasn't clear what happened next, if the floor jumped up to meet her or the ceiling fell down around her. In any event, the world went black and she slumped down into a maze of torn drywall and worn cardboard boxes.

****

"You sure you're okay?" Ryan asked, watching as Elena and the emergency physician, Dr. Fare, assessed Catherine one final time.

"Yes," Catherine pushed Dr. Fare's hand away from her chin. "I'm fine." She paused. "I think I fell over something and hit my head."

"You hit your head on a pipe that wasn't mounted fully to the ceiling." Aiden paused. "It was hanging very low and it looks like it dropped just enough to whack you."

"Thank God you weren't hurt any worse," Ryan added.

"Are you sure it was the pipe? Did anyone come out of the doorway?" Catherine paused. "I heard a noise before everything went black."

"It was probably the pipe slipping before it fell completely," Aiden reiterated. "Ryan was waiting for you at the west entrance and I entered through the east side. I didn't see anyone come in or out."

"Who found me?" Catherine asked.

"Aiden did. He called for help and the EMT's brought you from the building on a gurney."

"What were you doing in there anyway without a hard hat or glasses," Aiden asked.

"The door was propped open and I wanted to just make sure whoever was in there was authorized to be there."

"The workers were at lunch" Aiden explained. "One of them probably left the door propped open even though they know they aren't supposed to."

"Maybe." She thought feeling sorry she hadn't checked the area for the white van. "It just felt odd and I wanted to make sure everything was okay."

"Next time, you need to wait for security, Catherine," Aiden advised, looking quickly to Dr. Fare for reinforcement. "Right Doc?"

"He's right, Catherine." He handed her a prescription. "You could have really been hurt." He leaned in closer and smiled. "And I wouldn't tempt fate with the black cloud that seems to be hanging over us."

He patted her knee, "Take care and call me if you need anything." He disappeared through the doorway with his long white coat trailing behind him like a flag.

"I will," she mumbled, grateful the only casualty was the navy dress slacks she was wearing. No doubt the tear across the left knee wasn't repairable. She tugged anxiously at the two ends of the tear, grateful that was about the extent of the injury.

Her head felt better already, the bump hardly even noticeable, by the time she got home, it would be all but forgotten. At least she hoped so.

Chapter 19

Noah Reid was a good-looking man in a smart, nerdy kind of way. He was shorter than Catherine was expecting, pale with dark brown hair that he combed to one side that made him look more like a surfer than a CEO. She'd heard he was a smart man and she was sure the thin, wire glasses he wore contributed thoughts toward that notion.

"I'm very happy to be here." He explained to his administrative team. "I feel confident that we can put this ship back on the right path. We just need to reorganize and prioritize what's needed to open the new building on time and on budget."

"I've worked with Erin and Oliver previously." His eyes locked initially with Ryan's before he moved to assess Catherine. "Your reputation as an effective risk manager precedes you. Catherine." He smiled; his words as soft-spoken as the message. "I'm excited to be working alongside you."

"And I heard how willingly you stepped up to help out in the absence of a chief operating officer." His words were directed to Ryan but he looked quickly to Oliver. "I'm hopeful we can do some great work together."

"Ryan has done an amazing job, Noah." Oliver smiled. "What she doesn't have in experience she more than makes up for in heart."

Noah nodded. "I've spoken to your department heads. No one had anything negative to say about any of you." He scanned the room as if there were more people in the room and he was making eye contact with each one. But there weren't many people in the room, it was just the five of them. "We're going to do great things together." He looked again at Ryan. "All of us!"

He clapped his hands as if he were coaching a team. "I hope everyone has a great day." He handed his phone to Catherine as she passed by on her way out of the conference room. "Virginia has asked me twice for my phone." He smiled. "Could you give this to her on your way out?"

"Sure." Catherine took from his hand, noticing it was smaller, thinner, lighter than any of the phones carried by the other members of the administrative team, including Lindsey.

"Here," Catherine said placing the phone on Virginia's desk, out of her way but in a spot where she could see that Noah had given it up. "Noah asked me to give this to you."

"Corporate is having a fit that it's not ready for him." Virginia swiped the phone up and dropped it into a padded envelope.

"He just got here. How can you possibly have the phone ready for him?"

"I don't ask questions. I'm just doing what I'm told." She paused. "And if Lindsey doesn't return her phone by the end of business today. Her severance pay is going to be held until she turns it in."

"Why do they always make such a big deal about the phones anyway. It's like there has to be one in your hand the minute you come aboard and they want it back the minute you put in your papers." Catherine vented, smiling at the look on Virginia's face. "It's like a full-time job to keep up with the mobile device transfer sheets."

Virginia's face turned pale. "Oh no, I don't think Ryan's phone was upgraded when she became the COO." She wiped her eyes under the wireframe of the reading glasses perched on her nose. "I'm going to get disciplined for this, I'm sure."

"Were you asked to upgrade it?"

"No, but it's my responsibility to see that all the administrative team has a corporate phone that allows the team members to have continuous interaction with one another," Virginia said, almost as if she were praying out loud.

"It will be fine." Catherine comforted. "She's in her office, just ask her for it and send it out today with Noah's."

"Good idea," Virginia nodded, jumping to her feet and disappearing into Ryan's office only to return moments later with Ryan's cell phone in her hand. "She's not in there. I left her a note. Can you make sure she sees it before she heads out for the evening?"

"Sure, I think she's in the pharmacy office picking up a few things she wanted to bring over to the COO office." Catherine smiled, remembering Ryan's words when she'd moved into the office that she was bringing any more than what would fit into a small cardboard box.

"That reminds me," Virginia looked up from her computer screen, her hands still poised against the keyboard. "I asked Jay about that box we found in Andrew' s office."

"And?"

"He said he didn't see any box that looked like what I described and he had no idea how it got up in the ceiling tile. He did say there were other boxes mixed in the pallets when they were delivered. Facilities identified some of the boxes when they were delivered and pulled them from the pallet. There's a chance, it wasn't Cliff's or Andrew's."

"Did Andrew ever return any of your calls? We aren't even sure that's the box he was looking for. That box could have been up there for years." Catherine asked, knowing the probability of getting the answers was getting smaller and smaller with every day that went by.

"He wasn't real forthcoming with the specific when I asked him about it. Like you guys, he hasn't returned any of my calls so I really don't know if we found it or not."

The exterior door pushed open as Ryan walked through with a familiar looking woman that Catherine wasn't able to place but she'd seen her around before, recently. Ryan motioned to Catherine then to the visitor for reintroductions.

Ah, Catherine thought Healthcare Advisory Associates. She'd heard about the company in past discussions with Ryan. It wasn't an arrangement Ryan thought was beneficial to the hospital. By her own calculation, she'd assessed the hospital system had paid thirty-five million dollars over the last five years for a service that in her opinion wasn't worth a fraction of that amount. Catherine remembered how emotional Ryan had been when she completed the report and submitted it for Lindsey and Oliver's signature.

"We're paying this company," Ryan had said, "as if they are advising one hundred percent of the inpatients and outpatients discharged within our system."

"When in fact," She'd gone on. "This advisor group saw only 7% of the inpatients discharged and none of the outpatients during the given billing period."

"Five years!" Catherine remembered how Ryan had slammed her hand against the conference table for effect. "They've been performing this pitifully for the last five years, yet we've continued to pay them as if they were meeting every margin and maximizing every threshold."

Catherine remembered Oliver's smile as Ryan had recommended a proposal that the company return the biggest portion of the money and keep only the seven percent they were entitled to. No doubt, she mused this was the purpose of meeting with the owner of the company. She wanted the money back, it was a lot of money, and she wasn't taking no for an answer!

****

"How'd the meeting yesterday with Eleanor of HAA go?" Catherine asked, knowing some of the outcomes as she'd heard bits and pieces through the office wall of the angry conversation between them.

"Obviously, they aren't going to easily give up thirty-three million dollars," Ryan admitted. "Eleanor said everything was spelled out in the contract."

"The contract sucks," Catherine said. "But that's not a crime. Our corporate leaders signing it, sure is."

"I just want to get us out of the contract," Ryan said. "I told her to consider HAA notified of our intent to sever the agreement as soon as I can get everyone's signatures." She held up a handful of papers. "I only need one more signature before I forward it to Fleming for execution."

She spun around the room, smacking her jacket pocket. "Where's my phone?"

"Virginia needed to take it."

"For what purpose?"

"It has to be configured into a corporate phone."

"But I've had that phone for years since I first came to the system."

"Doesn't matter." Catherine nodded.

"When can I get it back?"

"She sent yours and Noah's together. Lindsey hasn't returned the company phone so he's using his personal phone for now. I'm assuming you'll get it back tomorrow."

Noah tapped anxiously against Ryan's door frame. "Sorry to interrupt but I have an email from the corporate office that the OIG officers are returning today to review all accounts payable invoices authorized over the last six months." He took a few steps into her office. "They are under the impression you require some time to arrange for your own legal representation prior to meeting with them."

"Yes," Ryan nodded. "These guys have already decided I've done something wrong. I don't think I have a choice."

"How about I sit with you then?" He smiled, his words were soft and reassuring. "I promise to look out for your best interests."

"Ok, Noah." She looked quickly at Catherine. "But I've left in the middle of their questioning the last two times they questioned me. I can't promise you it won't happen again."

"You do whatever you feel you need to." He walked to the door. "Have Virginia set up a time for them to meet with both of us?"

"Sure."

"Catherine," he paused. "They asked to meet with you again as well but separately from Ryan. I'm not sure why?" He turned to exit. "Would you like me to sit in with you as well?"

"If you think that's best. I'll do my best to be available when they arrive." She promised before taking her leave.

****

Instead of meeting in the conference room Catherine had Virginia show Agent Bronson and Inspector Winters to the small confines of the risk management office. Something was amiss the other times she'd met with them in the cold, sterile conference room attached to the CEO's office. Both times after the meeting with them she'd walked away feeling as if she'd lost a battle. She had the home field advantage this time and she was going to make the best of it.

"All the other times we've talked we've focused on the corruption and fraud accusations. That's not why we're here today." Agent Bronson spoke first.

"Why are you here?"

"We spent the last hour meeting with your COO and CEO regarding overpayments to specific vendors for services not rendered and mismanagement of the corporate pricing structure."

"I wouldn't know anything about either of those things?" She pointed toward the door. "If that's all?"

"Did you know Aaron Lewis was arrested last night in a beach house off the Bimini coast?" Inspector Winters didn't try to hide his amusement with her dismissal.

"No, again I wouldn't know anything about that." She waved at the door again. "Ready to go now?"

"Lewis is still insisting he's being framed and he swears Dr. Beliard was involved." Bronson ignored her previous statement.

"You don't think Beliard killed himself, do you, Mrs. Masters?"

"No, I don't. I've known him for over half my life. He's not the kind of man that would take his own life."

"What do you think happened to him?"

"Honestly?" Catherine bit her tongue, battling with the words she dared not speak. "I think one of you people killed him."

"You mean, the FBI?" Agent Bronson clarified.

"Yes, he told me was working with the FBI to uncover how deep the corruption ran. He was concerned that he was in too deep and couldn't understand why you weren't intervening. He felt as if he was alone."

"When did he tell you this?"

"About a month before he died."

"That's a very interesting story," Agent Bronson nodded. "Not necessarily a unique accounting of things but incredibly persuasive."

"I don't understand." She drank hungrily from a plastic water bottle.

"That's exactly the same story Aaron Lewis told us after he was arrested."

"What are you talking about?" She recapped the bottle and tossed in the recycle bin.

"He says he was working with Beliard to expose the lies and corruption within the system. Beliard thought Aaron could be more useful if it was believed that he was part of the covert, corrupt system."

"What about all the women he's accused of abusing?" she asked.

"Per Lewis, they were all fabricated," Agent Bronson answered.

"How could he get that many women to lie." She thought of Lauren Horseman, how she'd recanted her story.

"We aren't sure." Inspector Winters said. "But there's not one piece of hard evidence that Aaron Lewis sexually assaulted anyone. There are no hospital reports or police reports, everything is circumstantial. There is nothing except the words of these women, most of which we personally haven't been able to interview."

"In person?" she repeated.

"Of the twelve initial complaints," Agent Bronson flipped through his notes. "Three have recanted, six were interviewed over the phone. The remaining three have not responded to any of our calls or requests for an interview." He paused. "It's almost like they never existed."

"That doesn't make any sense." She shook her head. "Why would Beliard do that?"

"Because he didn't know who he could trust." Inspector Winters said. "I think he thought he could trust you, Ms. Masters."

"He knew he could trust me." She nodded. For a minute, she considered sharing the key Beliard had left for her and the box that was found in Andrew's office. But the thought vanished almost as quickly as it came. For all she knew, Winters and Bronson and had put the gun to Anwar's chest and pulled the trigger. They may have been the very people he was hiding the key from. She couldn't betray his trust no matter how afraid she was. She had to see it through to the end.

****

"I don't think I recognize anyone pictured in the corporate update newsletter." Catherine folded the shiny bulletin in half and dropped it in the trash can next to her desk.

"That's because Fleming has fired everyone and replaced them with her own cronies." Ryan fished the paper from the trash and ironed it flat against the desk. "I feel sorry for Kushion and Oscar. Both had given over twenty years of their lives to this place."

"Now, they're only years from retirement and pounding the pavement looking for a job." Catherine shook her head thinking they were about the same age as she was. She couldn't imagine how it might feel to be submitting applications at her age.

"I didn't know Kushion that well but Oscar was in charge of the cardiovascular program here many years ago before he became CEO of Pine Bluff. He was a good man," Ryan admitted.

"How'd the interview with the OIG agents go?" Catherine remembered seeing Noah first thing in the morning but she hadn't thought to ask him. She probably wouldn't have asked him anyway. Their relationship was too new. There were too many unknowns.

"It was okay," Ryan answered. "I didn't answer many of their questions."

"Why was that?"

"Noah took offense to nearly every question they asked. Finally, he told them to go through official channels to request the invoices for reconciliation against the contracts and accounts payment receipts. He implied they were lazy and expecting us to do the work ourselves." She laughed. "He told them not to return without specific questions regarding specific invoices and payments."

"He is the boss." Catherine's words came out like an afterthought. She didn't like him and she didn't know why. He seemed genuine and more than committed to being a part of the team. But there was something she just couldn't put her finger on.

Chapter 20

"You look terrible!" Ryan chanted from the doorway of Catherine's office. She disappeared for a second before reappearing without her briefcase or purse.

"I think I've got less than three hours of sleep last night."

"What's going on?" Ryan dropped into the empty chair and motioned for Catherine to pass a scrap piece of paper for her to use as a coaster for her coffee cup.

"I was here late last night reviewing a patient complaint."

"Something you can share?"

Catherine motioned for Ryan to close the office door before continuing. "We suspended Dr. Paine last night."

"Finally," Ryan took another sip of coffee. "That took long enough. Hopefully, the anesthesiologists will think twice before pilfering unused medications leftover from patient cases.

"No," Catherine shook her head. "His suspension has nothing to do with that incident."

"What then?"

"A patient undergoing a routine endoscopy made a complaint that Dr. Paine touched her breasts and genitals while she was sedated."

"If she was sedated how could she possibly remember anything like that?" Ryan paused. "I've had propofol. It's fast and quick and you're out like a light."

She says she recalled bits and piece as she was waking up."

"What about the surgical team?"

"For whatever reason, it was the last case of the day. The physician had completed the procedure and only one OR technician and Dr. Paine were left in the room with the patient."

"What did the technician say?"

"She had stepped out to obtain an additional roll of paper for the automated dispensing cabinet. When she returned to the room, she said the patient was fully awake and sitting up."

"Was the patient upset? Did anything seem wrong?"

"During the interview last night, the technician said both Dr. Paine and the patient were acting odd even before the patient was sedated. At first, the technician thought maybe the patient and Dr. Paine knew each other and given the nature of the procedure; they were embarrassed."

"What type of procedure was being done?" Ryan asked.

"Plastic, it was an elective procedure, facial mostly." Catherine tossed the patient's record on Ryan's desk and waited as Ryan read the history and physical section of the chart.

"This patient has had a lot of work done over the years," Ryan said aloud as she read. "Lipo, breast reduction, skin grafting." She handed the file back to Catherine, "Guess her face was the only thing left." Ryan laughed, "She'll be a completely different person once this is all said and done."

Catherine went on. "The technician reported she asked Dr. Paine after the procedure if everything was okay and did he want her to get the OR supervisor. Dr. Paine insisted everything was fine and indicated for the technician to call for patient transport to recovery."

"What was the patient's name?"

"Megan Cassidy" Catherine recited the name by memory.

"And the surgeon was?" Ryan asked

"Dr. Donald Randall. He was just recently given privileges." Catherine reached for the file, not remembering his name. "Medical staff just approved his appointment."

"Sort of an expedited appointment, don't you think?" Ryan leaned back in the chair, stretching her lower back and legs.

"Apparently he's somehow connected to Dr. Fare."

"The ED physician?"

Catherine nodded. "I don't know how they're connected, just that Morgan Fare is Randall's sponsor."

"What did Paine say?"

"He says there is no validity to the charge and he is comfortable the investigation will exonerate him." She paused. "What do you think?"

"I think it's odd that he was still in the room. Usually, anesthesia is the first in and first out once the patient meets recovery parameters."

"I reviewed the OR sheet." Catherine went on. "Based on the patient vitals, it seems appropriate that he would still be in the room. The patient's respiratory rate was below what would have been satisfactory for discharge. It would not have been policy to leave the patient alone with the OR technician given the patient's vitals."

"Paine's a lot of things but I don't think he's a sexual predator."

"Me either but we have to wait and see where the investigation leads us."

"Speaking of investigations, any updates on the syringes we found in the bathroom or the summary regarding potassium chloride in the vasopressor IV bag," Catherine asked, looking past Ryan to see who was in the exterior office area.

"Yes," Ryan motioned toward Catherine's computer. "I sent you the final summary from the chemist. He actually had it certified and signed it. And if you open up the incident report for the syringes we found in the bathroom, the contents were just as we suspected. They contained trace amounts of ketamine, midazolam, and fentanyl. The fentanyl syringe also had minute traces of glycopyrrolate."

"Paine's cocktail," Catherine whispered.

"Yes," Ryan folded her hands across the desk. "In a court of law, we'd say it's circumstantial. Everyone knows he mixes in glycopyrrolate."

"I know but it certainly is something to keep in mind."

The tap at the door startled them both and Catherine responded as if on autopilot. "Come in?"

Noah pushed the door open just enough to accommodate his head reminding Catherine of Jack Nicholson in The Shining. "When you're done, can I see you in my office?" His question was directed to Ryan.

"Sure," she said rising and ironing her skirt into place over her legs. "I'll be right there." She waited till he disappeared back behind the door before leaning in and whispering to Catherine. "If I'm not out in thirty minutes, you know the Drill."

Take your X-files stuff from your office and meet you at your house. Got it." Catherine laughed.

****

What was she doing? Catherine twisted forward as far as she could from behind the desk to see if Ryan's office door was still open, confirming she was still in the office. It had been almost an hour since Ryan had left Noah's office and slid back into her own. Why wasn't Ryan coming over and updating her on whatever Noah had wanted to talk about?

Catherine blew a sign of expiration and rose quietly to her feet before walking almost tenderly to the office two doors down. She didn't try to hide her surprise to find Ryan typing quickly on the keyboard.

"Let's talk later," Ryan whispered. "I don't want him to see the door closed and know you're in here."

"We can talk at lunch?" Catherine looked behind to ensure Noah's door was closed.

"Yes, but let's go offsite, I don't want to discuss it in the cafeteria."

****

"Alright," Catherine pleaded once the server had taken the order and walked away from the table. "What's going on? What did he want to talk to you about?"

Ryan turned around in the seat as if she were looking for someone specific. "Honestly, I'm not sure. It was all very odd."

"What did he want?"

"For me to explain the hospital's formulary process to him."

"Formulary? Why?"

"Because I removed Anodyne from the hospital's formulary three weeks ago." She paused and looked behind their table again.

"Removing it resulted in a 1.4-million-dollar positive cost impact to the hospital."

"Was he expressing gratitude?"

"At first I thought that was the purpose but then he asked me what the process would be if a physician wanted to order the medication for a patient."

"Nonformulary," Catherine interjected. "Click the box on the computer and it's ordered." She paused. "Why does the CEO of the hospital care about the formulary status of a medication?"

"Because his best friend is the representative for the medication."

"You're kidding?"

"I wish I was. Noah wanted to know why it was removed."

"Like 1.4 million dollars isn't a good reason?"

"He said he wanted to make sure it wasn't being removed simply because of cost. Which I assured him it hadn't been. And I went over the other, more cost-effective agents." She paused for the server to set the drinks on the table. "I felt like I was in trouble."

Catherine shook her head. "It's like we're in an episode of the twilight zone. And not a good one."

"Was there ever a good one?" Ryan smiled.

"Well, the X-files it's not," Catherine joked.

****

"I understand, Mrs. Crosby," Catherine explained to the caller for the fourth time. "Unfortunately, I can't make any changes to your bill at this time."

She listened as the caller went on before adding. "I'm sorry the food wasn't to your liking, Ma'am, but we can't adjust bills based on the temperature of your meals.

Catherine paused before explaining. "Yes Ma'am, I'm aware that the Governor is looking at our satisfaction scores. But as I said before, your food isn't billed as a separate item on your bill. It's all rolled up into your charge for the room."

"Mrs. Crosby," Catherine explained. "The director for dietary services will be contacting you to get a complete report of the issues you encountered." She paused. "No Ma'am, I cannot provide you a gift certificate to Outback for service recovery. I---"

Her sentence was cut short, distracted by the newcomer who'd entered the office. Catherine heard Virginia address the visitor. "Hi Eleanor, can I help you?"

"No!" Eleanor's response was brief and angry as she continued her route to Ryan's office. "I need to talk to her".

"HAA's agreement with us has been severed. You shouldn't be here without an appointment." Virginia rose and ran around the desk toward the door where Eleanor had entered. She stepped over Jay who was replacing a computer Drawer at Lorraine's empty desk and met Eleanor just in front of the small hallway between Catherine and Oliver's office.

"Settle down," Virginia advised, holding her hands out in front and pointing toward an empty chair just inside the office. "Take a seat and I'll get you some water."

"I need to talk to you!" Eleanor demanded and at first, Catherine thought was the request directed at her given the close proximity to her office door. Eleanor was dressed casually in jeans, a short-sleeved tee shirt, and sneakers. She was wearing little to no makeup and her hair was unruly, uncombed, and standing at its ends.

"What can I do for you?" Catherine rose and walked closer to the door, close enough to see that Eleanor had stopped short, standing just in front of Ryan's office.

"Not you!" Eleanor clarified. "I need to talk to her." She pointed toward Ryan's open door.

"What about?" Ryan appeared just inside the office door.

"You know what about!" Eleanor screamed, spittle spewing from her mouth.

"Come in and take a seat."

Catherine watched as Eleanor disappeared into the office with Ryan following behind her stopping just long enough to push the door closed but not completely. She'd left it open about four inches and disappeared from Catherine's line of vision.

"What's this about?" She heard Ryan's voice, calm and imagined she'd taken a seat behind her desk.

"Virginia?" Catherine whispered from the doorway. "Call security and have Aiden come to administration ASAP!"

Virginia nodded, dialing the phone before Catherine finished making the request.

"Jay ?" Catherine called, stepping from her office to where he was working on the empty desk in the middle of the room.

He stood up, tools in hand and turned to face her.

"Can you hang around for a minute until Aiden gets here?" She paused and looked toward Ryan's office where the voices continued loud and angry.

He nodded and stepped barely inside Catherine's office, his location just feet away from Ryan's office and made space for Catherine to stand close by.

They were able to hear Eleanor's voice was loud and clear from their nest. "I got fired yesterday because of whatever proposal you sent to your corporate leaders.

"Your employment," Ryan was saying, "is between you and your employer."

"You have to go back to the table and renegotiate something," Eleanor demanded. "You can't just terminate the contract and walk away. I need this job."

"I believe your company has breached the contract. It is within the scope of my responsibilities to review and assess contracts." She paused. "And take appropriate action."

"That's not fair." Eleanor words were thick with tears.

"What's not fair is how much money your company has sucked from the system over the last five years and yet, you've delivered nothing."

"You can't do this!" Eleanor's words were precise. "You're going to be sorry."

The exterior door opened abruptly as the lieutenant of the security team, Jessica, stepped briskly inside, one hand stationed on her belt, the other holding onto the radio fastened around her shoulder near the clavicle. "What's up?"

Catherine pointed to Ryan's office where the argument continued to escalate. "I think you should be nearby, just in case. The HAA associate was fired yesterday and she's blaming Ryan."

"You want me to intervene?" Jessica approached the door, still slightly ajar, and peered through the opening.

"No" Catherine shook her head. "Not yet, let's just be nearby." Her words drifted off as Jay strode past them headed for the office door. "Jay, can you stay? I didn't know Aiden was offsite today."

"He's downtown in a meeting with the other captains and corporate COO," Jessica explained.

"I hope this isn't about outsourcing the security detail again." Catherine looked back to Ryan's door hoping Eleanor had the answers she needed and was closer to leaving.

"Actually," Jessica explained. "I think it is about that."

"Oh no," Catherine turned back to her. "I think you guys do a really good job. It's unfortunate."

"I think the proposal was killed," Jessica interrupted.

"Killed?" Catherine repeated thinking she wished Jessica had used another term.

"Rumor has it, someone high up on the food chain put the whammy on it."

"High up?" Catherine said aloud but thinking about how it could be one of any number of people.

"You know, someone with some juice." She looked to the floor, "Aiden thinks Dr. Beliard rejected the outsourcing proposal. It was probably one of his last official acts."

"I see," she paused. "In any event, I'm glad you aren't going anywhere. It's ---"

Ryan's door exploded open and Eleanor marched out. "You're a bitch! Everyone thinks so."

"Maybe," Ryan responded calmly from behind the desk. "But for now, I'm an employed bitch. Have a good day."

Eleanor took a step back toward the office only to be intercepted by Jessica as she took Eleanor's arm and led her forcibly, yet gently away from Ryan's office and closer to the administrative door. "You're on private property," Jessica explained, letting her arm go and positioning herself between Eleanor and Ryan's office door. "I'm asking you to kindly leave the premises."

Jay moved closer to Jessica, his shoulder almost touching hers. He looked over to Catherine who seemed to be in a trance. Her gaze fixated on Eleanor.

"Catherine?" he nudged at her hand. "You okay?"

"Yes," Catherine cleared her throat. "You've been asked to leave the property. If you refuse, you'll be arrested for trespassing."

"I'm leaving." Eleanor opened the door, yanking it so hard it tapped the wall behind it. "But I'll be back."

"We'll be waiting for you with the police," Jessica advised, watching as Eleanor stomped through the doorway and into the administrative hallway. "I'll see that she vacates the property." Jessica disappeared through the door.

Catherine was quiet, unusually so. Jay continued to stand nearby as if waiting to be excused.

Virginia closed the distance between them, peering into Ryan's office before taking the place at Catherine's side. "Everyone ok?" She paused. "Do you still need Jay?"

When Catherine didn't answer right away, Ryan appeared at the doorway. "I'm fine." She looked at Catherine. "You okay?"

"Yes," Catherine cleared her throat. "Thank you, Jay, You're free to go."

"What's wrong?' Ryan asked, stepping past Virginia and pulling Catherine into the office. Catherine pulled away and practically ran into her own office, yanking filing cabinets open and flipping through folders.

"What is it?" Ryan followed her into the office, stopping at the door and watching as Catherine tore through multiple drawers before finally coming to rest on a specific file.

"This," Catherine flipped through a stack of black and white pictures until she tapped the one she was looking for.

"The pictures from the thief who emptied all the controlled substances from my dispensing cabinets?"

"Yes," Catherine turned the photo to face Ryan and slapped the photo again. "We already said we thought this was a woman, right?"

"Yes, but we've no way to identify her."

"The tattoo," Catherine advised, her words coming out so quickly it sounded like one big word. "Eleanor has this same tattoo in the same place as the woman in this photo. When Jessica took her by the arm and pulled her toward the door, her shirt was yanked over and I saw it on her shoulder."

"The photo is not very clear, Catherine.". Ryan surmised. "It could be a bird." She leaned in to get a better look at the picture. "And it could be a tree." She paused. "Hell, it could be a chocolate bar."

"It's a bird," Catherine repeated. "And I know she's the woman in the picture."

"How can you know that?"

"I feel it."

Chapter 21

It might have looked like a celebratory dinner. A group of friends positioned in a semi-circle of sorts with take-out cartons of food laid out among them like a mobile smorgasbord. The atmosphere wasn't party-like but it wasn't a work event either. There were partially empty wine bottles speckling the end and coffee tables of the living room and pieces of entrees left in Styrofoam containers. If there had been lively music and Detective Spencer wasn't wearing his sidearm, the gathering might have passed for a social event.

"Do we have any reason to believe Eleanor is involved in Dr. Beliard's suicide?" Cole asked, looking again at the photos from the surveillance cameras.

Catherine tried not to cringe when he used the word "suicide," but she understood. Without any other evidence to support otherwise, suicide was no doubt the accepted cause of death. "No, I'm not even sure she'd even met him."

"But you feel certain she's the woman in these photos?" Cole asked, looking across the room to Ryan.

"I do," Catherine took a sip of wine, holding the glass so tightly in her hands she could feel the dissemination of the energy. *I'm so tired,* she considered, thinking how much had happened in such a short period of time. *Four weeks,* the words sang on her tongue like a song. Anwar had been dead a little over a month. Yet so much had happened since the last time she'd been with him, it felt like a lifetime ago.

"Did you see the tattoo, too?" he asked Ryan.

"No, I was in my office," Ryan answered. She jumped to her feet and grabbed her briefcase. "I think I have photos from the holiday party a few months ago."

"So?" Catherine asked.

"Eleanor was there. She came in a very nice, sleeveless dress." Ryan flipped through the photos looking for the specific picture she was referencing. "I don't remember seeing that she had a tattoo but the party was here and I was very busy seeing to everyone's needs."

The rhythmic sound of the doorbell as it resonated through the house should have startled them but it didn't. Instead, Cole rose, "That's probably Erik." He held his hand out to Ryan for the photos. "You get the door; I'll look for the picture."

"Ok," she handed him the photos calling back over her shoulder. "A red dress. Look for the other pictures with the Christmas tree in it."

She returned seconds later with an older, distinguished looking man dressed casually in jeans, knit shirt, and a leather jacket.

Cole stood, his hand extended, "Erik. Thanks for coming?" He held a photo out to Ryan. "Is this the picture you were looking for?"

"Yeah," she moved closer to look at both photos. "I wish we had a better picture of either one."

"Wouldn't the pharmacist have known Eleanor; know she wasn't an anesthesiologist?" Catherine asked.

"Theo only works weekends and Eleanor works Monday thru Friday. Chance are, they'd never met." Ryan explained.

Cole lined the photos side by side to compare. "It's not possible to say definitively they are a match.

"They are similar." Ryan proposed looking at Catherine.

"That's about all we can say for sure." Cole closed the file with the photos inside. "I couldn't take this to court as evidence, it's just not enough." He motioned to Catherine. "I'm sorry."

"Don't be,' she smiled. "I don't need to compare the pictures. I told you I know it was her."

****

"What do you mean, you didn't bring anything objective, Erik?" Cole sounded almost agitated. "I thought you had something for me?"

Erik rubbed at the dark and gray hair overgrowth on his chin. "I have some data to share but everything I have to say is off the record so there are no documents of any kind." He paused. "And if it ever comes out, I will deny everything and swear you made it all up."

"What the hell, man?" Cole held his hands out for effect.

"I'm retired, Cole. My wife and I have earned some time together and I want to make sure we live to a ripe old age surrounded by dozens of grandkids and great-grandkids."

"Fair enough," Cole pointed to the box Erik had returned, the one with Beliard's photos. "Tell me what you got for me."

Erik sorted through the box until his fingers touched the photo he wanted. It was the one Beliard had sent to Catherine. "You already know who most of these men are." He tapped the second man from the right. Paul Rostock's daughter was Jacob Fleming's mother. Jacob was a toddler when Paul died, but he was very close to his mother, Evelyn."

He smiled as if he were reciting a bedtime story. "I know what you're thinking. How did the son of a Nazi war criminal become a high-ranking member of the CIA?" He cleared his throat. "It happens a lot more often than you might think. He wasn't the first and I doubt he will be the last."

"Tell me how Beliard and Jacob Fleming are connected?" Cole asked, trading glances with Ryan before taking the seat next to Erik.

"I found everything from elementary school report cards to marriage licenses with his name on them," Erik mentioned. "But something about the documents just didn't feel right to me."

"What do you mean, by feel right?' Catherine scooted closer to the group. "You don't think the documents are real?"

"No," he rifled through the box until he found Beliard's birth certificate. "I don't. They have the right look but not the right feel."

"I don't understand." Cole took the document from Erik's hand flipping it over several times before handing it back to Erik.

"This document is what fifty-five years, sixty years old?" Erik asked , holding it up for effect.

"Yes, I guess," Cole answered for the group.

"This thick, slick paper wouldn't have been used to print birth certificates."

"It seems worn enough, don't you think?"

"Yes," Erik answered, "but it seems staged to me like it was creased and folded to make it appear as if it's older than it is." He tossed the birth certificate back in the box and selected a marriage certificate. He held it out to Catherine. "You were his first wife?"

"Twenty-five years ago, yes," Catherine answered. "Want are you saying?"

"I don't think Beliard was his real name but I do believe he and Jacob Fleming were friends all their lives." He pulled a worn notebook from a leather satchel he'd dropped near the floor when he'd arrived. "In fact, unofficially, I believe Beliard 's real name was Reginald Anderson. He wasn't born was in Egypt while his father was serving as the ambassador but in rural New York. Young Reginald and Jacob met initially during the 1962 Scripts Spelling Bee where they were recognized as co-winners that year. Reginald was the youngest winner in the history of the competition. Evelyn took notice of the young man, intrigued by his intellect and took him in as an "adoptive son." "

Erik took several gulps of water. "Both Jacob and Reginald were groomed from early ages to assume leadership appointments in the CIA with Evelyn never far away from either child. Reginald had a photographic memory. He could recall large amounts of data in record time."

"You can't be serious," Catherine was pacing. "I knew this man, I loved this man, For God sake, I married this man." She collected her bag from the couch. "Why would you make up these lies?"

She waved to Cole. "I can't believe you'd support something this crazy."

"Catherine, wait." Cole took her hand. "Please hear him out. Why would he make this up? What would be the purpose of lying to you?"

"What purpose would Anwar have had to have lied to me?" She looked to Ryan, fighting back the tears. " I have to go. I'm sorry."

"Catherine, wait." Ryan pulled at her arm. "Please don't leave like this." She looked to Cole for assistance. "Do something."

"Let her go," Cole advised. "She needs some time to process it all."

"You better not spread any of these lies," Catherine warned. "I'll file the lawsuit myself." She couldn't get out of the door fast enough. By the time she reached the front door, she was practically running.

"Catherine?" Ryan called from the door. "Wait, I'm coming with you."

"Go back inside," Catherine warned. "I can't talk to you right now, about this."

"We won't talk, we'll just sit." Ryan offered.

"I'm tired, Ryan." She clicked the driver's door unlocked. "I'm going home. We'll discuss this in the morning."

"I don't want you to be mad at me."

"I'm not. I just need to think about everything Detective Spencer's friend said. Are you sure this man is a reliable source?"

"Cole trusts him. That's all I can tell you."

"And you haven't known Detective Spencer that long. Are you sure we can trust him? Is there any chance he could be a part of this?"

"I honestly don't know." Ryan shook her head and disappeared back into the house, watching as Catherine backed her car down the driveway and vanished into the darkness of the night.

****

She could have blamed her insomnia on the streetlight that bled through the curtains of the guest bedroom window or the digital clock that reflected the time onto the white wall on the other side of the room. She couldn't blame in on Gordon's snoring. He'd been sound asleep in their room for hours.

Truth was, none of those were the reason she couldn't sleep. Reginald Anderson? She repeated the name over and over trying to ignite a recollection, any recollection of hearing it in any capacity during the time she and Anwar had been together.

Had there ever been a time, even a whisper when his mother had accidentally called him Reginald or Reggie instead of Anwar? No, she told herself. Never. He'd never been anything other than Anwar Beliard to her. What motive could Detective Spencer's CIA friend have for delivering these lies to them? Maybe it was the CIA, not the FBI who'd played a role in his death?

She cataloged his last words in her mind, not that she hadn't done that already several hundred times. The last time she'd seen him, he'd hidden the key in her chair. What was it he'd said to her? Her mind replayed the scene like a movie. He'd mentioned something had happened, something to do with his past. She strained, pushing herself through the memory, trying to remember what else had he said. He'd talked about their first kiss. And how it was the only time he'd actually been afraid, afraid she'd slap him.

Catherine smiled and flipped over on her side, trying to recall the circumstances of that kiss. They'd attended a medical conference in Charlotte somewhere in the old historic part of town. After dinner they'd walked downtown to their hotel, deciding to spend the night instead of battling the traffic heading North.

There it was, its antique iron gate tucked carefully into the tree line behind the sidewalk so that it was nearly invisible. No doubt, the locals were aware of its existence. Just like fine restaurants, old graveyards were infamous. No one had been more surprised that she had been when the gate swung open and Anwar motioned for her to follow him inside.

She'd made a joke about him having a secret identity, maybe one as a serial killer. He'd laughed and pulled her away from the decrepit old tombstones that lined the ground for as far as could be seen in the light of the moon. Instead, he led her into the mausoleum, it's only light providing less than adequate illumination. Twice she'd tripped over loose rocks and stones, both times he'd caught her and pulled her upright to stand on her feet. She liked how he'd dropped his arm around her waist and pulled her the rest of the way into the dark dungeon like a corridor with moldy, smelly vaults on either side.

His kiss was warm and gentle and she'd fallen into his arms as if needing to be closer. She knew that night that she loved him. And if her memory served her correctly, it was also the first time he told her loved her. Her heart ached with the recollection; their time together gone almost as quickly as it had begun. She struggled to collect it all, every minute to fill up the places in her heart that had been empty since the day he'd left her.

She sat on the bed's edge, switching the lamp on the nightstand so that the room was lit like a fire. She'd didn't have many things left from her life with him. At first, she'd kept it all, she needed everything just as he'd left it in the house they shared. But as time passed, she found herself discarding more pieces of their life together until there was very little left. At some point in time, she didn't need the mementos, her time with him had been tattooed on her heart. With or without his personal belongings, his mark was there.

Catherine knew exactly where the book was, it was where she'd put it some twenty plus years ago. Quietly she climbed the step stool and pulled the book down from the top shelf of the closet. She'd never read the book, although she had planned to many times. Finally, years later. She opted for the movie instead. Gordon hadn't been impressed with the movie version of Alexander Dumas' The Count of Monte Cristo, but she had enjoyed it. The acting had been superb, the storyline exciting, although it was sort of a stretch that no one would have realized that Edward and the Count were one and the same person.

A coincidence her mind reassured her. It was all just a silly coincidence how he'd given her a book whose storyline was a man with two identities. Anxiously, she flipped through the pages, finally coming to rest on the last page where his handwritten message was still dark and prominent on the page. *I am my true self only when I am with you. I'll love you forever no matter where our paths take us. Anwar*

Oh God, his written words repeated in her mind. She replayed what he'd said to her the day he'd hidden the key in her chair. "It's just us," he'd said. "Anwar and Catherine."

She jumped from the bed as if the bed were on fire, pulling the thin pajamas off her body and slipping quickly into her clothes and shoes. She grabbed her car keys, cell phone, and Anwar's book, hoping she could get out of the house without waking up Gordon. She knew what the key went to and hoped Ryan would forgive her intrusion.

****

Catherine dialed the cell phone number by heart, surprised when a sleepy male voice answered the call. "I'm sorry Detective Spencer. I was hoping I could talk to Ryan. I'm parked in her driveway; I need to speak with her please."

"Who is this?" the voice was agitated.

"It's Catherine, can I speak to her please. I'm sorry it's so late. I know what Anwar's key goes to."

"Catherine?" the man asked. "Is that you?"

"Yes, Cole?" she asked, thinking maybe the phone carriers wires were crossed and she had the wrong number.

"It's Noah Reid," the man clarified. "Are you okay? Do you need some help?"

"Noah, are you with Ryan?"

"No, Catherine. It's three am. I'm in bed with my wife. You called my number by mistake."

"I see," she pulled the phone away and checked the number. Nope, she thought, seeing Ryan's name and number illuminated on the screen. Corporate must have gotten their phones mixed up and configured the numbers incorrectly. "I'm sorry, Noah."

"You okay, you need some help?"

"No, just dialed the wrong number. Sorry" She disconnected the call and selected Noah's number form her address book instead. Seconds later, she wasn't surprised at all to hear Ryan's sleepy words.

"Catherine?" Her words were slurred. "What's wrong?"

"I'm sorry to call you this time of night. Is Detective Spencer with you by chance?"

"Yes, he's sleeping. Are you okay?"

"I'm parked in your driveway. I know what the key goes to."

"Wait a second," Ryan said suddenly awake, "Let us get dressed and we'll be right out."

"I'll be here," she promised.

****

"We'll take my car," Detective Spencer instructed once he and Ryan were outside peering into the open driver's window of Catherine's car.

"I don't mind driving," Catherine offered and motioned for him to get in the passenger seat.

"We should take mine; it's equipped with a police radio and sirens. If there's trouble, we can get help quicker."

She nodded, pulling the car in reverse and parking closer to the garage door. "I'm really sorry about all this and for my reaction earlier this evening." She paused before climbing into the back seat of his car. "I do appreciate your help." She wiped her eyes. "I just can't believe he could have been anyone else than the person I knew and loved."

"What we've found doesn't mean his love for you wasn't genuine," Ryan whispered, turning around in the front seat to talk to her. She waited till Cole's car was on the highway headed south before asking. "What's going on?"

"I'm thinking that maybe some of what your CIA friend found out may have been true after all. At least the part about the multiple identities." Catherine had to swallow several times to finish the sentence.

"Why?" Cole asked. "What did you find?"

"I don't have many things left from our life together but I did keep a book that he gave me." She paused. "It was a gift he gave to me after we'd been divorced."

"What kind of book?"

"I've never read it but I did see the movie many years ago. It's by Aleandre Dumas."

"The Count of Monte Cristo?" Ryan whispered. "Is that the one?"

"Yes," Catherine nodded. "Do you know the story?" She handed the book to Ryan,

"Very well," Ryan smiled. "It's one of my favorite stories."

"Read the inscription on the back page."

"Wow," Ryan repeated the message for Cole. "You think it's a coincidence?"

"No," Catherine shook her head. "I'm not sure that it isn't."

"I know you said to head downtown, but where in Charlotte?" Cole interrupted,

"Go to the historic district, there's an old graveyard downtown."

"I know the place," Cole shook his head and motioned for the coffee thermos.

"I think corporate mixed up your phone with Noah's" Catherine added watching as the little bit of traffic that was on the road, sped past them, the headlights making her head spin.

"What?' Ryan pulled her phone from her pocket. "What makes you say that?"

"Because when I was in your driveway and called you, Noah answered." She paused. "At first I thought it was Detective Spencer answering your phone but it wasn't it was Noah."

Ryan flipped through the contacts, rolling her eyes when she realized none of the contacts listed on the phone were hers. "We'll need to get it fixed asap. I need my phone."

"First thing in the morning, we'll get Virginia to fix it," Catherine promised, watching as Ryan's expression changed to a frown.

"What is it?" Catherine asked.

"There's a text here. I didn't mean to snoop but it jumped out at me."

"Read it out loud," Cole advised, his eyes darting back and forth from the road to Ryan.

"It's from someone named Hoffmon and he's asking for an update on the formulary change."

"Formulary?" Catherine echoed. "You don't mean the Anodyne?"

"Yes," Ryan read the text again. "I think it is."

"Is it from the rep?" Catherine asked, not really sure why. She knew none of these people.

"No, the rep's name is Robin Carter." Ryan paused. "He's a nice guy, just pushy."

"How did Noah respond?" Catherine asked.

"He texted to sit tight, all good. Will be handled."

"Is he referring to you?"

"I think he is," she swallowed, sliding the phone back into her pocket.

"What the hell kind of medication is this that warrants a text at two am in the morning to the CEO?" Cole asked, his gaze off the road for longer than he intended so that he jerked the car back on the road.

"It's for pain," Catherine answered before looking to Ryan and adding, "Right?"

"Yeah, pain management." She answered but Catherine knew Ryan's mind was on something else.

"Some super painkiller?" Cole asked, not taking his eyes off the road this time.

"Not really," Ryan said. "It's not a controlled substance and it can be infused." She paused, "It was requested by the surgeons and obstetric physicians initially."

"Why'd you make it unavailable?" he asked.

"It was being used first line for everything," Ryan answered, pushing the hair out of her eyes and then dropping her head into her hands. "It's expensive and was becoming a huge piece of my drug budget."

"There's nothing unusual about her removing it, Detective." Catherine paused. "What is odd is that the CEO has taken such an interest."

"Was he a surgeon before he took the CEO position?"

"He's not a physician." Catherine answered, pausing before adding, "I'm not sure what his background is. Do you know?"

"All I know is he's a Fleming appointment." Ryan leaned her head against the window.

"You ok?" Cole asked.

"Just tired," She answered. "And I have a bad feeling about this."

"Going to the graveyard?" Catherine asked, not necessarily disagreeing with her.

"All of it," Ryan answered.
Catherine nodded, thinking to herself how she couldn't agree more.

Chapter 22

It was dark, but not as dark as Catherine expected it to be at four in the morning. Streetlights, she mused. They were placed strategically about every twelve feet so that the path below as well illuminated. If not for the full moon high in the night sky, it might have appeared as if the trio was taking a post-lunch stroll down Main street.

Cole parked on the street nearby placing his police credentials in the car window to dissuade any meter readers from issuing a fine. He led the way down the sidewalk, one hand on Ryan's arm and the hand stationed near his sidearm. "Let's cut thru here," He pulled her in the direction of the massive gate, it's large grotesque gargoyle statured at it's top like a mountain.

"That's creepy," Ryan paused and pointed to the gate. "If the outside is this scary. I can only imagine how frightening the inside is going to be."

"Maybe we should wait till daylight when there'll be more people about." Catherine stopped just short of the gate.

"We're here," Cole commented. "The dead things don't concern me." He pushed the gate open, its rusty hinges creaking and whining as it swung open enough to allow them entrance. "It's the living things, we should probably be looking out for."

He pointed at the line of trees just ahead. "The building's just thru there."

"You sure know your way around here, Detective," Catherine commented, thinking again how little they knew about the man.

"My first year out of the academy, I was on foot patrol down here in the historic quarter."

"I didn't know that," Ryan chimed in, exchanging glances with Catherine.

"I went to college here." He said. "I've been thrown out of just about every bar in this area." He laughed. He stopped at the thick, stone door of the mausoleum and pulled a small flashlight from his pocket. "It's not locked." He pushed the door open but motioned for Ryan and Catherine to wait, allowing him to enter first.

He stepped past the threshold, holding the light out in front and motioned for them to follow him. Almost in sequence, they began coughing, each one fanning the area around their faces as if that might help alleviate the smell.

"Boy scout," Catherine teased. "Got anything in there for this God-awful smell?"

"Hold your breath," he answered, letting go of Ryan's arm so that his free hand was positioned closer to his sidearm.

The building itself wasn't very big. In fact, Catherine thought as she looked up and down the walkway. There couldn't have been more than twenty, maybe thirty vaults in the room. She fingered the key in her pocket, hoping this wouldn't take very long. This place was giving her the creeps and she wanted to get out as quickly as they could.

Cole aimed the flashlight at the name plaque on the first vault. "Do we know what we're looking for?"

"Something to do with that book," Catherine whispered but she wasn't sure why. There was no one around for miles and probably wouldn't be for several hours. Once again, her thoughts turned to the detective. Maybe coming out here with him all alone at this time of the night had been a mistake. What if he wasn't someone she and Ryan could trust?

"Spread out," she heard him say. "Use the light on your phones to look around." He walked a few steps ahead of them. "I guess we'll know when we find it what we're looking for?"

Catherine stayed on the side of the building where they'd entered and walked slowly from vault to vault to read the names. She was aware of Cole just on the other side checking the names on that side. Where then had Ryan disappeared to?

"Here," Catherine heard Ryan's words about halfway up the room just inside a small corridor that held maybe an additional four vaults.

Cole's pace was quicker than her own and he reached Ryan a second or two before she did. "Who is it?" The beam from his flashlight lit up the entire vault, nameplate and all.

"Edmond Montes," she whispered looking at Catherine.

"Where's the key?" Cole held out his hand to her.

Catherine hesitated a second, her doubts bellowing up in her gut like smoke. "Give me a second." She exhaled and fished the key from her pocket before dropping it into his hand.

The key turned easily inside the lock. You'd think, Catherine thought, that after all the years had

passed, the big, thick, rusty, metal lock would have required more effort to unlock than what Cole had

used to open it.

The big piece of the lock dropped loudly against the concrete of the door and Catherine jumped as the sound echoed down the hallway and back around to where they were standing.

 Cole tugged the leather snap that held his gun in its holster so that his gun was accessible. "Ready?" he asked, stepping back so he could pull the door to the crypt open.

"Yes," they both said in unison.

It took a few minutes for the dust to settle and all three visitors leaned toward the vault for a better view. Catherine was the first to speak, "Thank god there's nobody."

"There's something on the ledge, there," Ryan said, leaning in as far as she could. "One of us has to crawl in there and get that." She paused, "I'll go but I'm warning you both, if there's anything slimy in there, I'll puke."

"You sure, I can go." Catherine offered but knew she wouldn't be able to climb in without someone giving her a boost and pushing her inside."

"I'm not sure I'll fit." Cole smiled and put his hands together in front and crouched just under the door. "Come on Honey, I'll give you a boost."

Reluctantly, Ryan stepped into his hands, preparing to use him as a ladder. "How am I supposed to get it and turn over to get out?" She shined the light into the crypt, "It's not that tall at all. I won't even be able to sit up."

"Go in on your belly and just grab it." Cole suggested. "Then we'll pull you out by your feet." He paused. "Just don't let go of whatever it is."

"Got it," Ryan stepped into his hands as he propelled her headfirst into the crypt. Once her torso was on the pedestal, Catherine watched as Ryan scooted so far into the vault, only the soles of her tennis shoes were visible.

"You okay?" Catherine asked, thinking again she wished someone else knew where she and Ryan were and who they were with.

"Yes," Ryan's voice was muffled. "It's hot in here, smells horrible."

"Can you reach it?" Cole asked, letting go of her ankles.

"Almost," her words were barely audible as her shoes disappeared past the threshold of the crypt. "Got it," she coughed. "Pull me out, quickly. No air."

Oh God, Catherine thought, digging in her pocket for her phone to call for help.

"Hang on," Cole called, yanking Ryan by the ankles from the crypt. Once her legs and buttocks were visible, he grabbed her around the waist and pulled her the remainder of the way out of the cubicle.

Ryan coughed several times, spitting at her feet as if she had a bad taste in her mouth. She slid down the wall coming to rest against the cool dirt of the floor.

"Call an ambulance," Catherine insisted dropping to her knees beside her.

"No," Ryan shook her head and waved her off. "I'm fine." She pulled herself to her feet. "Just let me catch my breath."

"Let's get out of here." Cole instructed as he pulled Ryan up by her arms. "Let's get back to the car. You can catch your breath there." He led them down the damp pathway out of the mausoleum and back toward the car.

Ryan continued to cough and choke, walking back to Cole's car with him wrapped around her waist. "Get in," he instructed, guiding her to sit in the front seat and adjusting the air vent to blow directly into her face. "Let me start the car."

Catherine watched as he ran behind the parked car and slid into the Driver's seat. "Maybe we should take her to the hospital." She paused, "We can have her seen in the emergency department very discreetly."

"Really," Ryan coughed. "I'm fine." She leaned into the car's vent so that the air blew her hair away from her face. "I'm feeling better already." She fell back against the seat cushion and adjusted the vent away from her face. "What's in the box?"

"Want to wait till we get back to your place?" He asked, but he fished in his pocket for something to open the box with anyway.

"No," Ryan and Catherine said unison.

"What's in it?" Cole flipped on the car's interior light and cut the thick, worn tape away from the boxes edges.

The box was filled with black and white pictures, each one wrapped in a plastic cover almost as if it had been laminated for protection. Ziploc bags of documents, each labeled with a year were stacked chronologically from newest to oldest.

"Look," Catherine held up the oldest bag and pulled its contents on the front seat between Ryan and the detective. A faded old birth certificate with the name Reginald Anderson fell face up on the seat. "Reginald," she repeated. "Here's his passport and some more pictures and papers."

Ryan held up a picture of two young boys and an older woman. "Catherine?"

"The one on the left is Anwar as a boy." Catherine smiled. "I think?"

"Yeah," Ryan flipped the picture over where written in thin black letters was printed. Reggie, Jacob, and Evelyn. "Look," she held up a worn, rotting catcher's mitt with the names Jacob and Reggie written in cursive in the palm.

"There are three other sets of identities," Cole held up the passport from one set. There was no debating the man in the picture was a younger, leaner version of Beliard. "And there's a dozen or so other pictures, not of Beliard. But at least a few of them I recognize." He held up a 4 X 4 black and white picture. "Lee Harvey Oswald." He fished for another picture, putting the first one back in the plastic bag. "And I'm pretty sure this is James Earl Ray."

"The man who killed Martin Luther King?" Ryan asked, her face pale and its nothing to do with air or lack of.

"Yes," the detective nodded. "Bunch of other papers. Some might be better interpreted by you." He handed the paper to Ryan. "It's some kind of chemical formula."

She turned the paper sideways assessing it from each perspective. "At first I thought it might be the chemical structure for serotonin."

"But it's not?" Catherine asked.

"No, it's not." She held it up to Catherine. "Okay if I hold on to this and try and figure out what it is?"

"Sure," she turned to Cole. "Can you get this box to your CIA friend?"

"I'm not sure Erik wants anything to do with an official investigation but I will ask him to take a look at the contents."

"Detective," Catherine's words were hoarse, soft. "I owe you and your friend an apology. I'm truly sorry for my behavior earlier tonight."

He waved her off. "It's nothing. You were upset." He paused. "But there is something you could do for me if you wouldn't mind."

"What?" She placed the contents back into the box.

"Would you mind calling me Cole?"

"Of course, Cole."

He went on. "I know this is hard for you and I can only imagine how difficult it is to find out something like this about someone you love."

"Loved," she corrected him.

"Loved," he restated. "I just hope we can get through all these clues and figure out what your friend wanted you to know." He tapped the box. "It's obvious he was trying to tell you something. I just hope we're able to figure out what it was."

"Me too," she smiled. "Me too."

****

"Have you had any sleep?" Virginia asked from her desk. Catherine knew by the way the question was asked, Virginia was trying not to laugh.

"No," Catherine yawned into her hand. "I was not able to fall asleep after I left Ryan's and then I sat up all night looking at old photo albums until about six am this morning." She hated lying to Virginia but there was no choice. For now, what they'd uncovered last night had to be kept confidential.

Virginia pointed to the phone lying on her desk. "I feel so bad about getting the phones mixed up." She shook her head. "Noah must think I'm an idiot."

"He probably just thinks you're overwhelmed trying to do the job of two executive assistants." Catherine paused. "Did he say anything about replacing Lorraine? I thought that maybe she'd return here and Fleming might pick her own assistant. God knows she's replaced everyone else."

Virginia laughed. "I know I've expected her back every day since Beliard passed away."

"Me, too." Catherine answered, "I—"

"Sorry I'm late," Ryan burst through the door. "We overslept."

"Haven't been in that long either," Catherine called out to her. "I told Virginia our evening ran a bit late." She hoped Ryan would take the hint and play along.

"Yeah," Ryan appeared in front of Catherine's open door and called back to Virginia. "By the time I got everything cleaned up, it was really late." She pulled the phone from her bag. "Did Noah already ask you about the phones?"

"Yes," Virginia explained. "I'm so sorry. I was waiting for you to come in so I could get yours." She dialed the landline on the desk. "Jay, I have both phones here on my desk. Are you still able to take them downtown and wait for them to be fixed?" She paused and listened to his response. "Great, thanks! Just stop by and pick them up."

Ryan reappeared at Catherine's door. "I'm not going to be able to meet for lunch today, after all." She paused, looking back to where Virginia was still at her desk. "I've got a few things to do for that project I've been working on with you." She stepped further into office. "Can you meet Cole and me tonight. Erik called already with an update."

"I'll go home and eat dinner with Gordon but I'll be to your place as soon as I can."

Ryan checked her watch. "I'm late for a meeting. We'll talk later."

Catherine nodded, not really seeing Ryan leave but hearing her address Virginia as she exited the administrative office. She spun the office chair around to check her emails hoping that the day might be an easy one. In truth, she was hoping to go home and rest a bit before meeting Ryan and Cole for tonight's update.

Odd, she thought as she perused the new incident reports that had been submitted for her to review, It was wishful thinking she knew hoping the report of Anwar's incident during his open-heart surgery might mysteriously disappear. Deep down, she knew it wouldn't. Whoever had tampered with it and ensured it wouldn't see the light of day ever again.

An incident report with a new sequence number caught her eye. Whatever it was it had just been reported. Eagerly she clicked it open to initiate the review. The report had been filed by an employee who worked in medical records and was complaining about another employee, also in medical records, who was utilizing company time to pursue a personal project.

Catherine picked up the phone and dialed the extension for the medical records department and asked to meet with the employee who had reported the issue. She'd just placed the receiver down when the code was announced loud and clear overhead. "Code rescue, OR 2. Code rescue OR 2." By the time Catherine was up and out the door on her way upstairs to OR 2, the announcement was repeated two more times.

Perfect, she thought to herself. All she needed was a code to review. And the rescue codes were the worst usually involving an emotional family member who had received the worst news they could have imagined. Odd, though, her mind was racing. How has the family member or visitor made it through the secured areas of the surgical suite and penetrated the operating room?

There was only one place in the entire hospital more secure than the OR. Catherine bit her lip and cringed thinking how they'd just welded the ceiling walls of the pharmacy closed as to deter any more intruders. Had the whole world gone crazy or was it just the world inside the hospital system?

"What is it? Hazel?" Catherine asked, as one of the operating room supervisors waiting just inside the mechanical doors of the operating room.

"It's bad," Hazel's hand went to her mouth. "He's dead. I'd say for a while, too."

Catherine took her suit jacket off and stepped into an OR suit, booties, hats, gloves, and masks and followed Hazel toward OR 2 where a group of employees had already started to gather.

"Get security up here and have Virginia call 911," Catherine instructed, as she made her way closer to the room. "I need everyone to step away from the door." She pointed to the other side of the hallway. "In fact, if you aren't participating in the resuscitation, please vacate the area and return to wherever you are assigned."

She turned to Hazel, "Please have April cancel all elective surgeries for the rest of the day and make sure the physicians are notified as soon as possible." She pointed way down the hall to OR 12, all other surgeries will need to take place in 11 or 12. We'll need to keep this area clear"

She pushed against the room marked OR 2 surprised that she couldn't get it to fully open. "What's blocking it?" She looked around the area frantically. "And where is Dr. Paine. He should have attended to the call for rescue?"

Hazel winced. "He's sitting up against the door. I could barely get through to get inside. I'm sure he's dead."

"Who?"

"Dr. Paine," Hazel cried. "Looks like he overdosed in OR 2. The syringe is still in his arm."

"Close the door," Catherine instructed before turning back to her just as Aiden and several officers entered the area. "I need this area cleared ASAP and a perimeter set up for the entire OR."

Aiden turned to his officers. "You heard her! Jessica, secure the scene. Kevin, clear the area." He tapped the radio on his shoulder. "I need the police to respond ASAP. We have a physician who has overdosed in the OR."

"Does he need medical attention?" the dispatcher clarified.

Aiden looked to Catherine who nodded no.

"Negative, he's going to be DOA. We need an investigative unit. ASAP. We've got the area locked down but cannot with confidence say the scene was not compromised."

"Units are in route,' the dispatcher reported before Aiden's radio went dead.

****

"You want some coffee?" Virginia's question was soft, almost harmonic. She'd stopped just inside the doorway, leaning against the frame. "I can't believe all that's happened, It's like we're jinxed or something."

"Another mysterious death," Catherine whispered, her heart racing against her mind.

"Are they thinking he committed suicide?" Virginia sat a steaming cup of coffee on Catherine's desk just within her reach.

"There's no note or anything," Catherine answered. "Preliminarily, they're ruling it an overdose." She tapped the keyboard so that the computer was awakened and she could input her password.

"Just odd after finding those syringes in the visitor bathroom a few weeks ago."

"I was thinking about that," Virginia admitted. "Is there any way we can tell if he discarded them?"

"Just checking to see if Ryan updated the incident report?" Catherine advised, reading the follow-up Ryan had entered just that morning.

"Looks like the meds came from our pharmacy." Catherine read on. 'But there's no way to know who put them there."

"How can she tell they were from our stock?" Virginia asked.

"Her note reads the lot numbers on the syringes were the same as the lots we currently have in stock. There's a high probability they came from here."

"Have you spoken to her this afternoon? Does she know about Dr. Paine?"

"I haven't talked to her since she left this morning for a meeting. She doesn't have her phone on so I haven't been able to tell her about Paine." Catherine paused. "I hope she doesn't blame herself. She's been pushing hard for his termination."

"He just came off suspension," Virginia added. "Noah signed off on the paperwork yesterday." Virginia jumped up. "Speaking of phones, I better check with Jay and get an update."

Virginia moved slowly, walking to the door almost on tiptoes. "I'm sorry you've got to go through all this again. Maybe you should think about taking some time off?"

"I can't," she shook her head. "But I appreciate the thought."

"Hello?" a voice called out from the front office.

Virginia accelerated and rushed out of Catherine's office to greet the newcomer. "Hi, Kelly, Who are you here for?"

"Me," Catherine answered, not getting up from her desk. "Have her come in."

The young technician from medical records seemed nervous as she made her way into Catherine's office and took a seat before Catherine had a chance to invite her.

"Hi Kelly," Catherine smiled, hoping Kelly wouldn't see how ingenuine it was. The last thing she felt like doing was smiling. In fact, all she wanted to do was crawl into her bed alone and cry. "You want a soda or some water?"

"No, what's this about, Catherine. I've got a lot of work to do." Kelly fell into the chair, scooting her butt against the back of the seat so that her feet hung loosely over the seat of the chair, shoes not touching the floor. She looked younger than she was and Catherine couldn't help but think of Gilda Radner and her big rocking chair.

"I'm following up on a complaint regarding utilization reports you've been running."

"I'm in medical records." Kelly's body language was defensive. Catherine knew the discussion was probably not going to go well. "I run reports all the time for all kinds of things."

"You run reports per request for specific projects."

"Yes, that's what I said." Kelly pushed her dark hair behind her ears before gnawing anxiously on the nail of her right pointer finger.

"So, tell me what reports you've run and for what project over the last two weeks." It was hard for Catherine not to notice how the nails of remaining fingers and thumbs were chewed almost to the quick, the skin red, swollen, and angry around each fingertip.

"All of them, that's going to take a long time to discuss." She checked her watch. "I'm supposed to leave at three today."

"Just the reports related to medications." Catherine clarified. "And we should be done in plenty of time for you to clock out on time.

"I had a request from the pharmacy for all opioids over the last 30 days." She paused. "And Chloe asked me to run Pitocin."

"Chloe's no longer working here and hasn't for almost a month."

"It wasn't specifically for her; I think it was for a committee. I gave it to Madison." Kelly blinked rapidly, her dark eyes darting back and forth as she alternated chewing on the other fingers of the same hand.

"What else?" Catherine transcribed Kelly's responses, looking up from the documents and waiting for her to continue.

"Infection control asked me to run utilization for all vaccines." She paused, rolling her eyes up in her head to indicate to Catherine that she was thinking about the request. "I think that was it?"

"What about Anodyne?"

"I don't think I ran a utilization report for that drug."

Catherine pulled a report, several pages long, from her satchel and placed it on top of the desk. "You did last week."

"I don't remember why I ran that one?" She didn't make eye contact with Catherine. Instead, Kelly's gaze was focused on the wall behind Catherine's desk.

"What about patients who had active orders for ketamine, midazolam, and fentanyl?"

"I can't recall who asked for that one either."

"What did you do with the data?" Catherine pushed the report closer to Kelly. "You ran this one nine days ago."

"I didn't give it to anyone."

"There's print encounters for both reports requested by you on the same dates as you run the reports. It was printed on the printer in medical records."

"I don't recall running the report or printing it?" Her words were short, precise, as if she were speaking to a child. She dropped her hands to her side, tucked slightly under her legs as if she needed her hands to be restrained.

Catherine dialed the phone on her desk without breaking eye contact and spoke calmly

into the receiver once the call was answered. "Jamie, Can you walk over to my office?"

"What's going on?" The medical records department manager's words were easily audible through the phone.

"I have Kelly in my office and I'm placing her on suspension pending the results of a HIPAA breach."

"I'll be right there," Jamie advised before the line went dead.

"Virginia, Can you call HR and ask someone from HR to join us, preferably Brittany?" Catherine called from inside the office, still seated at her desk.

"Already have," Virginia responded, her words transported through the open space between them like the wind. "She's on her way."

Brittany appeared about ten minutes after Virginia had made the request. Unlike the last early morning encounter when Catherine had seen her, this time she was dressed to the nines in a slim fitting sleeveless yellow dress, a strand of white pearls hung from her neck, the middle pearl placed strategically between her breasts. Her earrings matched the necklace, pearl studs stuck glue-like to delicate her ear lobes.

Sometimes, she pinned her long blonde hair up, either in a single ponytail in the back or pinned above each ear with shiny, sparkly hair pins. Today, it hung loosely around her shoulders, framing her face so that she looked almost angelic.

With minimal make-up and feet encased in off white heels with a thick heel, she would fit perfectly as if she were participating in a California photo shoot. All that was missing was a picturesque beach as a backdrop.

"Hey," she announced coming through the front office door and making a beeline for Catherine's office. She stopped short at the office door after seeing Kelly sitting comfortably in the chair at Catherine's desk.

"Hi," she drug the one-syllable word out, as if it were two, maybe three syllables and held her hand out toward Kelly and Catherine. Even with Brittany's hands palm up, Catherine could decipher all five perfectly manicured nails.

"I'm going to need you to wait outside, Kelly," Brittany said, wasting no time with peripheral conversation or small talk. "If you'll have a seat in the waiting area, Catherine will come and get you after we talk with your department manager." The way she'd interacted with the employee was as if she'd directed her to wait for a table at a crowded, popular club.

"Jamie is on her way," Catherine advised, wondering what was keeping her.

"Great," Brittany said again, making the word seem longer than it was. She smiled, revealing two rows of perfectly aligned white teeth.

Brittany waited until Kelly had vacated the office before closing the door and claiming the seat she'd vacated. "So, what's this about?" She checked her watch, "I may have to leave before we finish here. I'm expecting corporate to come and participate in the discussion with the OR staff and the police regarding Dr. Paine's overdose."

"Hi," another woman said as she slipped between the door and the frame and pushed the office door closed again. "Sorry, I wanted to see what other reports Kelly's been associated with since Dr. Beliard's suicide."

"Before we talk about that," Brittany interrupted, her words spilling over her tongue as if she were leading a discussion. "Tell me what brought us to this point."

"I'm not sure," Jamie said, folding her documents dismissively in her lap.

"How were you alerted to Kelly's unauthorized document searches?"

"A staff member in medical records completed an incident report that included a complaint that Kelly was using corporate time and resources to work on a non-work-related project," Catherine answered, handing the incident report to Brittany. "I had IT run her report history for the last 4 months and these two searches stood out as unusual."

Brittany looked to the report at the two searches Catherine had indicated and tapped the top one. "Obviously, this one caught your attention because of the investigation going on in the OR?" She tapped the remaining one. "What was it about Anodyne that made you curious?"

"I'd rather not say," Catherine answered. "It's part of something we've just started looking at."

"We've?" Brittany repeated.

"It's very early in the review, Brittany." Catherine sighed, sitting back in her chair. "Just a practice pattern that seems odd at this point. It would be preemptive to discuss it."

"I'm the director of human resources," Brittany barked sounding more like one of the college mean girls. "There's not a situation where withholding anything from me would be appropriate."

"With all due respect, Brittany" Catherine stood to her feet, hands braced against the top of her desk. "Your primary scope of service deals directly with hiring and firing of employees. Quite frankly, that's really all your entitled to be involved in."

She shuffled several folders into a straight pile. "We have a dead physician upstairs who overdosed on the exact combination of medications this employee ran reports on. This same remnant combination of products was found in the public restroom here on site."

Catherine picked up the receiver of the phone on her desk. "This employee is going to be suspended without pay until she tells me who she gave the utilization report to." She waited as the phone rang at the other end. "The only question I have for you is do you want to do the suspension or shall I have someone from corporate come down and do it?"

"Hang up," Brittany's face was red. "Tell me what you need me to do."

"She's to be suspended pending the outcome of our investigation, or until she tells us who she provided the data to." Catherine handed Brittany a copy of the incident report.

"Nothing about the other report?" Brittany's words were short and precise.

"Not at this time." Catherine replaced the received and reclaimed her seat. She turned to Jamie. "Can I see what your results were?"

Catherine scanned the document quickly, eyeballing each row for anything that seemed to be related to what she and Ryan had termed, the suicide conspiracy. Nothing stood out as peculiar to her but sometimes a second look was warranted. "Can you make me a copy of that?"

Jamie nodded. "You can have this one. It's a copy." She paused. "Should we call Kelly back in and suspend her till she complies with the directive?"

"Yes," Brittany said but didn't move.

"Are you delivering the suspension to her?" Jamie paused. "Or am I?"

"You are the department head. "Technically you have to be the one to suspend her or terminate her."

"Really?" Catherine questioned, remembering that Bailey had been fired without Ryan's participation. "Is that written down in some policy somewhere?"

"Yes, I can provide you a copy."

"I'd like that, thank you." Catherine didn't look away from Brittany's glare. If she'd been keeping score, she'd have tallied one for her side.

Chapter 23

"Why are we meeting here at the Walk again?" Ryan asked, her heels clicking in perfect rhythm against the concrete sidewalk. She pointed to a table and laughed, noticing it was the same table they'd shared the previous time when they'd run into Dr. Paine and the reporter, Tim Hartmann.

"I can't take the risk of Noah, Erin, or Oliver, overhearing anything about the key or the vault's contents. I still can't really believe it." Catherine explained. "And I feel as if I'm drowning in that office."

"Is there anything conclusive regarding Dr. Paine's death?" Ryan asked, motioning to the server that she wanted a drink menu.

"Not yet, the police did report there are no other fingerprints except Paine's on the syringe used to inject the medications or on the vials used to draw up them up."

"For all intents and purposes, he overdosed?" Ryan asked, finally settling on a mixed drink.

"There was no note and nothing to indicate foul play," Catherine explained. She gave her drink order to the server and waited for the server to vacate the area. "How did it go downtown?"

"It was an odd meeting; I presented an update that we'd termed the agreement with HAS." She spread a series of documents on the tabletop. "We asked that HAS return eleven million back to us."

"Congratulations!" Catherine reached across the table and playfully punched Ryan's shoulder. "That's quite a feather for your first cap, don't you think?"

"I thought so," Ryan looked around. "But to tell you the truth, Fleming seemed almost angry that we were pulling out of the contract. She kept asking if there was any way the relationship could be salvaged. If HAS was able to obtain the market points in the contract, could they be allowed to continue in their current capacity."

She paused as the server delivered their drinks. "Fleming seemed bored with my presentation. She couldn't have been less interested, she played on her phone almost throughout my entire discussion.

"What about Erin or any of our other administrators?"

"Erin was only slightly more interested." She smiled, trying to hold back the laughter. "I thought Oliver was going to bust, he was already counting how much of that money he was hoping to get as part of the capital budget."

"What about Noah?"

"He just sat there, in silent indifference." She took a big gulp of her alcoholic drink. "He didn't ask a question or applaud. He simply sat there sucking up the air."

"So, what happened? Did the commissioners and other corporate executives accept your recommendation?

"Yes," she smiled. "After the corporate meeting, I drove to Charlotte and met with Calvin."

"Calvin?" Catherine repeated.

"My chemist friend, the one I've been sending the samples to. We went to pharmacy school together. He runs a lab locally that works closely with the police and FBI as well as local hospitals and businesses."

"He provided us with the full report for the potassium chloride."

"What do you mean?"

"We seldom infuse more than 10 milliequivalents in 100 ml of fluid over less than one hour. In some cases, where a patient might be severely fluid restricted, you could give up to 20 milliequivalents."

"What was the concentration of potassium in the bag you sent to Calvin's lab for testing?"

"The concentration of potassium in the IV bag was well over what would have been considered therapeutic."

"Meaning?"

"The amount of potassium in the 100ml bag was almost as much as what we'd have put in a liter bag and infused over about four hours."

"How much was that?"

"About forty milliequivalents."

"And we are sure pharmacy didn't add it to the bag?"

"No, like I said before. We don't add anything to a premixed product."

"And the syringes found in the bathroom?"

"Fentanyl, Midazolam, and glycopyrrolate," Ryan paused, "in the exact concentrations as in the vials that we carry."

"Did you receive the results electronically or hard copy?" Catherine asked almost as an afterthought. The recent issues with IT were heavy on her mind. She was sure someone at a high level was involved with the disappearance of Anwar's variance report. No doubt these results would be similarly tempting.

"Calvin was going to forward the results to me electronically but I told him to wait a bit. Instead, I have a hard copy results of both Beliard's IV bag and for the syringes that were found in the bathroom."

Catherine patted Ryan's satchel, "Good thinking. Are you keeping them in a safe place until Cole can collect them from you?"

"Yeah, but not in there and not in my office, either office."

"Good," Catherine smiled. 'Did you check your email before you left for the day?"

"No," Ryan shook her head. "I try not to read any emails during the last hour of the day. Why?"

"Noah sent an email that Fleming will be touring tomorrow with a guest?"

"A guest," Ryan repeated. "You mean, like a celebrity guest?' She thought of Dr. Randall's plastic surgery cases and hoped it would be someone she'd know; someone she'd be excited to meet.

"No, we could never be so lucky," Catherine whined. "The governor's aid is expected to stop by sometime tomorrow. Noah asked that each department head ensure their areas are ready to be visited in case they stop by."

"Wonder what the governor is up to?" Catherine finished her drink and motioned for the server to bring her another.

"I don't suppose he's coming to reassign Fleming?" Ryan asked, pulling out her phone and dialing Cole. "I did hear a while back that he was shopping the system."

"Yeah, I heard that too." Catherine nodded, "but who's going to buy us with all the problems we have. Even if there was a flashing blue light on top of the roof, I doubt we'd get any takers."

"Guess that depends, given all the issues, I'm sure the sale price would be competitive. Think of the possibilities if some of the challenges were corrected, what the profit margin might be." Ryan dropped her phone back in her satchel and drummed her fingers atop the table.

"You sound more and more like a COO and less like a pharmacy manager with every day that passes." Catherine laughed.

****

"Sorry, I'm late," Cole pulled the empty chair between them out and slid into it, motioning for the server before his backside was flush in the chair. He kissed Ryan on the cheek and loosened his tie almost in the same motion.

"Beer, whatever's on tap." He mouthed to the server before she was fully to the table. He pointed to Ryan and Catherine's empty glasses. "You guys want another?"

"We've had two already," Ryan smiled, taking his hand. "Do you have any news for us?"

"Yes," he tossed a few peanuts in his mouth, looking anxiously past Ryan to see if the server was on her way back with his beer. "Erik is joining us as soon as he can, he's caught in traffic." He paused. "I heard about your overdose. That was the doctor I met last time we were here, right?"

"Yes," Catherine shook her head and asked the server to refill her and Ryan's water glasses.

"I'm sorry for your loss," he said to them both, but his eyes were fixated on Ryan's.

"Honey," he said moving as close to her as the table would allow. "I've soon news about your friend."

"Did he finally turn up," Ryan laughed. "I'm going to bust his balls for not returning my calls." She pulled her phone from her pocket. "Where was he, visiting with his family in New York?"

"No, honey, he wasn't" Cole looked to Catherine, licking his bottom lip before continuing. "I'm so sorry, honey. I know you'd been friends for a while."

Ryan disconnected the call and slid her phone back in her jacket pocket. "What are you saying?"

"His body washed up along the river this morning. Some fishermen found him tangled in a fishing net and stuck within the rocks along the bank."

"There must be some mistake." She stopped, looking pleadingly back and forth from Catherine to Cole. "He can't be dead. I mean, I saw him a few weeks ago." She pulled her hand from Cole's and took Catherine's. "You were there. You spoke to him. He was fine."

She wiped quickly at the tears as they trailed down her cheeks, her words softer and softer until she couldn't repeat it anymore. "He was fine. He was fine."

Ryan was silent, looking past Catherine to the shops on the other side of the busy street. "Could you excuse me for a minute?" She stood and walked behind the table, leaving her purse and satchel on the table.

"Where are you going?" Catherine asked, spinning around in the chair so she could hear Ryan's response.

"Bathroom," Ryan answered, walking away from the table, her eyes locked on the small coffee shop across the street.

"I'll go with you," Catherine jumped to her feet and followed behind her, taking her by the arm just as she stepped from the curb and into the crosswalk. "The bathroom is this way." She pointed back toward the direction they'd came, past the table where Cole was still sitting.

"I want to go to the one at the coffee shop." She pulled her arm away. "Nathan's probably over there. We've met there before for coffee; he likes the swing."

"Ryan," Catherine stepped in front of her, prohibiting her crossing the street any further. "He's not there." She took her hand. "Let's go back to our table. Cole is waiting there for you."

Catherine watched as Ryan's head turned toward the restaurant and she waved to Cole.

"I'll be right back." Ryan pointed behind him to the ladies' room inside the restaurant and stepped back onto the sidewalk, making her way back to the table.

Catherine walked alongside her, stopping once they reached the table. 'You want me to go with you?"

"No," Ryan shook her head. "I'm fine. Just give me a minute."

"Of course," Catherine took her seat and watched as Ryan maneuvered through the sidewalk tables and disappeared into the restaurant.

She turned to Cole. "How did he die?"

"He was shot, execution style, back of the head." Cole motioned to the server and held up two fingers indicating he wanted two more beers. "The ME's preliminary report is that he died instantly. There was no water in his lungs indicating he was dead before his body was dumped in the water."

"Any idea on how long he's been dead?" Catherine couldn't help but remember him just a few weeks ago, healthy and alive in Ryan's office.

"Hard to say without an autopsy but the officers working the crime scene seem to think it's been in the water for at least a week."

"A week?" Catherine repeated. "He'd probably been dead the entire time the FBI's been looking for him."

"Probably," Cole motioned to the restaurant where Ryan was making her way back to the table. "She's coming back."

He waited for her to get comfortably seated before asking. "You okay?"

"Yes," she took a big drink from his beer. "I just can't believe he's gone." She wiped her eyes as if she could will the tears not to fall. "I can't help but think this is all my fault. I'm responsible for what happened to him."

"That's not true, Ryan." Catherine took her hand. "He brought you into it when he reported what happened with Aaron and the sales representative."

"Nathan wasn't sure he should say anything." Ryan swallowed the knot in her throat. "I convinced him to make a statement."

"You were bound by subpoena, Ryan" Catherine reminded her. "You had no choice. You were legally bound to share what he told you with the FBI and the OIG."

"All that seems little in comparison to the fact that a man is dead, a man I cared about." Ryan took another drink and folded her head into her hands.

Catherine nodded, knowing exactly how Ryan felt.

"Excuse me." Everyone including Ryan turned toward the voice, waiting as the newcomer came to a stop near the table.

Catherine knew the stranger was familiar, someone from work maybe but she couldn't be sure.

He was short for a man, with dirty blonde hair that hung just to his shoulder and black plastic glasses that made his eyes look large and round. His plaid shirt was buttoned almost to his Adam's apple, he looked more like a college laboratory technician than a well-seasoned pharmacist.

Any reservations she had were answered seconds later as Ryan wiped her eyes and leaned closer to Cole. "What do you want?"

"I just wanted to talk to you." His words were soft as he held out his hand to her. "I need you to reconsider."

"Jayson, "Ryan looked across the table to Catherine even as she said his name. "There's nothing to discuss. We've severed the terms of your employment."

"But it's not fair," he stepped past Cole, drawing as close to Ryan as he could. "I didn't do anything wrong."

"I'm sorry," she said again. "It's out of my hands."

"You have to reconsider." His teeth were clenched, his face reddening. "I have a family to support."

"I'm sorry," she said again.

"Listen," he grabbed her shoulder. "I---"

"Back off!" Cole pushed himself to his feet and pushed Jayson from behind away from her. "It's time for you to leave."

Jayson took two big steps back to where he'd been standing, close enough to touch her again. "I'm talking to her," He pushed his glasses tight against his face and stared down Cole. "Not you."

Cole shoved him harder away from the table so that Jayson stumbled backward, his feet tangling together so that he nearly fell to the pavement.

"I'm not going to ask you again to leave." Cole advanced closer to him.

"Cole?" Ryan said, taking his hand and pulling him back to the table. "Come and sit down." She looked back to Jayson. "He's leaving, weren't you Jayson?"

Jayson took several steps backward, pointing to the table as Cole reclaimed the seat next to her. "You're going to be sorry," He finger-combed his hair from one side to the other. "Just wait and see."

Cole stood up again, pulling his jacket open to reveal his sidearm. "Are you threatening her?"

Ryan pulled at Cole's arm again, urging him back to his seat. "He's just venting, honey."

"You'll be sorry," Jayson screamed again as he walked backward away from the table, his words growing louder with the widening space between them, until he disappeared behind the building.

"We'll need to notify Brittany tomorrow morning when you get into work." Catherine watched the space between the buildings as if she expected him to reemerge maybe brandishing a weapon of some sort.

"He's harmless," Ryan added as she turned in her chair to check the last place she'd seen Jayson.

"Those are always the ones you have to watch." Catherine drank the last drop of wine in her glass and motioned for the server to bring her a refill.

****

The sun had made its way down the sky and dropped below the horizon about an hour or so before Catherine saw the older man approaching their table. With the sun in her eyes, she couldn't really make out his face but the purposeful way he walked closer to where she, Ryan, and Cole sat as well as the custodial way he clutched the worn satchel against his hip alerted her to the notion, it was Erik.

He looked older than she remembered from the last time she'd seen him, at Ryan's place. His hair seemed gray, griseous even and thinner as it was secured against his neck by a narrow hair band. He was wearing jeans, faded and worn, from use not because they were designer. Even odder was his shirt, it seemed out of place as if he'd been wearing a suit and tie but decided to utilize only the dress shirt.

By the time he'd approached the table, Cole turned to investigate what had Catherine's attention. He was aware she'd been looking past him toward something or someone further down the sidewalk.

"Erik," he said, standing and walking about half the way to where the man was before stopping and waiting. Once the man approached him, they shook hands and made their way back to the table.

It took only a few minutes for Cole to reintroduce everyone before he pointed to the empty seat beside him. "Grab a seat." He waved the server over. "You want a drink?"

"Just water," Erik answered, his voice soft, yet gravelly as he folded his long, lean body into the chair, his hands never letting go of the satchel.

"I'm sorry," he leaned forward so that he was nearly in the table's center. "I've been following the news," He paused and exchanged glances with Cole. "It's disheartening everything that's happening to your corporation."

"Do you live around here?" Catherine asked, pushing the basket of the bread closer to him.

"Yes," he smiled, displaying perfect white teeth. "Most of my life," he looked around. "And both my kids went to school here locally."

"How did you two meet?" Catherine smiled and waved back and forth between Cole and Erik.

Erik paused, looking at Cole for an extended period of time before answering. "We worked a case together, many years ago." He patted Cole on the shoulder so forcefully, Cole's body rocked back and forth in response. "Boy's like the son I never had."

He laughed and exchanged another glance with Cole. "I have two daughters." His hand fell away from where Cole was sitting and wrapped around the water glass placed in front of him by the server. "Almost became my son-in-law but that didn't work out."

Catherine's attention moved quickly from Cole to Ryan, noticing the flush that came over them both. "That might have been a bit awkward?"

He gulped the water as if it were spiked and shrugged, rolling his eyes as if he were a teenager. "Not really, they parted as friends?" He looked to Cole, "Right?"

Cole nodded and looked across the table to Ryan.

"How'd you two meet?" Erik indicated to Ryan and Cole.

"At a charity run," Ryan answered, moving her glass to the side and wiping at the wet place it had made on the tablecloth.

"Did you outrun him?" Erik nudged Cole, laughing as if he'd told a joke.

"Actually," Ryan cleared her throat. "Neither of us finished the race."

"Why's that?"

Catherine looked up from her drink, anxiously awaiting Ryan's answer. They had talked a lot about Cole over the last few months. There were several things she knew about him, except how they'd met.

270

"One of the runners behind me had an event and needed help." Ryan began. "I stopped and went back to help him, Several people stopped to help me, Detective Spencer was one of them."

"So," Erik gloated. "Technically, she was ahead of you, when the runner went down?"

"Yes," Cole answered; his eyes locked with Ryan's.

"So, she probably would have finished before you?"

"Not necessarily," Ryan smiled. "There was still a lot of race left to run." She looked away before looking back to him. "And he was just a few paces behind me." She took a long drink of water, looking over the glass to Cole. "It was still anyone's race."

This was a new side of Ryan, Catherine thought, a flirty, sexy one that she liked very much. She glanced quickly to Cole, hoping he didn't turn out to be another disappointment for her.

****

"You sure you want to talk about this here?" Erik asked, pushing his water glass more fully into the center of the table and holding on to his satchel possessively.

"It's loud," Cole pointed toward the front of the Greek restaurant next door where a small band and several dancers were engaging the crowd. "And be discreet."

"We could go back to my house?" Ryan offered; her eyes glued to Erik's satchel.

"No," Cole shook his head and watched as Erik unfastened the satchel and sorted through its contents. "What did you find out?"

Erik placed the photo Beliard had sent to Catherine's face down on the table. "We already identified most of these men in the photo." He tapped an image in the middle of the photo. Unlike the other men in the photo, he wasn't wearing a black suit and white shirt. This man was younger than the others and was adorned in a long white laboratory coat.

Erik scooted his chair as close to the table as he could, looking more like a jack-in-the-box than a man. "This guy in the middle—" he turned to inspect the immediate behind his chair. "His name was Sidney Gottlieb." He exhaled. "He led a project in the '50s called MKUltra."

"What kind of project?" Cole asked, picking the picture up and pulling it closer for a better look.

"It was a CIA mind control project. It was known by other names as well but that's the most widely accepted name for the project."

Cole handed the photo back to Erik. "Go on."

"Project MK-ULTRA was a joint partnership between the CIA and the US Army Biological Warfare Lab. It was officially sanctioned in 1953, downsized twice, once in 1964 and again in 1967. It was supposedly halted in 1973 but there are documents that contradict that," Erik whispered, and motioned to the server that he wanted a beer.

"Mind control?" Catherine repeated rubbing her head. "How's that even possible?"

Erik waited for the server to deliver his beer before continuing. "The program manipulated people's mental state by using drugs and other chemicals, hypnosis, sensory deprivation, isolation, verbal as well as sexual abuse." He took a long drink from the bottle and tapped the bottom on top of the table. "The research took place in multiple places including universities, hospitals, prisons, and pharmaceutical companies. The CIA operated by using these organizations as a front for the experiments."

"How could something like this happen?" Ryan words were hoarse. "Why would our government allow this?"

"To defeat the Soviet Union during the cold war," Cole added.

"Initially, but once the CIA realized its utility, it served other purposes." Erik shook his head in agreement. "In 1975 its secrets were exposed by the church committee of the Senate. At that time, the CIA director, Richard Helms, ordered all the documents destroyed."

"This is madness," Catherine said, her mind spinning with the implications. "If everything was destroyed how did you find all this out? And how was Dr. Beliard involved in all this?" She held her breath as she asked the question but deep within the chambers of her heart, she knew.

He would have been too young to have been in the picture he'd sent to her or the others he'd hidden in the vault but she knew just as surely as if he'd been standing there with him. He was one of the doctors who performed those hideous experiments. He'd willingly raped other human beings of their ability to choose a journey, he'd taken away their free will and instead merged their minds with the will of others.

"Documents continue to be declassified as they surface, bits and pieces mostly but enough to know the program did exist and continued long after 1975. One document mentions getting close enough to Fidel Castro to change his behavior. And another more recent document speaks to an ongoing study with dogs whose behaviors were modified by remote-controlled after having implants surgically placed." He paused, "And I suspect you've already formed an opinion of how your ex-husband was involved."

"I have a theory," she whispered, "but I'd like to hear it from you."

"Jacob Fleming was a high-ranking military officer with deep ties to both the CIA and the US Army, most specifically the biological research unit of the US Army." He paused. "Jacob was the details man. Once an assignment was approved by his CIA superiors, he set the wheels in motion. He devised the plan and selected the personnel, some willing, others weren't." His attention turned to Catherine. "When they weren't willing, especially if they were in a position to advance the cause, that's where Dr. Beliard came in. He supervised the medical treatment of both the soldiers and non-military participants."

Erik folded all the documents together and slid them into a padded envelope, handing them to Cole. "At some point, Beliard wanted out, he wanted to retain the identity he'd been assigned."

"That's when he and Jacob started having issues?" Catherine asked but she didn't wait for an answer. "He thought he'd just slip into this pseudo-life and everything would be okay,"

"Jacob loved him like a brother," Erik nodded. "It certainly seems as if Jacob was willing to let him out, let him have the life as fake as it was."

"The CIA killed Jacob?" Cole asked.

"At some point, I think the pressure of having Beliard out in the open was a weak link and they fear they'd be exposed." Erik tapped the envelope. "There's no evidence to support that claim but knowing how the CIA operated back then, I'd say it's a definite possibility."

"Do you think they had Beliard killed?" Catherine asked, her lips barely able to form the words.

"I think his death is related to Jacob Fleming and the MK-ULTRA program," Erik answered, not making eye contact with her. "I can't say for sure he was killed or if he knew they were going to call him back to duty and couldn't return to that life?"

"He told me he was waiting for the FBI to help him?" She whispered but not so that anyone could hear.

"This is like a movie or something." Cole shook his head, leaning as far against the He back of the chair as he could. "I can't believe any of this is real, is just too much." He dropped his hands atop the table. "There are drugs that can assimilate this?" Cole paused, his fingers rubbing his brow. "My God, what kind of drugs would be used to do that?"

Before Erik could answer, Ryan responded as if on autopilot. "LSD or an LSD- like medication." She looked up to face the others, her face pale. "LSD can do that."

Chapter 24

"Why didn't you come to bed last night?" Ryan asked sleepily as she yawned and made her way down the steps. The floor against her bare feet was cold and as she tied the belt of the worn fuzzy robe she'd thrown on, she wished she'd thought to step into the Christmas slippers tucked under the bed as well.

"I meant to," Cole pointed to the sofa where the cushions were smashed strategically against one another, the indentation of a body was clearly visible as if had been chalked at a crime scene. "But I wanted to finish go over everything we found in both boxes." He waved to the coffee table where several stacks of pictures and documents were visible.

"Knowing the pieces Erik was able to provide," He paused. "It's starting to make some sense."

"You're kidding," she fell close to him, "I don't understand any of this," She took his hand. "And Catherine must be beside herself realizing she really didn't know Beliard at all."

"Maybe she really did know the real him," he said. "Perhaps, it was all those other personalities that were fake." He kissed Ryan's hand. "Look who he turned to when the chips were down."

"Tell me again, why you slept down here?"

"Do you have a video camera?" He dropped her hand gently against her lap.

"Somewhere upstairs in the closet maybe?" She held up her phone. "Can't we just use my phone?"

"No, I want to make a recording of everything we know so far and then put it in a safe place."

"Cole," she pushed his hair away from his eyes. "You think that's really necessary?"

"Yes, I do." He wandered toward the kitchen, stopping at the coffee maker. "What's the name of the FBI agent that you've been talking to?"

"Bronson," she answered, jumping from the couch and pulling a business card from her briefcase. "What do you want to talk to him for?"

"Is his first name Frank?" Cole looked away from the coffee maker, as if testing the theory, it might begin to brew once he wasn't watching it.

She checked the business card and nodded. "Do you know him?"

"Very well," he nodded, trying to contain a smile. "We've been friends for a long time."

"He's not my friend," she broke in. "He's trying to discredit me and convince everyone I'm committing fraud."

"He's just doing his job, honey. You'll see, once he sees you've done nothing wrong, he'll move on to the next lead."

"What could he possibly do to help us?"

We're out in the open here, exposed without any backup," he poured two cups of coffee and pushed the lever of the toaster down. "It's time to call in some reinforcements I think." He reclaimed the seat next to her. "Once I've made the tape, I'm going to put it someplace safe and give him a key. He won't know where it is, but in the event, something happens to us, he'll be notified where the security box is."

"Maybe we should drop this, just get out," She joined him in the kitchen. "Take McKenzie and leave, start again somewhere else."

He wrapped his arms around her, resting his chin on the top of her head. "It's too late for that now, I don't think that's an option." He kissed her forehead. "All we can do is try and expose them."

She fished the bread from the toaster and spread a spoonful of grape jelly on both before refilling both coffee cups. "I've got to get to work." She slid the plate with the toast toward him and checked her phone. "There's an issue with one of the technicians."

"What kind of issue?" he asked.

"Not sure exactly, something about automated dispensing cabinets not getting refilled last night." She disappeared back up the stairs. "I'll know more once I get there."

"Is McKenzie home tonight?" He called upstairs as he sat the cups and plates into the sink.

"Yeah," She called back, over the running water of the shower.

He smiled, throwing his shirt in the plastic hamper as he climbed the stairs and passed the laundry room. By the time he reached the landing upstairs, he'd stepped out of his jeans and underwear.

"Room for one more?" he asked, opening the shower door and stepping inside, his arms open wide to her in the invitation.

She fell hungrily against him, grateful for his warmth and support. Her kisses were at his neck, hands roaming up and down the long length of his back.

"I love you," he moaned against her throat, holding to her as tightly as he could.

Even if she hadn't been naked, her body on his, he would have felt the change. It wasn't that she froze, she didn't. It was more of a pause, a moment of indecision before he felt her pull away.

"What's wrong?" he asked, as the water from the shower fell like rain between them.

"Nothing," she didn't meet his stare. She brushed the wet hair from her eyes, "I just—"

"You aren't sure if you're in love with me?" He took a step back, his back colliding with the thick plastic wall of the shower stall.

"After my divorce," she stepped closer to him, almost touching his chest, but not. "I was so lost, so broken. I didn't think I would ever be whole again."

Her hand touched his chest gently, "For so long, I wasn't interested in a relationship with anyone, anyone that wasn't my ex." She kissed his chest and pulled him from the wall closer against her, "Then I met you and things started to change."

"I'm not asking you to make any commitments but I have to know this means more to you than just sex?"

His truthfulness took her by surprise and she flinched as if he'd hit her. "It does. And I'm so grateful to have you in my life right now but for now, this is all I have to give."

Cole collected her in his arms and pushed her against the wall, lifting her up and sliding himself between her legs in a single motion. "At some point," he mumbled against her breast, "I'm going to want more." He licked and suckled at her breast, satisfied at the soft hum she sang as he slid himself into her.

At first he pumped slowly against her, however, his pace became more frantic as she urged him with her body to move his more quickly. His thrusts became faster and harder to meet hers until he was lost, lost in the heat between her legs and the smell of her skin as her body cascaded around his.

He pulled her arms as high over her head as he could and pumped furiously into her until he was empty and felt himself falling around her. He gave her a few minutes to recover, held on until her breathing return to normal and eased her down the wall. He didn't let go of her until he was sure her feet were on the floor, then he backed away and flipped the shower off.

"You want to dinner tonight?" he asked. "If McKenzie wants to join us, she can pick the place."

Ryan looked curiously at him. "I'll ask her. Are you angry because I didn't say I love you back?"

"No," he rubbed the towel over his head as if he were in a hurry. "I understand, I do." He stepped into clean underwear and dress pants. "But I meant what I said, I don't want to be just a quick "fix" for you." He pulled on a dress shirt, buttoning it quickly. "I want to build a life with you and McKenzie. We can't do that if we only get together for sex when she's with her Dad." He sat on the bed, sliding his feet into dark colored socks and shiny leather dress shoes.

With necktie in hand, he leaned into her and kissed her on the cheek. "I'll see you tonight for dinner."

She smiled, "Dinner tonight, the three of us." She kissed him again, "No sex, Huh?"

"Not tonight," he waved before disappearing down the steps.

"Be careful," she yelled down to him from the landing, bending to collect his jeans and underwear from the floor.

"You too," she heard him say just before the doorbell chimed throughout the house.

****

Ryan carried his clothes into her bedroom, pulling the closet door open to where she kept the upstairs hamper. It wasn't unusual for her to remove items from his pockets before tossing them in the laundry with hers. Most of the time, the items were of little consequence, loose change, a piece of gum, watch batteries and other similar accessories. Once he'd left his wallet in the back pocket, she'd driven the twenty plus miles to Providence to drop it by the police station.

Ryan knew whatever was in his pocket wasn't change or even a wallet but it was a document of some kind, folded several times as if he'd put it away for safekeeping. She removed it before tossing his clothes into the hamper and made her way absentmindedly to the bureau, planning simply to lay it there for safekeeping but something caught her eye and she found herself unfolding it hurriedly.

Her schedule? It was her work schedule for the last two weeks, every person she'd met with and for how long was printed in black and white on an excel spreadsheet. She folded it back like she found it and replaced it in his jeans pocket as if she'd missed it.

The hospital used different software for scheduling, not the spreadsheet version he had in his possession. It was almost as if he'd "hacked" into some other application and downloaded it from her computer at work.

What was he up to? For God's sake was he following her? Maybe Catherine was right, maybe Cole Spencer had been a part of this scheme all along, maybe he still was?

****

"Why didn't you just ask him why he had it?" Catherine asked, moving around in her chair as if she were cold, and looking to see if the vent in the ceiling over her desk had been modified. The office was always cold but today it was downright freezing.

"He'd already left when I found it," Ryan explained. "What was I supposed to do, run outside naked, wrapped in a bath towel, and ask him?"

"No," Catherine smiled, "You could have called and asked?"

"You're the one who questioned if we could trust him?"

"That was before?"

"Before what?"

"Before he started working with us. Besides, he seems to really care about you." She checked her own schedule for the day. "I've got a meeting at corporate in an hour, you are going to be okay?"

"I've got to meet the architect in an hour to finalize the layout of the medication rooms in the new building." Ryan nodded. "I've got to talk with Louis before he leaves for the day."

"Isn't he one of your night technicians?"

"Yes, he works seven shifts on and then seven shifts off. Today's the last of his seven and I don't want to make him come in on his day off while I investigate the variance."

"What variance?" Catherine perked up, she thought of her Gremlin analogy again. She'd just closed out two variances since yesterday, no doubt there'd be at least six new ones submitted after she left for the night.

"May not actually be a variance," Ryan explained. "I don't know yet. One of the OR rooms in preop called me last night reporting that they were having challenges getting the automated cabinets filled with medications."

"They called you at home for that. Why didn't they just call the pharmacy and address it with the pharmacist-in-charge?" Catherine asked.

"Apparently, they did but the pharmacist was not able to convince the technician to complete the request."

"Is this the technician that has a twin?"

"Yes," Ryan explained. "His brother, Levi, is a transfer in from IT but they both work for me in the pharmacy."

Catherine checked her watched again. "I'm going to get on the road. Call me if you need help with Louis."

"I will," Ryan rose to her feet.

"And give Cole a chance to explain about having your schedule, maybe there's a very innocent reason."

"I hope so," Ryan smiled, exiting Catherine's office and pulling the door closed behind her. Her heels were loud against the tile floor as she passed by her own office, the door open wide. Everyone else's office door including Noah's was closed tight, she paused near the administrative door and looked to Virginia. "I have a meeting in the new building, I shouldn't be gone for more than an hour."

"Don't forget the grab a safety pack," Virginia pointed to a large box on top of the credenza on the wall outside of Noah's office.

"I hate wearing the helmet and glasses," Ryan whined but moved toward the box anyway.

Virginia laughed. "My favorite is the bright orange vest and the shoe covers." She stopped typing on her keyboard and rose to meet Ryan at the credenza. "Let me help you, the vests are so hard to zip."

Ryan stood still like a child as Virginia brought the two ends of the vest together at Ryan's waist and yanked the zipper up as hard as she could until the garment was snug around Ryan's chest.

Virginia handed her the helmet with plastic glasses and paper shoe covers stuffed inside before pulling Ryan's phone off the desk. "Don't forget your phone.

"Are you going alone?" Virginia asked before sitting back at her desk.

"Yes and no, I'm meeting the architect, but I think it's just us."

She pointed to Ryan's shoes. "Be careful in those shoes, that building is not a place to wander around in wearing those heels."

"I will," Ryan promised as she wandered out the door and down the hallway.

She saw his retreating figure about thirty feet down the long corridor outside of the pharmacy. He was just rounding the end of the hallway, stopping when he heard her call out. "Louis?"

She watched as he stopped and looked curiously from side to side. "Louis," she called again before he turned back to acknowledge her. "Hold on a second," she asked, moving the hard hat to the other hand and nearly running to catch up to him.

Louis was tall and thin, with dark eyes and hair cropped close around his forehead and ears. He was dressed in blue hospital scrubs and carrying a black hoodie over his arm. "Hey Boss," he smiled. "Wait, what do I call you now, since you aren't exactly my boss anymore."

"Until I get a replacement for Bailey, looks like your stuck with me." She motioned for him to step closer to the wall, out of the traffic of the busy walkway. "What happened last night with the OR?"

"Nothing," he shook his head. "Was actually a pretty quiet night."

"Why didn't you fill the automated cabinets with Anodyne when they called?"

"I told the pharmacist that we were out, there was none to put in the cabinet."

"Oh," she nodded, knowing that happened more times than she'd like. "I didn't realize we were out of stock. I'll talk to Bryan and the amount we're ordering."

"Yeah," he nodded, "I told him he might want to increase the amount we keep on the shelf."

"I'll see that he does," she said, as she motioned toward the hallway that led to the employee entrance. "You on your way out?"

He nodded. "Meeting my brother at the gym, then I have to get to class."

"How are classes going?" It was a small talk and she knew he was aware. The truth was, she didn't know much about the young technician and that fact that he worked nights did nothing to improve her ability to get to know him.

"I'll be done in the fall." He held the door open for her before following behind her. "You off to meetings already?"

"No, I've got some things to do in the new building." They were still walking in step, their pace almost even which given the difference in their height, she knew he was walking slower so she could keep up.

"Quite a building," he stopped on the sidewalk, at the periphery of the employee parking lot and looked behind them to the new building.

"Have you been able to take one of the staff tours?" She fumbled with the shoe covers and glasses stuffed in the hard hat.

"I did," he seemed excited. "The night shift doesn't also get an opportunity to participate but there was a tour starting last week just as my shift was ending and I asked the guide if I could tag along."

"It's pretty impressive, huh?" She balanced herself against the wall and pulled the covers over her shoes.

"It will be, once it's finished." He stepped off the sidewalk toward the first row of parked cars, where she knew a lot of the overnight staff parked.

"I heard there will be a big grand opening party or something like that?" he asked stopping near an older Toyota was parked.

"Yes, a gala," she answered, pushing the glasses over her nose and setting the hard hat gently on her head. She was having a very good hair day; it would be a shame to mess it up so early in the morning for the hour it would take to walk through the medication rooms on all three floors.

"Will the staff be able to come?" he asked, sliding the key into the door lock and pulling the door open. He threw the hoodie into the passenger's seat and leaned against the top of the car awaiting her answer.

"I don't see why not," she smiled and waved before making her way closer to the new building's entrance. "Thanks for letting me follow up about the service item."

"No problem," he waved back and climbed in the vehicle.

Chapter 25

Ryan tapped her fingers against the phone, checking again to see if she'd missed the architect's call. It wasn't like him to miss a meeting or even be late. In the short time, she'd been the interim COO, she'd interacted with him frequently. He was nothing if not prompt, efficient, and professional.

The building was massive, stretched across the property to mirror the existing building so that the halves converged together to appear from a distance as if it were a single entity. However, upon closer inspection and with an all-knowing eye, it was easy to pick out the seams where the old and the new met. Smoke and mirrors, she thought again and smiled.

She made her way toward the front of the new building to where she knew a working elevator was and she felt confident, she'd be able to lower the safety barrier and work the winch to move it up or down. There were only two buttons, one marked up and another marked down. How difficult could it be?

Ryan gripped the blueprint tightly in her hand, thinking she probably wouldn't need to use them. She'd been in and out of the building several times in both her capacity as pharmacy manager and chief operations officer, she knew which rooms on the new floors had been designated as medication rooms, even without room tags outside each door, she'd have no problem finding them.

She kicked several pieces of plasterboard from the doorway of the first room and turned the knob, hoping none had been keyed yet. Like the pharmacy areas in the old building, once the rooms were in use, no staff other than pharmacy personnel would have access.

She breathed a sigh of relief when the handle turned and the door snapped open as if by magic. It was dark and she used the ray of light that bled into the room from the hallway to find the light switch on the wall and flipped it on. The fluorescent lights flashed on, bathing the room in thick white waves so much so she felt like she needed sunglasses. She took a moment to surveil the room, giving her eyes a minute to adjust to the bright lights.

She walked the longest wall, counting the steps as she did so, and mentally adding the space she needed along the wall for the automated cabinets. Yes, she thought to herself. All the dispensing equipment would fit perfectly on the wall.

Pretending the empty spaces between her hands were disposal bins for regular trash, pharmaceutical waste, and hazardous waste, she measured the area allotted near the sink to validate they'd left enough room between the wall and the cabinet.

She paused at the door and took one last look around to make sure she'd verified everything on her mental list. She smiled and checked her phone again to see if the architect had made it over to the building after all and perhaps was waiting downstairs on the first floor for her. She wasn't really surprised to find there were no missed calls. She slid the phone back in her pocket and wandered down the hall in search of the other two medication rooms on the third floor.

The dimensions of the remaining rooms were similar to those of the first room which meant the layout would also be similar. She just really wanted to appease Nurse leadership and assure them everything they wanted in the medication rooms would fit. With everything that was going on, she didn't want to give Fleming a reason to fire her.

As she made her way down to the other floors, it was interesting to note how each floor was less finished than the first one she had toured. So, by the time she traveled down to the first floor, it was little more than a skeletonized frame of wires and beams mirrored by exposed plasterboard and pipes. The first floor looked more as if it were ground zero for demolition than a building preparing for a corporate gala in less than a month.

Ironically, the grand ballroom stood oddly out of place amid the rest of the floor. It was nearly completed and in grand style, no less. The interior designer had been hard at work, placing furniture, hanging window treatments and acquiring a vast array of artwork.

She intended only to take a peek inside the ballroom, but the time had gotten away from her as she roamed through the space, admiring the decorations, especially the artwork. There were grand pictures adorning every wall, some so large they took up most of the wall.

The sound of her heels was loud against the ceramic tile of the dance floor and the emptiness only made the echo louder as it bounced from wall to wall before finding its way back to her. Once the vibration had stilled, she turned to go back out the way she'd entered pausing for what she thought was someone approaching from the hallway on the other side of the room.

"Elvin?" She called out wondering if the architect had finally realized he'd missed the meeting and was hoping to catch the tail end of it.

She took a few steps toward the hallway, knowing that once she left the ballroom, space would be as before with open walls and wires hanging everywhere. And she knew the lighting in that part of the building wasn't good, recalling they'd needed flashlights when she'd met with the building inspector a few days ago.

"Mr. Hills?" she called again, louder this time and retracing her steps out of the room just as she'd entered. She reached for her phone and dialed Virginia's extension, wanting someone on the line as she made her way down the hallway and back to the exit.

"Virginia?" she said as soon as Virginia answered. "I'm in the new building –"

Her words were cut off by the whine of a metallic door as it closed against its frame, she turned to the direction of the noise. "Elvin Hills didn't show up for our meeting." She said as calmly as she could, feeling as if she were a child again and frightened by a storm outside.

"Everything ok? You sound a bit flustered?" Virginia asked.

"It's a bit creepy over here." She answered, hoping Virginia wouldn't pick up on the way her words shook as they crawled out of her mouth. "I'm on the first floor, nearly done."

"You want me to walk over?" Ryan knew Virginia was standing up from her desk as she'd asked the question. She could see it in her mind's eye.

"No, no" Ryan answered although she really wanted to scream, yes, yes. "I'm walking down the length of the long hallway now, just stay on the line with me."

"Did you see something, what's got you so out of sorts?" Virginia words were intermingled against a small piece of gum.

"A door or something closed a second ago."

"Was probably one of the construction crews."

"I thought that too, but I didn't see anyone and no one answered when I called out"

"Catherine's white van ghost stories got under your skin, too. Huh?" Virginia laughed.

If she only knew, Ryan thought but instead, she answered. "Maybe," she paused. "I'm at the exit. Thanks."

"Are you coming back to the office?" Virginia paused. "You left the door open, if you're out for the day, I'll close and lock the door."

"I'm going to a meeting at corporate, I'm not sure how long I'll be there." She pushed against the exit door, expecting to be blinded by the sun hanging high in the sky. Instead, she welcomed a cool breeze that hit her in the face. "Go ahead and lock it. If I come back, I've got my key."

"Will do," Virginia said before hanging up.

Ryan knew she was probably already making her way to the office door and securing it for the evening. There was no sense in leaving it to chance that she'd forget that's just the type of person Virginia was and Ryan knew she could rely on her.

****

Catherine watched Virginia pass by the office and heard Ryan's door clicked shut. "Is she gone for the day?" Catherine checked her watch wondering what time Ryan and Cole wanted her to stop by tonight. Although the meeting last night with Cole's CIA friend had been incredibly productive, everyone was nervous and jumpy, especially when a stranger or the server was near to their table. She was glad they were meeting in a more private location; Ryan's house was becoming more and more like their headquarters since the investigation had turned into a full-time project.

"She's not sure," Virginia appeared at the door and leaned against the doorframe, her arms folded across one another as if she were posing for a picture. "She just left the new building, the architect never showed up."

"Bet she gives him an earful tomorrow." Catherine smiled. "That empty building gives me the creeps."

"That's what Ryan said, too." Virginia pushed herself away from the door. "Ryan's on her way downtown, she wasn't sure if she's coming back or not today." Virginia pointed behind her to Ryan's office. "I closed and locked her door."

"Oh good." Catherine nodded, knowing Virginia didn't know about the items related to Beliard's code and Dr. Paine's suicide in Ryan's office. She hoped Virginia didn't realize how interested she was in the status of Ryan's locked office.

"Did I tell you Governor Smith's aid was this afternoon while you were out of the office?"

"No," Catherine's interest piqued, like a child on Christmas morning. "What did he want?"

"He stopped by to let Noah know that Governor Smith will be attending the gala. He'll need several tables reserved to seat about fifteen, preferably the best seats for the night."

"Anything else?" Catherine was trying not to laugh but it felt as if there only laughing or crying, nothing in between.

"Oh, and he wants to deliver the keynote address."

'But didn't we get that celebrity –"

Virginia cut her off, "Yes, she's already been paid and everything."

"What will you do?" Catherine felt bad for her; Virginia always ended up "fixing things."

"I'm sure we'll do as he requests, I'll wait for Noah to tell me to cancel the celebrity."

"I'm sorry," Catherine turned attention back to her work. "Anything I can do to help?"

"I'm going to get some soup before the cafeteria closes, you want anything?" Virginia asked, only halfway into Catherine's office.

"No, I ate leftovers from dinner last night." Catherine snatched her glasses from the top of the pile and slid them precariously across her nose as she waited for the newly submitted variance reports to load on her computer screen.

"You had dinner with Ryan and her friend last night?" Virginia hovered near the doorway.

"Yes," it wasn't a lie. They had eaten while they were at the restaurant listening to the details Erik had uncovered.

"What's he's like?" She paused. "I heard he's very good-looking?"

"He is, I guess," Catherine blushed. "She seems to be very happy with their relationship,"

"Good," Virginia nodded. "Can you listen for the phone? I'll just be a minute."

"Of course." Catherine's attention was drawn to the screen where four new variances were awaiting her review.

Luckily for Ryan, only one was related to a medication. Catherine scanned the data quickly recognizing it as the incident Ryan had mentioned before she left, the one she was hoping to catch the night technician before he left for the day.

"I'll just tag this one for her," she said to no one. "So, she doesn't forget to go in and complete the follow-up."

Catherine had just finished moving the report to Ryan's in the box when she heard the outside door open and heavy footsteps on the carpet, stopping at Ryan's door.

She jumped to her feet, taking several large steps to the doorway, hoping to catch whoever it was before they turned and left.

The man was tall and stocky, dressed in khaki pants and a polo shirt with the construction company's logo on the left breast pocket. He was breathing heavy and holding a hard hat against his hip.

She knew he was with the construction company but wasn't sure in what capacity. "Can I help you?" She asked, moving closer to him.

"Is she gone for the day?" He pointed to Ryan's door.

"Not sure, she's in a meeting downtown. Is there some time I can help you with?"

He shook his head and wiped droplets of sweat from his neck and the area of his chest at the shirt's open collar. "She was supposed to meet me at the new building. I've been over there for almost thirty minutes."

Catherine bit her lip, "You are?"

"Elvin Hills," he offered his hand to her. "I'm the chief architect for the project. We were supposed to measure her medication rooms."

"I think there's been some sort of scheduling hiccup." Catherine smiled. "She went over there early this afternoon to meet with you. She mentioned you didn't show and she did the measuring herself."

"Well," he stuttered. "That doesn't make any sense."

"What time was your appointment with her, Mr. Hills?"

"Was supposed to me today at 11 am but there was a note taped to my computer this morning that she changed the meeting to 2pm, instead." He rubbed his forehead, making the skin crinkle and turn stark white.

"Do you have the note?" Catherine asked, wondering who might have left it.

"No," he patted his pockets. "I didn't see a need to keep it." He moved the hat to the other arm. "I guess someone got their wires crossed." He smiled. "I'm glad she got what she needed, would you give her my apologies, please?"

"Of course," Catherine nodded, jumping back as Virginia burst into the room holding a small white container of soup in her hand.

"Mr. Hills," Virginia said, in her best Lucy Ball accent. "You got some splainin to do."

"We were just talking about what happened." Catherine motioned to Elvin. "He received a note that Ryan had changed the meeting to 2 pm today." She pointed with her thumb. "He's been over at the new building waiting for her."

Virginia took hurried, small steps to her desk and set the soup on the top before flipping her computer on. She pulled up Ryan's calendar. "I'm sorry Mr. Hills but her calendar reads 11 am this morning."

"I'm so sorry," he explained.

"I'm sure it's fine, Mr. Hills." Catherine cut it. "We're just glad you're okay and I think Ryan got what she needed."

"I'm glad," he said waving to them as he headed for the door. "Would you tell her to call me if she still needs something, we'll get it figured out. I promise."

"Of course," Catherine turned back toward her office only half listening. Instead, she was thinking of Detective Spencer and Ryan's calendar. She couldn't help but wonder if the two events were somehow related.

****

Catherine tapped at the door again, twisting and turning at the door as if she could see into the smoked glass at either side of the big double doors. Maybe she'd gotten her wires crossed again. Perhaps Ryan didn't intend for them to regroup tonight at her house. She took two steps off the front patio, wondering if she could tiptoe and peer into the garage window to determine if Ryan or Cole's car was parked inside.

She spun back around and returned to the door just as it swung open and Ryan peered around the door, cellphone at her ear. Catherine waited for Ryan to step back just enough to slide through the open door and snapping it closed behind her.

"Come in," Ryan mouthed and motioned Catherine further into the room. Ryan turned back and retreated to the family room, adjusting pictures and other mementos before coming to the kitchen counter and leaning against the hard surface.

"I already told you, Jayson," she said into the phone. "There's nothing I can do, it's out of my hands."

"Please," he said, his words crisp and clear through the phone. "It wasn't my fault. The nurse told me to administer the med, I was just trying to help."

"His account of the event is very different," Ryan's words were sharp. Catherine could imagine her pacing back and forth in a courtroom, hammering the other side's witness. "And unfortunately, it's your word against his."

"Why are you doing this?" His voice was loud, the syllables jittery as if he was medically ill. "I didn't mean to imply you're doing anything wrong with the medications. I'm sorry."

"I don't know what you're talking about," she poured Catherine a glass of wine and handed it across the kitchen counter to her.

"The expired meds," he whispered, "I won't mention it to anyone else, I promise."

"I'm sorry, Jayson," Ryan explained. "I really am but I've no idea what you're talking about."

"If you don't make this right, Ryan." He warned, "I'll call AHCA or the Joint Commission and make a complaint. I bet they'll be intrigued with what you're doing."

"Don't call me anymore, Mr. Jamison." She moved the phone to her other ear. "From now on, you'll need to go through human resources."

"You're going to be sorry," His words hung pregnant in the air.

"Are you threatening me?"

"No," he said. Catherine could imagine him shaking his head as he'd answered the question. "Let's call it a premonition." He paused, "You have a nice day," before the line went dead.

****

Ryan pointed to the front door just as the front buzzer chimed. "Can you get that?" She asked Catherine before turning away and positioning herself against the counter, watching the phone as if she was expecting it to ring again.

"You okay?" Catherine asked from the foyer, looking back to Ryan. "Should we call Aiden and let him know what's going on?"

"Jayson's harmless," Ryan answered, still perched against the counter with her eyes closed as If she might be meditating." "There's no sense in bothering him tonight but I will file a report in the morning."

Catherine opened the door, not feigning surprise as Cole Spencer stood at the ready, a large bag of take out in one hand and holding a case of beer against his hip. She motioned him in and opened her arms to offer assistance. "Can I help?"

"I hope you haven't eaten," he didn't respond to her offer of aid. Instead, he barreled past. "I'm starving," he said once he was past the dining room and nearly to the kitchen where Ryan was still standing.

"And apparently thirsty." Catherine joked, finally taking the bag from him.

"Well, I wasn't sure who else was coming." He looked to where Ryan was still standing her back to them. "I didn't want her to have a lot to do."

"Who else are we expecting?" Ryan spun around as if she'd gotten her second wind and came around the counter smiling before planting a soft kiss on his cheek.

"Everything ok?" he asked, hoisting the beer atop the counter like a lumberjack might toss a tree stump, all that was missing was a red flannel shirt and hat.

"Just a problem at work," she nodded before exchanging a glance with Catherine.

"What kind of problem?"

"It's nothing," She unrolled the top of the bag open. "You didn't answer my question. Who else is coming?"

"You didn't answer mine, what's going on at work?" He met her stare.

"You first" she held her ground.

"Erik is coming by and I left a message for that reporter."

"Hartmann?" Ryan and Catherine both answered, one looking to the other as if to say, jinx.

"Yes," he nodded. "Now you go."

"Just an issue with a former employee that I terminated." She lined the takeout containers along the counter, pulling the tops loose and stacking similar items together.

"Not that creep from the other day at the restaurant?"

"Yes," Catherine answered for her. "He's continuing to call and harass her." She looked at Ryan. "He told her tonight she was going to be sorry."

Cole pulled out his phone. "What's this guy's full name? I'll have his ass picked up now!"

"Don't do that, you're only going to make it worse." She touched his arm, urging him to put the phone away. "I'll notify the captain of security tomorrow. Catherine and I can work with him to put together a plan."

"He knows your routine, honey. I don't like it." Cole said, pulling her closer against him.

A warning bell went off inside Catherine's head. Ought oh, she thought. Ryan was sure to bring up the schedule she'd found in his pants pocket that morning. Hurriedly, she handed each a paper plate. "Let's eat before it gets cold."

"Speaking of my routine," Ryan pulled out of his arms and walked toward her satchel, the one she'd dropped at the table when she'd arrived home from work.

"Ryan," Catherine warned, hoping she could dissuade her from bringing it up now.

"It's okay Catherine." Ryan's fingers were on the folder piece of paper. "He's always said there could be no secrets between us."

"Maybe it would be better to talk about it later, privately?" Catherine questioned; her eyes hopeful.

"What's this about?" Cole interrupted, dropping the paper plate of noodles on the counter and folding his arms across his chest.

Ryan handed him the paper. "Are you following me?"

"Why would you think that?" He was angry, there was no question about it.

She pointed to the paper and took a step away from him. "How did you get that?" Her expression was sad. "And why do you have it?" She paused, eyes looking down. "If you don't trust me-"

He cut her off. "It's not that. I trust you." He paused. "More than you trust me apparently."

"I'm not the one walking around with your itinerary in my pocket." She countered and gave him ample time to respond. When he didn't she went on, choking back the tears. "Maybe you should go?"

"No!" he took several steps to her, his hands out just enough to take her by her arms. "Stop doing that!"

"Doing what?" Ryan yelled back, jerking out of his hands.

"Pushing me away, every time you get scared." His next words were calmer. "I'm not him." He paused, words barely above a whisper. "I'm not going to hurt you, I promise."

"Then why are you following me?"

"I'm not sure what we've stumbled on." Initially, his words were intended for Ryan but as he went on, it was obvious he was talking to both Ryan and Catherine. "It could be that we've uncovered some horrendous act of the past or maybe we're just being played."

"Played?" Catherine repeated.

"Maybe someone Is trying to keep us busy from uncovering the truth about your ex-husband's death. It's a real-life game of smoke and mirrors and while we're busy chasing our tails with this ridiculous mind control plot, the real evidence, the real truths are being destroyed or buried so far under, they will never see the light of day." He swallowed and popped the top on one of the cans of beer. "I don't know what truth is or even what is real, what's been fabricated." He moved closer to her, taking her arms again but gentler this time. "I don't want you to get hurt. So, until I figure out what the truth is, I put a protective detail on you."

"You have a bodyguard on me?" She wasn't happy, Catherine could tell by the way Ryan pulled away and moved to stand closer, her arms folded, hands at her elbows. "Someone's following me?"

"Yes," he nodded as if to emphasize his point. "Someone I know I can trust."

"Who?"

"Knock, knock?" came a familiar voice from the front foyer. "I tapped at the door but no one answered." Erik walked more fully into the room. "Door was unlocked. Hope you don't mind.?"

His gaze focused on take-out containers. "Hope you got enough for me; I'm starving."

"There's plenty of food, "Catherine motioned him further into the room. "Come on in and I'll get you a drink." She squeezed between Ryan and Cole, each at the ready as if one were about to draw on the other in a gunfight.

"Am I interrupting something?" Erik asked, his hands reaching out to take the drink from Catherine's hands and looking back and forth between Ryan and Cole. "I didn't mean to intrude."

"It's no intrusion," Cole took a few steps away from Ryan and looked down to the floor as if he'd lost something. "I was just explaining how I'd assigned a protective detail to make sure she's safe."

Catherine watched as Cole moved closer to Ryan and locked his fingers into hers, she could tell by their body language that the gunfight was over, it had been a draw. Neither could claim it as a victory.

"She's uncomfortable with having a tail?" Erik asked, spooning a mouthful of fried rice into his mouth.

"Not exactly," Cole answered.

"I'll be discreet," Erik said to her, moving closer to be at her side instead of across the room. "Of course, you almost caught me this morning when you were roaming around that empty building."

"That was you?" Ryan broke in. "You were following me this morning?"

"Yes," he nodded. "But when you circled back I thought you were on to me so I waited until you were almost back to the end of the hallway before I tried to get back on your tail."

"I don't remember circling back," she shook her head. "I was just going from room to room measuring the room's dimensions."

"Mr. Hills stopped by around 2 pm looking for you," Catherine explained. "I told him your appointment was at 11 am and that you'd collected what you needed without him."

"Why'd he come at 2 pm," Ryan asked.

"He said someone called and change the time of your appointment from 11 am till 2 pm. He didn't get the name or why, just that you couldn't meet him until 2 pm."

"That's obviously incorrect." She paused. "Did you check with Virginia?"

"Yes, Virginia was there when Mr. Hills arrived. She told him there'd been no change to your calendar."

"That's odd," Ryan said. "Who would do that and why?"

"Someone's messing with your head, honey." He looked at Erik. "I'm glad you're able to help us out."

"It will be easier for me now that you know," Erik advised Ryan. "I promise I'll blend into the background of your life. You won't even know I'm there."

Chapter 26

"So," Erik asked, as he motioned for a container of sweet and sour chicken and scooped the remnants on his plate. "You think Dr. Beliard's death is somehow related to some left-over CIA mind control program from the '70s?"

"What you shared with us last time makes perfect sense," Cole explained. "It's just going to be hard to prove; these things aren't exactly well documented. No doubt a lot of these people have died off."

"Maybe the widow Fleming has continued to act on his behalf?" Erik added; his attention drawn to Catherine. "I know this must be difficult for you." He paused. "I was only recently informed that Dr. Beliard was your ex-husband."

"Was a long time ago," she whispered, looking away.

"Well, in any event, I think having a detail on you as well is a good idea."

"Pardon me?" She interrupted. "What do you mean?"

"Erik," Cole shook his head as if he were a child and was being grounded. "I didn't get a chance to discuss it yet."

"Now might be a good time," Catherine added, taking a large sip of wine instead of the small, delicate tastes she had been taking.

"I just think there are too many coincidences," Cole argued. "If what you've uncovered is, in fact, real, your lives are in danger, all of our lives are in compromise."

"So, where's your security detail?" Ryan asked.

Cole patted the holster against his hip. "Erik and I are armed, always." He looked back to Ryan. "I just don't want either of you hurt." He paused. "I have an agent on McKenzie as well but I think it's best if she does not know the agent is on her."

"How is a grown-up man going to integrate with a bunch of teenagers?"

"The FBI agent is a woman and she looks like a child." He smiled. "She'll fit in perfectly."

Erik collected the trash from dinner. "It's best if everyone just goes about their routines and pretends we aren't there."

Catherine whispered under her breath. "Yeah like that's going to happen." She dropped several empty boxes into the trash. "So, who's going to be responsible for my life."

"A friend of mine," Cole answered. "I've known him most of my life, our father's served in the military together. He and I went through the police academy together. My dad went into the secret service while his dad worked with the FBI." He paused. "His name is Darrin James but he goes by D.J."

"D.J.?" Catherine repeated. "As in music? How old is he?" She knew she was procrastinating, hoping to avoid the inevitable. A bodyguard? She didn't want or need a bodyguard.

"He's my age. He's a good guy and a great cop."

"I don't care." Catherine stopped at Ryan's side. "I don't want anyone following me around, how awkward is that?"

"You'll get used to it. I don't think we have a choice, really. It's for your own safety." Erik's words were soft, gentle. It was easy to picture him reading a bedtime story to his grandchildren.

"I took the liberty of asking him to stop by tonight so that you could meet him," Cole added.

"Catherine, I think you should listen to him." Ryan's words were sharp and cut short by the ringing of her phone. "Excuse me," she disappeared into the kitchen, looking down to identify the caller."

"Dr. Allen," she said into the phone, looking back anxiously at Cole as if he were about to be grounded. "How can I help you?"

"Ryan," the voice on the phone said. "It's Morgan Fare."

"Hey Dr. Fare," she slid upon one of the wooden bar stools and folded her ankles together. "What's up?"

"Having an issue tonight getting the automated cabinet in the trauma room refilled."

"Did you call the pharmacy?" she asked, stepping off the stool.

"Yes, they said they were busy and would get to it as soon as they could." He paused. "I explained to them how the emergency department has to get priority."

"What are you out of?" she asked, grabbing a pen and paper to make notes.

"Anodyne."

She waited for him to continue. "Anything else?"

"No, but we've been out for hours."

"Let me call the pharmacy and I'll get back with you."

Catherine watched as Ryan moved back into the kitchen, phone tight against her ear after punching in the central pharmacy number.

Ryan walked the short distance between the sink and stove, her steps short and in sync waiting for someone in the pharmacy to answer the phone.

"Hi Levi," she said, once the phone was answered and the employee identified himself. "It's Ryan."

"Hey boss," he said, sounding oddly like Louis had earlier that morning. "What's up?"

"Just got off the phone with Dr. Fare."

"I'm going to pull it now," he said sounding far away as if the phone wasn't fully at his mouth.

"Why isn't it coming out on the refill report?" She asked, looking across the counter to Catherine and Cole. "I don't like all these reactive resolutions." There was a pause before she added. "We need to work proactively to ensure the departments have what they need to take care of the patients."

She listened to his steps on the against the tile and his breathing as he roamed from one area of the pharmacy to the other. It was easy for her mind's eye to track him as he stopped at the places in the pharmacy where it was normally stored.

"There's none," she heard him breathe into the phone.

"What?" She asked even though she'd heard him very clearly. It was as if she was hoping he'd say something different the second time around.

"We're out," he said. "The shelf is bare."

"Is there any in the back, any in another machine, on another unit that we can share with the ED until some more product arrives?"

"Let me check?"

She heard him typing against the keyboard before he returned to the phone. "No, it's zeroed out in all the machines.

"Okay," she exhaled. "I'm going to call the buyer at home and inquire what's going on."

"Sorry," he explained before the line went dead.

Ryan selected one of the preset numbers of her phone and waited until the pharmacy buyer answered his phone. " Hi Ry," he said before she could say anything.

"Sorry to bother you at home, Bryan." She glanced anxiously at her guests, feeling as if all eyes were upon her. "Just got a call from the emergency department about Anodyne not being refilled tonight."

"Is it Levi or Louis?" Bryan asked before she could get the rest of her question out.

"Levi," she said as if on autopilot. "Is Anodyne on backorder?"

"No," he answered. "There's plenty on the shelf. I checked myself before I left for the day."

"You checked today?"

"Yes, I ran into Louis this morning in the parking lot. I was coming in and he was leaving." Bryan paused to give direction to his daughters as they placed their dinner orders with the server. "I don't know if it came in the order this morning or what but the shelves are full."

"Let me call back and speak to the pharmacist, thanks." She explained hanging up before Bryan could respond.

Surprisingly the pharmacist answered the phone after several rings.

"David," she said. "It's me."

"Hey," he breathed as if he'd been running. "What's up?"

"The Anodyne," she began. "Levi said we're out but Bryan insists there is drug on the shelf."

"I don't know," he explained. "Levi said we didn't have any so I called the emergency department and asked Fare to change it to something else." He paused; she could hear him entering data into the computer. "It's done and everyone's happy."

"Thanks," she answered. "I'll see you in the morning."

"Everything ok?" Cole asked, popping the tab on another beer.

"Yeah," Ryan took a sip from his opened can and handed it back to him. "Dammed Anodyne, everywhere I turn it's an issue." She paused. "First Noah and his rep friend are on my ass for trying to remove it from the formulary. And now it seems like every patient in the system is in a situation to need it."

The chime of the doorbell startled her, she motioned to Catherine who was closest to the front door. "Can you get that?" She turned three sixty to Cole, "Maybe you should get it, no doubt it's your friend."

"I got it," Cole shrugged and opened the door to Officer Darrin (D.J.) James.

DJ was tall and physically fit, with dark hair and blue eyes. No doubt during the workday the artwork that covered his arms would be concealed under a shirt or jacket. Tonight, however, he was dressed more casually in a short-sleeved knit shirt that not only enhanced his muscular physique but displayed numerous colorful tattoos that ran the length of his arms.

"Come on in, DJ." Cole motioned past the foyer. "Everyone's in the kitchen."

"How'd your friend take the news that she was getting a bodyguard for a while?"

Cole looked past DJ into the kitchen where everyone including Catherine was gathered. "About as well as you can imagine."

"I figured as much," DJ laughed.

"Come on, I'll introduce you." He stopped and laughed. "You are armed, right?"

D.J. nodded and followed Cole for introductions. "Always."

****

Ryan had never thought much about size, it wasn't something she prioritized on a daily basis but given there was all of six inches between her toe of her quarter- heeled shoes and the tip of Levi's sneakers, she thought maybe next time she wanted to meet with the staff, she'd suggest using her other office. The COO's space was much bigger. Luckily, the pharmacist, David, had chosen a seat against the other wall but still, the space was only slightly larger.

And the room was warm, hot, especially with so many people confined in the small space. Levi looked exactly like his twin had earlier that morning, down to the black hoodie hanging off his shoulders. To the untrained eye, they were, in fact, identical twins. However, Ryan was sure if asked the question, the twin's mother would be able to tell them apart. But Ryan couldn't, if it weren't for the hospital pharmacy badges that identified him as Levi, she'd just as easily assumed he was Louis.

To further complicate the issue, both were tall and thin with dark eyes and hair that curled perfectly framing their forehead, ears, and neck. Neither had piercings or any visible tattoos that might have offered aid and there was no discriminant jewelry. The only distinguishable factor was the color of the hospital scrubs they usually wore. Louis usually dressed in tan colored scrubs, while Levi normally reported to work wearing navy blue. Other than that, they were like blank pages in a book.

David, on the other hand, wasn't a youngster. Pharmacy wasn't his first career and as a result, he was older when he'd graduated from pharmacy school. He'd put on a little weight, too, over the years since walking across the stage and accepting his diploma. His sedentary lifestyle had contributed to his expanding waistline as well. He'd go for hours without leaving his chair in the central pharmacy.

His hair had probably been thick and dark when he was younger but not as he approached middle-age, it was more salt than pepper and thinning, especially around the forehead. Unlike Levi, David was more professionally dressed in khaki pants and blue shirt, adorned around his neck was a tie that matched both slacks and shirt. Like the twins, a hospital issue badge hung precariously from the pocket of his shirt.

It had taken several attempts before Ryan had been able to drag herself from the bed. Even though she'd slept alone, getting up had been challenging, partly because of the late hour everyone had taken their leave last night but mostly it was a result of the amount of alcohol she'd consumed.

As a result, she'd dressed in a hurry and hadn't realized she put on black shoes instead of navy ones until she'd sat down to meet with her staff. She smiled thinking Catherine must have surely noticed, she seldom missed even the smallest of details.

"I'm trying to understand what happened to bring us all together this morning." Ryan began, smoothing her skirt more fully over her knees.

David spoke first, pushing his glasses high up on the bridge of his nose, making his eyes look huge. "I already told you on the phone."

"Tell me again," she asked, smiling but there was no humor in her words.

He sighed as if he were bored. "Emergency department called the pharmacy late yesterday afternoon to let me know the Anodyne needed to be refilled." He looked across the room to Levi. "I asked Levi to refill it, he said we were out. So, I called Dr. Fare and asked him to change the order to something else." He paused. "He wasn't happy but he did it anyway."

"I spoke with Bryan last night and he assured me there were plenty of medication to fill up the cabinets. Why are you letting them be zeroed out?"

"It was a blue bottle and there weren't any blue bottles to fill it with," Levi explained.

"The shelf is filled with plenty of product." David stood and pointed to her office as if he were going to show them.

"But the pocket was a blue pocket and the blue bottles were all gone," Levi repeated.

"What's he talking about?" She looked to David for a response.

"I've no idea, there's plenty of product to fill the cabinets with," he said again.

Blue bottles? She thought, where had she heard that before. What had Jayson said about the technicians and blue dots? He'd said he was being paid back for asking about the blue dots.

Rvan stood and squeezed into the empty space between the desk and the door, opening it to David. "Would you give us a minute, please?"

The pharmacist rose slowly, his expression confused as he met her at the door. "You're done with me?"

"Yes," she nodded. "If there's something else I need, I'll pull you out of central."

"I can go back to work" He waited at the door for her approval.

"Yes, please. I appreciate your time." She waited as he slowly took his exit, looking back several times at Levi before pulling the door closed behind him.

"Tell me more about the blue dot," instead of taking the seat behind the desk, she took her seat vacated by the pharmacist.

Levi twisted his fingers as if he were wringing a towel dry. "I'm not doing anything wrong."

"Then, there should be no problem with you telling me what's going on. What do you mean by blue dots?"

"The bottles of medications with the blue dots are going to expire soon," Levi answered, biting his bottom lip. "There's a special pocket inside the automated cabinets where we stock the Anodyne bottles that have the blue dot."

"Under whose authority?" She paused thinking of Bailey, knowing Bailey wouldn't have initiated something like this without input from the rest of the team.

"The drug rep for the medication," Levi whispered.

"Why would you take direction from him. You don't report to him." She thought back to the conversation she'd had with Noah's friend, the rep and recalled how arrogant he'd been on the phone. She knew exactly whose authority her technicians were working under.

"He pays us five thousand dollars a month," Levi answered again, "to help him get rid of the product."

"Show me these bottles?" She rose to her feet and yanked the door open thinking about Jayson, and what he'd said about his termination being a payback for asking about the blue dots?

"The rep said we weren't to tell anyone and if we did, he wouldn't be able to compensate us."

"Who is us?" she asked, although she felt as if she already knew the answer.

"Louis and me." Levi stood and walked out of the office and into the main pharmacy.

She followed him behind him. "What purpose did the representative give for having you load these specific bottles with the blue dots?"

"They're expired," Levi offered. "But they're still good, the FDA always makes you toss stuff away before it technically has no effect."

"The Anodyne rep asked you to help him get rid of the expired product so you've tagged these bottles with blue dots and loaded them in the fast-moving areas?"

"No," Levi said as they came to a stop next to a counter with multiple shelves, several of which were filled with Anodyne bottles. These bottles, however, did not have any blue dots. "The bottles come with the blue dots, Louis and I just load them in the special pockets."

He paused and shuffled his feet from side to side where the plain bottles had overflowed onto the bottom shelf. The space next to it was empty. "We don't usually store them together like that. Some must have gotten mixed up because we are missing a few blue bottles. It's safe to say they were loaded into areas without the bins for the blue dot."

"Haven't any of the pharmacist questioned what the blue dots mean?" Ryan motioned him back toward her office and waited by the door as he entered and reclaimed his seat.

"Just Jayson," he answered. "He's the only one who noticed."

"Did you have anything to do with the incident that resulted in his termination?"

"No," Levi shook his head. "But the rep was notified that Jayson was questioning the significance of the blue dots." He paused. "Next thing I knew, you termed him."

Ryan grabbed the phone from her desk and dialed, waiting for someone in human resources to answer. "I need to speak to Brittany." She said into the phone once someone finally picked up the phone.

"I'm suspending two technicians immediately." She watched as Levi dropped his head, hands pushed snug into the pouch of the hoodie.

"What's the justification for the corrective action?" the familiar voice asked.

"Distribution of expired medications to patients." She answered and looked to Levi again. "I'm sending one of the technicians to HR now, you'll need to call the second one in to deliver the suspension."

"Where will you be? Aren't you going to meet with the employees over here in HR?"

"No," she answered. "I'm not meeting with anyone until I find out what the hell is going on."

Levi had only been out of the office a few minutes before Ryan logged onto the computer and completed a variance report. Over the course of her career, she completed hundreds of reports, ranging in severity from no harm to death. She literally could have answered the questions wearing a blindfold, she was just that familiar with the form. And the process for tagging two reports together was seamless.

Which is why the fact she couldn't find the report she'd completed regarding Jayson's incident was so alarming. She searched several times using his name and multiple times using keywords related to the incident. Just like the variance report for Dr. Beliard's code in the OR, it was nowhere to be found. It had simply disappeared.

Chapter 27

Tim Hartmann was a good-looking man especially dressed casually in faded jeans and a University of Miami sweatshirt. He'd had his hair trimmed since the last time she'd encountered him and had grown a thin beard that barely covered his chin.

Catherine couldn't help but think how easy it would be to shave it off, watching as the soft hairs filled the sink and knowing they couldn't be washed down the drain.

"I must admit I was surprised by your invitation." He refilled his container, pouring the last of the red wine into his glass. "I didn't really know what to say when I replayed your message." He paused. "It was all I could do to write down the address correctly."

He fell into the easy chair closest to the couch and pushed himself as far back in the chair as he could. "You have a lovely home, Dr. Allen." Hartmann took a large drink and sat the glass gently on the side table. "So, tell me what brings me here."

"We want to tell you a story," Catherine answered.

Almost an hour had ticked away and they'd shared it all. Beliard's secret past and alternative identities, the potassium additive in the vasopressor during his code, the key to the vault in the mausoleum, and the pictures of the war criminals who'd performed unsanctioned experiments on human subjects.

"That's an interesting story," he explained. "And as much as I'd love to be the one to break it, I never post anything I can't substantiate." He laughed. "It would take one hell of a fact-checker to validate that story."

"We need your help," Cole explained. "If anything should happen, no one will know the truth, know what really happened."

He tapped his phone. "I recorded everything you said and if anything should happen, I'll do my best to make sure whoever is responsible is held accountable." He poured himself another glass of wine. "How about I tell you a story now?"

Cole leaned against the couch, lifting his arm over its edge and around Ryan's shoulder. "We're all ears."

****

"You have proof of this?" Catherine asked, leaning forward off the couch and sitting her drink gently atop the wooden coaster on the glass coffee table.

"I do," Hartmann pushed himself fully against the back of the big chair's cushion and rested his right ankle atop his left knee.

Catherine noticed he wasn't wearing any socks; his feet were bare in the worn leather upper. "You can prove the Governor intends to break up the hospital system and sell it to the highest bidder, specifically a bidder he owns significant shares in?"

"I do," he smiled again. Catherine thought back to their encounter in the office, the day she'd come to Virginia's rescue. He was wearing the same arrogant smile as he'd asked about the hospital system's transparency.

"And I can attest that during his campaign when he swore he no longer had any financial interests in GHF, he lied." He rubbed his chin in deliberation, pulling at the tiny hairs of goatee that was just beginning to peek through the skin. "He indicated to the Senate overview committee that he'd sold all of his GHF stock and no longer had any financial interests in the corporation."

"And that's not true?" Cole asked

"Yes and no," Hartmann lurched forward quickly, and grabbed a partially full beer from the coffee table. "Technically, he did sell his shares of the stock."

"So, what's the problem?" Hartmann didn't look up to meet her eyes but Ryan went on just the same. "He sold it, so how is that still a conflict of interest?"

"Legal documents name the buyer as John Candle Corporation."

"And?" Catherine added, looking anxiously to Ryan.

"It was almost impossible to trace this corporation to its shareholders. There were no actual names, just endless lists of more companies and empty storefronts."

"There's no such corporation?" Ryan asked.

This time, Hartmann met her gaze. "Yes, there is and the one and only corporate officer is listed as none other than Daniel Ventor."

"Do we know him?" Catherine asked, looking around to Cole and Ryan and hoping the name wasn't lost on just her.

Hartmann's mouth opened to respond but Cole interjected before Hartmann could get the words out. "He's the governor's brother-in-law."

"You can't be serious?" Ryan asked, her voice tinged with sarcasm. "Why would he be so obvious?" She shook her head. "He's a lot of things but he's not an idiot. There has to be a mistake, some other justification."

"Oh, it's getting better." Hartmann smiled as if he was a cat who'd just swallowed the canary. "Daniel Ventor died in a skiing accident eleven years ago."

"Governor Smith has only been in office for eight," Catherine explained. "He sold his shares to a dead man."

"It would appear so," Hartmann smiled and reached for another beer.

Smoke and mirrors, Catherine thought but instead, she mumbled. "Hidden in plain sight."

"You're going to print this?" Cole asked, jumping as Ryan's cell phone came to life.

"Yes," he nodded as Ryan squeezed herself between his knees and the coffee table, her phone tight against her ear. "I am, it's with the copy editor as we speak."

"Your editor is okay with being on the wrong side of the Governor? He's a powerful man." Cole asked, stretching to see where Ryan had disappeared to.

"Nickolas has never been much of a political player as long as I have the facts to validate the connections and draw my conclusions, he'll support the story's publication."

Hartmann held his hand up before Cole could answer and went on. "I'm not afraid to write your story and Nickolas will support the publication, if the facts check out."

He paused and finished the last of his beer, sitting the empty bottle on the table but missing the wooden coaster. "I promise."

****

"I don't know what to make of any of this," Catherine yawned as she dried the last of the dinner dishes and stacked it with the others. "Although I've seen the clues Anwar left for me, I'm still having a hard time believing he'd be involved in this."

"He was young," Ryan answered, taking the stack of dry plates and stretching to place them on the top shelf of the kitchen cabinet. "I'm thinking he didn't realize what he was into until it was too late." She leaned against the hard surface; her arms folded defensively around herself. "Maybe that's why he wanted out, wanted a different life."

Catherine tossed the drying towel on top of the counter. "Why'd Cole run off? Doesn't he usually stay when McKenzie sleeps at her Dads?"

"Yes," Ryan rubbed her eyes, "he's making a point."

"About?"

"He told me he loved me the other night," Ryan paused and looked away as if there was someone else in the room.

Catherine knew it was a ploy, her friend was stalling, thinking about what she wanted to say before actually saying it. "And you didn't say it back?"

Ryan shook her head and bit her bottom lip.

"Why not?" Catherine moved closer to her. "I know you have very deep feelings for him."

"I like things the way they are," Ryan answered, looking around and snatching one of the newly dried wine glasses from the drying rack. "I'm not sure I want to complicate it by giving it a label."

"Loving him is akin to labeling him?" Catherine smiled hoping her reply was received in the same jovial spirit that she'd given it.

"I can't go through that again," Ryan drank from the wine glass as if she was thirsty. "I don't think I've got another battle in me."

"You mean your divorce?"

"That's a part of it yes but only a small part." Ryan moved to retrieve another clean glass but Catherine dismissed the offer.

"Those first few weeks after Logan moved out of our house, I was so lost. I'd never felt more alone." She refilled the glass. "I'd sit for hours and watch our wedding video and wonder where it went wrong, was there a sign I missed, something I should have seen and addressed before it came to his leaving." She wiped her eyes, taking the stilled tears away. "If not for my Mom, I think I'd have lost my mind."

Ryan smiled at the memory. "She practically moved in with me that first year. My Dad used to joke that he was a bachelor again."

"I know you miss her," Catherine's words were gentle and soft like a song.

"I do," Ryan answered, choking on the words. "All the time."

"Your ex is a selfish bastard," Catherine announced. "Isn't this written down somewhere?"

Ryan laughed and wiped her running nose with a paper napkin. "Cole wants to be more in my life than just the guy I have sex with three times a week when my daughter's with her Dad."

"What do you want?"

"I don't know, honestly."

"So, he's given you some space to figure it out?"

"Something like that," Ryan wiped at her nose again.

"He's a good guy, Ryan. I think he might be a keeper." Catherine cleared her throat, changing the subject after seeing how Ryan's eyes glazed over. The last thing she wanted was for Ryan to be hurt again.

At the same time, she didn't want her to shut the world off, either. "What happened with the twins?"

"I suspended them this morning until I can speak with the representative and find out who the hell he thinks he is." She paused. "That was the call I got while Hartmann was here, Brittany didn't sign off on the suspensions. She wants to talk to me first thing in the morning."

"What's there to talk about?" Catherine picked up the last piece of banana bread that was left from the loaf Ryan had served her guests tonight. "That's the best banana bread I've ever had. Did you make it?"

"No," Ryan rinsed out the wine glass. "Aiden brought it in for me."

"Aiden?"

"Yeah, a few months ago we were talking about how differently commercial and homemade products taste. He brought it back from wherever he was on vacation." Ryan wrapped the little bit that remained and handed it to Catherine.

"He mentioned growing up on a farm with his grandparents, somewhere up North I think." Catherine folded the edges of the plastic wrap tightly around the bread and placed it in her purse.

"I guess, looks like the old homestead is still in his family. I got the impression he returns there often to reconnect with his youth."

"That's nice." Catherine turned back to face her. "Back to the twins and their suspension, what's the plan?"

"I'm meeting with Brittany in the morning, I've no intention of changing my mind. They are suspended pending the outcome of my investigation of this expired Anodyne situation."

"I'm not sure why Brittany's being so hard-assed about suspensions. I had the same scenario with her and the medical record technician that I suspended." Catherine moved toward the front door with her jacket and satchel in hand.

"What was the outcome of that?" Ryan followed behind her, switching the kitchen lights off as they made their way through the living room and to the front foyer.

"She's still suspended but I am meeting with Dr. Paine's wife tomorrow." Catherine opened the door but waited at the threshold for Ryan to catch up to her.

"What would his widow have to do with the medical records information?" Ryan opened the front door and motioned for Catherine to proceed first before stepping into pace behind her.

"Nothing actually," Catherine explained, "but she called and asked if I could meet with her." Catherine descended the three steps before her foot touched the soft ground. "I thought it was the least I could do."

"I'll see you tomorrow. Drive safely." Ryan waved, before climbing the steps and disappearing through the front door.

"Have a good night," Catherine's lips formed the words but her mind was on autopilot. Her thoughts had moved on, thinking instead about the meeting tomorrow with Dr. Paine's widow and remembering the meeting she'd had with Melinda Beliard. How ironic, she thought. So much had happened in such a short time. Two women, both widows who's physician husbands committed suicide within the same healthcare system. What were the chances of that, she pondered and were the odds of winning the lottery better?

****

"I appreciate you seeing me on such short notice," Wynell Paine said as she sat perfectly in the chair Catherine indicated, the one usually empty across from her desk,

"It's no problem," Catherine answered, waiting until Mrs. Paine was seated before taking a seat on the other side. "What can I do for you, Mrs. Paine. And please know how sorry I am for your loss."

"Call me Wynni," she smiled, her words soft, barely audible. "Tyler spoke of you often."

"Me?" Catherine hoped she'd been able to curtail the surprise in her voice. She and Dr. Paine had battled many times over the years, about different topics. At one point, Andrew, the former CEO was ready to terminate Dr. Paine's contract as a result of the frequent altercations with both her and Ryan.

Ryan hated how lackadaisical he was with controlled substance record keeping and Catherine was almost as concerned with how he approached policies and procedures, especially if the surgical case had an unexpected outcome.

"Yes," Wynni cleared her throat but her words were still soft, almost as if she was whispering. "I know you and he didn't always see eye to eye but he respected you." She paused. "He thought you were the kind of woman who always did the right thing."

Catherine blushed, she hadn't expected that and felt a tinge of sorrow for how badly things had sometimes gone down between them.

"That's why I'm here." Wynni went on. "I'm hoping you'll be able to help me."

"Help you with what?" Catherine answered.

"Find out what really happened to my husband." She answered, her eyes hopeful and tear-free.

"I'm not sure what I can tell you, Mrs. Paine, that you probably don't already know."

"He wasn't a drug addict, Mrs. Masters," Wynni announced. "He hated drugs of any kind."

"You know Dr. Paine was suspended for a few days after a variety of medications were discovered in the anesthesiologist's sleep room."

"That room is used by all the anesthesiologists," Wynni pointed out. "There was never anything to suggest he was utilizing any of the medications." She paused. "My understanding is that these were medications that were removed from the automated cabinets for patient cases but not used and not returned."

"Yes," Catherine answered. "That was my understanding as well."

"Tyler was suspended because as the medical director he had an obligation to ensure the medications were returned to the pharmacy and when they weren't, he was suspended for violating that particular hospital process, yes?"

"Yes," Catherine nodded, thinking how Mrs. Paine should have been a lawyer.

"Then I don't see how that event has anything to do with his death."

"I was just pointing out that there is at least one other situation where access to medications that weren't intended to be used on any of his patients did occur." She paused. "And then there was the ongoing investigation regarding the incident with the female patient who said your husband assaulted her while she was under anesthesia."

"I would like to hear more about that event later." she rubbed her thumbs together impatiently. "But for now, I'd like to hear more specific details about the events surrounding his death."

"Can I call someone for you, Mrs. Paine, someone who can help get you home safely?" Catherine's words were calm and soothing but inside she felt like screaming loud enough for Virginia to hear from her desk out front. Perhaps this would have been a good meeting to have Aiden or one of the other security officers hiding in an adjacent office like they'd done the day they fired Cliff.

"I'm fine, Mrs. Masters." She smiled as if reading Catherine's thoughts. "And I assure you I'm no threat to you, I mean you no harm."

There was a pregnant pause before she went on. "My husband was a good man, an amazing father, brother, and son. He didn't deserve to die on the floor in the back of some operating room with a needle sticking out of his arm."

She fought back the tears, her armor broken and in compromise as if first blood had been drawn. "He was a good man." Mrs. Paine pulled herself higher in the chair, it was as if she'd willed herself not to cry. Her composure was intact again. "A man who would never violate the oath he took to do no harm. He would never have touched anyone, willing or unwilling, that he was treating in a medical capacity."

She scooted closer to the desk and folded her arms on top so that she was nearly face-to-face with Catherine. "Could you give me the details of that event, please?"

"Of course," Catherine looked away only long enough to bring the variance report up on her computer screen. "But I can't give you the patient's name, just the distinguishing aspects of the complaint."

"Megan Cassidy." Mrs. Paine said with great conviction.

"What?" Catherine asked even though she was able to read the name from the open variance report on her computer, a screen Mrs. Paine couldn't possibly see from her vantage point on the other side of the desk.

"The patient's name was Megan Cassidy." She paused but it didn't seem as if she was awaiting validation from Catherine that the name on the complaint and the name she'd given were the same. "Tyler was very upset the night he came home after finishing that case."

"Upset how?" Catherine looked around for a pencil and paper, hoping Mrs. Paine wouldn't mind if she took a note or two.

"Tyler finished his medical residency in Philadelphia. He worked with several other anesthesia groups over the years but he got his start in Philadelphia."

"I don't understand," Catherine stopped writing. So far nothing Mrs. Paine had said was noteworthy.

"His last shift as a resident, there was a party, organized by the medical director of the anesthesia department. In attendance were several women whose purpose that night was to reward the residents for completing the program."

"Hookers?"

"Yes," Mrs. Paine nodded. "Tyler did mention that they were hookers and that he, like the other residents had enjoyed the gift'."

Catherine retrieved the pen and loved the paper closer so she could document what Mrs. Paine was saying. "Dr. Paine recognized this patient from the resident party that night?"

"Yes, she was one of the hookers but Megan Cassidy wasn't the name she was using then."

"Tyler said it was Courtney something." She paused, "He couldn't remember the last name or If she even gave one that night."

Catherine tossed the pencil down again. "I'm not sure what the mystery is here, Mrs. Paine. Megan Cassidy, Courtney, whatever her name is was embarrassed about running into Dr. Paine again after all these years. Maybe she had a different life now and didn't want anyone to know about what she did before."

She was trying to remain calm and refrain from being angry at this woman. God knows, she's suffered a horrendous loss, But truth was, there was no smoking gun here. The woman's past caught up with her. There was nothing to suggest Megan Cassidy had anything to do with Paine's suicide.

"We all have secrets, Mrs. Paine." Catherine thought of Anwar. "I'm not sure running into an old John is justification to murder someone and set it up as a suicide." Her words were softer. "Is that what you are suggesting?"

"That's only part of what Tyler told me." Mrs. Paine pulled a faded photograph from her purse of several young men in white lab coats, their arms locked around a number of scantily dressed women. In the picture everyone was smiling, even a blurry figure in the background, one not meant to me in the picture but captured in its frame just the same.

"Tyler mentioned someone who works here at a very high level and who'd been at the party that night as well." She tapped the blurry figure in the background. "This woman was the owner of the escort service; she'd put the girls with the residents that night."

Catherine held the picture closer, hoping to definitively identify her. "Was she also a hooker?"

"No, she was the madam, in charge of all the girls and the money."

Mrs. Paine went on. "Tyler mentioned he'd ran into someone recently but couldn't place where he knew her from."

She pointed to the picture still in Catherine's hands. "After Mrs. Cassidy made her complaint, it hit him. He remembered where he knew her from."

"She's the woman from the picture but like Megan Cassidy, that's not the name she was using back then either."

"Did he say who she was, what name she was using then or now?"

"He died before he could tell me." She paused. "I know his death is somehow related to that woman." She pointed to the picture. "I know he didn't kill himself."

"Mrs. Paine," Catherine moved anxiously in the chair. She genuinely liked this woman and felt sorry for her loss. "I don't mean to be insensitive or invade your privacy in any way." There was a pause as she worked up her nerve. "I'd heard a rumor that Tyler was recently diagnosed with cancer. Maybe the thought of the impending treatments and chemotherapies ---."

"His cancer was not life-threatening Mrs. Masters." Mrs. Paine broke in. "He was diagnosed and treated within the same month. He was not a candidate for chemotherapy, he was surgically treated." She paused. "I can have his oncologist; Dr. Derrick Carter get in touch with you to validate what I'm saying."

"No," Catherine shook her head. That's not necessary." She swallowed, not able to make eye contact. Guilt had an amazing way of leveling the playing field.

"I know Tyler didn't kill himself accidentally or on purpose and I don't think Dr. Beliard killed himself."

"Why would you say that?" Catherine dropped the pen and picture as if she'd been slapped.

"A lot of people don't think he killed himself." she stood up from the chair. "Things are seldom as they seem, Mrs. Masters, don't you think."

"I don't know what to say to your claim, Mrs. Paine, but I will call Mrs. Cassidy and ask her to come in and make a statement about her charge. I can ask her if she and Dr. Paine knew each other in any capacity. I will definitely be watching her reaction."

Catherine handed the picture back to her, leaning across the desk as far as she could. "I'll need to update the variance report with the information you provided to me."

Mrs. Paine pushed the photo back to Catherine. "You can keep it. I've no need for it anymore. I'm trusting you, as my husband did, to do the right thing."

"Of course, Mrs. Paine. I will do my best to see that the truth comes out, whatever that may be."

Mrs. Paine turned to leave but she stopped at the door as Catherine added. "With your permission, I will need to share these details with the proper authorities?"

"Of course," She waved a faint goodbye and disappeared through the door.

Chapter 28

"It's Rachel Fleming," Ryan squinted at the picture, turning it from side to side as if it were an etch-a-sketch and turning it might reveal a better image.

"You don't know that," Catherine admonished, motioning for the picture to take a second look.

"It's that same arrogant smirk. The one she has on her face every time she walks through that door." Ryan argued. "Same hair and body composition."

She paused, "Didn't Paine say during her chief operations interview that he knew her from somewhere but couldn't place her?"

"Yes," Catherine smiled. "And you've said that about half a dozen times about other people since the beginning of the year. We all have deja vu at one time or another. It's a fact of growing old."

"It's her. I know it." Ryan made her way back to the door. "And so, do you –"

"Code Assist! Emergency Room!" came an announcement overhead.

"Code Assist! Emergency Room!" it repeated again.

Ryan followed as Catherine led the way out of the offices and down the hallway toward the emergency department where several hospitals workers were trying to subdue an irate patient from the hallway and get him back into the examining room.

The man looked relatively normal, Catherine thought as she and Ryan made their way to assist the emergency department staff. The man was probably in his mid-thirties, dressed in jeans and a long-sleeved denim shirt and construction boots.

He was clean shaven and well-kept, not the type at all Catherine expected to see throwing med carts out of the way with hospital staff clinging to both legs and at least one of his arms. The arm not attached to a staff member was wrapped in gauze from his elbow to his wrist. A worker's compensation accident, Catherine thought once they were close enough to fully assess the situation.

"Security in route?" Catherine asked, as she made her way close to the young wild-eyed patient.

"Yes," Aiden answered from the end of the hallway, running the rest of the way.

"What's his name?" Catherine called out to no one in particular, and noticed Ryan disappear into the medication room.

"Anthony." Someone yelled back.

"Anthony?" Catherine called calmly, "I'm Catherine and I'm here to help you."

"They're trying to kill me!" he screamed, fighting to free his arm from the grip of a male nurse.

"No," she answered. "You've had an accident I see at work?"

He wiped at his face with his gauzed hand. "Yeah but that was earlier, before."

"Before what?"

"Before they tried to kill me!" he screamed again, his words hoarse and pained.

"We aren't going to hurt you, Anthony." Her words were calm. "We're here to help you."

"He's got a gun pointed at me!" Anthony screamed again, motioning to Aiden.

"Aiden?" Catherine said, moving closer. "Down but close, ok?"

She watched out of the corner of her eye as Aiden lowered his gun but kept it at the ready just in case. "Doctor," she called over the crowd. "We need a verbal order for something before this situation gets out of control."

"Haloperidol 10 mg IM," a young African American female physician called out from the other side of the nursing station where several of the staff had moved safely out of the way.

"Got it," Ryan moved back into Catherine's line of sight, drawing up a syringe filled with medication. She handed it to one of the male nurses, one not already involved in quarantining Anthony.

"Locked and loaded," Ryan said, stepping away. "It's ready to go."

"On four," Catherine said.

"Back off!" Anthony screamed. "I swear to God I'm going to kill someone."

"One, Two, Three," Catherine counted stepping closer as the others swarmed Anthony. He didn't go down easy as it took all of them to hold onto him still. Catherine caught Anthony by the arm as he swung at Aiden, she'd diverted the blow but didn't expect Anthony to get his other arm free from the hospital staff.

The punch wasn't that hard but it caught her just under the chin and she went down like an Ali opponent in the mid-seventies.

"Catherine!" Ryan screamed, running toward her friend just as Aiden was propelled through the plexiglass window that overlooked examination room twelve.

"Oh my God!" Ryan screamed helping Catherine to her feet and pulling her behind the nursing station just as several other security officers arrived on scene and piled on top of where the nursing staff was struggling to keep Anthony on the floor so that the medication could be administered.

After several minutes, Anthony's body stilled, he was calm, awake and alert.

"We should get another dose ready," Ryan advised watching as Anthony began to move around more freely.

"Go get another dose," Catherine instructed, holding her arm as she pulled herself to her feet."

Ryan nodded and returned to the medication room, returning moments later with another dose and handed it to the physician who was also ordering physician restraints.

Catherine and Ryan watched as Anthony was returned to his examining room, given a second dose and restrained to the bed.

"Let's everyone convene in the conference room while this event is still fresh in our minds," Catherine instructed. "I need everyone who was taking care of him and everyone who responded to the code available for debriefing."

****

"Who wants to go first?" Catherine asked as she pushed a large ice pack against her elbow. After a moment of silence, she added. "Who triaged him?"

"I did," Elena Stalinski said pulling her chestnut colored hair out of the way to raise her hand as if she were in a classroom. Elena was a pretty woman with grey eyes and a full figure not easily disguised under the hospital issued scrubs she wore. She was feminine but at the same time comfortable enough to indulge in a pick-up basketball game after lunch in the parking lot behind the emergency room where someone had fashioned a basketball hoop.

"And he was fine." Elena went on as she flipped through her notes to provide the team with his vital signs and her assessment at the initial encounter. "He came in from the Port, workmen's comp case. Saw blade broke and cut across his forearm." She paused. "The doctor ordered one dose of Demerol for pain and a gram of cefazolin in case of an infection. I did the sutures myself. Everything was fine, I was getting ready to do the discharge paperwork when I realized he needed a dose of Anodyne before he left. I gave him the medication and handed him his prescription to have filled at his pharmacy for oral pain meds." She rubbed her forehead. "When I came back to take out his IV line, he went crazy."

"After you gave him the med, is when the altercation started?" Catherine restated.

"Yes," she rubbed her neck. "Do I have to be seen? I'm fine, you know."

"Where'd you get the Anodyne?" Ryan asked, before Elena had left the conference room. "Dr. Fare mentioned you were out frequently. I know he has issues with how often my department is refilling the machines."

"I got it from med room four," Elena answered, laughing. "The other nurses don't like getting meds from there, they say it's too far away." She stepped into the hallway. "Which means most of what I need is available in there since no one else goes in there to get what they need."

"Med room four?" Ryan stood up. "I'll be right back." She joined Elena at the threshold of the hallway, "Did you discard the bottle from the dose you gave Anthony?"

"Yeah, it's in the trash can in room ten."

"Thanks!" Ryan disappeared down the hallway.

"Okay," Catherine asked once the door was closed. "Who arrived first to the code assist?"

"I did," another nurse explained. "I was already in the room trying to help Elena when the code was actually called." She laughed. "Thank God, it was called quickly because we were getting our assess kicked."

"Did we get a tox screen back yet?" Catherine asked.

"Yes," the same nurse answered. "It was negative, no drugs or alcohol. Nothing."

"So, he just lost it?" Catherine asked.

"Maybe a reaction to the Demerol?" a voice at the table asked.

"He didn't indicate he had any allergies when Elena triaged him."

"That was fast thinking on Ryan's part to go get the Haldol before the doctor even ordered it."

"Yes, luckily she thinks quickly on her feet." Catherine nodded.

"She'd have made a good nurse," everyone laughed.

"Until there's blood, piss, puke, or slime, then she's done." The laughter grew louder until the opening of the door resulted in everyone turning quiet again.

"Aiden?" Catherine jumped to her feet and pulled an empty chair closer to him. "Have a seat. Did you just get cleared by the doctor?"

"Yeah," He held up his arm where a bandage covered the area from elbow to wrist. "Few stitches here and there." He tapped his head where a smaller bandage ran the gamut across his forehead. "I'm fine." His shirt was torn, hanging off his shoulders where the collar had been all but ripped away.

He addressed Catherine, "Did you have any questions for me?"

"No," she answered, her words thoughtful, slow, almost methodical. "I was already on scene when you arrived."

"What's wrong?" he asked, leaning in closer to her. "You okay?"

"Yes," she pulled away putting distance between them. "I'm just admiring that tattoo on your shoulder." She pretended to lean closer for a better view but she didn't need to, she'd seen it before. It was identical to the one woman who stole the controlled substances from the dispensing cabinets weeks earlier."

"Very nice," she nodded. "Why'd you pick a red bird?" She smiled, "Seems like a heart or military insignia, something like that would be more your style."

He laughed and yanked his other sleeve up when a large army service tattoo was etched into a bicep. "I got that one when I was a kid, that's why it's so small and faded. It's really old."

She nodded, "Seems odd a little boy would get a bird, a cardinal even."

"My grandfather's farm was full of them, everywhere you looked. Some kids that lived nearby and I did these ourselves when we were about nine, I guess."

He laughed. "My grandfather tanned my butt. I don't know if they got in trouble or not. I didn't see them again after that."

"Seems odd, sad even. You never thought about looking them up? Reconnecting, it's such a sweet story."

"Wouldn't even know where to start. He was my age, a lot of people thought we were brothers." He paused, squinting as if it might help him remember. "His name was Jaxson or James, something like that." He stood up, "I don't remember anything about her, they might have been siblings."

"It really is a sweet story," Catherine added thinking of Eleanor's tattoo. "Too bad you lost touch with them." Had Aiden and Eleanor known each other as children, were they involved now as adults? It was just too coincidental they'd have the same hand-made tattoos.

"I went away a lot to different schools so it wouldn't have mattered much anyway. We wouldn't have had that much time together anyway."

"I didn't realize you went away to boarding school?"

"Yeah on and off until I joined the Army." He yawned, "My pain meds are kicking in, you need anything before I go?"

Pain meds? She heard his words echo in her mind. Were he and Eleanor involved in the theft of the controlled substances from the operating room's automated cabinets? "No, go get some rest. You did good work tonight." It was just too much, she thought. What were the odds he wasn't involved?

"Thanks," he headed for the door. "So, did you."

****

"Catherine?" She heard her name before even realizing Virginia was at the office door. It wasn't that she wasn't listening. By all accounts, she simply "zoned" out. Who wouldn't? she thought. With everything that had gone on in the last few weeks, maybe she, Ryan, and Cole could all use a little psychiatric R&R.

"Sorry, Virginia." Catherine pulled her glasses off and dropped them on the desk. "I didn't hear you, what's up?"

"There's a doctor here to see you." She leaned closer into the office. "He says he's on staff but I don't know him so he must be a new appointment.

"What's his name?" Catherine asked, rising from the desk and adjusting her jacket.

"Carter," Virginia said. "Dr. Derrick Carter."

"Oh," Catherine didn't try to hide her surprise or disappointment. "I'll be right there."

She waited a few minutes before exiting her office and venturing out to engage him. "Hi, Catherine Masters," she offered her hand and motioned for him to follow her into her office.

"I'm sorry to come without an appointment," he said waiting on the other side of the desk for Catherine to offer him a seat.

Derrick Carter was a handsome man with dark hair that he spiked into a shallow peak. His eyes were a deep shade of blue, his jaw sharp as if it were simply put there to house the dark mustache under his nose. By all accounts, he could have been a model. Catherine cleared her throat and hoped he didn't notice the flush that covered her face.

"It's fine, Dr. Carter. What can I do for you?" She pointed to the empty chair.

"I wanted to inquire if there was anything you need from me regarding the unfortunate passing of Tyler Paine." He paused and ran his hand over the black stubble of thin beard on his chin. "I didn't know him very well but I've known his wife for many years."

"As I shared with Mrs. Paine, the police are handling the events associated with her husband's death. There's really nothing I can ask of you or share about the case."

"I see," he stroked his beard again. "It's very important to her that you understand Tyler was cancer-free at the time of his death."

"I did indicate that on the report I shared with the police. They have your name and contact data and will contact you directly if there are any follow-up questions."

"I understand," he rose to his feet and held his hand out to her again. "Thank you for your time."

"Was nice meeting you." Catherine motioned toward the office door and watched as he disappeared out of the office. She heard him exchange pleasantries with Virginia as the outside door snapped almost delicately closed.

"Is he the new oncologist on staff?" Virginia inquired not moving from her desk. "He seems nice enough."

"Yes, he does," Catherine answered, hoping unlike most everything else that had happened lately, he was exactly as he seemed.

****

"I thought you'd left for the day?" Catherine asked as she passed Ryan's office and found her sitting behind the desk, brows furrowed in thought.

"I stepped out for a while but I needed to come back. I'm waiting for Leon to come by before he starts his shift." She checked her watch. "I thought you had to leave early today?"

"I was but I got an unannounced visitor that took up some of the afternoon."

"AHCA again?"

"No," Catherine leaned against the desk. "Dr. Paine's widow mentioned having his oncologist validate that his condition wasn't serious enough for Tyler to be considering suicide. Even though I tried to convince her it wasn't necessary, Dr. Derrick Carter stopped by earlier to confirm what Mrs. Paine reported about her husband's condition."

"Not life-threatening?"

"Not at all, he wasn't even seeing Dr. Carter anymore." She slid into the empty chair.

"Did Megan Cassidy ever respond to your emails or calls for a follow-up to the complaint she made against Dr. Paine?" Ryan asked, checking her emails to see if the night pharmacist had canceled his appointment with her."

"No, she didn't, "Catherine ran her hand through her hair, thinking she needed a trim. Her hair was getting too long and stringy. "The only communication we've had with her post-complaint, is when Virginia called to inquire if she was available to meet. Mrs. Cassidy told Virginia she was just too upset over the ordeal to schedule anything at the present time and would follow up with us a future time."

"And she hasn't. That's odd, don't you think?"

"Maybe now that's dead, she's not as worried about her past life coving to the surface. Perhaps she thinks it's not a good idea to bring it all out in the open again." Catherine pointed out the window where a middle-aged man carrying a white lab coat over his arm was walking up the sidewalk from the employee parking garage. "Is that the night pharmacist you're waiting on?"

"Yes," Ryan turned in her chair to look out the picturesque window beyond the parking lot to where the safety lights of the new building were barely visible against the harsh light of the streetlights that lined the parking lot between the two. "Hard to believe the gala is just a week away? With so much of the building yet to be completed, it seems odd that the priority would be a ballroom."

"Everybody in politics has got an agenda, you know that, right." Catherine stepped closer and watched as the headlights of the cars on the busy street passed by.

"Yeah, I know but it just seems odd that we've got patients holding in the hallways waiting for a bed in an actual patient room. Yet, the party room is done and ready to go." Ryan's words were more like a chant than a statement. She stopped and considered her next words carefully. "I'm going to get to the bottom of the blue dot bottles, if it's the last thing I do."

"Where'd you step out to?"

Ryan motioned for Catherine to shut the door and used the phone to fill the confines of the office with music. "There was a single bottle left of Anodyne in med room four and it has a blue dot on it. I removed it from the premises where it is safe in a secure space."

Catherine made as if to speak but Ryan held up her hand. "The bottle that was used on Anthony also had a blue dot on it. I retrieved the used bottle from the trash can of examining room ten. I drove it myself to Charlotte and placed it in the hands of my chemist friend, Calvin."

She turned the music up a tad louder. "He promised he would do the analysis tonight and send me the results first thing in the morning."

"You think it's related to what's going on?" Catherine bit her lip thinking she needed to update Ryan on Aiden's tattoo and what she thought it might mean.

"Yes, I do and this time tomorrow I think we'll know how."

"Speaking of," Catherine added. "Did you know Aiden has a tattoo?"

"He was in the military, don't all soldiers?"

"This one is a red bird just like the one on the shoulder of the woman in the photo who emptied the machines of controlled substances while you were away."

"You mean the same one as Eleanore has?" She paused. "Apparently, a lot of people have similar tattoos?"

"No," Catherine shook her head. "He said he and some friends did them themselves when they were kids."

"You think Aiden and Eleanor are responsible for the breaking into the OR?"

"I think we need to find out more about our handsome, young captain of security."

The loud rap against the wooden door startled them both. Ryan turned off the music while Catherine answered the door.

"You guys alright, locked up in here with music playing?" Virginia laughed. "Thought for a minute Ryan had that hot cop in here and she was making out."

"No," Catherine jumped in. "Just trying to decompensate after the event in the emergency room."

"You two were lucky you weren't hurt," Virginia added. "Running down there like you were twenty years old again."

"Everyone okay?" Noah stuck his head through the door, his attention on Catherine's swollen arm. "Maybe you should take a few days off?"

"You too," he motioned to Ryan.

"No," Catherine advised. "We're good. Just a few bumps and bruises."

He clapped his hands together as if he had good news to share. "I suppose you heard about the keynote address?"

"Not really," Catherine answered for them both. "We've been kind of busy."

"Governor Smith is going to deliver the address for the gala next week. Pretty cool?"

"Ryan," Virginia cut in, "Your appointment is here."

"Is it Leon?"

Virginia nodded as Noah disappeared past Ryan's office door and into his own office. "Do you think it's cool?" she whispered before taking her to leave back to her desk. "What are we seven years old?"

Chapter 29

The pharmacist, Leon, was an older man, tall and thin with thick white hair that probably could have been a tad shorter, especially in the back where it fell against the back of his neck. His fat, black glasses weren't old but they certainly looked that way, as if he'd had them since the sixties.

To say he seemed nervous, was probably an understatement. He sat cautiously in the seat across from Ryan's, hands in his lap as if he were preparing to say grace before dinner.

"I'm trying to understand the operational processes around the bottles of Anodyne that are marked with a blue dot," Ryan said, sounding more maternal than she probably meant to.

"I don't really know anything about that, those two have the entire loading and unloading of processes down to an art. They don't really seem to need a lot of help. I just match the drug to refill paper, really not much else to do with all the automation and stuff you have over there."

"By those two, you mean, Levi and Louis?" Ryan asked.

"Yes," he laughed. "They are really good technicians, hard to believe they haven't been here that long, new to the system and all."

"Are you aware of anything different about the ones with the blue dots?"

"No," he shook his head. "I thought since they only put them in certain drawers of certain areas, the shape of the bottle's neck must be different."

"The bottle's neck," she repeated. "You thought there's a physical difference in the design of those bottles meant to fit a specific aspect of automation?"

"Yeah," he answered. "Why else would it matter?"

"I really don't know." She said. "What about Louis and Levi? How is it working with them?"

He laughed. "They are good boys and I don't want to get them in trouble."

"But?' she encouraged him along.

"They have such attitudes, big sense of humor, both of them."

"How so?"

"You have to promise you won't say anything to them?"

"I can't make that promise," she explained. "If it's a patient safety issue or anything related to safety, I would have to alert the appropriate parties."

"Sometimes, I think they switch places." He paused, sensing her confusion. "You know one works for the other and vice versa?"

"Why would you say that?"

"Because sometimes, I swear I told Levi something and then the next time I see him, he acts like he doesn't know anything about what I said. Same with Louis, too." He looked around as if assuring no one else could hear him. Odd, because they were alone in the office.

"Levi has a small scar over his eyebrow and Louis doesn't. The other night I see Louis is written on the schedule and wouldn't you know there's that scar over the eyebrow. I know it's really Levi but I don't say anything. I figure you're paying someone for the twelve hours, it shouldn't matter who's working them, right?"

"Why would they switch places?" she asked, it didn't make any sense, not really. If Louis needed to be off, why not just ask if his brother could cover the shift, why all the covertness.

"You know that Levi Is technically the oldest, right?"

"I didn't but go on, why would that matter?"

"Levi is in line to inherit the family business when his old man dies."

"Is their father ill?" She asked the question before thinking. She knew he was ill; she'd given the twins Christmas off even though they didn't have seniority and should have had to work the holiday.

"Do we know what the family business is?"

"I heard a rumor; his father is somehow related to the mob."

"Like the New York mob?"

"Yes, something like that."

"I've suspended them both until I get to the bottom of whatever's going in with the dots."

Leon smiled. "That's what I've always liked about you."

"What's that?" Although she wasn't sure wanted to know the answer.

"You've got balls of steel." He jumped to his feet. "Can I go clock in now?"

"Yes, and everything we've talked about is confidential."

"Got it, Boss." He pulled the door closed behind him.

One more thing, she thought to herself, to do before she left. It was almost an involuntary sleight of hand and eye coordination to pull up the variance reports. It would only take a minute to pull up the variance for the Anodyne and update it with what she'd uncovered about the blue dots and how the twins had been suspended.

It shouldn't have been a surprise to discover, it was gone, erased like the others. It shouldn't have surprised her at all, yet it did,

****

"I'm going to terminate them both," Ryan said into the phone, using her shoulder to hold the phone to her ear and grabbing her satchel from the back seat.

"You sure you have enough justification? You know bleeding heart Brittany will make it harder than ever to fire them." Catherine's voice from the phone was clear.

"I'd think sending up medications they believe to be expired should alone suffice. Now with this claim that they are fraudulently signing each other's timecards, do I really need anything else?"

"Hi Dr. Lee," Ryan said to the short, thin physician exiting the physician's entrance with a grocery bag full of snacks from the doctor's lounge."

"Shopping day?" she heard Catherine say, just about the time Dr. Lee grunted back at her and quickly slid into his car, his new car she couldn't help but notice. It was a silver Mercedes with expensive

335

looking tires that were nearly clean enough to eat from. Ryan turned and watched him pull away, following his vehicle with her eyes until it trailed off like smoke in the distance.

She felt rather than saw him, his fist actually as it collided with the side of her face. Ryan fell to her knees, tearing her pantyhose and scraping the skin away from her knees.

"Ryan?" she heard Catherine's voice but it sounded odd, far away. Ryan crawled to the sidewalk, clawing her way to her feet only to feel another blow to her head from behind. She fell face first against the pavement, feeling the strap of her satchel being yanked off her shoulder.

"Ryan?" she heard the voice again, "Ryan?" it repeated, anxiously, desperately.

Her face was wet, the sprinklers must be on she thought, why else would her hair and face be so damp. Odd, her mind raced. She hadn't noticed the sprinklers when she parked her car.

"Over there," she heard Catherine's voice again, but not on the phone this time. "She's here, on the sidewalk," her voice was louder, near the physician's exit.

"Oh god," Catherine exclaimed dropping to her knees next to Ryan. "She's hurt. Call an ambulance."

In her peripheral vision, Catherine saw Erik rounding the side of the building, almost running to where Ryan had fallen. She didn't know why, but she waved him off, thinking it would be better if everyone didn't know about the security detail Cole had put on Ryan.

Catherine watched him, retreat back to the front of the building where a line of visitors was waiting to enter through the front entrance. Discreetly he made his way to the back of the line, no doubt where he'd have plenty of time to overhear a patient name and gain a visitor pass into the hospital.

"No, no," Ryan's words drew Catherine's attention to the few emergency workers as they struggled to keep Ryan reclined against the sidewalk. "I'm fine." Her thoughts were more organized, her words better structured. "I hit my head when I fell. Help me up."

"No," Aiden knelt to her side. "You have a head injury, let's wait for the backboard."

"I am not climbing on a backboard in this skirt," Ryan stated. "Now help me up!"

"And just like that, she's back," Catherine nodded, "Let's walk her to the emergency department."

"Police is in route," Aiden added, taking Ryan by the arm and walking slowly with her as Catherine guided her by the other arm.

"Did you get a good look at him?"

"No, but I did see the van."

"The white one?"

Ryan nodded. "How did you know where I was?"

"I heard you address Dr. Lee. I knew you must be in the physician's lot and when you didn't answer." She paused. "I could hear the sounds of the struggle."

"Wasn't much of a struggle. Two punches and I was down. He took my satchel."

"That's two more than I could have probably taken."

"Who are you kidding? I saw you in the Emergency room, you were one hundred twenty pounds of pure terror." Ryan laughed, spitting blood from her mouth.

"Didn't Virginia say we were too old for this crap?"

Ryan nodded, "Something like that."

****

"I'm not going to admit you," Dr. Fare's words had her attention. She was sure he'd admit her even if only for to observe her for twenty-four hours. "But," he went on, "You have to stay in bed and rest for the next twenty-four hours."

"I will," her words were jumbled mostly because her bottom lip was swollen to about twice its normal size.

"I mean it," he smiled. She always found him to be good-looking, dark curly hair and blue eyes, muscular physique, she could tell he worked out by the outline of his shoulders and chest against the blue scrubs. "Nothing strenuous." He leaned in closer, smiling. "And when I say in bed, I mean alone."

"Please, I'm so sore that's the last thing on my mind." She tried to smile but wasn't sure her lip was cooperating. It was best to just sit still and stare at him with a stupid, blank look on her face.

"Speaking of my mind." She touched the small piece of gauze on her forehead. "Am I going to need to see a plastic surgeon?"

"You are in the presence of a super talented emergency room physician who just happens to dabble in plastics." He tapped his chest as if he were Tarzan, "You won't even have a scar."

"What about the back of my head?" She turned herself gently to the left and then the right. "My neck is killing me."

"Excuse me?" a young laboratory technician stopped at the doorway holding several vials and a long, skinny strip of blood results.

"What is it?" Dr. Fare asked, holding out his hand as if he expected to sign something. "The results from her blood work are back already. She doesn't need any more to be taken."

"No," the technician shook his head. "I just need to confirm for the blood bank that your Rh negative."

"Yes," she nodded.

"Do you anticipate she will need a transfusion during this visit?"

"No," Dr. Fare nodded. "She's already been sutured and there was very little blood loss."

The technician pushed the strip of paper toward Dr. Fare. "Can you sign this for me? It's just acknowledging the blood bank doesn't need to procure blood for her."

Impatiently, Dr. Fare scribbled his name and handed it back to the technician. He turned to face Ryan as the technician exited the room. "X-rays and CT scan were negative." He ran his hand down the length of her neck, stopping at its base. "I ordered a consult with Dr. Parker, just as a precaution."

"The neurologist?" She repeated. "You think that's necessary?"

338

"I didn't see anything on the CT." He scribbled on a piece of paper. "But I'm not an expert. You do have one hell of a turkey egg on the back of your head. I imagine it's whiplash kind of reaction." He turned and typed something else onto her medical record. "Let me get you something for that."

He turned to leave and then leaned back into the room. "You want visitors?"

"Depends on who it is?" She pulled at her hospital gown. "I'm not really dressed for visitors."

"It's me and I've seen you in less." Cole slid past Dr. Fare. He stopped once he was fully into the room, his jaw tight, eyes narrowed. "I hope to be the one who catches this son of a bitch."

"It's not as bad as it looks." She opened her arms to him. "How'd you know?"

"I heard the 911 call on the radio, I knew from the description it was you. And Erik called about the same time. I was on a stakeout in Charlotte. He kissed the top of her head. "I may be looking for a new job in the morning." He looked around the room. "Where is he anyway?"

"I saw him for a few minutes as they were bringing into the examining room." She pointed into the hallway. "Probably lurking out there somewhere."

"Sorry to intrude," a husky voice called from the hallway. The tall, fit physician offered his hand to Cole as he advanced into the room. "Jeriad Parker. Morgan asked me to stop by and take a look, Ryan. I think he's hoping to discharge you."

"Did you review the CT, Dr. Parker?" Ryan asked, pulling the hospital gown tighter around her shoulders.

"I did" he smiled. "And I don't see anything on the CT. As Morgan said, it's negative." Dr. Parker flashed a ray of light from a penlight into both her eyes. "Your responses are fine. Other than an egg on the back of your head and some skinned knees, I think you're good to go."

He offered his hand again to Cole. "Virginia has access to the medical staff's cell phone numbers. If she needs anything or something concerns you, just give me a call." Dr. Parker disappeared out of the examining room with his white coat trailing behind like a banner.

"Excuse me?" Dr. Fare returned with a syringe in his hand. "Just let me give you this injection and I'll sign the discharge papers." He smiled but it wasn't a genuine smile, it was sadder. Gone was the jovial banter back and forth he'd exchanged with her minutes ago. It was all business, almost as if he were a completely different person.

Her mind drifted back to what Leon had said about the twins switching places when the situation demanded. She wondered if Dr. Fare had any siblings, a twin even. Her mind was spinning like a rat on a treadmill, she knew it was the pain med he'd already given her.

"What are you giving me now?"

"You pharmacists," he joked, only half-kidding. "Steroid, should last a day or two, just long enough for the pain you're having to resolve." He used an alcohol swab on the skin at the back of her neck.

"You're giving it to me in my neck?"

"Into the articular joint space." He gently slid the needle through the skin and emptied the contents of the barrel. "All done," he rubbed the place where he'd injected and tossed the syringe into the red sharps container. "Call me if she needs anything. My number is in her cell phone. And let me know if she does go and see the neurologist."

"Will do," Cole offered his hand. "Thanks for everything, Doc." He turned to Ryan. "A neurologist?"

"It's nothing, I've no plans to see him. I'm fine." She waved at him dismissively.

Cole waited until Dr. Fare had left the room to discreetly check outside for Erik. It only took a second to spy on him, sitting in the middle seat between two sets of families awaiting news of their loved one. To the outside observer, it appeared as if he could have been with either of the families. Erik was a master at blending in, if nothing else.

Cole motioned with his head for Erik to join them in the examining room. Once Erik was fully inside, Cole shut the door and pulled the privacy curtain around the bed. "Where were you?" His words were precise, short, and angry.

"I was right behind her, I swear," Erik answered looking anxiously at Ryan. "She parked in a secured lot. I don't have access to that area, I had to circle around the side and park in an adjacent area." He looked to his feet. "I saw him just as he ripped the satchel away but by the time I got around the building, he'd jumped into the van and it sped away."

He toyed with the hair hanging into his eyes, smoothing it into place to one side. "I'm sorry."

"It's not his fault, Cole," Ryan said, around her swollen lips. "I shouldn't have parked in my regular spot, it's just a habit."

"We have to be more careful, watching each other's back all the time," Cole said, sounding more like a coach than a cop. He looked around the examining room. "Where's Catherine?"

"She was here," Ryan answered. "She's with the cops."

"Did you already give your statement?"

She nodded that she had.

"Then let's get you dressed and home into bed." He motioned for Erik to step out and poured Ryan's clothes from a big plastic hospital bag onto the bed.

"I'm not putting that back on, just ask for a set of scrubs," she said, swinging her feet from the tall bed as if she were seven years old or an adult pretending to be a child, like Lily Tomlin.

Chapter 30

"My God," Coles words were soft as he folded the newspaper and placed in on the nightstand beside her bed. "I can't believe Hartmann wrote this story. I bet the phones at the state capital are buzzing."

"He said he was going to print it," Ryan said, taking another sip of coffee and trying not to agitate her swollen lips. She reached for the newspaper again. "Did you doubt that he would?"

"No, he said it was his practice to only report things he could prove. He was pretty sure about his facts the other day." He slid fully clothed into the warm place next to her. "I did not enjoy sleeping in the guest room last night."

She adjusted the blankets more fully around her waist. "I told you to sleep in here with me." She paused. "I had a long talk with McKenzie the other night, she's old enough to understand our relationship. You shouldn't have to sneak in and out of the house depending on when she is and isn't home."

"After yesterday you needed to rest," he explained. "I'm so afraid something's going to happen. This thing we're in the middle of, is dangerous."

"What do you think they were hoping to take?" she asked, yawning into her hand, mindful of her lip. "There was nothing in my satchel important enough to warrant a mugging."

"I don't know, the results of Beliard's code medications, the contents of those syringes. Catherine's key, the pictures, stuff from the crypt." He paused. "I don't know.

"Why would I have Catherine's pictures or the key?" she asked, her thoughts racing. "She's got those in a safe place."

"What about the guys you fired?"

"The twins?"

"No, the pharmacist," he paused. "What twins?"

"It's a long story. And I've always said Jayson was harmless. I--"

Her cell phone startled them both as he jumped to his feet to grab it for her.

She checked the number before answering the call. "Hey Calvin," she said into the phone as best as she could, with the injured lip.

"Hey Ryan," his words were easily audible through the receiver. "I finished that assay you wanted on the medication you dropped off."

"Anything interesting?"

"The partial bottle and the full unused bottle both contain the same chemical entity but it's not the product that is currently commercially available as Anodyne."

"What is it?"

"I couldn't identify it," he went on. "It most closely resembles the chemical structure of serotonin but it isn't. There are also characteristics similar to lysergic acid diethylamide but again, it isn't."

LSD, she thought to herself, her silence took him by surprise as several minutes passed before he asked. "Ryan, you still there?"

"Yes," she said, her words hoarse, her mind on overload as she recollected the chemical drawing in Beliard's crypt. She'd known right away the structure in the drawing was similar to serotonin. "Calvin, if I send you a picture of a chemical structure can you rule it out or in as probable."

"Yeah," he answered. "Probably down to a side chain or two."

"I'll send it within the hour." Her mind was spinning, Was it possible, Beliard and his friends had reactivated a CIA cell here in the hospital before his death? "Thanks, Calvin." She disconnected the call.

"You can't be serious?" Cole asked, "You think the stuff in those bottles you sent to your friend and the medication used in the MKUltra studies are the same?" He didn't give her a chance to answer. "You must have hit your head harder than I thought. Where's Dr. Parker's number again?"

"I think it's beginning to make sense," she said, as she threw the blankets back and moved toward her closet.

"What are you doing?" He followed her into the big walk-in closet. "The doctor said twenty-four hours." He checked his watch. "It's barely been twelve."

"I'm a terrible patient," She stepped out of her pajamas and into black dress pants and a light sweater. "Everyone knows this is a fact."

"Seriously," he got her around the waist. "Go back to bed, you're still recovering."

"I was mugged, Cole." She stepped into her shoes. "It looks worse than it is, really. And Erik will be close by and at all times."

"Yeah," Cole whined. "That plan didn't work out well at all yesterday." He stepped into his shoes and grabbed his leather jacket from the dressing chair. "Where are we going?"

"To get a copy of the chemical formula we found in the contents of the crypt. It's in a safe place. I've got to get it over to Calvin as soon as I can."

"You're not thinking about driving all the way to Charlotte?"

"Yes, I am." She stopped at the door. "What if the experiments didn't stop when the CIA says they did? What if they continued and Beliard was a part of it and wanted out? Jacob Fleming was a high-ranking official in the intelligence branch of the US Army." She paused. "Maybe that's what they fought about, what caused the rift between them."

"And after he died, someone took the program over?" Cole walked quickly to keep up with her, even in heels she could outpace him.

"Yes, and reactivated Beliard. He didn't want to play and they had him killed."

"Maybe," he followed her down the steps. "But as Hartmann said, if you don't have the proof, you don't have anything."

"I guess we'll just have to work harder to find some proof then. And we're starting with this chemical structure." She grabbed her purse. "I'll call Catherine." The sentence was barely out of her mouth when she staggered and fell into the door frame.

"What's wrong?" he asked, holding her at the waist and pulling her toward the sofa. "Maybe I should call Dr. Parker, honey?"

"I got up too quickly, I'm just a little dizzy." She used the back of the sofa as leverage to stay on her feet. "It's okay, really—"

Her hands flew to her head, the pain was blinding as she fell against him but she pushed him away and stumbled toward the bathroom, retching with each advancing step. She'd only barely positioned her face over the toilet before emptying the contents of her stomach into the porcelain bowl.

Cole waited patiently at the door, stepping in and out of the bathroom several times to pull her hair out of her face or make an offer of water or a wet compass.

"Feel better?" he asked, once she'd struggled from the floor and was back on her feet.

"Yes," she looked around the hallway. "Where's my satchel?"

"Your what?"

"My satchel?"

"Did you get a new one?" he peered into the living room where she usually dropped the old room once she'd arrived home.

"No, of course not. I've had that one for years. It was a graduation present from my Dad."

"Honey, you were mugged yesterday and someone took it, remember?" His face contorted with concern as he reached for his phone. "I getting Dr. Parker's number."

"Don't be silly," she pushed at his chest. "I forgot, that's all." She grabbed her purse from off the floor by the front door where she'd tossed it when the wave of nausea had struck. "Haven't you ever forgotten something?"

"Of course," he nodded. If she'd been watching his face, reading his eyes, she'd have known he didn't mean it.

"There you go, then," she said. "Let's go, I've got to sign off payroll or no one in the pharmacy is going to get paid."

"You're going into work? I thought we were going to see Catherine and then come back here so you can rest."

"Oh yeah," her words were mechanical. "What did I want to talk to her about, again?"

He stopped. "You're not well. Maybe you're having a stroke or something."

"No," she slid into the passenger seat and handed him the key. "I just a little dehydrated I think. I'll get some water and I'll be fine."

"I hope so," he smiled, before adjusting the driver's seat and pulling out of her driveway, praying that Catherine was in her office and could talk Ryan into a more in-depth evaluation than the one she'd received from Dr. Fare.

****

By the time Ryan and Cole completed the fifteen- minute drive to the hospital, she was more like her usual self. Gone was the disorganized rambling and forgetfulness. In its place was the critically thinking and methodical person he'd come to know over the last few months.

"You sure you're okay?" he asked again, as they pulled into the physician's lot and waited as the electronic bar code reader scanned the sticker on her back-passenger window.

"Yes, whatever it was, has past."

She turned and looked out through the back window. "I don't see Erik. Is he close?"

"Two cars back," Cole watched in the rearview mirror as Erik turned into an adjacent lot and parked on the exterior as close to where Ryan usually parked as was possible.

"He's parking." Cole pulled her car into a spot near the physician's entrance.

"Are we waiting for him?" she asked, leaning in minimizing the space between them to determine where Erik had stationed himself.

"No," Cole parked and made his way quickly around to her side and opened the door. "Since I'm with you, he'll maintain surveillance from his vehicle."

She scanned the area, "Is D.J. somewhere nearby as well keeping an eye on Catherine?"

He nodded and motioned her toward the door. "He better be."

****

"You look like hell," Catherine said from Ryan's doorway. "I thought Dr. Fare said twenty-four hours."

"He did," Ryan nodded. "I averaged the time plus or minus ten hours, so I'm good. And you only look slightly better than me. How's the arm?"

"Much better. This isn't a clinical trial, you know. You should try and be a better patient."

"Are you familiar with the pot and kettle analogy?"

"Yes, and I don't like either." Catherine laughed. She cleared her throat. "I watched the video from the camera that faces the physician's lot. Your entire assault was captured on tape but the license plate of the van isn't readable and there's nothing about the men who mugged you that we can use to identify them."

"I'm not surprised."

Catherine went on "The first man runs into the frame and punches you, while you are down and fighting him off, another man enters the frame and hits you from behind before ripping the satchel from your shoulder. The entire event took less than 45 seconds."

She paused. "What do you mean, you aren't surprised?"

"They've been one step ahead at every turn, it's like they've got eyes and ears on us at all times, even though we can't determine how."

"Speaking of eyes and ears, where's Cole?" Catherine held up her phone. "I got a text from him asking to send your CT scan to a neurologist for a second opinion." She paused. "It's not necessary, I'm fine."

"So, you don't want me to have Dr. Fare forward them to –" She checked her phone. "Dr. Parker?"

"You can, but I'm sure nothing's wrong with me."

"Where'd you say Cole was again?" Catherine asked, and moved around to her computer to facilitate sending the CT scan electronically to Dr. Parker.

"He went to take something down to Charlotte for me."

"Your chemist friend, again?"

"Yes, guess what's in the Anodyne bottles with the blue dots?"

"No idea but I'm guessing it's not Anodyne."

"You are right again, as usual. It isn't Anodyne."

"What then?"

"I'm not sure but Calvin said it had a chemical structure similar to that of serotonin and features similar to LSD."

"My God, "Catherine's hand went to her mouth. "You think it's the MKUltra Drug?"

"I do," she pushed back in her chair as far as she could go. "I don't think the CIA's testing stopped when it was supposed to, I think someone or some group has continued the program and is testing it on patients here at the hospital."

"For what purpose?" Catherine could hardly put the words together. As much as she wanted to deny what Ryan was saying, tell her how ridiculous it all sounded, she knew in her gut, it was beginning to make sense finally."

"I think Beliard and Jacob Fleming were recruited at a young age by the CIA, Beliard wanted out and Jacob let him go. After Jacob's death, for whatever purpose, Beliard was called back to action and declined. I think they killed him because they feared he was going to expose them. His meetings with the FBI had nothing to do with corporate corruption, he was feeding them information about MKUltra."

"Speaking of corruption, I think we need to notify corporate compliance that we suspect Aiden and Eleanor were responsible for diverting the controlled substances from the operating room."

"You really think Aiden is involved in this?" Ryan dropped her hands to her side as if she were surrendering.

"If you think about it, he's always the one who reviews the tapes and reports nothing back. What if he's involved and manipulating the evidence?"

"What are we going to do?" Catherine whispered before stopping at the door. "I'm scared."

"Me too," Ryan mumbled, hoping Cole returned soon.

****

"You wanted to see me?" Brittany tapped on Ryan's door frame but didn't wait for an invitation to enter. Instead, she plopped herself down into the empty chair, careful to pull her form-fitting, tight skirt discretely over her thighs.

"Yes," Ryan motioned to the chair out of habit not because she hadn't realized Brittany was already seated. Ryan supposed Brittany could be classified as pretty, at least if she weren't so annoying, so preppy, and school-girlish all the time in any given situation.

Brittany was tall and blonde, at least for the time being, that is. Last year when Brittany first moved into the role of director for the human resources department, she'd come into the job as a blonde. Within a few months, she was a brunette, a red head by Christmas and for the last four months, she was back to being a blonde. Ryan smiled, thinking if there were any colors left that Brittany could try out. Hospital policy stated hair had to be of a color that occurred naturally in nature. She supposed Brittany could dye it black next time, but with her crystal blue eyes and fair skin, she'd probably look more like Elvira than a professional healthcare associate.

"Your message said something about suspending two pharmacy technicians, but I asked Mira, the associate who manages any and all corrective actions, and she had nothing documented so I suppose you've decided against the corrective action –"

"I suspended them already two nights ago." Ryan didn't blink, she was hoping her battered face and swollen lips would give her the edge she needed to face down Brittany. No way was Brittany going to mess with her when she looked as if she'd gone five rounds with Mike Tyson.

"Ryan," she exhaled, as if she were disciplining a child. "We've talked about this before, you can't just suspend people at will. There's a process."

"Actually, I can," Ryan flopped an open manual under Brittany's nose and tapped the policy titled Patient Safety. "This reads that in the event the action is so egregious as to compromise patient safety, the employee may be suspended immediately without satisfying any other component of the corrective action procedures."

"How do you believe patients may have been compromised?" Brittany asked as if she had a bad taste in her mouth.

"Louis and Levi are engaged in an unsanctioned distribution of a medication. It has not been procured in a manner that promotes the best interest of the patients. I cannot validate neither the chain of custody nor the integrity of the products they have been dispersing."

"There's also a question regarding fraudulent timecards."

"How so?"

"The staff believes at times they are working shifts as the other twin and then signing at the end of the week they worked a shift when in fact, they didn't. The other twin did."

"What action plan are you working under?" Brittany's bottom lip curled up, Ryan couldn't help but think of Cruella Deville but without the cute black and white dalmatians.

"I've sent a sample of the product out for analysis. Both employees are suspended pending the results of the outside laboratory."

"And for the issue of fraud?"

"One twin has a scar, just over his eyebrow, the other doesn't. Aiden has the timecard report and is reviewing the video to see if he can determine which twin is working and which twin is signed in as working."

"You will have all this data available for the final corrective action if termination is recommended?"

"Yes, of course."

****

"It's late we should head home, D.J. and Erik are probably rethinking this assignment." Catherine laughed, pointing to the window behind Ryan where the sky was illuminated only by the half-full moon.

"They're probably in Erik's car together, waiting for us to come out. They know we both exit through the physician's exit." Ryan flipped her computer off.

"Yeah, but one of us has a really great parking spot, while the other has to hike it across the street to the medical office building."

"I'm sorry, you should ask Noah about parking in the doctor's lot. Your hours alone probably warrant it."

"No, that wouldn't be fair. A lot of the nurse managers work the same hours and they aren't parking isn't convenient. I guess I should have gotten a doctorate, right?"

"If it were up to me, I'd let you park there, right alongside of me." Ryan folded the day's newspaper and stashed it under her arm. "I read this quickly this morning when I first woke up but I didn't retain much. I'm going to read it again."

"What do you mean, you didn't retain much?"

"I had a horrible headache this morning with vomiting, and a little dizziness. I thought I might have to come back in, maybe Fare missed something during my assessment but whatever it was passed and I was fine."

"It's a good read for sure, definitely one you'll want to remember. Virginia said the phone was ringing off the hook this morning." Her words were mechanical, her thoughts lost in the gratitude that she'd sent Ryan's CT scan for follow up with the neurologist.

"Who was calling?" Ryan pulled her office door and waited for Catherine to secure hers.

"Other reporters, patients, staff," Catherine says. "It's not every day an article comes out that pretty much demands the Governor steps down after being charged with corruption."

"Guess will be looking for someone else to do the keynote speech at the gala?"

"No, Virginia said his aid stopped by this afternoon and stated the Governor is still planning on delivering the speech. I think you were in with Brittany." She paused. "How is the princess?"

"Blonde today," Ryan laughed. "She was giving me grief about suspending the twins without a proper investigation."

"You showed her the patient safety clause?" Catherine waited at the physician's exit for Ryan to swipe her badge through the reader and followed her out the door and into the night air.

"Yes, and there's no way she could argue with my concern about them switching places."

"That's going to be hard to prove, don't you think?"

"Aiden is watching the tapes and comparing it to the schedule and the time reports. One has a scar over his eyebrow, the other doesn't."

"Aiden's watching the tapes. "Catherine repeated, her mind spinning with the implication.

"Did you complete the compliance report regarding your suspicions about Aiden?" Ryan asked

"I did and I got a call not twenty minutes later from Peter asking for more details." She paused, "Right before I left my office I received notification from compliance that the complaint was closed."

"That's odd," Ryan added. "They were able to investigate it so quickly and close it out so soon. Maybe we're just being paranoid? Everything can't be a chimera, maybe some things are exactly as they seem."

"Almost verbatim what Peter said when he closed out my concern." She paused. "He said the picture is clearly not Aiden and thousands of people worldwide probably have a tattoo that is the same or similar to someone else's."

"Did you tell Peter that the tattoo was handmade?" Ryan asked.

"Yes, and he said for all we know, it's nothing more than a birthmark or a scar."

Ryan looked anxiously around them. "Maybe all this secret agent stuff is starting to get to us? Maybe he isn't involved at all, everything is as it seems and his scar is just a scar?"

"What's funny, Aiden has a scar over his eyebrow. Said he got it playing basketball but I heard a rumor he had some plastic surgery done and removed a birthmark."

"I'm glad I won't have to dish out extra cash for a plastic surgeon, Fare said he sutured me so well, I won't be able to find the scar." She paused. "Did you know he dabbled in plastics?"

"I did hear that somewhere." Her mind wandered, trying to recall where. "But I can't remember where."

"Anwar had a scar too, right over his brow." She smiled, remembering how he'd recited the pig slopping story and the injury that resulted. Recently Anwar had said the new scar was the aftermath of a birthmark removal but thinking back to the fact both scars were on his face maybe neither of those stories were true. Maybe, he'd had a little plastic surgery of his own. She couldn't help but consider if Reggie's face might have been different. So different, in fact, she might not have known him.

"Ladies?" Erik stepped out of the new building's shadow. "Calling it a night?"

"Yes, I'm beat." Ryan looked to where her car was normally parked. "I forgot Cole dropped me off this morning. I'm afraid I'm going to need a lift, Erik."

"I can take you," Catherine offered, pointing across the street.

"That's okay, I'd have to follow her anyway. Taking her up to the door's really only an extra step or two."

"You sure?" she looked to Ryan for approval.

"Yeah, it's fine." Ryan nodded. "D.J.'s waiting for you in the other lot. I see him over by your car."

"Oh yeah, I see." She smiled. "I'd wave to him but he lectures me about pretending he's not there. So, I better not." She stepped off the step and across the physician's lot, coming to a halt at the sidewalk. She looked left and right to ensure nothing was coming. And then stole a last look to her let before stepping into the street.

She wasn't exactly in the middle of the street, but would have been had she taken three, maybe four more steps. There was no horn or squealing of brakes, nothing except a tunnel of light so bright, she almost didn't realize it was coming from a car, the car speeding up and heading right for her.

It was like a scene in a movie, she thought, frozen in place, unable to move or scream, although she could hear herself screaming in her mind to move. But as she stood there caught in the car's high beam, all she could consider was would it be better to try and run ahead or fall back to get out of its path.

Closer, she considered again, the car was coming closer. It was nearly upon her. She should make a decision, move one way or another before it was too late. She didn't see D.J. didn't really hear him either but she did feel him as he flung his body against hers as if they were on a football field and she was holding the ball.

They fell against the pavement, out of the car's path, the force of D.J.'s movement taking them almost back to the sidewalk.

It took a minute for Catherine to realize what had happened, acknowledge that she was safe albeit dazed. She struggled to sit up and push herself away from him. Like her, he was unhurt, just stunned and trying to push himself to his feet at the same time.

"Are you hurt?" He asked and offered his hand to her.

Ahead of them, the traffic continued, moving up and down the dark street as if nothing had happened. "No, my arm is hurting but I don't think it's broken." She turned her wrist to check the time. "My watch is broken."

"Watches can be replaced," he said grabbing for his gun once he heard the sounds of someone else approaching them.

"My God, D.J.!" Erik called once he was close enough for them to hear. "You guys okay?"

"Yes," I think so," D.J. answered, but waited for Catherine to respond as well.

"Yeah, a bit bruised for sure." She rubbed her hip with the hand that wasn't hurting knowing her ass and back would be black and blue in the morning.

"Catherine?" Ryan exclaimed, finally coming upon them. She pointed to her shoes. "I'd be dead meat in these heels." She took her friend's hand. "You okay?" And looked to D.J., "Are you hurt?"

"Did you see what kind of vehicle it was?" D.J. asked, looking down the street where it went as if he might still catch a glimpse.

"Not really," Erik answered. "larger model SUV, dark color."

"Not a van?" Catherine asked and exchanged looks with Ryan,

"No, maybe an expedition, something like that." Erik offered. "I think it's pretty safe to say that was no accident."

"Maybe the driver didn't see her, playing with the radio or texting?" Ryan suggested.

"It was parked with its lights off on the shoulder of the road." D.J. paused. "He was waiting for her."

"He?" Erik questioned, "Did you get a look at the driver?"

"No," D.J. shook his head. "It could have been a woman, I guess. I couldn't tell the lights were too bright."

Erik took Catherine's arm. "You sure you don't want to go back to the emergency room and left the doctor take a look?" Once D.J. was at their side he added. "Either of you?"

"No," D.J. shook his head. "I've taken much harder hits." He assessed Catherine. "But you're a tiny thing, you sure you don't want to get checked out?"

"I'm sure," she walked toward her vehicle with him only a few steps behind. "I'll soak in a hot tub for a bit once I get home. I'll be fine."

"You want me to complete the variance report?" Ryan called out once Catherine was to the car.

"I'll do it when I get in," Catherine chuckled nervously. "I've already written the action plan in my head."

"What's that?" Ryan called back, walking with Erik to his vehicle.

"Contract that catwalk company to start on a crosswalk." She smiled. "See you in the morning."

Chapter 31

"Not another article by that reporter?" Ryan heard Virginia complaining from her desk. "Jesus?"

"Everything ok?" Ryan asked, getting out from behind the desk and walking toward the exit, stopping at the doorway.

"This guy Hartmann has it bad for the governor." She popped loudly on a piece of gum in her mouth. "I can't believe the editor allowed him to print something like this." She paused and added quickly. "Again."

"Hartmann doesn't hit me as the type of man who takes a stand about anything he can't support."

"Maybe," Virginia mumbled; her face buried behind the opened paper. In the same motion, she swatted the paper away and folded it into uneven quarters. "Did you speak with Catherine this morning?"

"Yes," Ryan nodded, stepping close enough to collect the paper to read as she wandered back on her side of the office and through her door. "She's running a bit late."

"She's lucky she wasn't badly hurt last night. That street is crazy at night, the people drive like they've lost their mind."

"Or just had it altered," Ryan whispered under her breath. "Did you get the mail yet from the mailroom?"

"Yes," Virginia nodded. "You only had a few things." She pulled a small padded envelope from her inbox. "This came for you as well." She turned it so Ryan could read the front where CONFIDENTIAL was printed in big, black, and bold letters. "I'll get it in a minute." She continued reading to herself. Hartmann had taken off the gloves for today's article. He'd implied nothing, instead, he spoke to every rumor and complaint ever made against the governor since he'd taken office.

Her cell phone rang twice before she pulled it from her pocket, tossing the paperback to Virginia. "I'll take this in my office."

"The hunky cop?"

"No, a friend from school. A bunch of us get together once a month for dinner and catch up."

"That's nice," Virginia said, without looking up.

"It can't be for that, we just met two weeks ago." She pulled the phone to her ear. "Hey, Stacy."

It was obvious the caller was upset, crying even. "Stacy, what's wrong?"

"It's Calvin," the caller cried. "He's dead."

"What?" Ryan fell into her chair, the phone still tight against her ear. "What happened?"

"Someone broke into his lab and stabbed him."

"There must be some mistake." Ryan's mind was traveling, thinking Cole has just dropped off the diagram of the MKUltra." The words repeated, silently in her head.

"There's no mistake," Stacey went on through the tears. "Apparently they were looking for drugs, didn't even know Calvin was still in the lab."

"How do you know this?"

"They arrested someone already." She paused. "A junkie who lives on the streets near the airport."

"I've got to go, Stacy. I'll call you later." She dialed Cole three times, hanging up once it went to voicemail. There was no way she could leave this on a message. She'd killed him, just as surely as if she plunged the knife into his heart herself.

She tossed the phone on top of the desk and ran her hand through her hair before walking slowly to the chair and easing herself into it.

"Everything ok?" Noah's voice from the doorway was soft as if he was in church.

"No, just got some bad news about a friend of mine. He was killed yesterday."

"I'm sorry,"

She jumped, he moved stealth-like from the door to her empty chair. He hadn't made a sound, not even the sound of air expelling from his lungs.

"Yeah, me too." She rubbed her lip gently, aware that it was still sore and bruised from the mugging. "He was a good guy, a great friend." She cleared her throat. "Did you need something?"

"Yes," he clasped his hands together in his lap as if he were meditating. "I want to talk to you about your friend, the reporter."

"My friend?" she repeated. "I wouldn't call us friends."

"The leadership team and I met yesterday evening and we're extremely concerned about these articles." He paused. "We'd like them to stop."

"I've nothing to do with the articles or with Mr. Hartmann."

"Are you his source?"

"Me?" she couldn't help but laugh. "You think I'm the leak?"

"I think there's a probability that you are, yes."

"Where would I even get that kind of information? I've no knowledge of the intricacies of the GHF corporation or the governor's ties."

"Do you and Mr. Hartmann engage one another outside of the working environment?"

"Who I engage with outside of work is none of your business."

"You're suspended?" His words were flat, they were no different than if he'd asked her to pass the butter.

"You can't be serious; you have no grounds to suspend me."

"Captain?" He stood and looked toward her office doorway where Aiden sulked into the picture.

"I'm sorry, Ryan." His head was bowed, arms at his side. "If you'll just grab your things, I'll walk you to your car."

"This is ridiculous." Ryan blushed, her fair complexion betraying her once again as the embarrassment set in from her forehead and traveled all the down to her chest. "Why don't we talk about your Anodyne friend instead?" She was surprised how confident her words came out, all she wanted to do was run back in the office and shut the door.

"Anodyne?" Noah stopped and turned back around to face her. "I'm afraid I don't know what –"

"Don't play stupid Noah," She cut him off. "You're not a stupid man!" Ryan stepped into his personal space. "I know about the blue dots."

"I don't know what you're talking about Dr. Allen," he turned away from her. "Captain?"

Aiden stepped in between them and took her gently by the arm. "Let's just go, you can sort this out later. Okay?"

"You could at least tell me who's giving you your information." She grabbed her purse and an old briefcase she'd stashed in her closet. She hadn't had time to get a new one and thought at the time, the old one was better than nothing.

"As I said," Noah's tone and cadence was a decibel above the piano. "It is the consensus of the management team."

"There's no way Catherine would support this, Erin's been away at a conference all week. That just leaves Oliver." She paused, "He rarely comes out of his office anymore, does he even still work here? Brittany.." Her words trailed off; this was Brittany's payback for suspending the twins without HR approval. "Is Brittany behind all this?"

"She is the HR director." He motioned Aiden toward the door. "Obviously, she's been involved but no more or less than anyone else."

He smiled at her as if he was expecting her to hug him goodbye. "Go home, get some rest. Brittany will call you to set up an appointment after the investigation is complete." He waited until she was out of her office before pulling the door behind him closed. "It will all work out, you'll see."

Ryan stopped at Virginia's desk. "Can I get that envelope please?"

Virginia handed it toward Ryan's extended hand but it was swept up by Noah before it touched Ryan's hand. "This is hospital property." Gone were the soft, whispered words. This time his statement was bold and loud.

"It's addressed to me and marked confidential." Calvin's results, she thought to herself. Dammit, she wished she'd taken it when

Virginia initially offered it to her. "You don't know that it is hospital property until you open it."

He held on tightly to it. "And you don't know that it isn't."

Noah wandered in front of Virginia's desk, stopping just short of his office door. His words were soft again. Mr. Hyde had banished Dr. Jekyll away again. He was just a shadow away from smiling. "If it is indeed your personal property, it will be returned to you."

He opened the door and disappeared inside, taking the envelope with him and tapping the door closed.

"Let's go, Ryan." Aiden offered.

"I'm so sorry," Virginia's face was almost as red as Ryan's.

Ryan walked silently in front of Aiden, considering that maybe she should fake a stroke and drop to the floor only to feel better and walk by herself out once she'd been transported to the emergency department.

As humiliating as it was, the saving grace had been that Noah nor Erin was there to escort her out the door. Ryan could picture Erin's canary eaten face as she was being escorted from the office.

Yes Ma'am, the contributing factor for avoiding a rapid response code today had been that the only person escorting her out of the building was Aiden. And she liked him. At least she thought she still did. Until they could confirm his tattoo wasn't the same as Eleanor's, he was an ally. Although it was still up for debate.

****

"They fired you?" Cole looked quickly back and forth from the road to where Ryan sat in the passenger's seat.

"No, I've been suspended pending the outcome of reviewing where the leak for Hartmann's article came from."

"Why would they think it came from you?"

"I can't even begin to answer that. I'm hoping once Catherine gets back to work, she can find out for me. Virginia and she are close. If Virginia knows anything, she'll tell her."

"Isn't Virginia, the CEO's executive assistant?"

"Yes."

"Aren't you afraid he might fire her as well?"

"I hadn't thought of that, you're right. Catherine will have to do this on her own."

"How is she." He paused. "I mean, she could have been killed last night, that has to weigh heavy on her mind."

"Speaking of, I know Calvin's death is related to the formula you took to him. I'm responsible, aren't I?"

"You aren't responsible, but I do agree with you that it's related."

"How so?" She turned in the seat to face him better.

"When you called me this morning to tell me about getting suspended and Calvin's death. I felt so bad for you. It's just so much to take it all at the same time." He adjusted the volume on the radio and went on. "I got a friend in BSO and she told me where the guy the arrested for Calvin's murder was being held."

"You interrogated him?"

"No, it's not my case but I was allowed to watch the interview from the observation room."

"Observation room?" she repeated.

"There's a one-way mirror into the interrogation room and I was on the other side watching."

"I see" she nodded.

"The guy who was arrested, admitted to killing your friend. But he claims he was high as a kite when he broke into the lab."

"Why would he break in, it's not a pharmacy. It looks more like an office building."

"He says a friend of his gave him the smack but it was stronger than what he usually gets." Cole paused, checking his rear-view mirror.

"Are you looking for Erik?"

"No, I gave him the night off since you were already home and I'm here with you."

"You can't stay the night, McKenzie is home."

"I thought you said—" His words were tinged with frustration.

"I did and I will, but I haven't yet." She rubbed his arm. "Give me till the weekend" and motioned in the air with her hand. "Go on."

"So, after the guy gets really high on the smack, the friend mentions a place where a lot of product is stored and there's no guards, alarms, nothing. Even mentions the address to him."

"The junkie goes to the lab to collect the smack, isn't expecting Calvin to be there and ends up killing him in response."

"What about that seems odd to you?"

"The junkie is a confidential informant; he works with the detectives a lot to get some really bad players and drugs off the street. His rap sheet contains mostly possession related charges, he'd never hurt anyone in his entire life."

"Sounds convenient."

"Once the detectives finished with him, they let me talk with him. You know what he said?"

"What?"

"He said the chemist's death must have been a payment of some debt because there was no way he'd have gone into that place looking for drugs if he hadn't been high." Cole shook his head. "He said it was almost like his friend set him up to do this murder and he couldn't figure out why."

"I think we know why and it was Calvin who was set up not that murderer."

"Was Calvin able to tell you what you wanted to know before he died?"

"No, but an envelope came for me today marked confidential."

"Great! What was in it?"

"Noah confiscated it as hospital property."

"I'm sorry, that was the only real evidence we had to prove what you believe is happening."

"I know, I'm hoping Catherine can sniff something else out while I'm on suspension."

****

Catherine looked again through the walkway out of the office and into the hallway. If she spun to the left in the chair she could almost make out the door to Ryan's office, the closed door that is to the still empty office. In fact, it hadn't been opened all day and no one had been inside.

Virginia had tears in her eyes when she updated Catherine on what happened with Ryan earlier that morning and how embarrassed Ryan was to have to be escorted out.

And poor Aiden, Virginia had wiped at her eyes, he couldn't even look up at her. He'd kept his head down for the entire distance from Ryan's office to the exterior hallway. Virginia had said she imagined he'd walked like that with her all the way to Ryan's car.

No doubt, Erik would have an earful to tell them all when they next met. And she couldn't hardly wait to see what Hartmann had to say about all the feedback from the articles.

She wanted nothing more than to call Ryan and inquire if there were any new developments but something in her gut told her to hold off and her gut was seldom wrong.

"Hello?" she heard the man's voice loud and clear even though he was still outside of her office standing at the main entrance into administration.

"Can I help you?" She made her way quickly around the desk, trying not to scream out when her knee tapped the edge of the desk.

If the man noticed her limp, he gave no indication or apology for the intrusion.

"My name is Sherman Hanks. I am—"

"I know who you are, Mr. Hanks. I recognize you from the many pictures you're in with the governor." She paused. "And you've been in before, yes?"

Sherman Hanks was a small man, dressed in a brown suit that was almost a size too large for him. And it looked cheap, not blue light special cheap but not designer expensive either. His brown hair was thin, so thin there were places you could see his scalp, even though he'd tried to cover the balding areas with the longer, greasy hair that he'd combed over.

There was very little of the shirt visible under the thick, wide tie he was wearing. It reminded Catherine of one her grandfather used to wear before he died. And he'd died thirty plus years ago. He wasn't wearing a wedding ring but that didn't always mean a man wasn't married. Gordon seldom wore the one she'd put on his fingers twenty years ago. There was, however, and expensive watch around his left wrist and several thick, gold chains hanging from the other.

What he lacked in financial consideration for clothes, he more than made up for in jewelry. Catherine was pretty sure the Rolex he was wearing wasn't a knock-off. She was confident it was the real thing.

He smiled. "Yes, I came a few days ago to announce the governor's request to speak at your upcoming gala." He looked around the office as if he was looking for someone, his attention focused on Virginia's desk. "I believe the lovely lady who sits at this desk was here to assist me."

"Virginia's already gone for the day. Is there something I can do?"

"As his aid, I have to make sure all the arrangements are in accordance with his requests."

"His requests?"

"Yes, you know. Which table he wants to be placed at and who he'd like to accompany him at the table, his food choices, and wine selection."

"Did you provide these details to Virginia?"

"Yes," he smiled revealing a small gap between the larger teeth on top.

"Then I am confident everything will be per the governor's request." She paused. "I hate that you've wasted your time, made this trip for nothing."

"There's also the matter of the recent articles that have surfaced regarding alleged connections between the governor and his former employer." His words were arrogant, he was diving into the deep end of the pool, clothes, shoes, and all.

"I can't speak to that Mr. Sherman." Catherine positioned herself more firmly against the empty desk by the front office.

"From what I understand, you and Dr. Allen are very close?"

"Is there a question in there somewhere, sir?"

"No, no," he was backpaddling, the water was deeper than he was expecting. Catherine was thinking maybe he couldn't swim after all. "The governor was just wondering that maybe you could consider speaking to her and convincing her to share where Mr. Hartmann is getting his information."

"Why do you think Dr. Allen would have information about Mr. Hartmann's source for the investigation?"

"Because that's what our sources have shared with us."

"I think your sources are mistaken." She turned away from him. "Good day, Mr. Hanks. It's late, I'm going home for the night."

****

Ryan knew it was a dream, it began like all dreams do, blurry, dark, and smoky with distorted images that seem to float on air in and around the immediate area. There was an unfamiliar odor, it smelled as if someone had let a fire burn out and the ash was still circling in the air. But she knew she was in her bedroom, at least some of the furnishings were familiar. There was her bed, and dresser, both nightstands at either side of the bed, pictures of her Mom and McKenzie poised at angles so that she could see them from any place in the room.

Wait, she thought, if the bed was over there were it normally was, then what was she laying on? A gurney maybe, a massage table perhaps? Had Cole planned a night of romance after all? No, she moved her lips but the words didn't come. He'd left hours ago, whatever she was dreaming, it didn't feel romantic at all.

Wake up, she told herself again and attempted to pat herself awake with a free hand. Why couldn't she move her arms or legs? She craned her neck just enough to see she was restrained, it looked just like the ones they used sometimes in the emergency department.

She pulled at the restraints, her mind screaming within itself, Wake up! The bed under her rocked back and forth gently, perhaps she'd wake up if she fell out of the bed.

"It's okay," his voice was soft and familiar as he stepped from the shadow toward the back of the room. "Calm down, it will all be over soon and everything will be good again for you. I promise."

Wake up! she demanded, jerking so hard against the restraints, her wrists were hurting.

"You're going to bruise, if you don't stop that." He wrapped a strip of gauze around her wrist several times just under the leather bracelet and repeated the action on the other wrist.

She saw the syringe in his hand when he turned back to her. "No," she whined. It was the first time she thought she'd actually said the words instead of thinking them.

"It won't hurt, you have my word." He pulled her hair away from her neck and injected as close to the base of her neck as he could with her laying on her back. "There," he said, massaging the area. "You're all done. Time to sleep now but I'll see you soon."

She felt a burning at the back of her neck before the room went dark and her head slumped to one side as she succumbed to the darkness.

****

"Mom!" Ryan heard her daughter's voice before she felt the not so gentle shaking at her shoulder. "Mom, wake up!" McKenzie said again, falling into the bed alongside her and almost trampolining Ryan out of the bed and onto the floor.

"What is it that can't wait till morning, McKenzie?"

"It is morning, Mom," McKenzie explained. "Are you going to work today or what?"

"Or what" Ryan flipped over in the bed so that her back was facing her daughter.

"You're not going in, seriously?"

"No, I was suspended."

"Suspended?" McKenzie's words were full of intrigue. "My never-color-outside-the-lines Mom was suspended?" She slid further into the bed to lay alongside her mother. "For what?"

"Did you read the articles about the governor?" Ryan words were muffled under the blanket.

"Yes." She toyed with her mother's hair.

"My boss thinks I'm the sources for all the information the reporter mentioned."

"You?" She paused. "He obviously doesn't know you very well."

McKenzie leaned in close to her mother, it was as if she was going to kiss her neck. She smiled and pulled away so that a comfortable space was left between them. "Maybe your boss and I both have lots to learn."

"What's that supposed to me?"

"Mother, you have a hickey."

"I do not," Ryan sat up, the blankets falling away to collect at her waist.

"Yes, you do, on your neck."

"That's ridiculous –"

"Please Mom, I heard Cole sneaking out this morning, it was early before sunrise."

"McKenzie, he never stays over when you are home, you know that. I was alone last night."

McKenzie laughed and slid out from under the blankets to stand at the side of the bed. "I thought I heard a man's voice last night. I heard your voice as well, but it was different."

"You were dreaming," Ryan explained, her own dream suddenly popping into her mind.

"Mom, it's no big deal, you're an adult. I'm—"

"Fourteen," Ryan interjected. "Too young to be discussing your mother's sex life."

"So, you admit it, you do have one." McKenzie held up arms up in the arm as if she were Rocky on the steps of the Philadelphia capital.

"Yes, I do have one but I didn't have one last night." Ryan scooted to the edge of the bed and stood up. "Now go get ready for school."

"You're not going to admit that you had company last night, are you?"

"No, because I didn't. I told you I was alone."

"Mom," McKenzie said as she exited her mother's bedroom. "I even heard the chime on the front door engage when he left."

"The chime?" McKenzie had her attention now. "The chime for the lock on the front door?"

"Yes."

"That's not possible, McKenzie. Cole doesn't have the code for the lock, you and I made a deal that no one gets the code, not even Daddy."

"And I kept my end of the bargain."

"McKenzie, you sure you didn't give it to one of your friends?"

"No Mom, it's on my phone. I don't even know how to share it if I wanted to." McKenzie picked up her mother's phone from the nightstand and pointed to the chime application on the phone. "It's here on your phone, too. Has anyone else had your phone?"

"No," she lied, thinking back to Virginia's confusion with the phones.

"So, you admit, Cole was in the house last night?"

"Yes," she lied again. It seemed like the lesser of the two evils.

Chapter 32

"And just like that, your suspension is lifted?" Catherine asked, pointing to a concrete bench by the lake, one that was seldom used by the employees, even though it was only a stone's throw from the parking lot.

"Yes, he called me around lunchtime and asked me if I could come in and talk."

"I thought I was coming to be fired, imagine my surprise when he told me the suspension had been negated and I'd be paid for the time I was off yesterday.

"Did he say what changed his mind?"

"Just that new information had come to light that refuted the charges that had been made against me."

"Wonder who?"

"He didn't say and I didn't ask." Ryan looked away and rubbed the back of her neck where it was starting to ache. "He still hasn't addressed his friend giving instructions to my staff regarding Anodyne."

"His friend?"

"The drug rep, Robin Carter." Ryan's words were loud and anxious.

"What else is going on?" Catherine sat back to observe her friend. "You aren't yourself today."

"I'm tired, I didn't sleep well last night." She paused. "I had the weirdest dream last night."

"What kind of dream?" Catherine didn't really believe in the mythology of dreams and she knew Ryan didn't either.

"I was tied to some kind of examining table and injected with something by a man dressed in scrubs." She paused. "I couldn't tell who he was because he was wearing a surgical mask the whole time but his voice, it was so familiar. I know it was him."

"Who?"

"Noah."

"You had a dream about Noah?"

"Yeah and that's not the weirdest thing, McKenzie mentioned hearing Cole leave early this morning, hearing us together last night and the chime this morning when the door closed."

"So, you talked in your sleep?"

"What about the chime?"

"She drifted back off to sleep. I hear our dogs barking in my sleep all the time. I get up to let them out only to discover Gordon has them and they aren't even in the house." She laughed. "It happens."

"Maybe –"

"Hi Girls!" the voice erupted from behind them, before either noticed they weren't alone.

"Erin?" Catherine hoped the disappointment wasn't evident in her voice. "Welcome home. How was the trip?"

"San Francisco has always been one of my favorite places. It was my good fortune that the nursing leadership conference was there." She pointed to the tiny spot on the bench between them and indicated she wanted to sit down.

Ryan and Catherine moved to opposite ends of the bench to accommodate Erin between them. Once she was settled in place, she looked to one then the other. Ryan's facial bruises were almost healed, the color had transitioned from dark, bloody-black to brown and yellow.

Catherine's, however, was more acute and less healed. She'd removed the wrist support from the event in the emergency department but the scars and bruises from nearly being run down were more prominent.

"Speaking of good fortune, doesn't look like you gals have had much?"

"We're breathing," Ryan added. "So that's something."

"I was sorry to hear about your suspension, Ryan." Her smile was genuine. "I know we haven't always seen eye to eye but I've never doubted your loyalty to the hospital. I know you would never compromise your integrity by leaking anything to the papers."

"No, I wouldn't."

Erin went on. "It isn't your nature to run and hide behind anonymity. You're much more likely to burn the barn down to save the stall." She paused. "And I like that about you."

She looked off into the distance, across the lake and smiled as if something far away had caught her eye. "Sometimes you just got to let things go, you know?" She patted Ryan's leg. "Forget the stall, save the barn."

Erin pulled herself up to her feet. "Nice talking to you both. I'm glad neither of you were hurt very badly. I enjoy working with you both very much."

She nodded and strolled off behind the bench, in the direction opposite of which she'd come. If she had on a long dress and hat and sipping a glass of tea, she'd look like any one of the women from Steel Magnolias, except of course for Julia Roberts.

Catherine waited to be sure Erin was out of earshot. "What the hell was that about?"

"I think we've just been warned off."

****

"Are you sure this is the same package that was in my mail the day I was suspended?" Ryan rubbed her forehead; she was getting another headache. It was the second one in two days and acetaminophen did nothing to help alleviate the pain.

"I haven't seen anything else come from the mailroom," Virginia answered. "Why don't you think it's the same?"

"I thought I remember seeing a return address on the other one. I was hoping it was from a friend of mine."

"I'm pretty sure it's the same one, maybe your friend is just late in mailing it and will get it to you soon."

"I don't think so," Ryan mumbled under her breath before returning back to her office and falling into the chair. "He's dead."

It was hard not to smile when she thought of Calvin, he was always smiling, a generally happy person with a positive and optimistic outlook. It had been his idea to sneak the mechanical rubber hand into their cadaver lab when they were in college. Even knowing the professor was an ex-nun with little to no sense of humor, he'd carried it in and placed it discreetly under the sheet near the hand of the cadaver and waited patiently for the professor to begin the lab.

Ryan was still smiling when Catherine stopped at the office door. "I just saw Louis heading toward the pharmacy?"

"Yes, I reinstated them both late last night." She looked away, not wanting to meet Catherine's stare. "Brittany called me at home and asked for a status."

"Why would you do that? You –"

"I didn't have a choice." Ryan interrupted her. "There's no evidence they've done anything wrong except bend to the will of a drug rep." She shook her head and rubbed her neck, twisting it from side to side as if she had a crick. "Doctors and pharmacists do it all the time."

"That doesn't sound like you at all. You're a stickler for the point of a matter."

"Don't worry," Ryan reached for the envelope Virginia had given to her. "I'm not going to burn down the barn or the stall. I'm just trying to house the crop."

"You okay?" Catherine stepped further into the room. "Is someone pressuring you to –"

"No," Ryan cut in again. "I'm tired, physically, emotionally, mentally. I'm just tired." She ripped the top the envelope open, Dropping the part she'd torn away in the trash and pouring the contents onto her desk as a zip drive and folded note fell atop a stack of file folders.

"What's that?" Catherine asked moving around to the desk and standing behind Ryan.

"I don't know." Ryan exposed the port and placed into her computer, unfolding the note almost at the same time. "Put everything back the way it was." She read aloud before turning it over hoping for a clue to the identity of the sender.

"What does that mean?"

"Beats me –"

Ryan's computer screen exploded to life to reveal a light enhanced video of a bedroom. It took her a few seconds to realize it was her bedroom and the couple withering in the bed was her and Cole making love. "Oh my God," Ryan jerked the zip drive from the port and the screen went black again. "What am I supposed to put back, rehire Jayson, return Anodyne to the formulary, undisciplined the twins? And what if I can't or don't? Am I supposed to assume this video will go out over the Internet?"

"Can you tell when or how it was filmed?" Catherine asked.

"I didn't see enough of it to really determine that." She looked away awkwardly. "I'll have to watch it in its entirety and see if I can figure it out."

Catherine hesitated before leaving, looking back at Ryan with a worried expression. "Is there anything I can do to help you with this?"

"Obviously, I don't want you to see the video," She closed her eyes and exhaled. "I wouldn't want anyone to see this, it's private."

"I understand," Catherine walked back to the desk and patted Ryan's shoulder. "I'm just next door if you need anything."

"I know," Ryan patted Catherine's hand and then pulled away.

Catherine knew it was a signal Ryan wanted to be alone, wanted to watch the video independently. She cleared her throat and took her to leave, opening the door abruptly, so quickly Noah jumped on the other side.

"Sorry," she said, hoping he wouldn't pick up that she really didn't mean it. Had he been listening at the door.

"It's okay," he tapped hands together in front of him and peered into the office. "I was just about to knock when you opened the door."

"I was just leaving anyway," Catherine slid past him, "excuse me."

"Hi," he said stepping further into the room. "I wanted to check in on you and make sure there's no hard feelings about the suspension."

His cadence was soft, like a preacher on Sunday morning giving the final prayer.

"There's not." Ryan didn't look up at first. Her words were spoken directly into the desk, lost around the empty packing that had been the envelope.

Seconds past before she looked up to face him. "You did what you felt you had to do." She paused. "Right?"

"Yes," He leaned against the wall, standing almost beside her instead of taking the empty chair in front of the desk. "I spoke to my friend and I instructed him that he is to have no interaction with you or any member of your department and that he should make an appointment with you, regarding any and all formulary issues."

"I appreciate that," Ryan didn't look up. It would be easy for him to see that she didn't believe him if she met his eyes.

"If he's violated any policies or procedures, I trust you've made the appropriate notifications. I don't expect him to have any special privileges." He leaned in closer to her. "I see you got your package."

She nodded, wondering why he hadn't opened it already. He'd suspended her for leaking confidential information to the media. Why wouldn't he, at the very least, opened the envelope to investigate its contents.

"Do you know anything about this?" She held up the zip drive.

"No," he paused. "Is it something I should be privy to?"

"I meant do you know how to determine when it was delivered or where it came from?"

He reached across her to collect the torn pieces of the envelope before returning back to his stance along the wall. The scent of his cologne was familiar, unique, it was a cross between musk and burning wood. It reminded her of the way the room in her dream had smelled and she had the same autonomic nauseous response.

Her stomach turned as the bile climbed up her throat and threaten to spill out her mouth. "I'm sorry." She jumped to her feet, "I'm going to be sick."

"Use my private restroom," he called to her as she flew past him and disappeared into his office.

****

"I don't see a barcode on the envelope so I don't think it was sent through interdepartmental mail," Noah said once Ryan returned to her office. He hadn't moved a muscle except to drop the packaging back on her desk. "Feeling better?"

For a minute she panicked, thinking she'd left something on the desk, something that might reveal what they'd discovered about MKUltra or Beliard. A quick glance around her desk, eased her mind, and the calmness settled over like a gentle rain.

"Yes, thank you" she answered before taking the seat across from where he was standing instead of the chair behind her desk, the one closest to him. "If came from within the system, there'd be a barcode?"

He nodded. "So, it was either dropped off in the mail room or here in the office. Virginia might know?"

"She said it was in my box when she came in yesterday morning."

"There's so many people in and out of here right now, with the gala only a few days away. Anyone could have left it." He pushed himself away from the wall and made a move toward the office door. "You may never know."

"I'm really glad you're back, Ryan." He smiled. "I'm not your enemy, although at times it certainly might seem that way." He paused at the door. "We all have jobs to do and just like you, sometimes I don't like mine much either."

"Good to know, thanks." She forced a smile.

"If you need anything, let me know." His words trailed off as he left the room.

She wasn't sure what was more unnerving the subtle apology for suspending her or the fact he hadn't asked what was in the envelope.

****

The view from the lakeside bench was unusually soothing she thought, looking behind her to the physician's entrance where she knew Catherine would eventually make an appearance and wander over to join her. There were only a few ducks on the lake, swimming close to her bench, waiting patiently for some food to be thrown their way. She crushed a pack of saltine crackers and threw the pieces into the air around the ducks in spite of the sign that read not to feed them.

"Did you not read the sign?" a familiar voice asked, still a fair distance away.

"Better to ask for forgiveness than approval." Ryan crunched another handful of crackers in her hand and threw the fragments at the ducks. They swarmed like flies to where the pieces floated snow-like on the water.

"Did you watch the video?" Catherine asked, sitting down gently beside her.

"Every agonizing moment." She clapped her hands together before wiping them down her thighs, leaving a white trail of crumbs down the side of her skirt. "I'm not sure what the attraction is for making a sex video," She paused. "It was horrible. I'm actually considering never having sex again."

Catherine fought back a smile. "I can't say I understand but I am sorry. I know it's a terrible invasion of your privacy." She waited for Ryan to respond but added once it was obvious Ryan had nothing to say. "Were you able to figure when or how the video was made?"

"It's not like we have sex every night, so yes. I think I've narrowed it down to a few nights ago. The last time Cole stayed over." She added before Catherine could ask. "My navy suit jacket is draped over the chair to the right of the bed. And I'm pretty sure, my camisole is hanging on the footboard of the bed. I can tell by the clothes I wasn't wearing."

"What about how?"

"It's hard to say, from the angle, it almost looks like it's being recorded from something on or near the desk."

"Your laptop?"

"No, it's on the workspace in the kitchen. I don't take it to bed anymore, I was staying up half the night reviewing departmental budgets."

"What's usually on the desk when he's there?"

Ryan shrugged her shoulders. "Nothing out of the ordinary, a digital clock, his weapon, and our phones." She rubbed her head, feeling the pounding at the base of her neck that signaled a mother of a headache was coming. "How am I going to tell him?"

"About the video?"

Ryan nodded and massaged her forehead, right above the eye sockets.

"Guys don't have the same privacy issues as we do. If it were Gordon and someone taped us, he'd just want to make sure he got a copy."

Ryan tried to fight back a laugh but felt the sides of her mouth curl up in defeat. It was true what they say, she thought. You either have to laugh or cry. What she hadn't known, couldn't admit, was that somethings, both emotions felt exactly the same.

****

"There's no way to track it?" Cole asked pacing back and forth from the kitchen hallway into the living room with the envelope and zip drive in his hand. "Did you ask the security team to check the video in the mail room?"

"It didn't come from within the system, so no it can't be tracked." She answered and motioned for him to give her the package. "Aiden watched the video in and out of the mailroom. There's lots of traffic but no he couldn't see a circumstance where the envelope was placed in my mailbox."

"So, someone just waltzed into the administrative offices and dropped in the box to be distributed?"

She nodded, "It would appear so, yes." She dropped her head. "I'm so sorry."

He gathered her into his arms and folded himself around her small frame. "It's not your fault. You're on the video, too." He kissed the top of her head. "I think it's actually a good sign."

"What?" She pulled away from him as if his body was on fire. "What does that mean?"

"You've made someone very nervous. So that means something we've uncovered must hit pretty close to home." He took the envelope and poured the zip drive into his hand. "Grab your laptop and let's go upstairs and try and determine where the camera is or was."

Obediently, she collected the laptop from the kitchen alcove and followed him up the stairs and into the bedroom. The distance to the bedroom had never seemed longer and she thought of the movie the green mile when the inmates were led down the hallway to the death chamber. She knew she was being extreme, but she felt just like she imagined the inmates had as they made their final walk toward the chair.

"I think the camera was over here somewhere on the desk," Cole said, looking back and forth from the desk across at the foot of the bed and the laptop he poised on the long counter of the bureau.

He watched a few more minutes before turning to her. "This is from a few days ago?"

She nodded but didn't look at the video, she didn't need to. It would be forever burned into her mind, like a tumor.

"What's not on the desk that would normally be?" He scanned the immediate area, walking closer to inspect the window and curtain that hung to the floor behind the desk. "I guess if the curtain wasn't completely closed, they could have gotten a shot through the window with a high-resolution lens."

He pulled the curtain open and looked out the window to the row of houses who's back yard faced hers. There was nothing out of the ordinary or unusual, no flashing neon sign that read, this is the house. We're the one.

"The only items usually on the desk is that clock." She pointed to a digital clock-radio. "And our phone, sometimes you drop your watch and wallet on the top."

He picked up the clock. "Is there a camera in this model?"

"No," she laughed. "I had it in college. I don't think everything had cameras back then the way they do now."

"Same with my watch," he spun his wrist around. "It was my grandfather's. Worth nothing to anyone but me." He ran his hand through his hair. "Whoever made the video could have removed the device as well. I mean, they placed it fairly discreetly, I guess they removed it in the same manner."

She fell into his arms again, feeling oddly exposed as he wrapped his arms around her waist. "What are we going to do?"

"I'll send one of the locksmiths we work with to change the locks and have Erik run the wand to make sure the rest of the house is clean. Wouldn't hurt to have a security system in place so that if someone enters the house while you and McKenzie are out, you'll be notified."

"I like that idea."

"I'll make the calls; I can have everything completed tonight."

Chapter 33

"I've swept everywhere twice, Cole," Erik explained. "If there was any listening or camera device it's not here now." He looked around to where several workers were replacing locks while others were on ladders placing security cameras and motion detectors strategically throughout the house.

"Is there something I should know about?"

"Ryan got a video in her mail at work today. The nature of the video leads us to believe someone planted a camera in her bedroom.'"

"Were you able to test the resolution to determine the type of camera?"

"Way above my paygrade, CIA man," Cole commented, looking back at Ryan.

"If I could see it, I might be able to tell you what type of camera was used. Might give us a lead on what we're looking for."

Cole looked behind to Ryan, his face pale. "I don't know how she feels about that –"

"It's fine, honey. Let him see it. I'm going to the mailbox."

She grabbed her jacket and made a beeline for the front door. "I'll be back in a few minutes."

"I won't need to watch the entire thing, just a minutes worth will do."

The door closing behind her was all the response she gave.

****

The breeze through her hair was nice, as was the little bit of sun still left of the day. Although it had dipped low in the sky almost behind the horizon, there were still enough rays radiating through the clouds that she wished she'd have remembered to bring sunglasses.

Bill, she flipped through the mail, another bill, junk mail, bill. It was the same every day, no one sent letters or cards anymore, it was always the internet or text. No one sent out anything else, everyone was just too busy and self- absorbed.

Calvin? She recognized his handwriting before she saw his return address on the left corner. Urgently, she checked the post date. It was the morning he'd died. No doubt, he slipped out and mailed it prior to the break-in.

It took every bit of self- control she had not to run the rest of the way from the mailbox to the front door as she tore open the envelope. A note fell out first, in scribbled cursive, he'd written. Sent one to your work and one to your home, just in case. Hope this helps, See you soon, Calvin.

She yanked the results from the envelope as she stepped into the foyer. Her eyes traveled the length of the paper, taking in every word.

"Cole," she yelled, her legs not able to move. Like her dream, she was frozen in place only this time she was wide-awake.

"What's wrong?" he nearly collided with her at the door.

"It's a match." She held the paper out so he could see it.

"The Anodyne I sent and the chemical formula for MKUltra. It's a match."

He took the paper from her hand. "My God, you can't be serious."

"I am and we've got our proof."

"I'll call Hartmann," Cole handed her the results back. "Put this in a safe place."

"I'll call Catherine."

****

Tim Hartmann looked as comfortable as Ryan could ever recall seeing him dressed in khaki shorts and a black t-shirt that emphasized his chiseled chest and arms. He'd already finished one beer and was working on his second when the doorbell rang.

Ryan jumped to her feet to get the door, pushing Cole feet out of the way as she maneuvered around him heading to the front foyer.

"Check the camera," Cole called out.

"It's probably Catherine," She called back almost to the front door. "Or Erik" once her hand was on the doorknob."

"Hey," Catherine said, sliding a grocery bag into Ryan's arms. "I picked up some finger foods. Hope you don't mind." She pointed to the street behind. "I think I saw Erik at the gate."

"He left to investigate something he saw on the video."

"You let him watch it?"

Ryan motioned her in and shut the door. "I didn't think I had a choice. He knows a lot about surveillance equipment. He thought he might be able to tell us how it was filmed."

"That would be great." Catherine added, "That's good news about identifying what's really in those Anodyne bottles." She smiled.

"Yes, I can't believe we finally have something concrete, something to support what's going on." She paused and indicated to the family room. "Hartmann is here. He's writing everything down. I just gave him copies of everything we have to date." Ryan paused. "And I called Brittany and Noah to let them know that I'm resuspending the twins and I've reported the drug rep, Carter, to the FDA for suspected drug tampering."

"You did what?" Catherine stopped in her tracks, her face pale.

"You heard me, I've sent McKenzie and my ex away for a few days. Cole has arranged for them to stay in a safe house until this is over. You should consider the same for Gordon and the boys."

"Gordon will never agree to that but I will ask D.J. to stay a little closer in the interim."

"I want to make sure I have this all down correctly," Hartmann was saying as Ryan and Catherine approached the living room.

"You believe Jacob Fleming was mentored by his father and grandfather when he was a very young boy to eventually take over a leadership role in the CIA mind control program utilizing a drug known as MKUltra. Jacob's first recruit was Reggie, who later assumed an alternate identity as Anwar Beliard. As a physician, like many of the original scientists who created MKULtra, he was in a unique position to identify potential candidates to carry out specific assignments within the program. Some of these assignments were akin to government-sanctioned assassinations. One of the most widely recognized was, in fact, Lee Harvey Oswald but there were operatives positioned elsewhere to fulfill a political strategy as well. The distribution method for the MKUltra is being accomplished by its substitution for an FDA approved drug for pain. The MKUltra is marked uniquely different and is loaded into specific automated cabinets where an MKUltra physician would select appropriate candidates for the program and subsequently administer the drug.

After the death of Beliard's second wife and son, he had a change of heart and wanted out. He went to his good friend Jacob and asked for help. Jacob wasn't happy with Anwar's decision and it is the start of a life-long rift between them but Jacob let him out anyway and arranged for Anwar to keep his current identity and lifestyle.

After Jacob's untimely death, the other members of the program decided to reactivate Beliard, he refused and ultimately, he was murdered and made to look like a suicide.

Before his death, he left a picture of the original scientists who designed MKUltra as well as a key to a vault where he kept documents of his true identity."

He paused, "You don't know how Rachel Fleming is involved but you believe she is and the death of the anesthesiologist is also related as is the death of your chemist friend who identified the structure in the test bottles of Anodyne as MKUltra." He closed his notebook, "And you've no idea who actually killed either of these men or how but you believe you are on the right track because of Ryan's mugging and Catherine nearly being run down by a car on a dark road late at night."

"It doesn't seem as believable when you put it all together and say it out loud," Catherine said.

"That's the cool thing about a lot of our covert government programs, they sound so unbelievable, a normal person would never accept any of it as fact," Hartmann advised. "It's also what makes it so hard to prove, they hide everything in plain sight. It's real but it's not." He paused. "It's a chimera."

"A chimera?" Cole repeated.

"Yes," Hartmann nodded. "It's parts of three creatures spliced together to become one but it could never exist naturally."

"What three creatures?" Erik asked, reaching in and grabbing a bear.

"Head of a lion, the body of a sheep, and a serpent's tail," Catherine answered before Hartmann could. She traded glances with Ryan.

"It's quite a story and it will be a fascinating read once we put the final pieces into place." Hartmann hesitated. "We have to know who actually killed Beliard, it's a vital piece of the story."

Hartmann tossed a thin book on the table. "I know this guy who runs one of those government conspiracy newsletters." He took a long drink from the bottle. "I don't believe most of what he writes about but there are a few pages in this book about a government-sanctioned mind-control program managed by the CIA in the seventies. He doesn't call it MKULTRA, instead, he refers to the drug as EA227 but what he describes sounds exactly like what you've been talking about, He's retired and lives about two hundred miles south. I'm thinking we drive down and pay him a visit tomorrow?"

Although he'd asked the question of everyone, it was obvious it was waiting for Cole to answer.

Cole hesitated and rubbed his chin to such extent; it left the skin red and marred. "I don't know, it's three hours there and then another three hours back. I'm not sure I want to be that far away."

"I'll be fine," Ryan added, letting him finish speaking but just barely. "I'm working a full day, meetings on site. I'm not traveling at all tomorrow."

He looked to Catherine, "Are you going to be close by?"

She nodded, "A few meetings but nothing that will take me off-site. And Erik will be around as well, yes?"

"Yes," Cole picked up the book and read the back cover. "He and D.J. will both be at their posts tomorrow." He flipped through the pages, stopping somewhere in the middle and read silently. "You sure this guy warrants a six-hour excursion?" He tossed the book back on the table. "If he starts talking about little, gray aliens, I'm out of there."

"He's very enlightening,' Hartmann retrieved the book. "It will definitely be worth the trip."

****

"What did you find out about the video?" Cole asked before Erik was even completely through the front door. Erik paused at the foyer and peered around the corner to determine where Ryan was.

"You aren't going to like this."

"What?" Cole shifted his weight from one foot to the other. "What is it?"

"I need to make a copy before I can tell you anything. Whoever's watching you has some top-notch equipment at their disposal. I've never seen a clip not leave some kind of tag, a footprint of some kind."

"There's no way she's going to let us make a copy."

"Would she have to know?"

"Yes, I wouldn't do that without telling her."

"Tell me what?" Ryan turned the corner just in time and repeated. "Cole, tell me what?"

"Erik can't tell anything about the video without making a copy."

"Absolutely not, if that were to get out, I'd die." She wiped her hands up and down the sides of her jeans. "My professional life would be over."

"I promise, there wouldn't be any chance of a leak." He swallowed. "I'll do the tests myself and destroy it when I'm done."

She bit at her bottom lip and closed her eyes, wishing she could start the day again. "Are you certain there's no other way?"

"I'm sure I can't tell you anything about the video without running these tests."

"The zip drive is upstairs in the top drawer of my bureau, there's a box just under some college t-shirts."

"I'll get it and make a copy while I'm upstairs." Cole stopped about halfway up the stairs. "You do have a blank zip drive?"

"Top drawer of the desk,"

Cole returned a few minutes later and handed the duplicate zip drive to Erik. "I hope I don't live to regret this."

"You won't, I promise." He pocketed it. "When I'm done, you want to destroy it or you want me to?"

"Bring it back to me," He pointed to Ryan who had returned to the kitchen. "I'll let her destroy it." He paused. "I think it's the only way she's ever going to have any kind of closure."

Erik nodded, patted his pocket where the zip drive was, and turned for the door to take his leave. "You're probably right. It will be cathartic for her." Once he'd stepped through the door, he turned back to Cole. "You and the reporter making a trip to the keys in the morning?"

"Yeah, I think Hartmann's set us up to meet one of the lone gunman." He laughed initially but his expression turned serious. "You and D.J. will be on your own for the biggest part of the day. Don't be afraid to call in reinforcements if you need them."

"I know D.J. updated his ASAC on what's been going on, just in case we were to be in an accident or something," Erik admitted. "I wasn't sure if it was wise to include anyone else till we know who we can trust but D.J. believes he can trust her."

"I trust D.J. Do you?" Cole asked, walking out and closing the door behind him.

"Yes," Erik nodded.

"Then we really have no choice. We have to let him do what he thinks is right."

"Have a safe trip and keep your eyes open. You're going in without any backup."

"I'll be fine," Cole answered before disappearing back into the house.

****

"We swept the house, honey," Cole explained, falling into the empty place next to her on the sofa. "There's nothing, here. It's clean."

"I'm tired," Ryan explained, twisting around on the sofa to look into the spotless kitchen where the only item out of place was a worn holiday towel draped over a wire drying rack.

"I told you the kitchen could wait until morning." He adjusted himself more comfortably beside her and took her hand into his. "You're wearing yourself ragged with these get-togethers." He brushed the hair from her eyes. "I'm worried about you."

"I'm fine." She moved as close against him as she could. "Once we put all the pieces together, I think I'll sleep for a year."

"We should head upstairs earlier rather than later," he kissed her knuckles. "Let's take a shower before bed."

"We can't have sex here." She sat up, rigid against the sofa. "The video –"

"There's no surveillance devices. Erik scanned the entire house, both floors, even the garage."

"I wouldn't be comfortable –"

"We could go to my place," he kissed at her neck.

"You have a typical bachelor pad," Ryan returned his kisses. "I'm not sure your bed will accommodate us both."

"Think of the fun we'll have trying." He captured her lips with his and pulled her as tightly against him as he could. "Put a bag together and let's go."

"I don't know," she whispered against his lips.

"I've got to meet Hartmann early in the morning, tick, tock."

"Alright," she answered, pulling away and pushing to her feet. "Let me grab some clothes. I've got an early meeting tomorrow with the director of the operating room. I won't have time to come back here, I'll have to leave from your place."

****

There wasn't much light in Cole's bedroom. Even with the thick beam that radiated from the streetlight on the sidewalk, there was barely enough illumination to see her hand in front of her face. Her hair was still wet from the shower, draped over one shoulder and barely covering her breast.

Cole was quiet as she slid one leg over his hips, using his arms as a pillow and repositioning himself under her as she moved aggressively against him.

"God, your beautiful," his hands found her breasts, pushing and pulling at the sensitive skin before sliding his hands under her arms and pushing her close against him.

He kissed her neck, holding her tightly against his chest. "Don't rush," he mumbled against her breast, as his hands traveled up to her neck, twisting at its base until she groaned and arched forward in response.

Ryan pulled her knees so closely against him, she heard him groan, moan, actually. She only hoped it wasn't in response to something he found uncomfortable. "I'll have to reconsider the tight quarters," she said against his chest as she ground against him as hard as she could before feeling him jerk in response and empty himself into her. Seconds later, she felt herself falling around him until her body was slick and wet with her own satisfaction.

"That was amazing!" he pulled her in his arms and spun her over on her back, falling against her in the same motion and kissing her shoulder and back of the neck.

"There's a small knot here on the base of your neck." He ran his fingers tenderly over the skin, the tips stopping on the head of the knot.

"What kind of knot?" She ran her hand up to where his was, so she could feel it for herself.

He turned over on his side and flipped on the light by the nightstand. "Actually, it's a scar."

"A scar?" she sat up, pulling the blanket around her chest.

"Looks fresh," he noted. "Maybe from the event in the parking lot?" He caressed the area again. "You were hit in the head."

"I was seen in the emergency department. Dr. Fare didn't mention it," she reminded him, before she settled back against him. "I'll see my primary care doctor in the afternoon."

He wrapped his arms around her waist and pulled her as close against him as he could. "I love you," he whispered into her ear.

"Love you too," she answered almost mechanically.

****

Dr. Crystal's exam room was colder than usual or at least it felt that way to Ryan. Twice she'd jumped down from the table and moved to wait in the chair for the doctor, at least the chair was out of the direct flow of the air conditioning's cool air through the vent.

Ryan yawned into her hand, wishing she'd had a few more hours of sleep before Cole's alarm had gone off. She was torn between pulling on comfortable traveling clothes and joining him to interview the conspiracy doctor and dressing in her conservative suit for work. In the end, she donned the charcoal grey suit and black heels, splashed a bit of make-up on and made a dash for her car. If she hurried, she'd only be a few minutes late for the meeting with the operating room physician and she could blame it on the traffic.

The door burst open as Dr. Crystal strode past the threshold. "I had to check the schedule twice," she joked, before dropping a thick, fat medical record atop the counter. "You're three months early instead of two months late."

"I'm not here for my annual check-up," Ryan explained. "I was mugged last week in the parking lot." Seeing Dr. Crystal's expression, Ryan added. "I was seen in the emergency room and received a clean bill of health."

"So, what brings you in?" Dr. Crystal asked, leaning against the counter with her coat trailing open, stuck at one side against her hip.

"I've got something in my neck," Ryan rubbed the area as if the mere mention of the wound provoked a painful response.

"Let's take a look." Dr. Crystal approached, pulling on examination gloves and flashing a small penlight at the base of Ryan's neck. She ran her hand over the small jagged scar.

"I can feel it just under the skin." She flicked the light off and searched the cabinets until she found a small bottle of lidocaine and syringe. "Let's see what it is."

Ryan squirmed as Dr. Crystal swabbed the area and injected a small amount of lidocaine just under the skin. "You shouldn't feel anything," she advised, making a small incision and pulling a small piece of metal from the area.

"What is it?" Ryan asked, watching as Dr. Crystal dropped in into a clear test tube.

"Looks like a piece of whatever you were hit with got lodged under the skin. I see this a lot in soldiers and law enforcement personnel. "Most of the time, the material is so small and thin, it lodges into the skin without any fanfare."

"You got it all?" Ryan asked.

"Yes," Dr. Crystal said. "It went in clean and came out clean." She pulled the gloves off and dropped them in the trash receptacle. "I'll send it out but I'm pretty sure it will come back as some kind of scrap metal."

"Let me know when you get the results." Ryan rubbed her neck.

"Did they catch the guy?" Dr. Crystal asked, making notes on Ryan's chart.

"No, and he took my satchel."

"Took your briefcase but left you with your purse?"

"Yes."

"That's odd, don't you think?"

"Very," Ryan answered, thinking to herself, *you don't know the half of it.*

Chapter 34

"I was thinking you might take the morning off?" Catherine asked, watching as Ryan made her way through the administrative office and into the chief operating officer's area. She tossed the keys on the desk and fell into the desk chair.

"I was in earlier but I had an appointment with Dr. Crystal." She flipped her computer on and waited as the screen flashed to life.

"Everything ok?" Catherine set a Styrofoam cup of coffee on the desk of the front of Ryan.

"Yeah, Cole felt something on my neck last night and I wanted to have it checked out."

"What do you mean by something?"

"A small knot, scar actually." Ryan rubbed the tiny bandage at the base of her neck. "Crystal thinks I was most likely injured last week during the mugging and a piece of whatever he hit me with penetrated the skin."

Catherine nodded, "You'd think Dr. Fare would have seen it when he saw you in the emergency room?"

"Probably wasn't swollen when he saw me, it's probably an inflammatory response to whatever got lodged in there." Ryan's computer hummed, it's internal drives whining and churning as it came to life. She sipped at the coffee and waited for it to finish booting, watching as the icons and applications lined up along the bottom of the screen.

As usual, she clicked on the email icon and waited as the new messages loaded into her email box. "What did you send me?" Ryan asked as Catherine walked toward the office door to leave. "It's taking forever to load."

"I didn't --- Catherine turned back to face her, wandering around the desk to stand at Ryan's side and see what file she was referring to.

The images that flashed across the screen were familiar, Ryan froze unable to even click the stop button. "Oh, God."

"Ryan?" Virginia called from her desk, "You better come here, quickly."

"I can't right now." Ryan smacked at the keyboard trying to stop the video of her and Cole making love. It was the same as the one she had hidden in her bureau drawer. No matter how many times she clicked stop, the video continued to play.

"Catherine?" Virginia was persistent. "It's playing on my screen, too!"

"What?" Catherine ran out, stumbling over her own feet to get to Virginia's computer. She nearly ran over Erin tripping at the door to her office, Erin's face was pale, ashen even. "It's on my computer, too."

"Call IT and have it taken down, ASAP!" Oliver yelled, not stepping from his office.

"I'm calling Mason's office directly," Virginia screamed back, twisting in her chair so she could see better into Ryan's office. "I'm so sorry."

****

"Two minutes," Mason's words, like his apology echoed in her mind. "We were able to get it off the network but it played for almost two minutes." He paused, Ryan heard him swallow, as if he was drinking something. "I don't know how but it was downloaded directly to the server and sent to every active email recipient in the system."

"I'm so sorry," his words were soft, apologetic and he spoke to her as if she were a child. "I can only imagine how you must feel." He cleared his throat. "I promise you I will personally investigate this breach and those responsible will be held accountable."

"What about the emails that weren't opened yet?" Her mouth moved but every other part of her body including her eyes were stuck as if in a trance.

"We isolated the file and it was removed."

"I see," she closed her eyes, thinking of a time when McKenzie was a baby, how soft the kisses were, how warm and tickly the smiles were. She doubted anything would ever feel that good again.

"The video was attached to an email in my mailbox that appeared to have been sent by a colleague of mine, Catherine. It didn't have the warning about it originating from an outside source."

"Whoever sent it attached it to a virus that penetrated the firewall. It duplicated the address from the last email in your mailbox. The last email sent before the one with the video must have been from Catherine."

"A trojan horse," Ryan whispered.

"Something like that, yes." He paused. "I feel so badly, if there's anything you need –"

"Let me know what you find out, Mason." Ryan broke in, her words eerily calm as she hung up the phone and looked to Catherine. "I should have known this wouldn't end well."

"It's not your fault," Catherine moved closer. "You're trying to do what you think is right."

"By bullying a bunch of madmen?"

"You've never been the kind of woman who backed down from a fight." She checked her watch. "I've got to get to a meeting. You going to be alright?"

"Yeah, go ahead. I'm going to try and get out early today."

"That's a good idea," Catherine walked slowly to the door. "I'll check in on you later."

Ryan waved her off, looking wistfully at her computer as if she could will it rewind the last half hour and delete it from her memory. But she knew the images were burnt on her mind like a tattoo. And not the cute, romantic kind. Instead, the image was as a skull and crossbones, one with snakes streaming from the empty eye sockets.

She wasn't sure how many times her phone rang before her cognitive recollections caught up to the annoying ring of the cell phone in her pocket. She checked caller identification before answering and spoke into the receiver once the line was open.

"Hi, Erik, What's up?" she asked, hoping the call wouldn't take very long. What she'd said to Catherine about leaving early hadn't been a lie. She had every intention of calling it a day as soon as she could.

"I have some news for you about the video." His voice was crisp and clear, even without being on the speaker.

She exhaled. "I bet my news beats yours?"

"Huh?"

"Never mind," she shook her head as If he could see her through the phone.

"The video was made using the camera from a cell phone."

"Were you able to determine who's?"

"Yes," he hesitated. Something she heard in the background noise led her to believe he was nearby.

"Who's phone made the video?"

"Yours."

"Mine?" She said, her voice tinged with tears. "You're sure?"

"Yes," he answered. "the meta data from the video is your phone."

"I certainly didn't record myself having sex."

"Of course not." He said in a way that made her think he only half believed her. "If not you, who else has access to your phone in your bedroom?"

"Thanks, Erik," she hung up without giving him an opportunity to add anything else.

A thousand alarms went off in her head, her phone, sitting on her desk, in her bedroom. There were only two people who'd have the access to utilize her phone to record them having sex. Only she and Cole would have the opportunity. Obviously, she hadn't made the recording. Question was, why would he? Sick, she felt ill all over but the biggest source of discomfort was her heart. Had he been deceiving her from the very beginning. Had Catherine's warning come to fruition?

****

It was hard to look at the pictures and not remember the good times they'd shared before their marriage and divorce. She flipped through the pictures of the small photo album in her top drawer. After his death, it felt wrong to hide Anwar's pictures in the small trunk on the shelf in her bedroom closet. It seemed better suited to be stored in her workspace surrounded by the tokens of her twenty plus year career.

"Hey?" Jay stuck his head into her office while the rest of his torso remained at the doorway. "Ryan's phone has been ringing like a half hour."

"Her phone?" Catherine rose, pushing the chair out of the way and closing the short distance to Ryan's office. "Why isn't it with her?"

"I don't know," he answered as he followed her into Ryan's office and watched as she picked up the phone and checking the missed call list to see who the persistent caller was. "It's Cole," she said to no one specifically. "I'll call him in a bit to let him know she must have accidentally left her phone here at work."

The phone rang again as if he'd heard his name mentioned and wanted to respond.

Catherine took the phone and made her way back to her own office before she answered the phone. "Hi, Cole," she said taking her seat at the computer.

"I've been calling her the better part of an hour?" He said before Catherine was able to exchange even the simplest of pleasantries.

"She left her phone in the office," Catherine explained. "I'll drop it off to her when I leave."

"It's not like her to leave without it."

"She had a rough morning." Catherine considered not telling him about the video's broadcast at work. After all, it was Ryan's private business and she should be the one to discuss it."

"What's happened now?"

"The video was sent to all active email recipients here at work." It was as if her words had thoughts of their own and escaped from her mouth before she could stop them. She was instantly sorry but at the same time, relieved. She knew he couldn't help Ryan if he didn't know all the truths, her truths.

"God no," she heard him exclaim, his words farther away as if his lips were far away from the phone.

"It took IT two minutes to take it down but hundreds of people viewed it before they could pull it off the server."

"She must be devastated." His words were sincere, she could hear the concern in his voice.

"Actually, she was surprisingly calm."

"That doesn't sound good ---" His words cut off by the visitor at the door.

Virginia stuck her head through the entrance. "There's an urgent call for you. Something's going on in CCU."

"Cole," Catherine interrupted him. "I've got to go; I'll talk to you later."

She disconnected Ryan's phone, and dropped it in her jacket pocket as she dialed CCU from her own desk phone.

"It's Catherine, what's going on?" she barked into the phone sounding more like a police officer than a risk manager.

"I think you should come up to the floor," the nurse manager said, almost whispering.

"Do I need security to come with me?"

"No, I'm hoping not."

"What is it?"

"It's Ryan," the nurse's words were tight. "She's having some kind of event."

"Did you call a code?" Catherine was on her feet, heading to the door with the phone cord draped as far away from the desk as it would go.

"Not that kind of an event." She paused. "She's sitting in room 4, in the chair next to the bed. She's talking to herself but is really out of it."

"I'm on my way." She hung up the phone and ran through the office, calling to Virginia. "Have Aiden meet me in CCU. Tell him to be discreet."

****

Normally, Catherine would have taken the stairs from the first floor to the second where CCU was located but there was nothing routine about anything that happened in the last few weeks.

Luckily the elevator's door opened and she stepped inside, glad she hadn't had to utilize the firemen's key she was toying with in her jacket pocket. It seemed like it took forever for the fat, heavy doors to close and for her to feel the elevator churn and grind as it made its way to the second floor.

She was already off the elevator before the doors were fully open, her heels clicking against the tile floor as she practically ran down the brightly lit hallway and turned the corridor to arrive at the secured door of CCU.

Catherine tapped the buzzer and replied to the speaker before the voice on the other side of the door could even ask. "It's Catherine, let me in."

The door buzzed and she yanked it open in a single motion, stepping through the door and heading directly to room four. From the nursing station, she could see Ryan through the glass wall, sitting just as the nurse over the phone had described, in the big, leather chair next to the hospital bed.

The patient in the bed was oblivious to her visitor, she slept amidst the whine and moan of the machines that pumped air into her lungs and fluids into her veins. The heart monitor tapped out a distinct rhythm but neither the patient nor Ryan was privy to it. In fact, one was just as unresponsive as the other.

Ryan had taken off her jacket, it was draped over the foot of the bed and the top three buttons of her shirt were unbuttoned to reveal the outline of a black bra and the curve of her breast.

If she was aware Catherine was in the room, it wasn't obvious. Instead, she sat mostly still, rocking gently in the seat and whispering something Catherine couldn't make out.

"Hey," Catherine said once she was close enough she was sure Ryan could see and hear her. "What are you doing up here?"

Ryan smiled as Catherine took the empty seat across from her as if they hadn't seen each other in a while. "I'm waiting,"

Catherine looked around the room and into the hallway to where several of the nursing staff were gathered at the nursing station. Aiden stepped into the station, his hand cautiously on his sidearm as if he wasn't sure what to expect.

She waved him off and scooted her chair a little closer toward Ryan. "Waiting for what?"

"My mom, she'll be here soon."

"Your Mom?" Catherine repeated her eyes growing wide and watery. "Honey," she dropped her hand on Ryan's knee. "Your Mom's not here."

"I know," her voice was hoarse. "But she will be."

"Ryan," Catherine fought back the tears that threatened to fall. "You lost your Mom a few months ago, remember."

"This is where she'll come to get me." Ryan's words were hoarse.

"You aren't making any sense," Catherine looked awkwardly around to determine who was listening and wishing they weren't. Everyone here had no doubt seen the video this morning and knew Ryan was having some kind of dissociative event. "Let's go downstairs."

"No," Ryan pulled her hand from Catherine's. "She'll come here and get me." The tears began to fall. "She always said if I was ever lost to go back to the last place we were together and that's where she'd come to find me."

Catherine paused, wiping at her own tears as Ryan's fell freely down her face, dropping from her cheek, and pooling on her chest.

"This is the last place we were together; this is where she'll come to find me."

Catherine turned to Aiden, taking one of Ryan's arms at the same time. "Can you give me a hand?"

Aiden moved to assist her but Ryan pulled her arm free. "No, I can't." she cried. "I have to wait here for her. She'll come here."

"No," Catherine choked. "She's not coming, honey." She paused. "I'm going to call Cole to come and get you."

"No!" Ryan was on her feet, pulling away from them both. "He's not who he pretends to be at all."

Dr. Fare stepped closer toward them. "Can I help?"

"What are you doing up here?" Catherine asked, trying to hold tighter to Ryan's arms and knowing Dr. Fare only worked the emergency room and participated in situations where a code was called.

He traded glances with the nurse manager. "I got a call downstairs, that there was an issue and could I come up and assist." He took a step closer to them. "Do you want me to give her something to calm her down?"

"I think she'll be fine." Catherine offered, pulling Ryan closer against her. "She's had a rough day and is a little confused." She nodded to Aiden. "I'm taking her home to rest. She'll be fine."

"I heard about the video." Aiden made eye contact with Catherine.

"You sure you don't me to take a look." Fare stepped in front of the door. "Maybe we should Baker act her until one of the psych guys can get here and talk with her."

"She's not a danger to anyone, Morgan." Catherine's words were harsh. "I'm taking her home."

"That may not be your call," Dr. Fare maintained his stand at the door, effectively blocking the exit. "You aren't a doctor."

"You and I both know she doesn't meet the criteria for baker acting and I have the follow up from the neurologist to support that. His consultation was posted to her medical record this morning. She's fine." Catherine stepped closer to him, her face near to his. "Now back away from the door."

"You heard her, Doc." Aiden's hand went to his sidearm again, his fingers resting against the leather of the holster.

"I'm only trying to help," he stepped away from the door.

"Then move," Catherine barked again, wrapping her arms around Ryan's shoulder and pulling her toward the door.

"Where are we going?" Ryan asked, sounding almost juvenile. "I have to wait here for my Mom."

"Ruby will make sure anyone who asks about you is made aware where you've gone." She nodded to the nurse manager standing patiently behind the nursing desk. "Right, Ruby?"

"Of course," the nurse manager nodded, replacing the desk phone back to the cradle. "I hope she feels better."

"Me too," Catherine's words were cut off as the big, heavy door of the coronary care unit slowly clicked to a close and locked behind them.

Chapter 35

"You sure she's still sleeping?' Cole asked, pacing in and out of the hallway that led to the kitchen. "I don't want her to be laying up there alone and confused." He pushed his hands into the pocket of his leather jacket. Catherine knew by the outline his hands made in the pocket that his hands were clenched into fists. "I feel bad I wasn't here to help with her, it must have been hard for you knowing she was waiting for her Mom."

"It was," Catherine pulled at his arm, bringing him to a step closer to her than she intended, and she took a step back in response. "But not as hard as it was on her."

"Maybe we should check on her?" He moved to the bottom of the steps with his hand on the knob of the banister.

"I've checked about every half hour," Catherine answered. "I gave her a half a glass of wine and put her to bed. She's exhausted, I think you should let her sleep."

"Do you know anymore the video?" He paused and tapped at the floor with his shoe. If they'd been outside, she was sure his shoes would have kicked up dirt from the ground. "How it got onto the hospital server or who filmed it?"

"No," she looked up the stairs as if she could see into the bedroom upstairs. "But it's safe to say, getting it on the server required some juice by someone."

"What about who filmed it?"

"Not that I've heard of," She pointed to a big chair on the other side of the room and waited for him to follow her. "Did you and Hartmann find out anything."

"Rudolph Brown, Hartmann's friend was quite interesting." He fell into the chair, his expression one of a surprise when the chair scooted loudly across the tile floor. "I'm not sure how credible anything he said was but I'm sure it will make a good read."

"What do you mean?" She licked her lips nervously and hoped whatever Cole had to share with her would be a short conversation.

She was tired and she wanted to lie down on the sofa for a few minutes while Ryan was resting upstairs. Catherine wasn't sure what kind of shape Ryan would be in when she woke up. There was a fifty-fifty chance Ryan would need supervision tonight and she wasn't sure Cole would be the appropriate sitter for the job. Not tonight.

"Brown really didn't us much that we didn't already know." Cole went on. "He was able to identify all the men in the photos Beliard saved and he was more than familiar with the MKUltra program although he refers to by a different name, EA 227."

Cole rose steadily to his feet and grabbed a beer from the refrigerator. He offered a bottle to Catherine and waited for her to decline before popping the top and returning to the chair. "Brown did say, the EA 227 program was being sanctioned now by the next generation." He smiled. "He also said the people in charge of the program are also conspiring with the gray aliens to prepare the earth for colonization."

She nodded and stifled a yawn. "I see."

"You look tired," he finished his drink. "Why don't you go home and get some rest. I'll stay with her."

"I'd rather wait and see how she is," Catherine explained. She patted the pillow on the sofa. "Why don't you head home and I'll stay here with her. I can nap here on the sofa for a bit"

"Don't be ridiculous," he jumped to his feet and slid out of his jacket. "I don't mind—"

"Cole," she cut him off. "I appreciate that you're concerned about her, I am too. But she wasn't herself today." She paused. "I wouldn't feel right leaving her with anyone until I know that she's okay and fully able to comprehend everything that's going on around her."

He tossed his jacket over the back of the sofa. "Then I guess we will both wait here together."

"I guess so," she said, lying back against the sofa.

****

"Are you sure you wouldn't rather I leave?" Catherine asked, as she moved awkwardly in the chair and reached across the table to refill her coffee cup. "Maybe this is something you need to discuss in private?"

"No," Ryan shook her head. "I'd like you to stay." She looked across the table to Cole and held her hand out as if she were handing him something but her hand was empty. "Did you talk to Erik about the video?"

"No, I was with Hartmann in the Keys to interview the guy who writes those conspiracy books." He answered her and looked curiously at Catherine. "Is there a new development?"

"I don't know," Catherine said. "Ryan?"

"Erik called me yesterday morning before I went up to CCU." She averted her eyes in embarrassment. "He was able to trace the metadata to a specific device."

"This is great!" He rose to his feet, the chair sliding out from under him. "Who's responsible?" He pulled his phone from his jeans pocket. "I'll have them picked up."

"It came from my phone," Ryan said, her words tense, arms folded across her chest.

"What?" He took his seat and pulled his chair up against the table, almost choking his gut.

"The video was recorded on my phone."

"How's that possible?" His face contorted in confusion until his expression changed to one of concern. "You don't think I had anything to do with--?"

"Who else would have access to my phone and me during sex?" Ryan cut in, her words bitter, hurt, and angry. She looked away from him, unable to meet his gaze any longer.

"You really think so little of me?" He was on his feet again before he'd finished the question, jacket in hand and jabbing his feet into his shoes. He walked to the door with the shoelaces dragging behind him. "I thought there was more between us than just sex."

"What else would I think?" Her words were wet and breathless, ladened with pain.

"Ryan?" Catherine stood up and walked away from her, stopping close enough to Cole so that she could touch him. But she didn't. "I think we all need to calm down and take a step back."

"Don't waste your time," Cole answered from the doorway. He turned to Ryan. "I would never hurt you like that!" He opened the door. "You really don't know me at all."

Ryan blinked and he was gone, out the door in a flash. If she hadn't heard the door slam behind him, she might have thought she'd hallucinated the encounter. However, when she turned to face Catherine, it was the look on Catherine's face that told her, it had not been imagined. Cole was gone, out of her life just as quickly as he'd entered.

"Are you sure you know what you're doing?" Catherine asked, her question little more than a whisper. "You aren't yourself."

"You're the one who said we couldn't trust him." Ryan pointed out, her words stung as if they'd been dipped in acid and flung into the air.

"That was before." Catherine gathered the used cups still partially full of coffee and walked them to the kitchen sink.

"Before what?" Ryan added. "He videotaped us having sex and shared it with the world?"

"How can you be sure it was him?"

"Who else?" Ryan's words were loud, tinged with sarcasm. "I certainly didn't do it."

"All along, you've made a point of saying nothing is as it seems." Catherine paused and moved closer. "How can you be so sure this is any different?"

"You don't think he's to blame?"

"No," Catherine shook her head. "I don't. I'll admit, I had my doubts initially." She ran warm water over the dirty dishes stacked haphazardly in the sink. "But he seems sincere and I think he genuinely cares for you."

"What's done is done," Ryan made her way to the stair steps. "I've got to get ready for work."

"You're going in today?" Catherine's attempt at disguising her surprise was not successful as Ryan stopped about midway up the steps.

"Of course, aren't you?"

"Yes, but I thought that after yesterday, you might want to take a day or two off?"

"I'm getting ready for work," Ryan repeated, before disappearing up the stairsteps.

Catherine waited until she heard the shower upstairs come to life before she slipped quietly out the front door. She checked her watch and thought to herself if she hurried, she could still make the quality meeting with infection control. She knew talking to Ryan would be pointless, there would be nothing to say to convince her to stay home and recuperate. The best thing she could do was play along and pretend everything was okay even if everyone around them, including Ryan, knew it wasn't.

****

Today's newspaper folded neatly atop the far corner of her desk was still a distraction. Catherine glanced anxiously at it again, picking it up and unfolding it open atop her desk. It was hard not to react to the headline, LOCAL REPORTER KILLED IN AUTOMOBILE ACCIDENT. Tim Hartmann had never looked better than in the picture plastered on the front page.

Another accident, she thought, how ironic. She read it again, instantly feeling sorry for the reporter's family. She knew he had a young son, she remembered him sharing the events of a recent baseball game the last time he was at Ryan's. Based on the information provided in the article, he'd been involved in a head-on collision late last night on the interstate. Sources report, she read to herself, Mr. Hartmann was heading North from the downtown area following a meeting for an upcoming story. The paper went on to list numerous other stories Mr. Hartmann had contributed to as well as information on his upcoming funeral services. She couldn't help but wonder what other story he might have been working on. She knew there was no way to be certain if his death and Anwar's were related. But she felt it in her bones they were related. She just knew it.

"You have a visitor," Virginia's words sounded more mechanical than usual through the intercom system. It hissed and buzzed while Catherine searched her appointment calendar, finally becoming silent as her computer screen lit up into a series of columns and rows.

Quickly, she checked the day's calendar and called back through her open office door. "I don't have anyone scheduled."

"It's me," his voice was familiar. She knew who it was even before his lanky form appeared at the doorway and leaned against the frame. "I was hoping you might have a minute?"

"Cole?" she motioned to the empty chair. "Sure, have a seat."

He fell into the chair and rubbed his chin with his hand once he was fully into the seat. He hadn't shaved that morning; his chin and cheeks were only partially visible under the thin patch of beard. Instead of dress pants and a shirt, he was wearing blue jeans and a casual, worn shirt. She didn't think he'd went to work today. Was he upset about Tim Hartmann's death or his fight with Ryan last night? She wasn't sure, but she had a feeling he'd come to enlighten her on one event or another.

"You heard about Hartmann?" She asked, looking past him into the office area to where Virginia was sitting. Even from the distance, she could see Virginia's lips moving, watch her eyes as she read the words on the paper.

"Yeah," Cole nodded. "I feel bad for his family, especially his kid."

"Do you know any more about it?"

"Just what was in the paper," his words were dismissive. He slumped deeper into the chair, looking more like a teenager being disciplined than a decorated officer.

"You think it's related to MKUltra?"

"Based on what I read, they think he fell asleep at the wheel and collided with an oncoming car from the other lane." He paused. "I think we're looking for conspiracies everywhere." He closed his eyes and rubbed at his chin again. "It could have been just an accident."

"I guess," she closed the file folder in front of her. "What brings you by?" She asked although she already knew, the question had merely been an exercise.

"I'm sorry about last night, what happened at Ryan's. I know it must have been awkward for you."

"You were hurt by what she accused of; she's hurt over what she thinks you did." Catherine paused. "And you're both angry." She tapped at her phone to determine if she'd missed any calls. "I've known Ryan for a long time and she doesn't handle either of those emotions well." She dropped her phone and looked at him directly in the eye. "I'm wondering if you're any better?"

"I didn't make that recording." He pleaded, his eyes sad and defeated. "I swear."

"I believe you."

"Why can't she? Why doesn't she trust me?" He paused. "I'm not her ex-husband. I don't want any more of her than she's willing to give."

"They had and still do have a complicated relationship." She hesitated. "She loves him, she always will but she no longer likes him. They argue about everything now, especially about McKenzie."

She leaned back in her chair. "Do you love her?"

"Yes," he said without any hesitation. "I do and I've told her how I feel dozens of times."

"What?" Catherine knew he had more to say, she could see if in the way he sat on the front of the seat with the tip of his shoes against the floor.

"She's only told me once recently while we were making love." He looked away from Catherine's eyes. "It didn't feel right at all." He paused. "They were just words and I knew she didn't mean it."

"What do you mean, she didn't mean it?"

"The words came from her mouth but they weren't hers at all. It was like she was reciting the words."

"Are you sure you're not just being overly sensitive?"

"She hasn't been herself; you must have noticed that." He paused. "Even before yesterday's event in the CCU, she's not been herself."

"She's been through a lot; the tape was her straw and she broke." Catherine watched as Aiden, Noah, and Michele walked by her office door and disappeared into Noah's office.

"What do you want to do?" Catherine asked hoping Virginia would know what was going on with Michele."

"I want to work it out with her, I love her." He answered. "Can you talk to her for me? She'll listen to you."

"Ryan is one of the most pertinacious people I've ever known. I'm afraid she won't do anything she doesn't want to do." She stood up, leaned across the desk and placed her hand over his. "Go talk to her and make her hear what you have to say."

"She seems so fragile?"

"Ryan's anything but," Catherine pointed outside her office. "I've got to go and see what's going on in the CEO's office. Go see her, tell her the truth."

"Anything I can do?" He rose and adjusted his weapon more comfortably against his waist."

"No," she moved toward the door. "Let me know what happens when you talk to her. I'll stop by and check on you both tonight."

She waited until he had vacated the office before venturing out to Virginia's desk. "What's going on?"

"I'm not sure exactly," Virginia whispered. "All I know is that they are all in Noah's office waiting for the police?"

"Police?" Catherine repeated. "Why wasn't I notified?" She yanked her phone from her pocket and began texting Aiden quickly. "I'll ask if they want me to join them?"

Minutes later her phone's beep alerted her to his answer and she didn't even try to hide her confusion and disappointment. "What could Michele have done that would warrant a police investigation?"

Virginia leaned in. "I heard she was hiding a handgun in one of the vents in the grand ballroom."

"A gun?" Catherine echoed, "In the ballroom?" She paused. "The gala's tomorrow night, do they think it's related?"

"I don't know but I'm sure the governor's security staff will be on guard throughout the entire event," Virginia explained. "Who was the good-looking guy in your office, the one without an appointment?"

"That was Ryan's friend," Catherine answered, hoping that was still the case.

"He's really good looking," she smiled. "How's she doing?"

"I don't know," she was sleeping when I left last night and both times I've called tonight, it's gone to voicemail."

"My heart broke when I heard that she was in CCU waiting for her Mom,"

"Yeah," Catherine looked to the closed door of Noah's office again. "I'll stop by later tonight and see how she's doing."

Virginia moved closer to respond but her words stalled as the outside door opened and several police officers stepped into the office and walked to the desk where Catherine and Virginia were standing.

Virginia pulled away, leaning into the doorway and tapping against the door softly before opening it up. "The police are here." She pushed the door fully open and waited as the officers stepped into Noah's office.

Catherine stole a glance into the office as the door was closing, Michele was seated at the round conference table in the corner, Aiden was standing just behind her, hands on his hips. She couldn't be sure but she thought Michele had been crying.

The door snapped shut, vibrating the wall on either side as Catherine returned to her office. She checked her watch as she took a seat and swept the phone up in the same motion. She was going to stop by and check on her whether Ryan answered the phone or not. She supposed she could just wait. Right now, she needed to stay close to the office so she could catch Aiden when he came out and find out what the hell was going on.

Chapter 36

"I can't believe he's dead," Ryan said, pouring another glass of wine and handing it to Erik. "An accident, Huh?" She finished the last drink in her own glass and looked longingly at the partially full bottle on the table between Erik, D.J., and Catherine. Instead, she disappeared into the kitchen and returned with a plastic bottle of water.

"Last call kind of early?" D.J. asked, refilling his glass. "A toast to Tim Hartmann?"

Ryan poised her bottle into the air with the other glasses and made the toast.

"Is Cole running late?" D.J. asked.

Ryan looked awkwardly away, "I don't think he'll be joining us tonight. He's been inundated with work and --"

She jumped startled by a loud banging at the door and nearly tripping over her own feet as she tried to get to her feet and answer the door.

The older man standing at the door looked like a character from a movie, although she couldn't put her finger on which one, just yet. But, it would come to her, it always did.

"Can I help you?" She moved closer to the door wishing she'd checked the camera first. She could hear Cole's voice in her head repeating, check the camera, honey. Be safe, check the camera.

He pushed a fat yellow envelope between them and stepped passed the threshold uninvited. "Hartmann said if anything should happen to him, I was to deliver this package here."

"What is it?" She asked, stepping away enough for him to enter.

"I didn't ask," he made his way to the sofa and sat down collecting a handful of crackers and stuffing them into his mouth, not caring how the small bits and pieces fell from his mouth and onto the floor. "He said it was your story and you'd know what to do with it."

Ryan opened it up and held it out for the others to see. As Hartmann had promised he'd written it all down from beginning to end as he had known it. Attached on the front was a yellow sticky note that read. I did my part; you guys make sure you do yours.

Ryan made her way back to the table and poured a small amount of wine in the glass, "To Tim," she whispered, wiping away the stray tears that fell down her cheeks.

****

"I 'd heard all that before," Erik laughed, and dropped the empty bottle into the trash. "Mostly when I watched the X-files."

"You have to admit, he's quite a character?" Ryan smiled. "I finally remembered who he reminds me of." She paused. "The crazy doctor from the back to the future movies."

"You're right," D.J. slapped his leg. "Same wild, crazy hair and everything." He slid his bottle on the table. "I gotta go." He looked to Catherine and then to Ryan. "Cole was supposed to arrange my pass for the gala tomorrow, do you know if he did?"

"Same for me," Erik said rising unsteadily to his feet.

"He didn't say" Ryan answered. "And I really don't know," She looked to Catherine, "Are there any tickets left? I heard it was sold out?"

"I'll put you both on Aiden's list for security detail. Just be sure you have your badges with you." Catherine advised, looking anxiously at her watch. It was getting late, she really wanted to talk to Ryan privately but if Erik and D.J. didn't leave soon, it would have to wait till tomorrow.

Catherine waited for Ryan to walk Erik and then D.J. to the door before picking up the remnants of their meeting and dropping the leftovers in the trash and the wine and beer bottles in the recycle bin.

By the time she returned to the family room, Ryan was just stepping out of the foyer. "I know it's late but I was hoping to talk to you."

"About?" Ryan pretended not to know, although she wasn't sure which topic was on Catherine's mind. Either the breakdown in CCU or Coles' exit from her life. She knew one of these questions would be the first words that slipped from her mouth but she didn't know which topic would win out over the other.

"Were you able to talk to Cole this afternoon?"

Ah, Ryan thought, a clear winner. "I haven't seen him since yesterday when he stormed out of the house."

"He stopped by the office today and I got the distinct impression he was coming by to talk to you."

"He must have had a change of heart," Ryan folded the leftover pizza into a Tupperware container and placed it in the refrigerator. "I haven't spoken to him."

"He was hoping to reconcile with you." Catherine dipped her foot into the pool, testing the temperament of the water.

"Maybe he changed his mind."

"Ryan, I don't think he had anything to do with making or posting that video."

"Who else could have done it?"

"I don't know but I really don't think he did." She paused. "You haven't been in your usual state of mind."

"You aren't insinuating I made the video?" Ryan's words were slick as ice and no doubt just as cold.

"No, but yesterday –" Catherine explained.

"I didn't feel well yesterday," Ryan cut in. "I don't even remember going up to CCU or getting into room four. The entire event is a blur."

"What did your doctor say?"

"That I'm perfectly healthy and I need to minimize the stress in my life."

"Well," Catherine smiled. "We could both use a little less stress." She pulled the hair from her eyes and hoped to find a less uncomfortable topic. "What are you wearing to the gala?"

"Black dress, comes just over my knee and my Mom's silver jewelry. You?"

"Also, black dress, but mine is sleeveless and has a small black jacket lined with silver piping."

"Is Gordon still going?"

"Yes, but I'd rather he stay on the west coast where I know he's safe." She smoothed her skirt comfortably over her hips. "He's insisting."

"What happened with Michele?" Ryan asked, sitting gently on the couch and noticing how surprised Catherine looked at her as she asked the question. "I have my sources."

"I don't' have many of the details," Catherine explained, sitting nearby. "Michele was arrested today for possession of a firearm in a healthcare facility." She paused as if she were counting. "Michele was caught planting a handgun inside one of the vents in the grand ballroom."

"Has she said anything?"

"No, all she has said is she is taking the fifth."

"Scary? Huh?"

"Yes, the dogs were there when I left, sniffing around the ballroom." She grabbed her purse, "I gotta go." She pulled Ryan into an embrace. "I'll see you tomorrow?"

"Yes, I'm only working half the day. I don't want to rush to get ready." She paused. "I hate going alone, if it weren't mandatory, I'd bail."

"You don't think Cole will change his mind and show up to accompany you?"

"No, I think if he planned on a reconciliation, he'd have stopped by tonight."

"Maybe you should just take the day off, Ryan. You're still recovering from the breakdown in CCU?"

"I have to get the final measurements of the medication rooms in the new building to the automation company by tomorrow at noon." She shook her head. "Just because the grand ballroom is ready, doesn't mean the rest of the building is good to go."

"I'll see you tomorrow then," Catherine waved from the doorway. "Have a good night."

"You too," Ryan followed behind her, clicking the deadbolt and peeking outside the window. It wasn't a conscious act but she knew she was scanning the neighborhood looking for a familiar vehicle. To her dismay, Cole's car was nowhere to be seen.

****

"What the hell is going on?' Catherine asked aloud even though she was alone in her office and reading the morning email with disbelief and sadness. Could Aiden seriously be capable of embezzling millions of dollars from the hospital system? Maybe the emptying the automatic dispensing cabinets hand been a dry run for something bigger.

No, she thought. It didn't feel right. It was too easy; there it all was wrapped in a package like a present as if someone was saying. Here he is, here's the guilty man you've been looking for.

"Apparently Inspector Winters was waiting for Aiden this morning at six when he arrived for his shift. He was arrested in the security office." Virginia said, stopping at the doorway in response to Catherine's question.

"They're saying he wired several million dollars to a bank in the Bahamas from Oliver's computer." Virginia went on.

"When would Aiden ever have unrestricted access to Oliver's office?" Catherine didn't even try to hide her skepticism.

"Aiden has a key to every lock in the building except for pharmacy." Virginia reminded her. "I heard this morning that they are reopening the wire transfer thought to have been perpetrated by Cliff to determine if maybe that was Aiden as well."

"What motive would he have?" Catherine shook her head, no way. There was no way he was involved in embezzling; it was all wrong.

"Like millions of dollars wouldn't be a motive?" Virginia asked.

"You can't really believe he'd do this," Catherine asked, "you knew him."

'I don't think we ever really know anyone." Virginia walked away. "He had a zip drive in his jacket pocket with all the bank account numbers."

"A zip drive that could belong to anyone and has been dropped in his pocket." She paused, "If you had just embezzled millions of dollars from where you work would you carry the evidence around in your pocket?"

"I don't know," Virginia admitted, walking slowly back to her desk. "The whole thing is crazy."

****

"I made the rounds," Ryan advised, grabbing her briefcase and throwing her purse over her shoulder. "I'm going to the new building and measure the longest wall of each medication room." She stopped at her door. "Then I'm going home to shower and change."

"Any word from Cole?" Catherine called out from her office.

"I've left several messages but he hasn't returned any of my calls." She adjusted her purse higher on her shoulder. "I know he's angry and he has every right to be." She bit her lip, "I just wanted to make sure he's okay and tell him I'm sorry."

"Maybe he's off on assignment?" Catherine offered, only half considering that it might be true.

"He'd still have his phone," She reached for the door. "I'll see you tonight. Save me a seat at your table?"

"Of course," Catherine said, checking her watch to determine how much time she had before she needed to leave and get ready for the gala.

****

She knew she should really have donned the safety helmet, glasses, and orange vest prior to entering the new building but she didn't. She calculated the time it would take to "dress" and decided she'd be finished with measuring in half that amount of time. Besides, no one was in this part of the building to "rat" her out, they'd been gone for hours. And anyone still in the building was on the other side, setting up for the gala.

The walk up to the third floor wasn't as easy as she'd been expecting, partly because of the heels she was wearing but mostly because she was tired. Her heels echoed off the tiles of the flooring before bouncing down the hallway and back up along the other side of the wall. She turned the knob on the door and stepped inside not concerned with the footsteps she heard making trailing a ways behind her. Erik, no doubt, maintaining his surveillance post even though he'd been no more successful at locating Cole than she'd been. It's okay, Erik had said that morning on the telephone, I'm going to stay on task until we finish this thing. The last words he'd said to her before hanging up the phone had been, I've got your back.

Effectively she stepped over the numerous pieces of baseboard, tile, and silver stripping finally finishing the three medications rooms on the third floor. As she entered the hallway into the second floor, Erik steps on the stairs behind her was comforting. The medication rooms on these floors were more complete. In addition to the sinks and cabinets, most of the shelving had been placed. All she needed to do was measure the big open spaces between the cabinets to ensure the automated dispensing cabinet would fit snugly between them.

The medication room on the first floor was completely furnished except for the dispensing cabinets, even the thick formica countertops had been placed on the first floor. Plastic yellow and blue bins lined the shelves from top to bottom. Additionally, the waste management team had placed the black and purple hazardous waste receptacles in the room. The only thing missing in the rooms were her cabinets, medications, and supplies. Quickly she measured the space and noted the dimensions. Smiling at how accurate she and her team had calculated the width, length, and height of the devices.

Ryan didn't hear the medication room door open but she did feel the temperature of room drop as the cool air outside rushed inside the medication room. She half expected it to be Erik, checking in on her as she'd been in the room almost twice as long as any of the others but to her surprise, Jay pushed himself into the room opening the door just enough to squeeze inside. It was as if there was an imaginary dog or cat he didn't want to escape from the room.

"Hey," she said once he was inside, startled but not concerned. "What are you doing over here?" She turned her back and waved around the room. "This one is done, there's nothing pending in here for facilities."

"I came to check on you," he said moving closer.

Virginia or Catherine, Ryan thought, which one had sent him over. Virginia didn't know Erik was nearby, but Catherine did. Therefore, Ryan surmised, the culprit had to have been Virginia. "I'm fine, just finishing up." She grabbed her briefcase and flung her purse over her shoulder. "I'm on my way out."

"Change of plans," he answered, his words muffled.

"What do you mean?"

His answer was a fist, which made contact point blank in the middle of her forehead, just above the bridge of her nose.

Her head snapped back in response, her mouth moved to question his actions but, instead, it intercepted with his fist again.

"What the hell is wrong with you?" She asked as her mouth filled with blood as he spun her around and pushed her face first against the counter to such an extent that her feet were lifted off the floor.

"I was hoping it wouldn't come to this," he hit her again in the back before pulling her by the hair and slamming her face into the countertop. "You were warned off twice but you're so damned hard-headed."

The door opened again allowing Dr. Fare to squeeze through. "What are you doing?" He screamed.

"Thank God," Ryan stuttered around the mouthful of blood that spilled on the counter. "Morgan, call 911."

"Not here," he said to Jay. "Get her to the van. Carlos and Val are parked just outside the door."

She felt the needle prick into her thigh about the same time as the room started to spin. "Erik?" Her words were slurred. "Erik," it was little more than a whisper this time.

"He's not coming," Dr. Fare answered, as he helped Jay lift her off the counter and into his arms. Ryan felt herself being transported down the hallway, only slightly aware of the open ceiling tiles that seemed to rush by they carried her down the hallway and out the door to the van waiting just on the other side.

A ticket, her thoughts were jumbled as they dropped her into a white van with mismatched doors, they should get a ticket for parking so close to the door. It was her last thought as the light around her became smaller and smaller, until the light was no more than a pinpoint in the center of her eyeball. Then it was dark, the darkness was everywhere.

****

The smell, it wasn't unpleasant but it wasn't an appealing one either. It smelled clean, not springtime clean but medicinal clean. The odor was an aseptic one and the alcohol fragrance was still strong in the room. She opened her eyes slowly, closing them quickly as to evade the bright light. It was so white it hurt her eyes and she moved her hand to wipe the discomfort away. Neither of her hands, nor her arms would move. At first, she considered she might be restrained on a gurney or in a bed.

But once she opened her eyes enough, she found the source of her discomfort was a series of ropes that secured her upright in a chair. There was a movement to her right, she recognized the bulking figure of Dr. Fare, still dressed in scrubs. Instantly, she was angry with herself, many times she'd admired him in a meeting or walking down the hallway and considered how good looking he was. Watching him as he prepared a syringe at the counter on the other side of the room, he was anything but attractive.

"She's awake," Jay's voice from the other side of the room was authoritative. He pushed himself away from the wall where he'd been leaning and walked arrogantly to her. He shook his head once he was closer. "Didn't have to be this way but you are one hell of a pain in the ass."

He toyed with a strand of her hair. "A pretty pain in the ass, nonetheless."

She jerked her head away, watching as her hair fell through his fingers. She grunted something through the thick piece of tape they'd placed over her mouth.

"What's that?" he asked. "You're unhappy."

"Leave her alone and tell Sidney, she's awake," Dr. Fare barked, without turning around to face them.

"This isn't the emergency room, Doc. You aren't giving the orders here." Jay said, turning away from her to face him.

"And you are?" Dr. Fare turned to face him. Their eyes locked in battle, each waiting for the other to look away.

"That's enough, both of you." A man behind the surgical mask said as he stepped fully into the room. Like Dr. Fare, he was wearing scrubs but unlike Fare, his scrubs were covered by a pristine, white laboratory coat.

"She's awake," Jay pointed behind to where Ryan was bound. "Do you want her up on the table?"

"No," he answered Jay but turned to Dr. Fare who pushed the syringe into his hand. "What's this?"

"What do you think it is?"

The masked figure dropped the syringe on the counter. "We already know it's not going to work on her." He stepped closer to Dr. Fare. "Thanks to your unsanctioned trial."

"She was there in my emergency room. She'd been mugged, a head injury even. It was perfect. I thought –" Fare explained.

"You thought wrong." The masked man argued back, "And it wasn't your decision to make." He hesitated. "Your job is to bring me subjects for consideration. I decide who is a candidate and who isn't."

"She's perfect." Fare argued. "She manages the pharmacy and the formulary. The Anodyne, she can condone and approve it all. The program can continue here without any interruptions."

"It doesn't work on her." The masked man repeated again.

"Give her a higher dose," Fare argued, reclaiming the syringe and adding an additional amount of drug from the Anodyne vial.

"She's Rh negative, no amount is going to work on her."

"Rh-negative?" Fare repeated. "I didn't see that in her chart. I never select candidates seen in the emergency department who are Rh negative."

"You did this time. And put the entire program at risk." He adjusted his mask. "Jacob?"

Jay spun around. "Don't call me that ever again, Sidney." He fished for something hidden in the waistband of his pants. "Jacob Fleming was my sperm donor; he was never a father to me."

"We are all our father's son's Jacob." He looked awkwardly at Fare, "Except for you, Morgan."

The bullet from Jay's gun caught Dr. Fare square in the middle of the head, spilling blood and brain matter atop the counter and back wall.

Ryan jerked in rhythm with the gunfire, closing her eyes as Dr. Fare's body slumped backward to the floor. She watched in horror as Jay drug the lifeless body of the doctor out of the laboratory and noted the long, thick strides he had to take to avoid stepping in the trail of blood that pooled on the floor.

Jay returned only minutes later and stopped to wash his hands at the sink before returning to where Ryan was still subdued. "So, if she's not doing the deed tonight, who is?"

The masked man turned back to Jay, "I'm afraid our beautiful, pharmacy manager will be a casualty tonight during the event. Once the bullets start flying, there will be some unfortunates caught in the crossfire tonight when the governor is assassinated."

"Monday morning, "he went on, "We will mourn those we lost but life will go on as will the program."

"Who's going to pull the trigger?" Jay asked.

"We've lined up another mule." He wandered to the back of the lab where the figure of a man was barely discernible from under the sheets. He patted the shoe of the figure on the gurney. "After the detective assassinates the governor and mortally wounds several others, he will turn the gun on himself and take his own life."

"Are you sure this is going to work, Sidney."

The masked man, stopped with his back to Ryan and pulled the mask over his chin before removing the surgeon's cap. "We already know it can be done. Reggie didn't flinch at all when he pulled the trigger."

"Except he wasn't a very good shot and I had to step in and finish him off, "Jay said.

"That's why we have someone who will be a much better shot, this time, Jacob." The unmasked man said turning to face her. "I hear your detective friend is a very good shot, Ryan."

Ryan's eyes were wide with confusion as she came face to face with Noah Reid. Even if she hadn't been gagged, the words would not have come. She knew even though she couldn't see the face of the figure on the gurney. She knew it was him, she knew it was Cole.

Chapter 37

It was hot! Even as the sun dropped behind the horizon, the temperature outside was still blazing. Catherine waited for Gordon to park the car, watching for his tall, graceful form to appear from the parking garage.

She pulled at the long-sleeved jacket, the one that matched her black dress, and wished the silver glitter piping wasn't so itchy. If her dress hadn't been sleeveless, she'd simply removed the jacket and carried it over her arm. Most everyone, men included, would have their jackets thrown over the back of their chair at some point during the night, anyway.

She checked her watch again; it wasn't the casual leather one she normally wore to work. Instead, she had donned the one her Mother had willed to her, it was white-gold and very old, its thin bracelet-like links dainty and fragile. She smiled at the picture it made against the brown spots and veins of her wrist and thought of her mother. Theirs had always been a complicated relationship but she had loved her just the same. And despite their battles, she knew her mother loved her, too.

Lately, there were many lazy pre-coffee mornings when the words or expressions flew from her mouth she couldn't help thinking how much like her mother she had become. Catherine wondered if that's how it was in most families. Were we little more than genetic mismatched copies of our parents?

Her thoughts were interrupted as she spied Gordon exiting the parking garage and waiting at the crosswalk to cross the busy street. She wasn't sure why but the man behind caught her attention. There was something familiar about him but she couldn't put her finger on what it was.

There was nothing distinctive about him, no doubt he was attending the gala tonight, his black suit and tie and shiny, dark dress shoes were a dead giveaway. It wasn't until the traffic stopped, the crossing light turned green, and he stepped from the curb that it hit her, like a runaway train.

Gordon had stepped on the curb just as the light changed and was nearly half the way across the street while the familiar man was limping as he struggled to keep up with the crowd. The white van, she considered, he was a man who was always in the passenger's seat.

Instinctively, she leapt from the sidewalk and nearly ran to meet Gordon at the corner. He stopped and waited for her, thinking reasonably so that she was meeting him. Instead, she sped past him.

"Excuse me?" she walked into pace with the limping man, stepping around the other pedestrians who were passing him to get to the other side of the street. "Do you have some identification?"

"Honey?" Gordon asked, his hands stuffed into his pockets. "What are you doing?"

"Go ahead, Gordon." She said without taking her eyes off the limping man. "I'll be right there."

"Identification?" the man repeated, slowly as if English wasn't his primary language.

Catherine knew he could speak English; she'd heard him several times as he waved her off and sped away in the van. "Yes, something with your name and picture on it?"

"I got a ticket, lady." He patted the breast pocket of his cheap suit. "Tonight, that's all I'm going to need." He pushed past her. "Excuse me."

She watched as he struggled to step up onto the curb and followed the others as the line snaked down the parking lot and trailed into the ballroom like ants.

Gordon hadn't gone far, he was standing just on the other side of the street, waiting patiently on the curb. Predictably, he'd stripped out of the jacket already, it was draped over his arm while he held the other arm out to her. "What was that about?"

"That was one of the men who's been in and out of the new building without authorization."

He spun around to see where the limping man had gone to but he was nowhere to be seen. No doubt he'd already gained access to the ballroom. "Really? You're sure?"

"Yes," she said falling into place next to him, her legs stretching to keep in line with his longer ones. "But I can't prove it."

"Where's your detective friends?"

"Cole and Ryan had a falling out; he hasn't been around for days. I haven't see Erik since this morning when he followed Ryan into the new building to measure her medication rooms." She looked around them. "I never see D.J., the man's like Mr. invisible."

"Let's just hope he's around, somewhere." He took her arm in his and led her toward the growing line to enter the ballroom.

"I'm sure he is," she answered, taking one last look behind and around her before disappearing inside.

****

The convoy for the governor's brigade was about four cars more than was probably needed but then again, he'd always been most comfortable on display. It was difficult, sometimes to determine which limousine he was traveling in, all four were identical, even the interior was the same. Sometimes, he liked to ride in the second car, other times he'd step from the third car as if it were his second home. However, today, it was the last car that his security team gathered around and waited for it to come to a complete stop.

All of the security team were chiseled and bulky, even the two women looked as if they'd be more comfortable in a one-piece wrestling leotard than the dark, keenly pressed suites they were wearing.

Both waited at the rear of the vehicle as their male counterparts stood to watch on either side of the car door. Only a few minutes past before the governor stepped from the car, leaning into the crowd and shaking hands with the crowd that lined the sidewalk where the limousine had stopped. Like a well- choreographed dance, the security staff and the governor moved as one away from the vehicle and vermiculated toward a special entrance reserved for very special guests or VIPs.

Rachel Fleming wasn't a patient woman; she was even less so dressed as if she were presenting an Oscar or accepting a Grammy. Her long gown was hot and sticky, even though it was sleeveless, she felt as if her body was on fire. Three years into the change of life and she still hadn't grown accustomed to the hot flashes. Every time the door opened and someone entered through the VIP door, she'd hoped it would be the governor. Lord knows she needed to get away from the exterior door and back to the ballroom where she could easily dictate the temperature of the room. It had been more challenging recently to dictate other things.

The opening of the door caught her off guard and she stepped out of the path of the outside furnace. She was only half-surprised to see him enter and step to the side as if he planned to walk past her.

"Governor," she leaned in to shake his hand. "Rachel Fleming, CEO of the hospital system."

"I know who you are, Rachel," his tone was dismissive, as he motioned for several of his detail to move past them.

"We are so thankful that you agreed to deliver the keynote address tonight." She said loudly and pulled at his arm so they could talk more privately. "A word, please?"

"What is it, Rachel?" he asked, as they stepped closer against the wall and he motioned his remaining support staff away.

"I was hoping you'd be able to give me some insight into your plans for the system?"

"I'm not sure what you mean," he licked his lips, not making eye contact with her but instead smiling and nodding to other guests as they passed by.

"Come on, Tony," she said, as if they were old friends. "There's a rumor that you're looking to break up the system and sell it off to the highest bidder. One of those looking to buy it is none other than GHF, your old employer and one I believe you still hold financial interests."

"Even if I wanted to do that, what makes you think that I could?" It was the first time he'd actually made eye contact with her.

"Buy cheap and sell it off, pocketing a big profit. Isn't that how you do things?"

"Theoretically," he smiled, baring his teeth as if he were going to take a big bite out of her. "Let's say I was looking to break it up and remove the tax burden from the county. It wouldn't be a conflict of interest if another system bought one or all of the sites. Whichever buyer had the most money could make a bid. There's nothing illegal or immoral about that."

"There is if you're setting the system up to fail, hoping it will fall apart."

"That would make me a very smart man, Rachel, a man able to predict the future." He paused. "And we both know that you don't think that much of me."

"I'm asking you to reconsider," her words were genuine.

"All this theoretical talk has made me thirsty," he laughed, a hearty Santa laugh and took her by the arm. "Come on I'll buy you a drink."

"At least say you'll think about it?" she asked, pulling her arm from his.

"I've no way to predict how the ongoing OIG corruption investigation is going to turn out." He smiled. "Just know I'll do what I need to do, whatever that may be."

"I see," she backed away and offered her hand. "Thank you for your time, Governor. I'm sure I'll enjoy your speech tonight."

He nodded as she walked away. "Good to see you again, Commissioner Fleming."

Rachel walked briskly away from him, frantically rummaging in her pocket for something. She'd made it to the ballroom door before finally getting the phone to her lips and barking. "Proceed as planned."

****

Noah spoke softly into the phone. "Understood." He disconnected the call and dropped the phone on top of the empty examining table beside Ryan. He had removed the gag a while ago but she was still bound into the chair.

He turned to face her. "I was hoping she could reason with him, change his mind." He swallowed so loudly she could hear the saliva as it slid down his throat. "But that is not to be, the governor will surely die tonight."

"Why are you doing this?" She looked around the room. "There's still time to stop what you have planned." She paused. "It's the gala, isn't it?"

"My job is to complete the mission, just as if was my father's and his father before him."

"Which one of the MKULTRA physicians was your father?"

"What they say about you is right, you are very smart." He smiled. "And very pretty."

"Which one?" she asked again.

"Sidney Gottlieb," he said, and there was a pain in his eyes as he said his father's name.

"Is that why Jay calls you Sidney?" She was pushing him and she knew it but she'd lost all sense of reason. It seemed the only possible way to get out of this alive was to outthink him.

"Noah Sidney Gottlieb is what my real birth certificate reads," he bowed as if he were a prince and they'd just been introduced.

"And Jay is somehow related to Jacob Fleming?"

"Touché, Dr." He smiled. "It's too bad your blood is tainted; my serum isn't effective on you at all. You could be a valuable asset to the program." He shook his head as if he'd made a joke. "Of course, the young master is the spitting image of his father."

"My blood?" His words had distracted her and she knew she'd given him the advantage.

"When you were mugged, you were injected with MKUltra in the emergency room."

The steroid shot Dr. Fare had given her, she thought. It had left a residual piece in her neck, one not absorbed in the body. It also explained her odd behavior, some of it anyway.

"It should have last much longer but because you are Rh negative, the drug was degraded very quickly." He moved closer to her. "We'd have to inject you much more frequently and each time the medication would be less and less effective." He paused. "I thought maybe if I gave you a more potent concentration, it might correct the deviation." He was sad, almost child-like as he added. "But it didn't work."

The dream, she thought. It wasn't a dream. The male voice McKenzie heard and bell chime of her front door. The bastard had been inside her house! She struggled against the ropes, her anger building like a storm until she felt the hurricane force winds churning in her gut. She didn't care about the ropes; she was going to find a way to get free and beat that smirk off of his face.

He shook his head and made a face as if he smelled soured milk. "That's why we don't select a candidate with that blood type, but Fare was an idiot and injected you without my consent."

"Your consent?"

"Yes," he straightened out as much as his five feet, eight-inch frame would allow. "This is my program. I'm in charge and I decide who carries out the mission."

"And the mission tonight?"

"Will commence soon enough."

****

Catherine checked her watch again and moved the sign that read Table 12 away from the middle of the table so they could see each other better. "Where is Ryan?" she mouthed to Gordon. "The gala started an hour ago. Smith will be delivering the keynote address soon and Noah was specific that the event tonight was mandatory for all department directors."

Chimera

"Does she know that you gave me her date's ticket?" Aiden asked, pulling nervously at the sleeves of the white dress shirt under the black sleeves of his suit.

"No," Catherine nodded, "she doesn't. I haven't seen her since she left for the new building this afternoon." She checked her phone. "I've left several messages."

"You sure," he asked. "Maybe she doesn't want to be tarred with the same brush--"

"If you know anything about her, you'd know she's that last person that would do that. If anything, she'd sit with you just to make a point."

"A point?" Aiden asked.

"That she doesn't give a shit about what they think."

"How'd you break out anyway?" Gordon asked. "Last I heard they escorted you out in handcuffs."

"I didn't upload any funds," Aiden smiled. "I wouldn't even know how to do that." He took a long swig of beer from the bottle on the table. "But, I think I must have hit on something that made someone nervous."

"What do you mean, hit on?" Catherine asked.

"I got a buddy who is really into technology, he's always designing these really cool devices that sweep for bugs." He laughed. "He's convinced everyone is spying on him, the government, his boss, his wife, everyone he encounters."

"Is he someone famous?' Gordon asked.

"No," Aiden laughed. "He's just crazy as hell." He took another drink of beer. "Anyway, I was at his house the other night and I pulled my phone out of my pocket and dropped it on the table." He looked around the room. "My friend goes bat crazy and starts turning on all kinds of musical devices, to such an extent I thought my eardrums were going to burst."

"Next thing I know, he's pulled out some weird ass surveillance device and tells me my phone has been modified to act as a receiver."

"A receiver?" Catherine repeated; her hand went to her stomach to quell the churning pain that had just started.

"Yeah, a bug of sorts." He fidgeted with his tie. "And someone was listening to everything that was going on."

"Everything?"

"Yes, every word, discussion at work and at home was being listened to by someone within the hospital system, someone at a very high level."

"You can't be serious?"

"Give me your phone." He took it from her outstretched hand. He swiped on the flashlight function of his phone and aimed its beam at the face of her phone. "See that metallic reflection in the upper right-hand corner?"

She nodded and moved in closer so she could better see what he was doing.

"Someone is listening to every word you say or that is said to you." He handed her the phone back. "The day they arrested me; I'd put in a formal complaint." He paused. "They invaded my privacy, recorded my non work-related conversations without my consent and it's illegal."

One step ahead of us, she thought of the numerous conversations where she and Ryan had discussed how they always seemed to be a step behind what they were investigating. It also explained corporate's fascination with phone protocol. No doubt, they wanted to reconfigure the phones so they could have access to whatever felt they needed to.

The video, she went on, her thoughts spinning as if caught in a hurricane, they'd probably done something similar with the camera, devised a way to remotely operate it and video Ryan and Cole having sex. He'd been telling the truth when he said he didn't make the recording. They'd set him up, set Ryan up to distrust him and send him away.

But why? Her thoughts were troubling on many levels. She checked her watch again and started to worry. Ten minutes, she decided. Ten minutes and she was going to Ryan's house and look for her, something was wrong.

****

"It's time to get them ready," Noah stepped into her view again but this time he wasn't wearing scrubs and a laboratory coat. Instead, he was dressed to the nines in a black tuxedo, white shirt, and black bow tie. He had shaved, the skin of his cheeks still pink from the razor's edge. His unruly, surfer's hair was combed perfectly into place as if were fearful of what might happen if a strand dared to move.

He tugged at his shirt sleeves and toyed with the gold cuff links under each wrist. In addition to his gold wedding band, a gold link bracelet peeked from his right sleeve. He cleaned up well, she thought, especially for a psycho-killer.

"Here," Jay practically ran into the room, dropping a plastic bag with a black suit and dress shoes on the table in the back. "He's waking up, you want to sedate him again?" He asked of Noah.

"No," Noah said. "We need him wide awake to complete his mission tonight. Just make sure his restraints are secured. Once he's fully awake, I'll give him the dose and he'll do whatever he's been programmed to do." He held up a sealed bottle of Anodyne. "When the smoke clears in a few weeks, everything will return to normal."

"What about Fare? Who's working point in the emergency room now?"

"No one is indispensable." He smiled. "I'll have his replacement selected before the morning." He looked around the room, "Where's Eleanor?" She should have returned from the house by now. We need Ryan to be dressed as if she were a guest and in attendance tonight."

"I'm here," Eleanor tore through the room like a whirlwind, dropping a black dress and heels on the table by Ryan. "I brought her makeup and jewelry." She knelt, hands on her knees, so that she was eye level with Ryan. "The bitch has a walk-in closet bigger than my apartment."

Ryan looked away, not because she was scared but as a result of Eleanor's foul-smelling breath. It took a few seconds before she spoke. "You were in my house?"

431

Ryan cringed thinking of Eleanor rummaging through her personal belongings and those of her daughter. Oh God, she prayed, Cole wake up and get us out of this.

"Too bad the little bitch wasn't home." Eleanor added, "her room's pretty nice too. When I was her age I was lucky if I had more than two pairs of shoes. There's more in her closer than I had over the entire year."

"I'm sorry that your childhood wasn't ideal—" Ryan began.

"Ideal?" Eleanor screamed. "Jacob and I were raised on a farm in the middle of nowhere. There was only this one little boy for miles around to play with and he just disappeared one day."

"Miss Blome!" Noah warned. "Help her get ready, she needs to look perfect, her hair, makeup, everything."

"I have to untie her," Eleanor answered, her eyes narrow and mouth curled in a frown. "And I've asked you not to call me that. No one in my family uses his name, ever." She paused. "I'll need help with her. Jacob, can you help?"

"He's getting the detective ready," Noah smiled. "I'll help you with her."

"Jay?" Ryan repeated. "Please don't do this." She paused, her mind racing. "I only know pieces of your story but you don't have to be like your parents. Whatever Jacob was or Rachel is --."

Jay threw Cole's clothes against the counter. "That bitch's not my mother! She doesn't even know I exist. The sperm donor got one of the program doctor's daughter pregnant." His smile was arrogant as he bent to collect the bagged clothes. "My 'father' hid me away here within the program, rather than fess up to his infidelity and tell her what he'd done."

Jay tossed the clothes on the next gurney. "His perfect family?" He laughed. "Nothing perfect about them especially my spoiled, fat, half-brother." He snapped his fingers in the air. "Almost got rid of him, too but—" He trailed off.

"You deleted the allergy information on Justin Turnhill's prescription?"

He nodded and turned his back to her, pulling and tugging at Cole' shoes. "And I injected the potassium into Beliard's IV."

"But why?"

"Because I could," she heard him say.

"Did you murder Dr. Paine and the chemist, too?"

"No," he smiled. "That was all Eleanor."

"What about Hartmann?" Ryan asked.

"The late Dr. Fare took care of the reporter," Jay laughed.

"Jacob?" Noah pointed to the back of the room where Cole was regaining consciousness. "Check his restraints and shut up."

Jay hesitated and for a minute Ryan wasn't sure he was going to do as Noah had instructed. However, only seconds past before Jay turned and returned to his task.

"Untie her, Eleanor and help her get undressed." He smiled and pulled a handgun from his suit pocket. "I'll make sure she behaves."

****

"Something's wrong," Catherine pulled out her phone and dialed. "I'm calling in reinforcements."

"Here, use my phone," Aiden said. "Who are you calling?"

"I'm having D.J. call in the Feds. Erik isn't answering, I fear something has happened to him already. I can't wait and let the same fate befall Ryan and Cole, if it hasn't already."

"What can I do to help?" Aiden asked.

"One of the men in the white van is here, I saw him come in but, I haven't seen him since. I think something is going to happen tonight." She paused. "It started with Anwar's death and I have this feeling that it's supposed to end here tonight."

"Okay," Aiden stood up. "Describe him, who am I looking for, I'll find him."

"Maybe you should wait for the federal agents?" Gordon asked, wiping his mouth with a linen napkin and tossing it atop the table.

"I'm just going to poke around," Aiden answered, disappearing into the crowd on the dance floor.

****

"You look beautiful," Noah said, twirling several strands of her hair between his fingers and smiling to her as if she were his shelter during the storm. "Such a waste."

"Get your hands off of me," she pulled her hair from his hands and took a step backward nearly falling as one foot snagged on the heels of the other shoe. "There's no way we're helping you do anything."

"Here," Noah handed Jay a folded piece of paper the outline of a seating chart clearly visible from the other side. "Most of the incidentals are at table twelve."

"She's there, too?" Jay asked, stepping into her view so she could see he was dressed as one of the male servers.

"Yes," Noah answered, 'Black dress, has a silver lining all around the jacket." He paused, "Her husband is there too as is our former director of security. And your stepmother is safely out of the way a few tables away so make sure you're on the mark." He rubbed his chin. "Just take out everyone at table 12."

"You want me to eliminate Aiden, too?" Jay's words were slow, deliberate.

"Yes, is that a problem?"

"No," Jay shook his head. "I think about when we were young a lot. I know he doesn't remember, but I do." He rubbed his shoulder, pulling his shirt down enough to reveal a faint red outline of a red bird was just visible under the skin. "He's not supposed to be here, he was suspended."

"And you did a fabulous job of incriminating him, Jacob, but he's here at the gala never-the-less."

"Wasn't supposed to be here, Jay mumbled again.

"Did you get the detective dressed?" Noah asked.

"Yes, and he's really out of it," Jay said. "I'm not sure he's going to be awake enough to pull the trigger."

"Then you'll have to pull it for him and then finish them all," Noah said, and Ryan was sure she saw him smile as he finished his recommendation. "I have to go," he checked his watch, "the keynote address is getting ready to start."

"Ryan?" Cole moaned from the other side of the room where Jay had sat him up in the chair and tied his hands through the slats in the chair. "Ryan" he called again, more frantically than the first time.

"I'm here," she said, straining to make eye contact with him across the room,

"Are you hurt?" his words were slurred and she could see his head bobbing up and down as he tried to focus not only his thoughts but his vision as well.

"No, are you?"

"My head is spinning," he answered before his head fell backward against the back of the chair.

Ryan was sure he was asleep again and a small part of her hoped he stayed that way. If he wasn't conscious, they couldn't give him the MKULTRA.

"There's a room, to the right of the serving room. It's very small and not on any blueprint." Noah advised as he stepped between Ryan and Cole. "There's a door into the room between the old and new building, it looks like a mechanical vent but it's not. "Take them and wait there for the signal. Then take the shot."

He took Ryan by the arm and pushed her toward Eleanor." Secure her hands behind her back and gag her for now."

"Should I sedate her?" Eleanor asked, adjusting the black tie around her neck and pushing the white shirt more fully into her black skirt. She would no doubt blend nicely into the surrounding as a server to the gala guests.

"No, there can't be any sedatives in their system when the medical examiner completes the autopsies." He paused. "Just keep them quiet. We're almost home-free." He slid the handgun back into his jacket pocket and pointed to a large bag in the back of the room. "You don't have any extra cartridges, whatever's in the rifle, is it. So, make the shots count."

He made his way to the door. "You should go find the vent and get inside the room. It's getting ready to start; the governor will be at the podium for only twelve minutes."

"Good luck, Jacob." Noah disappeared through the door and closed it quietly behind him.

Chapter 38

The ballroom was packed to full capacity with only an empty seat scattered here and there as guests roamed on and off the dance floor and lined several deep to indulge of the open bar. Servers dressed in black pants or skirts and white shirts with small black bow ties wandered from table to table, taking food orders and delivering drinks.

The lights were plentiful but, dimmed to such degree that some areas were darkened more than others. The food table was well lit not only by the fluorescent lights on the ceiling directly above the food table but, also by a dozen or so candles that were lit and lined down the center of the table.

The stage, too, was illuminated so that it appeared at any minute as if a famous band was about to take the stage. In its center was a small podium with several microphones mounted on top and the hospital system's logo on the front of the podium. Behind stage, it was dark, dark as night, with only the red lights of the exit signs bleeding through the darkness.

At either side of the ballroom was the kitchen and serving areas, both had swinging doors and it was obvious one side was meant as an entrance while the other door served as the exit. Servers passed in and out with such frequency neither door was closed for very long and the tables closets to the doors were fortunate enough to enjoy the cool rush of air as the door was forced open as the servers went in and out.

Noah took his seat at the corporate table number eight just as Rachel pushed herself to her feet and walked confidently toward the stage with her hand up to her face blocking the sharp rays of the stage lights. Once she was at the podium, she opened a crumpled piece of paper and ironed it against the top of the podium.

Rachel leaned in toward the microphone, her lips only inches away from the metal edge. "I'd like to thank everyone for coming."

A hush settled over the ballroom as guests collected their drinks and food and rushed back to their tables, balancing their plates and drinks in their hands. The servers paused, taking their stations near the doors and along the periphery of the ballroom.

"My name is Rachel Fleming. I am the chief executive officer of Ridgepoint Health System. It is my great pleasure to welcome you all here tonight to celebrate the grand opening of the Cardiology expansion for our flagship hospital."

She leaned against the podium and crossed her feet. "As most of you know, this expansion has been a collaboration with so many of you and has spanned some six years of blood sweat and tears."

Fleming looked to her right hoping the governor was on the stage and ready to accept the podium and deliver his speech. "Please join me in welcoming the governor of the great state of North Carolina, Governor Tony Smith."

She waited and looked again, left to right and then left to right again. An aide ran from the other side and whispered something in her ear. Rachel looked out toward the gala guests and laughed nervously into the microphone. "If he doesn't come soon, we'll approve next year's fiscal budget."

There was scattered laughter and several of the commissioners clapped, before Fleming's attention was drawn back to her stage left. She smiled and waved toward the waiting figure. She announced and waved. "Ladies and gentlemen, Governor Smith."

Once again the crowd applauded as the governor stepped out of the shadows and into the spotlight, walking briskly as if followed him to the podium. He waited for the applause to settle, before pulling reading glasses from one pocket and a piece of paper from the other. Like Fleming, he opened it out and rubbed it effectively against the top so that he could easily read it.

"Thank you, everyone, for allowing me this opportunity to share this very momentous event with you and to tell you all how proud I am of everyone who has had a role in the creation of this cardiology hospital."

He waited once again for the crowd to settle, for the servers to return to their stations, and for swinging doors of the kitchen to stall.

Chimera

"I wanted to share a little bit of what I think this hospital will mean not only for this county but, for several surrounding counties as well."

He paused, looking out into the crowd and for a second it seemed as if he'd forgotten what he wanted to say. He was as if he was paralyzed and unable to move his discussion any further. He leaned into the microphone and adjusted it so that he wasn't bent over the podium. "Can I get just a little lighter up here? I can't read my notes."

The lights around the stage illuminated brighter but, only for a second. After the initial surge in brightness, the room fell black, even the emergency lights were silent.

"Can we get the lights back—" the governor said around the first series of shots as the room exploded into gunfire and confusion. Crowds of people battled for the thin beam of light from a single emergency lamp in the center of the room, while others hid in the darkness of the shadows and under the tables and behind the chairs. Some escaped through the kitchen and server's doors while others lay unmoving on the floor.

Some made it out on their own, while other guests were carried or drug from the building. It was mayhem as SWAT, FBI, and other officers appeared at the scene shouting instructions to those who had yet to vacate the building and to offer aid to those who weren't able to vacate the area on their own.

"Governor?" one of the female bodyguards screamed, rushing back into the room only to be stopped by a SWAT officer. "He didn't get out," she screamed at the officer. "He's still inside."

"We'll see to him; we are assessing the scene." The SWAT officer stood his ground. "Once the shooter or shooters are in custody we will secure the scene."

"But we have injured people in there," Noah stepped from the crowd. "Some of our own friends and coworkers are still inside."

"The main ballroom has been secured," an FBI agent appeared and motioned for several other agents to set up a perimeter. "We are in the process of triaging the injured, several have been transported around to the back of the building to the emergency department."

"I'll go over and see," Noah said stepping away.

"The hospital is on lockdown, sir." The Agent informed him, crossing his arms as Noah contemplated the agent's words.

"But I'm the CEO," he said.

"Then you should know the rules, they're your rules."

****

"I can't believe this has happened, "Rachel Fleming wiped her eyes and cleared her throat as she addressed the board of commissioners. "The governor's dead, it sounds so surreal." She paused "Even though the FBI shot and killed the shooter, it's not enough."

"Do they know what his motive was?" one of the commissioners' asked.

"He'd been fired recently; he was the former captain of our security force." She paused, "Ironic, he was the only one of the security staff that was armed."

"Have all the families of the victims been notified?" Another commissioner asked.

"Dr. Allen's ex-husband and daughter were away but, my understanding is they've been notified." She turned the page of the report she was reading. "Catherine Master's sons have been notified that their parents were among the casualties. Jay Flowers must have tried to stop them when they went into the building as he was found outside the building, apparently, he was picking up extra hours in the kitchen."

She wiped her tears again. "I'm not sure if Dr. Morgan Fare or the detective's family has been notified yet but, I hope they have. It's a terrible thing to discover from the news media."

"I heard the FBI lost an agent as well?" Commissioner Greynolds asked, placing his hand over his heart as if he were pledging allegiance.

"I think he was CIA; his name was Erik something, he died on the scene." She closed the report. "There's was also an unidentified server, a female server, who has yet to be identified."

"What will the hospital do for the families?" Commissioner Greynolds rubbed at his chin. "We need to make sure the families are taken care of."

"We will see to it that they have what they need to get through this terrible time." She paused. "But we have patients to care for, people whose very lives depend on us." She took a sip of coffee and set the cup down delicately. "Life goes on, everything will go back to the way it was before."

****

The room was quieter than might have been expected given the number of people scattered about, tucked into one corner or another. There were blankets and pillows stacked atop small cots, some rolled into neat bundles while others lay loose atop the bed as if whoever had slept there had only recently rolled out. The air conditioning was set to its maximum and as result, the air was wet and damp, as if a winter storm was insight while just on the other side of the window, the sun was shining.

It smelled of greasy, fast food and there was a strong odor of garlic, pizza. No doubt with several dozen garlic rolls as an appetizer. Agent Frank Bronson and Inspector Winters sat anxiously at a small, round table near the back of the room. Although they were alone, they'd had visitors as was evident by the numerous empty coffee mugs that littered the table's top.

"How long are we going to keep them here?" Winters asked, looking to the farthest corner of the room where a figure was sleeping on a small bed. "The longer we wait, the harder it's going to be to keep it quiet."

Bronson pulled a small flask from his pocket and poured its contents into one of the coffee cups. "The arrests are being made today." He drank the cup's contents in a single swallow, grimacing as it traveled down his throat and tapped the cup against the tabletop. "This time tomorrow, they'll all be back home where they belong."

He looked into the hallway where the approaching voices grew louder and louder as they approached the room. "Lunch is here."

"Is he awake yet?" Ryan asked before stepping fully into the room and offering Bronson one of several brown lunch bags.

"He stirred a bit about a half hour ago but, I think he drifted back off to sleep." Winters answered holding his hand out for a bag.

"We're going to sit by the window," Catherine added as she walked into the room, pulling Gordon by the arm toward a rectangular table positioned by a large fake window. The window itself was real but, had been covered with animated pictures of the landscape. "Aiden said to save him a chair, he's in the bathroom. He'll be out in a minute."

"Hey," Ryan said as she claimed a small piece at the foot of the bed and pushed his feet as close to the wall as she could. "You need to get up and eat something."

"I can't seem to wake up," Cole said, struggling to get his feet on the floor and sit upright on the bed. He rubbed his eyes and pulled at the beard covering his chin. "Soon as I can stand up I'm shaving."

She ran her hand through it. "I don't know, I kind of like it."

"Then you grow one," he smiled taking her hand and holding it against his cheek. "I really don't know all that happened, I remember leaving your house after we argued." He paused, battling with his memory to recall what had happened after that.

"It's okay," she said. "We think you were abducted right after you left my house."

"We're in some kind of safe house?" he looked around the room.

"A safe room," she corrected him, smiling. "Let's go eat, I'm hungry," She stood up with her hand still locked within his.

"Wait," he held onto her hand, not moving from his sitting position on the bed.

"What is it?" she took her seat again and pulled herself as close against him as she could.

"What happened? How'd we get here? Why aren't I a walking zombie?"

"After Noah left to take his seat at the gala, Jay and Eleanor took us to the secret room where we were supposed to remain until they'd assassinated the governor." She blew a sigh wishing D.J. had packed a short sleeve shirt for her. Even with the air conditioning as low as it could go, she was still warm, hot actually.

"I was tied up and you'd been chemically restrained, I'd never felt so helpless but, I knew I had to at least try and alert someone, pray for some help to come our way." She smiled. "I'd just about given up when the door was pried open and Aiden burst into the room. I told him what was happening, who was involved and that they were going to assassinate the governor, everyone at table twelve, and then return to the secret room and kill us and make it look as if you'd murdered me and then killed yourself."

"All that happened very quickly," Cole nodded, "It takes hours to put a defensive like that together."

"Maybe, but Catherine had already called D.J. and Inspector Winters. Both SWAT and the FBI had already been dispatched." She helped him to his feet and walked him slowly toward the table where Catherine and Gordon were seated and pouring through the contents of their lunch bag, "Aiden had a radio and was communicating with the tactical teams."

"Are you catching him up?" Catherine asked as Gordon stood and held the chair in place for Cole to fall into.

Ryan nodded and handed him a bottle of water. "You should drink, you've had almost nothing in over forty-eight hours."

"What happened to the governor?"

"His team's first instinct was to pull him from the program and get him the hell out of there but, the FBI ASAC convinced everyone the best way to catch everyone in the net was to make them think their plan had been successful," Catherine answered. "The governor didn't take the stage right away, there was a delay while the FBI fitted him with a bulletproof vest."

"How'd they know the shooter wasn't going to take a head shot?"

"Because by then, both Jay and Eleanor were cornered. Neither would surrender, they both died at the scene." Catherine paused for a moment, remembering his laugh, his smile, especially when he talked about growing up at his grandfather's.

"When the lights went out," Ryan went on, "D.J. got Catherine and Gordon safely to the floor and out of the room while the SWAT sharpshooter fired blanks at the stage and table twelve."

"We were taken back to where you and Ryan were being held and we waited while the crime scene was secured," Catherine explained.

"How'd they explain the lack of bodies?"

"Fare, Reid, Eleanor and Jay's bodies were loaded into waiting ambulances and taken around the back entrance to the hospital. As is customary, all the bodies were covered for privacy. "Several of the officers pretended to be casualties and were carried around to the makeshift morgue the FBI had set up at the hospital."

"As far as the conspirators were concerned, they expected eight bodies counting Jay and Eleanor. Eight sheet covered bodies were transported from the gala to the morgue."

"What about the governor?" Cole asked, looking around. "I don't see him anywhere."

"He's in protective custody at a swanky hotel downtown guarded twenty- four, seven by a dozen FBI agents," Gordon added, leaning in and kissing Catherine. "You guys saved his life."

"Sorry, I'm late," Aiden chimed in, approaching the table and stepping over the back of the chair and sitting in the seat. "What did I miss?"

"We were just filling Cole in on the details of the gala shooting and the casualties," Catherine answered, she patted Aiden's shoulder. "Here's the real hero. If you hadn't caught Jay coming out of that secret room, you wouldn't have known where Ryan and Cole were being held, wouldn't have known about the intended shooting."

"Maybe," Aiden stuffed a quarter of a sandwich into his mouth and answered. "But you guys are the ones that figured the whole thing out. I just happen to be in the right place at the right time."

"You're a good man, Aiden, just like your father," Catherine said, barely above a whisper.

"What?" he swallowed the contents in his mouth and placed the sandwich on the table. "I don't know what you're talking about."

"I know who you are, Aiden. Who your dad was?"

"I told you I grew up on my grandfather's old farm—"

"After Mae died, Anwar's mom lied to him and told him you'd died. He never knew about you, I'm sure of that."

"How can you be sure of that?"

"Because I knew him." She took his hand. "And I loved him."

"My grandfather was a great man and growing up there was truly an amazing experience. Was out in the middle of nowhere, only a couple of other kids to play with from the farm across the way."

He rubbed his shoulder where the tattoo was, "It was obvious that all these families knew one another and as I got older I thought maybe it was a cult of some kind but, when I turned eighteen and wanted to leave, they let me."

"Can I see your tattoo again?" Catherine asked and at the same time called to Agent Bronson. "Do you have the picture of Eleanor's tattoo?"

Agent Bronson approached the table, not caring how heavy his boots sounded on the tile floor and dropped a black and white picture the medical examiner had taken of Eleanor's tattoo.

"The man has one as well?" Agent Bronson added as he looked over her shoulder.

"Jay had the same tattoo?"

"Yeah," Agent Bronson walked back to Inspector Winters and collected another black and white photo. "See." He dropped the photo on top of the other one.

"It's the same as yours Aiden."

"That's impossible, my friends and I did these ourselves. We were like nine."

"Noah kept calling him Jacob instead of Jay," Ryan added. "Jay said his father was Jacob Fleming."

"That's impossible," Aiden choked his words out. "Jacob was the boy who lived on the other farm across the way. He called the little girl, Nellie."

"Eleanor," Catherine whispered to no one specifically.

"The three of you were all there together, no doubt getting ready to take over the family business." Agent Bronson added. "But for some reason, they let you go."

"Anwar's mom, wouldn't have wanted that life for him. She knew Anwar wouldn't be strong enough to say No. So, she took you and hid you away." Catherine paused. "But something happened and they found out and took you from her to live in the compound with the other children." I'm sure she made some sort of arrangement with them but, for some reason, they let you go." Jacob Fleming, she thought, he must have intervened and paid the last debt to his oldest and dearest friend.

She took Aiden's hand. "When did you first suspect Anwar was your father?"

"There's was this old lady who used to visit a lot, about every other weekend. For a long time, I thought maybe grandpa had a girlfriend but I realized it wasn't like that, she wasn't there for him. She was there for me." He smiled, "I didn't even know her real name, I called her Babi."

"When I was in college, a few years after my grandfather had passed away, a box came for me. There wasn't a return address or anything I could use to determine where it came from but, inside the box was a bunch of old pictures. Some were of me and others were of Babi and a man. In some pictures, the man was young, very young. In others, he was older, grown. On one picture, was a handwritten name, Reggie. At the bottom of the box, there was a note from Babi. It read, I'm sorry."

"Over the next few years, I went through my grandfather's estate and found a reference to a man named Reggie. At that point, it was like putting a jigsaw puzzle together." He paused. "Eventually, it led me here to him."

"What did he say when you met him, told him who you were?"

"I didn't get that chance, he died before I could work up the courage to confront him."

"I'm sorry," Ryan leaned against Cole, "It's hard to lose someone you love, even if you aren't aware how much love them."

Cole kissed her forehead. "So, you think you, Jay, and Eleanor were supposed to be the generation to take over the program?" He checked his watch, "How's Rachel involved in this?"

"She took over after Jacob's death," Bronson added. "She was one calling the shots. We think she had Beliard killed because he didn't want to come back in and was threatening to expose the program If she didn't leave him alone." There's evidence to suggest she placed program participants in key roles within her organization that have targeted people for other purposes."

"Purposes such as?"

"Political overthrown, foreign and domestic assassinations, influencing everything from the stock market to the space program. We've reason to believe she has a vast resource of operatives in key strategic positions around the world." He looked at Cole. "They can make you do whatever they want once they give you that drug."

"Is Noah in custody?" Catherine asked.

"He was also a casualty of the scene, he died trying to escape through a series of tunnels he'd designed into the building's infrastructure."

"How did Dr. Fare die?"

"Jay shot him," Ryan answered, "before we even got into the hidden room."

"What about Tyler Paine? What was the justification for his death?"

"Paine recognized Fleming from the time she spent in Philadelphia, she was running a call girl ring than with the same purpose as Fare's emergency room. They targeted rich, influential men and administered the Anodyne to them. No doubt she gave the order to eliminate him."

"We may never catch them all. This has been going on for years?"

"Maybe," Winters nodded. "But it's a start. And the company that makes that drug will also be shut down by the FDA until they can determine how the MKUltra is being exchanged for Anodyne."

"Seems like such a waste," Ryan fell into Cole's arm. "I'm sorry about Erik, I know he was your friend."

"He was," Cole sighed, "And I'll miss him very much." He hugged her. "And I'll be forever I his debt." He released his hold just enough to grab one of the plastic bottles of water. "To Erik and Tim, may they both rest in peace. It was easy to imagine the clicking sound the bottles would have made had they been made of glass. Instead, the table was silent as each gave thanks to the heroes who had sacrificed so much.

Chapter 39

"Excuse me," an official-looking woman said as she made her way to the table where they were seated and stopped just behind where Aiden was sitting.

As if on cue, the group turned to acknowledge her, each hoping she was there to tell them they could go home, it was all over.

Instead, she held out her hand, waiting in turn for each one to take it. Catherine couldn't help but, admire the perfect manicure and she tried not to be envious of the expensive, designer suit.

"ASAC Cilla Walters, I'm the special agent in charge of the investigation. I trust everyone is well and a bit more relaxed than last night when we drug you all in here?"

There weren't any responses but, several heads bobbed up and down in agreement. Those seated with their backs to the FBI agents, turned their chairs around as if they were expecting a speech or presentation. ASAC Walters waited as everyone repositioned their chairs.

"I wanted to let you know that arrest warrants are being executed as we speak for all the known participants in the murder of Anwar Beliard, Tyler Paine, Tim Hartmann, Erik Horseman, Calvin Watson, and Morgan Fare. Another set of warrants are being executed to the same individuals for the attempted murder of Governor Smith, Ryan Allen, Cole Spencer, Catherine Masters, and Gordon Masters. There are other warrants being executed for felony conspiracy to the same individuals as well as other representatives of Anodyne Drug Company, Ridgepoint corporate IT, corporate communication, and Human resources."

Catherine waited for ASAC Walters to finish speaking, "Michele is that you?"

ASAC Walters smiled, a perfect row of teeth. "Yes, I was incognito. You have a keen eye, Mrs. Masters,"

"Why?"

"Getting a job with janitorial services was a perfect cover. They are in our lives every day, privy to the intra-workings of the system, yet unnoticed." She pulled her light red air away from her eyes. "We knew the mole was someone at a high level, possibly in administration. After we ruled out Cliff, we were looking hard at Aiden. He fit the profile; we weren't even looking at Jay. Funny how things turn out sometimes, Huh?"

"The day I caught you coming out of Cliff's office?" Catherine asked.

"I was looking for something I could trace back to who was embezzling, we knew the money was being used to fund the MKUltra program, just couldn't figure out who or how." She clapped her hands together. "Thanks to you, we have everyone associated with this cell."

"This cell?" Catherine repeated.

"Yes, there are dozens of other cells just like this one, all over the world."

"That's ridiculous, you know they're there and you just ignore them?"

"No, of course not. Once we've debriefed, we'll move to the next location and start again."

"How are you going to do that?"

"One day at a time."

****

"It's good to be home," Ryan dropped her bag at the door and kicked her shoes off in the same motion.

"I'm going upstairs and shower," Cole carried his bag through the living room and headed up the stairs.

"Mom!" McKenzie cried from the doorway, running the last few steps across the threshold to embrace her mother. "Mom, I missed you so much. Dad and I were crazy worried."

"I missed you guys, too." Ryan let McKenzie pull away only long enough to hug her ex-husband before grabbing McKenzie again and folding her into her arms so tight, McKenzie winced.

"Is it over?" McKenzie asked, taking her mother by the hand and pulling her toward the family room.

"Yes," they continued walking side by side as If they were at the beach, walking the shoreline.

"Where's Cole?" McKenzie asked, stopping at the kitchen. "Is he okay?"

"He went upstairs to shower." Ryan looked up the ceiling as if she could see through the plaster and wood. "I think so, thank God he didn't get the Anodyne. But he has had one hell of a hangover."

"Mom, "McKenzie took her hand again.

Ryan smiled. "Honey, are you proposing?"

"Mom, please," she said in a way only a fourteen-year-old girl can. "I'm trying to be serious."

"About what, honey?"

"I want you to know that you don't have to sneak Cole in and out of the house. I'm old enough to know how things are with adults. I know you love him and I want you to know it's okay that you want to be with him, in that way."

Ryan kissed her daughter's head. "When did you get to be so smart?"

"I love you mom," McKenzie cried into her mother's shoulder. "I was so scared."

"Me too, baby." Ryan rubbed her daughter's head. "Me too."

****

The air conditioning inside the corporate building where the commissioner's meeting was being held was on the fritz. Not only was it warm, hot actually, but more annoying was the thick, warm fragrance of musk and mold that seems to penetrate from the walls. If Rachel Fleming hadn't known better, she'd have thought there might have been a dead, decaying body behind the southern wall. It just smelled that badly. Worse yet, the agenda for today's meeting was long, they were going to be here for hours.

As frustrated as she was, the tap at the conference room door did nothing for her temperament. "It's a closed meeting," she barked at the door. "Thirty more minutes before we are open for the public to participate."

The door flung open, ASAC Celia Walters entered followed by at least a dozen other officers, half dressed like ASAC Walters, the other half donned in full SWAT attire. "Rachel Fleming?"

"You'll have to make an appointment tomorrow in my office," Rachel flung the next page of the packet against the desk. "I'm afraid I've nothing else to say about the unfortunate event."

ASAC Walters stopped in front of Fleming with the thick bench between them. "I'm afraid I'm going to have to insist, Ms. Fleming. Please step from behind the bench?"

"I'm calling my lawyer; you people are going to be so sorry."

"I think calling your lawyer is a smart idea." ASAC Walters motioned with her head for the officer to walk behind the bench and bring Fleming down. "You're under arrest."

"What?" Fleming asked, standing to her feet, only to have her hands pulled behind her back and secured with handcuffs. "You're making a terrible mistake."

"No, Ms. Fleming, I think not."

ASAC Walters waited for the officer to accompany Fleming down from the bench and onto the level ground with the others waited. "Have your lawyer meet us downtown."

"Can you at least tell me what you are charging me with?"

"Murder, conspiracy to commit murder, unlawful imprisonment, felony conspiracy. Here!" She stuffed a company of the warrant into Fleming's pocket.

"You don't want to do this," Fleming warned.

"Yeah," ASAC Walters nodded. "Yeah, I kinda do."

Chimera

****

"Is there any other business, items not on the agenda?" the good-looking middle-aged man asked the committee. He looked at his well-manicured fingers, wanting nothing more than to chew the nail of the pointer finger. But he didn't, he smiled to the woman sitting next to him, revealing, perfect white teeth that had probably cost a fortune.

He caught his reflection in the mirror that hung over the sink at the end of the room. He liked when the meetings occurred in the tropical room, the lighting was good and he knew what all the women were thinking as they finished up the meeting.

Mason Riley was attractive, so much so he could have been a model. Hell, unknowns to everyone in the corporation, he put himself through information technology school by doing a little modeling on the side. He lifted his chin just enough to gauge his reflection on the mirror, dam, he thought, the barber needed to trim just a tad more off of his beard. He didn't like it long under his chin, against his neck and neither did the ladies.

"There's someone at the door," the pretty woman in the brown polka dot dress said motioning to the door where a figure could definitely be seen through the small window in the door.

"Come in," he yelled, smiling to the group around him. "We're done."

The door flew open from the hallway as ASAC Walters and several officers entered the room. Like rats on a sinking ship, the room began to clear. "If I could ask everyone stay where you are and remain seated with your hands in plain view on the table."

"What's this about?" Mason asked, staying on his feet despite instructions from ASAC Walters to do otherwise.

"Mason Riley?" ASAC Walters asked as she moved closer and waved the warrant under his nose.

"Yes," he smiled. "Do I need a lawyer?"

"Yes," ASAC Walters nodded. 'You do, hands behind your back."

"You have to be kidding, is this some kind of joke?"

As if in answer to his question, the officer behind ASAC Walters stepped behind Riley and pushed him face down against the table. "Hands behind your back!"

Effectively, the officer secured Riley's hands and pulled him off the desk.

"What am I being charged with?"

"Illegal wiretapping and unlawful video surveillance to start. "She paused. "I'm not sure what to call manipulating the hospital's electronic medication order sets or deleting official incident reports as related to medication and patient safety, but, we will let the Federal prosecutor make that call."

"I need to talk to Rachel," he said, as he was pushed through the doorway by two officers.

"Don't worry," ASAC Walters almost laughed. "You'll have plenty of time to visit with her in jail."

****

Fifteen more minutes, Levi thought checking his watch again. No one could be more boring than Professor Daniels. The woman had to have little to no life, why else would she stay up the night before a test to identify the most insignificant, mundane pieces of information from the chapter on Neurological Pharmacology to test the class on. He was sure he'd failed the test; no doubt summer school was going to be in his future sooner rather than later.

He looked three rows behind him to where his twin, Louis was sitting anxiously at his desk. If Levi was reading Louis facial expressions correctly and he usually did, no doubt Louis faired equally poorly on the exam. Well, he tried to conceal a smile, he and his twin would be able to carpool back and forth to summer school in June.

Levi waited at the door, hoping Louis wouldn't be the last student out of the room today. He was in no mood for Louis' loitering about, they had to be at work in four hours and Levi wanted to shower, grab a bite and reread the chapter assigned for today. Professor Daniels would surely repeat the exam if the entire class were to fail.

Hurry up, Lou!" Levi said before Louis was to the door. "I've got a million things to do before work tonight and you know Ryan will write me up if I'm late."

"Coming," Louis answered absent-mindedly, his gaze on a convoy of police officers as they crossed the parking lot and headed for the science building. "What's going on?"

"Someone's busted," Levi answered, turning to watch where the officers gathered. He moved anxiously from side to side as the entourage grew closer and closer, finally coming to a stop at the bottom of the steps where Louis and Levi stood.

"Gentlemen, please turn around and put your hands behind your back."

"What's the problem, officers?" Levi asked, turning his back to the officers and following their instructions."

"You are under arrest." Both young men complied as they stepped down the steps and waited for the officers to handcuff them.

"What are we being arrested for?"

"You have the right to remain silent. If you give up that right --" The plain- clothes officer began to recite the Miranda rights.

"Just tell us what you're charging us with?" Levi asked, his face bowed as other students began to gather around them, watching as the brothers were led toward the waiting police cruiser.

"You are charged with violating the Federal Drug Supply Chain Security Act." ASAC Walters folded copies of the warrant and placed one in each cuffed hand. "I'm not sure how the attorney general will define the manipulation of the dispensing cabinets to dispense the happy juice." She smiled. "Some sort of conspiracy charge, I guess. He's a very resourceful man, I'm never surprised at the things he comes up with."

"There's a bunch of other technicians," Louis argued. "You can't prove that Levi and I are the only ones who sent up the medications."

"Actually, we have the Anodyne dispensing reports, we can prove it." She sounded almost joyful, happy. "Dispensing expired medications to anyone is a federal crime and you will be tried in a federal court."

With heads bowed, the twins were escorted past their friends and other onlookers and to the parking lot where they'd watched the cruiser park not more than twenty minutes ago. They were nearly to the door before they noticed the second cruiser parker about a hundred feet away from the police car that were being led to.

"Who's that?" Levi asked once they were close enough to see there was someone in the backseat. It was obvious he was a man and his head was bowed, in disbelief and embarrassment.

"Don't you recognize your co-conspirator?" ASAC Walters added, pushing at Levi's arm until he staggered into the car's door.

"My what?" Levi bent, peering into the window to get a better look. His dark complexion flushed pale, almost white as he recognized the sales representative for Anodyne. "I don't know him, not really. He's just the guy ---."

"The guy that paid you to dispense what you believed was expired medications to unsuspecting patients."

"I swear we didn't know it was anything else," his eyes met the drug representatives. "I swear,"

"Doesn't matter," ASAC Walters opened the door and motioned for the twins to slide into the back seat. "What's done is done, the fat lady is singing."

****

"You don't think having a wedding at our age is a little silly, self-indulgent? Ryan asked, pushing the pile of papers away from under her nose so that they clustered in the far- right corner of her desk. "Maybe it would be better to just go away someplace together for the weekend."

"What does Cole want?" Catherine asked.

"He doesn't care," Ryan answered. "McKenzie wants a wedding and an after party."

"There you go," she paused. "After all you've been through, you've earned it."

"I just can't help but, think that it's a waste of time and money."

"What? You're the COO now, permanently. You can afford it." Catherine laughed.

"How about you?" Ryan reached for the newspaper. Although it had been delivered in the morning, it was bent and folded to such extent, it looked as if she'd had it for days. "It's all out in the open now. His part, our part, the secrets, and the lies as well as the truths."

Catherine took it and unfolded it, ironing it flat atop the desk. "Tim put it all in his article and his editor filled in all the blanks. Anwars's true identity, Jacob Fleming's role in the CIA, their friendship and subsequent falling out, the feud that all but, destroyed them, Rachel's rise to power and the role her call girl ring played in her ascension to power. How the next generation made up of Jay, Eleanor and Noah stepped in and took over the program. And why after recognizing her from the escort service, Tyler Paine had to be eliminated.

Tim exposed Noah's role in directing Dr. Fare's candidate selection in the emergency department and how the MKULTRA, an LSD type analog, was disguised as an FDA approved the medication for pain and secretly dispensed to patients with the aid of an IT resource, Mason Riley, and several pharmacy technicians.

He left nothing to chance," Catherine went on. "He provided supporting documentation that the first attempt to murder Anwar was unsuccessful after his IV bag was injected with a subtherapeutic dose of Potassium. When that failed he was injected with MKUltra and programmed to commit suicide. Like the first failed attempt, it was not successful and Anwar was shot a second time by Jay Flowers."

"The report details how the death of a Charlotte chemist and a retired CIA agent were perpetrated by someone in the MKULTRA program." Ryan read from the paper. "And that unidentified hospital manager and as well as a Caswell county police detective were injured trying to bring the exploits of the MKUltra to light. "

Ryan tapped the paper. "Did you see who is listed as co-author with Tim?"

Catherine shook her head. "Michele House?"

"Wasn't that the name ASAC Celia Walters was using when she was posing as a hospital housekeeper?" Ryan asked.

"So, she was Tim's source?" Catherine smiled.

"Apparently," Ryan refolded the paper. "I took the fall for her?"

"It's odd, you know," Catherine scooted her chair closer to Ryan. "Sitting here and looking back on the last month, nothing was really as if seemed. It was as you said from the very beginning a Chimera."

"That's not true," Ryan said. "You are, I am, Cole is. Right?"

Catherine nodded, "And I will always be your friend, whether I'm here in this office next to you or retired a hundred miles away. This time, is and was ours. I don't want you to doubt that."

"I don't," Ryan spun around in the chair, taking note of the setting sun in the sky. "Do you think it's really over?" She paused. "Are we safe?"

"Walters seems to think we are, she said once they have been exposed, they tend to find another place to settle and set up shop." She paused. "And the Attorney general has filed insider trading charges against the governor. If he is trying to break up the system, he won't be able to gain financially. And I heard a rumor the Senate Ethics Committee was looking into any reelection plans he might be making."

"We sacrificed so much. Beliard, Tyler, Calvin, Tim, and Erik are all dead. Did we really change anything?" Ryan gathered her purse. "Come on, walk out with me. I'm heading home, I've a wedding to plan."

Catherine laughed and followed her out the door, pausing at the external door out of the administrative offices. "Night Virginia," Ryan said, watching as Catherine waved and exited first.

"Night ladies, get some sleep." Virginia answered, "See you in the morning."

She watched and waited for the door to snap closed, smiling to herself as she picked up the paper and read it again. Ryan was only half right, Virginia thought, things would go back to normal and everything would continue as it was, everything including the program's mission. She smiled and dialed a number she knew by heart.

"Hi Andrew," she said into the phone once he answered the phone. "Sorry, I mean Mr. Hoffmon, is it all set?"

She listened, nodding as he gave her instructions for cover and location. "So near? I thought we'd at least go farther North."

"No" she looked around. "I understand, I'll collect my things and meet you there within the next forty-eight hours."

Virginia collected a few things from the top drawer, leaving most of the framed pictures and trinkets scattered on her desk and credenza, they'd never meant anything to her anyway, not really. It was all for show; her husband had her left years ago and the children in the pictures weren't hers. She'd cut them out of a catalog. "Standard withdrawal protocol, I'm assuming?"

"Okay," she said, dropping everything into a small box. "I'll see you soon."

She tossed the office keys on top of the desk and grabbed her purse, leaving the office door unlocked behind her. There was a tinge of remorse as she walked the hallway for the last time, the years spent here had been meaningful and, at times fulfilling. There had been many a moment, the guise seemed almost real, but like the lion-serpent, it wasn't. It had been a role, one of many she'd played over the years. Nothing was as it seemed and, she wasn't naïve enough to think that it ever could or would be.

About the Author

Lisa Robin Phillips Colodny was born and grew up in the rural countryside of Kentucky. She attended the University of Kentucky and Broward College in Fort Lauderdale and graduated with a Doctorate in Pharmacy from Nova Southeastern University.

Her non-fiction publishing history includes numerous publications in the health and science industry. Other titles currently available by this author include an award-winning children's book, Ms. *Abrams' Everything Garden*, and adult fiction, *The Town Time Forgot*, and *Yellow River Pledge*.

Dr. Colodny currently works in the healthcare industry and resides in South Florida with her daughter and their Labrador retriever, Cooper.

About the Publisher

Kingston Publishing offers an affordable way for you to turn your dream into a reality. We offer every service you will ever need to take an idea and publish a story. We are here to help authors make it in the industry. We've been hurt by publishers in the past and we want to provide a positive experience that will keep you coming back to us.

Whether you want a traditional publisher who offers all the amenities a publishing company should or an author who prefers to self-publish, but needs additional help - we are here for you.

Now Accepting Manuscripts!

Please send query letter and manuscript to:

submissions@kingstonpublishing.com

Visit our website at www.kingstonpublishing.com

Extras

Dr. Jordan Chamberlain is a successful, beautiful, young medical examiner with the perfect husband, the perfect life, and perfect friends. Somewhat of a whiz, kid, she's younger than most Medical Examiners and enjoys a bit of glamour whenever her forensic data is sent to trial. To an outside observer, Jordan has it all, until that is, her husband, Jason, announces without warning that he doesn't want to be married anymore and Jordan's perfect life crashes and burns around her.

Jordan buries herself even deeper in her work, temporarily embarking on a career consulting with the FBI's Violet Crimes Division under the careful eye of college friends turned colleagues, who support her during her as she tries to rebuild her life.

Her future, however, is about to be compromised once more when she becomes the target of the serial killer she's been pursuing.

Milton Keynes UK
Ingram Content Group UK Ltd.
UKHW052140270324
440206UK00011B/853